FOREVER CHANGED

BY JIM SERVI

Editing and book design by Jansina of Rivershore Books

ISBN: 978-1-63522-086-5

Printed in the United States of America
10   9   8   7   6   5   4   3   2   1

Rivershore Books
8982 Van Buren St. NE • Minneapolis, MN 55434
763-670-8677 • info@rivershorebooks.com

FOREWORD

After living in a war zone for two of four years—first in Iraq and then in Afghanistan—and thinking of little but war in between or from the moment the planes hit the Twin Towers, I was admittedly lost when I returned. The world was different to me, and I didn't understand my place in it. The future that I had so carefully planned didn't excite me any longer. I didn't understand why such terrible things happened and why some people harbored so much hate. There were moments that should have been pure joy, like playing with my then one-year-old son after missing his first year of life, where I felt little emotion. It didn't make sense, so I blamed myself and fell into deep states of depression. After a while, I would return to my new sense of normal only to repeat the pattern of depression again and again. Like many veterans, I tried different avenues to find help, but nothing worked. Looking back, I realized that I didn't give them a proper chance. I was too prideful and stubborn, wanting to do it myself and not let anyone else in.

Finally, I turned to something that had always worked for me in the past: writing. In writing this, I became not only a better writer, but a better person. It helped me to reflect and put things into perspective, and it helped me to rise out of the depths of depression. My purpose in writing this book was two-fold. First, was for that personal reflection—to think more deeply about my journey and the time I spent in Iraq and Afghanistan. Second, was to put myself in others' shoes—friends, family, the people I served with and met along the way, and the Iraqi and Afghan people. I found that although veterans tend to get PTSD and struggle with depression more than most because of the nature of war, it was not only veterans who struggle. Nearly everyone I've met in my life has

DEDICATION

For Justin Ross and Ben Hall, who made the ultimate sacrifice in Afghanistan,

And for all those who tragically perished on September 11th,

And for all of those who bravely served in Afghanistan and Iraq,

You will never be forgotten.

This book is for you.

CHAPTER 1

Paul glided to his Global Perspectives class with the smile of a young man experiencing true freedom for the first time. No, he wasn't locked in a basement for years—although his makeshift room at his parents' house was now located in the basement—nor did he live a bad life at all. In fact, he was blessed to live in a safe, quiet town, with lots of friends, and a family that loved him.

However, he was finally out on his own. He was away from home, starting college, and no longer had to abide by the rules that came with living under Mom and Dad's roof. Never a rebel or renegade, Paul just liked doing things his own way. At five feet, eleven inches, Paul was average in most ways. Brown hair, hazel eyes, friendly but quiet, athletic but no superstar, smart but no rocket scientist. He tended just to blend in with the crowd. Yet deep in his mind was something far from typical. Paul knew he was going to change the world.

His parents had dropped him off earlier that month, along with his siblings, in what turned into a very sober occasion. Initially after arriving, Paul was lost in his excitement. Getting moved in, linking up with his dormmates, even visiting the cafeteria. It was all new and exciting. Then, reality set in. They'd all be gone. His family was extremely close and always had been. Paul was the oldest and always made it a point to look out for his siblings. He tried to include them in everything he did. They all knew that would be a lot tougher now. It reflected on their faces as they said goodbye.

"I'm going to miss you, bro," Paul began, hugging his brother Joel.

"Yeah, me too," Joel began, not really knowing what to say. "It's just not going to be the same."

"I know," Paul started, then stopped, avoiding everyone's

1

gaze for a moment, holding back a tear. "I know, it's tough, but I'll be home every chance I get and you'll have your license before too long and can come visit any time you want." Joel was just entering high school and hated having his brother living nearly 200 miles away. They wouldn't be able to throw the ball around after school or head to the river to go fishing. They had become more than just brothers, they were friends now, and that made it even harder to say goodbye.

"Sounds like a plan. I'll miss you, Paul," Joel said, trying to be tough, but the pain showed in his sad, misty eyes and the frown that overtook his face.

Matt didn't wait for Paul to turn in his direction to say goodbye. He wrapped his arms around him as Paul began to turn. Gail followed suit and they laughed as they wrapped him in a bear hug. Paul laughed, too. The embrace helped break the awkwardness for a moment.

"You two goofballs," Paul said. "How am I going to get by without you two keeping me on my toes?"

"Easy; we'll just stay with you," Gail grinned.

"Sure, I'll need someone to do my homework," Paul agreed. "But I think Mom and Dad will miss you a little too much. Maybe they'd let Matt stay, though." He wrapped his arm around Matt's shoulder to show him he was kidding. One thing about his family was that they always loved to joke. Paul would miss that, too. In fact, there wasn't much he wouldn't miss, he thought as he reflected.

"Sounds good to me," Matt shouted, his eyes twinkling at the thought of joining Paul at college.

"I wish, buddy," Paul whispered, avoiding their gaze again. "I wish."

With Matt and Gail, Paul almost seemed more like an uncle since he was almost a decade older than both. In fact, they went fishing on Father's Day earlier that summer and the guy at the bait shop thought they were his kids. Paul was only eighteen and the owner of the bait shop was a bit senile, but his mistake displayed their relationship perfectly. They both looked up to Paul and were going to miss the adventures they had together.

Having never really been apart and saying goodbye like

this for the first time, it seemed like the world was falling apart. It seemed like they would never be close again, or do all the fun things they once loved. Paul was going to miss all of them more than they would ever know. As much as he hurt inside, he tried to hold it in and put a smile on his face. That's what he always tried to do, but now it cracked.

His mother came to the rescue, just like she always did, wrapping him in a hug so no one else could see him cry. "No one will miss you more than I will," she whispered, her own voice cracking, but remaining strong. "I'm so proud of you and know that you're going to do great things. I want you to do all the things that I never got a chance to do." She was pregnant with Paul when she was his age and never got this opportunity. She knew that would keep him going, no matter what troubles came his way.

"I love you, Paul," she said, smiling despite the pain that was still written in her eyes.

"I love you too, Mom."

Paul's father loved adventures and teaching him all about life, but he wasn't one for emotions and definitely not one for hugs. Paul turned to find his dad's arms open, rather than just his hand extended for a handshake. Paul pounced. For a moment they embraced but said nothing.

"I love you. Now go out there and do great things," his father whispered quietly.

"I love you, too. I love all you guys."

And then they were gone.

Here, walking into his first class, the somber feeling lingered, but it was joined by a deep determination and unbridled optimism. He was going to make them all proud.

The classroom was modern, bright, and well-lit, unlike some of the aging buildings on the campus that was as old as the state of Wisconsin. The University of Wisconsin. He was finally here, in Madison, along with all the other Badger faithful. He had dreamed about this day since he was a kid, watching Barry Alvarez and the Badgers defeat UCLA in front of more than 100,000 fans during the Rose Bowl. Paul had worn that Rose Bowl championship hat everywhere. He was only in sixth grade at the time, but it made a deep-rooted impression.

Although he dreamed about being a Badger all his life, it was the superior education and top-notch engineering program that solidified his plans. Still, he had his doubts at first. There was no denying Paul was a country boy. He loved the outdoors and needed quiet places to get his thoughts straight. Too long without solitude in the great outdoors, and it wore on him. And now he was in the big city, where there were people scurrying around at all hours and traffic everywhere. He wasn't sure he'd ever get used to it, but he tended to find wilderness hideouts everywhere he went. Deep down Paul knew that if he didn't follow this dream he would regret it forever.

Paul arrived a full five minutes early and found a seat in the middle by the window, not too close to the front to be considered an overachiever, but not in the back, either, where he could potentially be labeled a slacker. He just wanted to blend in, for now.

The professor was there already, putting on his final touches and reviewing notes. With the few extra minutes before class, Paul glanced through his textbook. Although he'd never admit it out loud, the book sounded interesting and might actually relate to what he'd be doing after graduation. After graduation, Paul would not only be receiving his engineering degree, but he would also be receiving a commission into the United States Army as a Second Lieutenant.

He and his friend JD had both signed up for ROTC since neither could decide whether to go to college or go into the military. Of all the conversations he had with JD since they first met on the Little League baseball field, this was the one he remembered most.

"Hell of a party last night, huh?" JD said, smiling as he rubbed his bloodshot eyes. JD loved to party. In fact, the only thing he loved more than partying was his longtime girlfriend, Lynn. They had such a natural, easygoing love that they were the envy of all the drama-filled high school relationships. They were usually inseparable. Last night, though, she had to work, so it was just JD and Paul. Blending in was Paul's forte. JD was usually the life of the party. People naturally gravitated toward him, not just at parties, but everywhere. Sports, school, it didn't matter. He just had that presence. All their close high school friends were at the party last night for one last summer get-together before going back to school for their senior year. The few that remained were still sleeping.

"Sure was," Paul agreed. "I'm going to miss these days. Can't believe we're almost seniors."

"You ain't kidding, my friend. Hey, since we're up so early, wanna see if the fish are biting?"

"Have I ever said no to that?" Paul said, already walking toward the boat with the half of his breakfast bar that remained. It wasn't exactly an early morning sunrise. The sun was just beginning to show a little stronger through the trees, reflecting off the mesmerizing current of the Wisconsin River. This was JD's family cottage and their favorite place to party.

JD's dad is not going to be happy when he finds out, Paul thought, glancing over at JD.

The temperature was already warm, but as they motored downstream, the breeze made Paul shiver. Goosebumps appeared on his arms as he tucked his hands under his legs.

"You wuss," JD chided with a quick smile. Nothing ever seemed to bother him, or at least he never complained, just accepted things, and made the best of every situation. Paul's hands remained locked between his legs and the seat. JD's remarks only made Paul smile. The outboard idled to a stop as the waves crashed along the densely forested shore. Soon, it was calm. The morning was quiet as they casted.

"Heading back to school next week makes me start to think a little bit more about what to do after graduation," JD said slowly. "Any thoughts about what you want to do? If your baseball career doesn't work out, that is."

"I'm not worried. The Brewers came for a visit last week," Paul quickly retorted. "And if that doesn't work out, smartass, I've been torn about going to college—Madison hopefully—or maybe even joining the Army." Paul glanced over at JD quickly, trying to gauge his reaction. "I've actually been thinking about joining more and more lately. What about you?"

"Don't tell my dad or Lynn's dad, but I really want to join the Army, too. Actually, it's all I really want to do," JD confessed. Both JD and Lynn's fathers had been career military, and JD had always resisted any talk about him joining up. JD's dad was a career officer in the Wisconsin National Guard, and Lynn's dad spent twenty years in the Active Army as an enlisted soldier, travelling around the world. Both hailed from the infantry. This connection was just one of the many reasons JD and Lynn were inseparable. "I'm surprised to hear that from you though."

"Yeah, I know. It's weird, but I've been giving it more thought, too. Remember my uncle who lives down in Tennessee, you know, the one in the Gulf War and Somali and all that?"

"Vaguely," JD admitted. "Rick. Was that his name?"

"Yeah, that's the one. I remember watching Desert Storm on TV and thinking how cool it would be to do something like that. You know, serve our country, travel to places like that to help others. Everyone was so proud of him, talked about him all the time."

"I know exactly what you mean. As much as I"—JD smiled ruefully—"*clashed* with Dad, I was always pulled in by his stories and adventures. They always sounded like such a challenge. And I always thought to myself, 'I can do that, no problem.' Kind of makes me want to prove to him and myself that I can do it. Plus, and don't tell him this either, I never really realized it, but the uniform has come to mean something special to me. More than just a job, you know. You're doing something that truly matters."

"Definitely," Paul replied. "I kind of always figured that about you. Even though you never said it, you didn't exactly hide it either. Just wanted to piss your dad off all those times, didn't you? What about Lynn? How does she feel about that?"

"Tough to read. I think she's both excited at the prospect, but scared at that same time. Probably a pretty natural reaction. We've been talking a lot more about it and options."

For a couple minutes they just casted, their lures making a perfect ripple as they plopped in the water. The sun was over the trees now and hot on their faces. Warblers sang as they fluttered along the shoreline.

JD broke the silence, squinting into the sun as he spoke. "One thing that Lynn and I talked about was going the ROTC route. She really wants to go to college at Point and teach someday, and I really like the idea of going the officer route. I want to lead. Maybe lead troops into battle someday. How cool would that be?"

"Pretty sweet; hard to imagine, even," Paul agreed. "Bullets flying, killing bad guys, just like the movies. Plus, the great thing is that you'll have your degree without being $50,000 in debt."

"Sounds like you made up your mind, too." JD was smiling.

"What do you mean?" Paul asked.

"You just said you wanted to go to Madison and wanted to join the Army. This way you can do both. Plus, I'm going to need a roommate," JD said, smiling his trademark, overly big grin.

"Are you serious?"

"Sure, why not. Just you and me, like it's always been."

Paul pondered for a moment. The more he thought about it, the more he liked it.

"OK, let's do it."

And here they were, together. UW-Madison. Army ROTC. Roommates. Despite their plan coming together so serendipitously, their first physical training session earlier that morning showed how little they actually knew about the military. Paul showed up with a goatee. Although not much of one, his instructor wasn't too happy. He was a Master Sergeant with a Combat Infantryman's Badge and Master Parachutist Wings, and he was a badass that had been in Desert Storm a decade earlier. He started off nice since they were all freshman and didn't know any better but quickly changed his tune.

"I can't look at your face anymore," he scolded. "Go get rid of that and don't let me ever see it again." Paul obeyed as he would get used to doing.

The professor didn't waste time getting into his first lesson.

"Most of you grew up in a fairly quiet neighborhood where you were safe and felt supported by your family and friends," he began. "That's good and I wish that were the case for everyone. But it's not a reality. This is Global Perspectives and I'm Professor Hamm, but you already knew that if you looked at the syllabus in front of you." Many of the students looked down, noticing the syllabus for the first time. "I plan to open your eyes to what happens around the world every day. To those who are attuned to the news and world events, you may have a better understanding of issues that have occurred or are occurring around the world. If I had to guess, though, most of the things we'll talk about this semester will be something new for you, even though it affects our lives as Americans."

It was a new century, a new millennium, the year 2000, and most of the class was eighteen and fresh out of high school. In fact, as Paul looked around, everyone appeared to fit that description. At this point, they were all trying to just blend in. The professor went on to describe the class as self-absorbed, which, he explained, was normal for high schoolers.

"You're trying to determine what college to go to and, by the way, I'm glad you decided to come here. You're involved in activities, have relationships, hang out with friends, and are just trying to figure out who you are as a person. It's completely normal and good that you had that opportunity. Now, by a show of hands, how many of you know that America is the most loved and hated country in the world?"

No one raised their hand and, in fact, most of them looked surprised to be asked this question.

College is sure different than high school, Paul thought to himself as he pondered the question. Puzzled looks appeared on every face as students tried to understand the interrogation. Many began to look around the classroom, searching for answers maybe, or perhaps simply uncomfortable with this new reality. *There is no way that can be true,* Paul concluded.

"Okay, maybe not the most hated, but one of them. Now, how many of you know that there has never been peace in the world during your lifetime, that there has been war, violence, and terrorism constantly happening somewhere in the world since you've been born?" Again, no one raised their hand.

"Now, just for fun. How many people know about the Oklahoma City Bombing?"

This time, most of the class raised their hand.

"Why do you think you know about that particular incident?" The professor looked around. No hands were raised. Most of the students avoided direct eye contact as he looked their way. "Maybe we need to back up a little bit. There are no right or wrong answers in this class. Well, usually not. This is not high school. This is a discussion to help broaden your perspective. I expect you to think about each of these concepts and formulate your thoughts. They may not be the same as your neighbor's, or mine for that matter, and that's good. Now, who can tell me why you know about this event?"

"Ah yes, a hand. What do you think, Dawn?" the professor said as he glanced down at the name on the desk that he had them fill out earlier.

"I remember seeing it on the news with my parents," the girl sitting two seats over from Paul replied. She immediately caught his attention. Her confidence, the aura about her—she was very beautiful in a quiet way. Noticing her made Paul think about Marie. Despite the fact that they just couldn't make their relationship work and weren't together, Paul still felt guilty. He confessed his love one last time before leaving for college, but the timing wasn't right, at least according to Marie.

Nothing more you can do now, Paul reminded himself.

"Bingo!" The professor looked pleased. "When something is publicized by the media, especially over and over again like that event, we are more likely to know that it occurred. Of course, this comes with a bias that the media always brings, which is neither good nor bad, just their perspective. That's important to understand. The news they are reporting becomes the reality for many Americans." He paused for a second, then looked directly at Paul. "The truth is, events like this happen around the world on a regular basis, but we rarely hear about them. Some happen in nations that America is not concerned about, others that don't have a large media presence or the media is suppressed, and some just aren't a story that anyone wants to share, or no one wants to hear."

"Miss Dawn, we'll start with you since you were the first brave one in class. How did you feel that day watching the news with your parents?"

"Scared, I guess. Not sure what was going to happen in other places, like where I live."

"Definitely a natural reaction," the professor assured. "What about the rest of you? How did you feel?"

"I remember having this really uneasy feeling, wondering how something like that could happen. Wondering why the police, FBI, CIA, all those organizations couldn't stop this," a guy wearing red shorts and a Badger t-shirt behind Paul explained.

"I was scared, too, but I guess I started thinking about the future more, especially when I was getting ready to go on a trip after that. I guess I was more aware of things, always wondering what might happen," a blonde girl on the opposite side of the room said.

"Maybe a little less naïve?" the professor questioned. "Which is what happens as you develop and learn more about the world. That's my hope for you in this class."

"What about you?" he said, turning toward Paul. "You look like you might be a military guy with that haircut—former, ROTC, or am I completely wrong?"

"ROTC," Paul confirmed as he glanced at Dawn. She smiled. "I felt a lot of what everyone is describing, but more than anything I was wishing that I could do something to help. All those people that were killed, injured, and scared. I wanted to be there."

"A lot of people feel that way, too, and you might just be in the right line of work to do just that," the professor replied, but quieter and more distant than before. He paused as he glanced out the window. "Now imagine for a second that you lived like this every day of your life or at least in fear that something like that could happen every day. How would that change your life and the person you are at this moment?"

Before anyone could answer, he continued, "Please open your books to page thirty-two and see if there is anything you recognize there."

The book was *Terror in the Mind of God* by Mark Juergensmeyer and the page described the Oklahoma City bombing by Timothy McVeigh. In front of Paul a hand shot up and waved eagerly. The kid hadn't gotten the opportunity to talk earlier and was itching to now.

"My aunt was in Oklahoma at the time of the blast," he explained, "and had been near that building earlier that year. She said she will never go back."

"Another natural reaction, but people's initial response to terror often fades if they didn't experience it directly. Everyday life takes over once again and the details are forgotten. Everyone is different, though. It's generally the prolonged effect of violence or direct exposure to it that can forever change a person's life," the professor explained. Paul liked his straightforward approach to answering questions and he was clearly knowledgeable.

I wonder what his background is? Paul thought, but before he could continue the thought, the class began discussing the culture of violence that the chapter highlighted. It was sad to learn that many conflicts were the result of some form of religious ideology or extreme nationalism. The class knew about some of them: the Holocaust, the conflicts between Protestants and Catholics spanning several centuries, and the Crusades. What Paul hadn't realized was that there were also several examples of modern terrorism like the Aum Shinrikyo assault or numerous assassinations in India. Both were done in the name of extreme ideologies, and the class would learn more about them throughout the course of the semester. These examples were just organized violence and didn't include murder, rape, and assault that occurred all the time.

It's a scary world out there.

As the professor was closing up, Paul was overwhelmed by his thoughts. *This is a lot to take in for the first class of my college career.* For the first time, Paul began to think about the world outside of his previous realm of understanding. Beyond what was in front of him. Beyond his experiences.

"I'll leave you with one final question," the professor spoke to the class as they were getting their books packed up. "How many of you have heard of Osama bin Laden?" Again no one raised their hand.

"That's typically the response I get, but you'll find his name throughout this book. He's tried multiple times to attack America and American interests . . ." he trailed off, and then seemed to gather his thoughts, "But I'll let you figure that out for the next class. Look at your book and do some research to figure out why we should be interested in this guy."

Paul left class with a different feeling than when he walked in. He was excited for his freedom but beginning to realize the reality that was up ahead. *It's not always going to be a rosy ride, so I might as well just enjoy it while I can,* he thought. He couldn't help feeling fortunate to grow up in a place where he never had to worry about all this terror and hatred.

Paul strolled the city streets of Madison, dodging traffic, still pondering the last thing the professor said. *Osama bin Laden wanted to attack America—why?* He couldn't understand it. He couldn't understand why people hated America.

"There he is!" JD boomed as he walked into their shared dorm. "How was your first day of class, young man?" Always joking, always having a good time, JD loved life and that was one thing that Paul admired so much about him.

"Although I hate to admit it to you, because I know I'll never hear the end of it, it was actually pretty interesting," Paul replied. "Even you'd like it because it relates back to the military. I had no idea that it was such a crazy world out there. You ever heard of anyone named Osama bin Laden?

"Nope."

"What about you, Chad?" Paul asked. Chad Snow, coincidentally another ROTC cadet, was rooming with them as well. They roomed at Slichter Hall, where they claim that everyone knows your name with only twelve rooms, thirteen if you count the Resident Assistant, to a wing. Although they generally didn't put three people together in a dorm room, they were trying something new this year. They were putting more students in dorms the first semester, knowing many would party their way right to their parent's couch at the end of the semester. The first semester was the toughest and it was legendary how many went home. Paul had heard upperclass-man say it was like a ghost town at the start of the second semester. Not all rooms had three people, but none of them minded being part of the experiment.

The dorm room was fairly small, about the size of an average bedroom at home. It had a two-person desk with a divider in the middle, two plain dressers, a couch that doubled as a bed, and a closet. Engineers at work, they had quickly taken the bunk beds apart and turned them into a loft, to free up some space. In the end, it essentially looked like two top beds, with no bottom bunks, out of the bunk bed set. Paul and JD slept up in the loft, while Chad was on the futon. Chad also brought in his own small desk so they would each have their own study space. Quarters were tight, although they quickly made it a home.

"Can't say that it rings a bell to me, either," Chad said. "Why? Who is this guy?"

"Not really sure yet, but apparently he hates America and has tried to attack us several times," Paul explained.

"Just give me five minutes and I'll take care of this guy," JD boasted. "No more bad guy. Easy as that. Now are you guys ready to eat? All this talk is making me hungry."

"JD to the rescue! Sure you would; five minutes, huh, tough guy?" Chad couldn't resist. Just as quickly as they met, they had become close friends.

"Alright you jokers, let's eat." Paul shook his head, smiling.

They quickly settled into a routine during the first week, with each of them going their separate ways after PT in the morning and then linking up at noon for lunch every day at the cafeteria. Without fail, they would get ice cream for the walk back. Then, battle it out in Mario Kart on Chad's Super Nintendo. JD was usually the winner, with Chad keeping it interesting when they raced. Gaming rookie Paul was usually at the back of the pack. It didn't take long before Paul and JD felt like they had known Chad all their lives.

CHAPTER 2

"Oh shit, we're late!" JD shouted from their loft, hustling down the makeshift wooden ladder. Paul was right behind him. Chad was still clinging to his covers, trying to savor an extra minute or two of sleep. Nearly two months into their college careers, they still weren't used to getting up by five o'clock every morning to make it to their morning physical training for ROTC. It was especially tough knowing most of their non-ROTC classmates would be sleeping for at least another two hours, probably more.

"I forgot, this is the morning we've been waiting for, too. We're heading to Camp Randall for PT," JD called from the bathroom before appearing again briefly. "Should be interesting."

"The scenery may be interesting, but I'm not looking forward to those stairs," a groggy Chad mumbled, acknowledging that he had to finally get up by swinging his legs over the side of his futon bed.

"Chad, you forget, JD loves this stuff. He's not a mere mortal, like the rest of us," Paul said. JD was already one of the top performers, easily scoring more than the three-hundred-point maximum on their physical training test. He exceeded the standards in every category—push-ups, sit-ups, and the two-mile run. While many of the freshmen struggled to meet the minimum and pass for the first time, JD scored on what they called the extended scale, allowing him to rack up more than three hundred points, reserved only for those that went above and beyond. Yet, even with his natural physical ability, he trained harder than most.

"I'm dreading those stairs too and the run we'll probably have to do just to make it on time," Paul said. The stadium was just over a mile from their dormitory.

"What are you waiting for then, mortals?" JD bellowed, continuing the joke.

Dressed in their physical training uniforms, they raced out the door, and headed toward Camp Randall Stadium. Despite Paul's comment, he was looking forward to walking out onto the field where the Badgers played. The coliseum-like stadium loomed larger than life as they approached the *Home of the Wisconsin Badgers* sign and headed for the Camp Randall gate. The scene was surreal to the trio. Typically, it was a sea of red when they saw it on gameday. Now, it was quiet. Not a soul in sight other than the three of them rushing toward the entrance. Major Suter had coordinated the special event, always trying to find new ways to make things fun, yet challenge the cadets both mentally and physically. He was the first one they saw when they arrived, with seconds to spare, panting and out of breath. The rest of the cadets were already in formation near midfield.

"Nice of you to join us, gentlemen," Major Suter gently rebuked, letting them know their close call didn't go unnoticed. One of the first lessons they learned in the military was that early is on time and on time is late.

Falling in the rear of the formation, something was different. Usually one of the upperclassmen led the formation, called "out stretches," and led them through their physical training. That was one of the many approaches used to prepare the cadets for their future leadership positions. Paul knew that planning, organizing, and leading physical training while becoming comfortable giving orders to a large group was all part of that preparation. Altogether, there were more than fifty cadets. Today, Major Suter was out front.

"At ease," he called. "Camp Randall is one of the many beautiful places here on campus and I'm glad we get to train here today instead of back at the gym. We've got to mix it up every once in a while. Make it interesting. Keep you on your toes. Today is about more than physical training," he said, pausing to allow everyone to develop some thoughts about what was coming next. "Right now, most of the college is asleep, yet here you are. Why? Why are you here when you could be snoozing?" Again, he paused, looking around the formation. All eyes were glued on him. "Everyone's reason is different, but all likely leads to the same place. You have a strong desire to serve, to protect the things you love, to allow all of your sleeping classmates the opportunity to come enjoy the Badgers playing here next Saturday. There are so many great places in our country and so many freedoms to take advantage of, yet you will not always get that opportunity."

JD glanced sideways at Paul. Paul could sense his confusion from the furrow that formed between his eyebrows, yet his posture remained disciplined like a true soldier. Chad wore a similar expression. This was not what any of them expected as they raced to PT this morning. Major Suter had been purposely coy as to what they were doing, but they knew it would be exciting. Better than the usual running, ruck marching, sit-ups, and push-ups. What Paul didn't expect was something this deep, this early.

"You pledge to protect the freedoms we hold dear, yet you may be sent away to places where you will not be able to sleep when you want, nor eat or drink what you wish. Where you will not be able to see your family, friends, and loved ones. Where you'll miss holidays, birthdays, and anniversaries, and you may not even get to watch your beloved Badgers like your classmates." This got a few uneasy chuckles.

Major Suter continued, "It will be pure misery, you'll be tired and dirty, and it will be the hardest thing you've ever done, but that will only make you treasure those great things and those great moments in your life even more when you return. Hard to understand now, but trust me." Trust him they did after nearly twenty years of service, four enlisted and the rest as an officer. He was set to be promoted to Lieutenant Colonel soon. "That's why we're all up now, preparing for that moment, so we can make it back, lead our soldiers to safety, and treasure those things we hold dear even more. By a show of hands, how many people know what happened to the USS Cole yesterday?"

About a dozen hands immediately shot up, and three more reluctantly joined as they considered, clearly showing they had heard something, but not quite sure what. JD, Chad, and Paul's hands remained by their sides.

17

"You need to know this stuff," Major Suter continued, "because it affects you. If you don't have a habit of keeping up with the news now, then I suggest you start. Cadet Waylon, I saw your hand up. What do you know about the event?"

"All I know is that the USS Cole was attacked off the coast of Yemen yesterday. There is lots of damage and a few sailors died with lots more wounded, but I'm not sure how many," he replied.

"You are correct. At least fifteen sailors dead right now, but the report isn't finalized, so there will likely be more, plus twice that number wounded on a routine fueling stop in Aden Harbor off the Yemen coast. This is something they've done many times. A huge Navy vessel, state of the art, attacked by a small skiff of suicide bombers. There is nothing routine, cadets. Nothing you should take for granted. The lives of those you lead depend on it. Nine times out of ten, or sometimes ninety-nine times out of a hundred, or in the case of the USS Cole and other Navy vessels, much more than that—nothing happens. Combat is like that. It can be boring, boring, and then a moment that will change your life forever. That's what you're preparing for. That moment. Remember that. Anyone know who might be behind the attack?"

No hands went up this time.

"The first step is becoming aware, the next is trying to gain understanding, and then with that understanding, you need to determine what you can do to prepare for and prevent situations like this from happening to you and your soldiers," he stated. "Although reports aren't confirmed yet, all signs point to al Qaeda as the culprit, given the nature and location of the attack. These are some bad dudes with ties to terrorism on US soil, embassies, our allies, and US military personnel around the globe. Founded by Osama bin Laden, they want to destroy America, and they are not going away any time soon. Like I said, we need to prepare, and that's exactly what we're going to do today."

Both Chad and JD glanced at Paul, remembering that he mentioned that name after class earlier this semester. Paul was staring intently at Major Suter, deep in thought. *There it was again—Osama bin Laden—why do I keep hearing that name?*

"Alright, I need everyone to line up at the base of the steps," Major Suter directed. "It's a race to the top and the first five to the top and back are the team leaders. Ready, set—" and the whistle blew. They were off.

JD was the second to return and was one of the team leaders along with four of the upperclassmen. Although no one else could tell, Paul knew JD was dismayed by his second-place finish. He always wanted to be the best and it would only drive him that much more.

"Now, count off by fives."

"One!" "Two!" the remaining cadets began counting.

"Line up behind your team leader," Major Suter yelled above the growing noise from the eager cadets after the counting was complete. They instantly became quiet when he spoke. "There will be five stations spread throughout the entire stadium. You'll get a card to start and then you will discover your remaining missions when you complete that task. You'll need these tennis balls as well. It will make sense to you when the time comes. If, at any point, you are 'injured,' your entire team must return to the field to simulate a MEDEVAC request. Only then will you return to the game. If you trip as you run the stairs around the stadium, you just hit a land mine. Down to the field and complete a MEDEVAC request. You get the idea. Remember, nothing is routine. Be ready for anything."

Each team was handed the notecard with their first mission. Chad, Paul, and JD were all on separate teams.

"Hey, Paul! JD!" Chad yelled. Both looked as they assembled into teams. "Anyone want to make a friendly bet? Loser buys pizza tonight?"

"You're on, my friend," Paul said without hesitation.

"Are you sure you can afford to buy pizza, Chad? Look at this team; we're stacked," JD said to his team, giving them instant confidence as they began. "It's a deal!"

And they were off. Cadre members were attached to each team, acting as advisors. Some selected cadets served as role players.

The stands above the south end zone, with Badgers brightly painted in the end zone, contained a simulated minefield that the team had to navigate from bottom to top to reach a friendly village. Jumping from seat to seat, they could only touch certain letter-number combinations. The tricky part was that two of their teammates were blindfolded. Any missteps and they were hit. The safety message associated with that card also told them to be extra vigilant with the blindfolded cadets to ensure there were no injuries. As a result, they had to complete a verbal risk assessment to the cadre member that was monitoring this event. Cadets quickly learned that even with dangerous missions, risk mitigation was a vital component of planning operations. Methodically, JD's team navigated the course with no injuries. Each of the blindfolded cadets had a personal guide, their risk mitigation, while the rest of the team figured out the best route. At the top, they received their next destination.

Section E had a simulated sniper attack from the press box above. Tennis balls began raining down on them as they read their mission. JD was instantly hit along with two of his teammates. They ran back down to the field, called in the 9-line MEDEVAC request, identifying the extent and urgency of their injuries, and were miraculously returned to life. On the way back up, one of the upperclassmen tripped. Landmine. They had to return to the field once again.

MEDEVAC request complete, JD addressed the team. "Okay, we've got this, team. Let's be smooth and fast up the stairs. Half of us will go to the station, you five, and the other half of us will flank that press box. Suppress them with all the tennis balls you've got and stay low. Don't get hit. We'll take care of business when they're focused on you." It worked like a charm.

After defeating the sniper, they received their next mission. Gather intelligence and determine the undercover enemy. Five locations were spread out across the stadium. Decision time. Break into small groups and risk losing an entire team, or stick together. JD decided to stick with the same two teams they just utilized. Using their knowledge of the stadium, they mapped the locations. Evenly spread throughout the stadium, one team took the three close points, the other team the two far points. They would rendezvous at the bottom of Section P to decipher the message.

As they departed, he glanced around. Chad's team was approaching the sniper location for the second time, only to get barraged by tennis balls again. Back down they went. He didn't see Paul's team, but he saw a dejected team coming back down to the football field from the minefield.

Returning to Section P, they had found five letters. R, S, U, E, T. Written with one of the letters was the clue that there was an insider that was passing valuable information to the enemy. They must find and confront them. Trying a few different combinations, they were confused.

"It must be a person. Maybe one of the Badger players is playing along? Or one of the cadets? Cadre?" JD wondered out loud to the team, hoping someone could solve the mystery.

"I've got it!" Cadet Kelly Winchell yelled. "Suter, it's Major Suter."

"You're a genius! Nice work," JD said, seeing that it was obvious now. They raced to find him.

"Nicely done cadets," Major Suter said when they found him, near the marching band's designated location on the north end of the field. "Your next mission is a little more fun. Do you have any tennis balls left?"

Half of their team lifted tennis balls into the air.

"Good. Now, here is your mission." He handed them the card.

JD read it out loud. "Select one tennis ball and one tennis ball only. Each member of the team must throw it once and catch it once, but only once, no more. Your mission is to see how far you can move it down the football field. The team that moves it the farthest wins. If the ball hits the ground, it will be placed at the location of the person who successfully caught it last. At that point, you will get a one-minute penalty for each person who did not touch the ball. That time will be spent alternating between push-ups and sit-ups. No gimmicks and no using anything other than one tennis ball and your team."

JD paused after he read it. "Hmmm, simple enough in theory, but does anyone have any ideas on how to do it best, and avoid the penalty?"

"I say we line up the best throwers and best catchers first to get as far as we can," Cadet Limbaugh, one of the well-respected upperclassmen, offered.

"How about one throws and the entire group waits together in case the throw isn't accurate? Then call it in the air like baseball," another explained.

"Good thoughts," JD acknowledged, as he saw Paul's team heading toward Major Suter. They would now be watched, which was completely fine with JD. He performed better under pressure. "Any other ideas?"

"Not really an idea, but we need to have some kind of assessment of skill level. I played soccer and ran track, so I can run all day, but catching and throwing is another thing," Winchell confessed.

"Alright, I think we have some good ideas on how to proceed. How about we do this? Conduct a self-assessment, one to ten, on how proficient you are at throwing and catching. We'll start with the highest and work to the lowest. The thrower will direct the catcher on the range and the rest of the team will back them up, hoping to catch it if it goes astray or maybe on a ricochet, you never know. Then, we'll proceed down the field. No crazy shots either that might blow it in the early stages and get us penalized. Work for everyone?"

"Sounds good," Limbaugh concurred and everyone else murmured in agreement.

They lined up based on their numbers and proceeded down the field with the plan that JD laid out. After a couple bobbles and close calls, everyone caught it with throws ranging from twenty yards to five yards with some nice solid bullets and others that were carefully placed under-hand throws. They ended up near the twenty-yard line on the opposite side of the field. JD was proud.

As they read their final mission, he looked up just in time to see Paul throw a monster bomb, thirty to forty yards, to another cadet who had also played high school baseball. Right in his hands, then he dropped it. Both their heads fell. Their team was stuck back near the opposing twenty-yard line almost sixty yards away from JD's team, preparing for their penalty.

The last challenge was also completed on the field. Using the troop leading procedures, a military planning process to follow after receiving the mission, and a mission to assault the opposing field goal, they had to use the elements of drill and ceremony to march their team down the field in step. Any misstep, improper commands, or movements and they would be required to start again. Anyone could lead this event. Everyone turned to Limbaugh and Winchell, by far the most proficient at drill and ceremony. They would lead the two teams. Two early missteps by some of the junior cadets, including JD, caused them a delay. They needed to refocus and slow down. They aced it on the third time. Hurrying back over to Major Suter, they could see that they were the first ones complete. High fives all around, JD personally went and thanked everyone for the hard work. Now, he'd wait to see who was paying for pizza.

Oftentimes the one boasting and making the bet is the one paying at the end. And so it was the case here. After working off their penalty, Paul's team finished five minutes behind JD's team, good for third place. Chad's team finished last.

"Alright, what do you want on your pizza tonight, boys?" Chad said grudgingly, then quickly changed tone in typical Chad fashion. "You may have won, but we had the most fun."

Before they could answer, Major Suter shouted, "Fall in!" and they rushed to formation.

"Nicely done everyone. I hope you got some exercise and had a little fun, but most importantly I hope you learned something today. You will be the ones out there leading soldiers soon, preparing for unforeseen situations, and you must always be ready. Use your time wisely to prepare yourself mentally, physically, and emotionally. With that, enjoy your weekend. Dismissed!"

Immediately after PT on Mondays, Wednesdays, and Fridays, Paul had to hustle back to the dorms, shower if he had time, skip the rinse if he didn't, and hurry to his eight a.m. Global Perspectives classes. He didn't mind, though, for two reasons. First, he enjoyed this class more than any others. Class would be especially interesting today considering the events of the past twenty-four hours. During the course, Paul learned that his professor was a Vietnam veteran who had pursued his PhD and professorship after the war. He was an activist, not like the anti-war protestors of the 1960s and 1970s, but rather an activist for timely intervention to prevent larger conflicts and prudent use of the American military. His hope was to educate the next generation in anticipation of preventing future conflicts. That's why he was so passionate about expanding each student's worldview. After earning his doctorate in international relations, he served as an advisor to President Reagan and advocated for a strong military, committing to armed conflict only when necessary — the "speak softly but carry a big stick" philosophy of Roosevelt.

The second reason Paul raced to class was Dawn. His hustle had more to do with getting a seat next to her and less to do with being on time for the actual class. They weren't officially a couple, but they were more than just friends. It started with some initial conversations in class, progressed to studying together, and finally resulted in their first date last week. The date went well, better than either expected, considering they'd just met. Paul could tell by her no longer shy smile, and the excited way she talked when he arrived in class each day, that she was falling for him. Paul was falling for her, too.

"I imagine that you all know what we'll be discussing today," Dr. Hamm began, glancing at the clock. "If you don't, then I haven't been doing my job."

With that comment, Paul felt like a disappointment, as if he had let Dr. Hamm down. He knew of the attack now, but only because of the discussion this morning. He was oblivious before that. Tuning into the news was just not high on his radar. There were too many other competing interests, but he vowed to remain more attentive.

"Al Qaeda hasn't claimed responsibility for the attack on the USS Cole, not yet anyway, but anyone that has followed their activity in the region knows that it's pretty likely. We already know that Osama bin Laden has a strong influence as the founder of that organization, but what else do we know about him?"

"Let's recap." Dr. Hamm didn't waste any time making his verdict. "He's on the FBI's 'Ten Most Wanted' list. This is for his active connection to terrorist events around the globe—Sudanese terrorist training camps, Somalia, Saudi Arabia, Philippines, and Yemen once before, to start with. Plus, connections to the 1993 World Trade Center bombing and the 1998 attacks on the US embassies in Tanzania and Kenya. He also issued a fatwa, essentially calling on the Muslim community to kill Americans and their allies. What we haven't discussed is what he's doing now. Intelligence reports indicate that he travels to Afghanistan on a regular basis. Afghanistan was taken over by the Taliban a few years back, and they practice the most brutal interpretation of Sharia law in the world. Despite that ruthless influence on the Afghan population, Afghanistan remains relatively lawless even for terrorist organizations. One of these is al Qaeda, who currently operates terrorist training camps there. In fact, President Clinton ordered a Tomahawk strike on one camp, called Al Farouq, for their role in the 1998 embassy bombings." Dr. Hamm paused to catch his breath. His face was a little flushed and Paul had noticed he tended to talk faster and more passionately as he went along. His knowledge of the subject was only over-shadowed by his passion. "What does that mean in the context of what we've been learning? What do you think is their reason for this attack?" he continued.

No one raised their hand anymore. Instead a professional discussion broke out, just as the professor had been prompting them since the beginning of class.

"To scare people," one of the students near the front mentioned in a conversational tone. "That's why I think they did it. That way others will second guess their own safety, and in that way, they're in their heads."

"Some say that they are doing it for revenge," another began, "for our meddling in the affairs of other Muslim countries. Think about Iran, Desert Storm, our influence with Saudi Arabia, and I'm sure there are more."

"What about recruiting?" Dawn asked. "Maybe, by carrying out these events that are portrayed on major news networks, they are catching the attention of people who are angry about the same thing or maybe something else. That would be my guess as to why they claimed responsibility to events like this, even when they didn't do it sometimes."

"Yeah, I agree," said Paul. "That allows their cause to grow. More recruits equal more damage. More damage equals more publicity and then their cause keeps growing." Dawn smiled at his agreement as he finished.

"You are all absolutely right. All valid reasons," the professor confirmed. "They are trying to gain recognition and influence. The more they recruit, the more they spread their message, the greater their influence. They embolden those full of hate to act independently or join their cause. That message resonates with some and their cause grows. Hard to understand and even harder to stop. There are some experts who say that bin Laden wants to draw the US into another conflict in the Middle East, likely Afghanistan, so al Qaeda can prove to the world that they can defeat the US, just like they defeated the Russians in Afghanistan. That would again grow their cause and possibly expand their influence. To them Somalia was a great victory because we left after sustaining casualties."

He paused for a moment, looking around the classroom to gauge reactions, and then peered out the window. "This is something that most Americans don't like to think about. Some reports show that there may be terrorists, al Qaeda and others, in the United States right now, training, waiting for the right moment. I don't want to scare you, just want to make you aware." Seeming to sense their discomfort at that thought, he switched subjects. "OK, enough of that for now. We'll come back to this, but let's switch directions a bit. It's indirectly related, but something that is coming up quickly and can change the strategic direction of the country, specifically in dealing with terrorism. By a show of hands, how many of you voted in the last presidential election?"

No hands were raised. Most were just beginning high school, and not yet eighteen, four years ago.

"That's what I thought, and now you are going to have a big decision in front of you. On one hand, we have the current vice president as the Democratic candidate. Al Gore will no doubt have his own views and make some policy changes, but will likely follow in the same general path as President Clinton. George W. Bush is likely to do anything but follow the same path, being from the other party. Although on some issues, the status quo may stay intact for quite some time."

Dr. Hamm paused and glanced around the classroom. "So, the question to you is how do you feel about the direction of the country? That's often what the presidential vote comes down to, not necessarily just policies and the candidate's personality. Rather, voters who are seeking change are more likely to turn out to vote and that often makes all the difference. Generally, if the country is happy with the direction of the country, the incumbent party will win."

Dr. Hamm started pacing again in the front of the classroom. "In fact, I saw a statistic once that showed if the president's approval rating is over a certain percentage, then that party is highly likely to win. If it is under that percentage, the country almost always opts for a new direction.

"We're not going to discuss partisan politics here—much too dangerous—but I encourage you to do two things," Dr. Hamm said with a slight smile. "The first is simple. Vote. But more than just voting, the second thing is to get educated. Look at how much you've learned already in this class. I hope," he said, knocking on the corner of his wooden desk. "Get educated, look at their voting record, who's in their circle, positions they've held, whether they flip-flop. I encourage you to keep an open mind as you determine the best person to lead the United States. Try not to get caught up in the parties. Alright, enough preaching for today. Let's get to our presentations and then we'll discuss how the events of the USS Cole will impact the United States going forward."

Paul raised his hand.

"Yes Paul," he called, no longer needing the names on the desk as a reminder.

"What's your prediction with the election?" Paul asked, hoping to get a nugget of insight.

"Not that I necessarily would, but I don't want to sway anyone's decision. How about I'll write my thoughts on this paper, tuck it in the drawer, and we'll look after the election?"

"Sounds like a plan," Paul said, excited at the prospect.
On a note the class could not see, he wrote the following:

> Direction of the country is generally good—strong economic growth, low inflation, high stock market, no major wars. However, the Clinton scandals will undo Al Gore, and give George Bush the win in one of the closest elections ever.

> Another prediction: Al Qaeda will attack American again if nothing is done.

He tucked it in his desk and the student presentations commenced.

What a day, Paul thought as he lay in his dorm room that night. More often lately, he found himself pondering late at night like this, unable to sleep while connecting his future to events happening across the globe. He was developing a strong yearning, a calling, to prevent all this terrorism, violence, and all the hatred that he was discovering.

JD was busy chatting on the computer with Lynn, no doubt replaying the events of this morning and contemplating their future together. Despite being apart, it was easy to see that they were still head over heels for each other, madly in love. Like clockwork, they talked every night.

Often overhearing their conversations, Paul knew it was deeper than most relationships. They already had their dream life planned—JD's duty stations lined up for the next twenty years, where they would settle down after that, what their dream house would look like, kids' names, everything. Lynn wanted to be a teacher so she had decided to go to college at University of Wisconsin-Stevens Point because she felt that they had the best program. It didn't hurt that her parents lived just a short drive away. After travelling around the world while her father was in the military, her parents decided to settle down in a quiet location, away from the hustle and bustle. Merrill, Wisconsin was the destination where her father worked his way up to become an executive at one of the local window factories. Lynn was true to the term military brat; she didn't have many close friends and always got in a lot of trouble growing up. Her parents wanted to give her a chance to escape that lifestyle, make some friends, and have a normal high school experience. Quiet Wisconsin seemed to be the perfect place for that.

They were probably right too, until she met JD, Paul thought, smiling to himself, knowing her parents were skeptical of the relationship. He had to admit, they were good together, even if her parents would not acknowledge that fact. Maybe they were scared to see their daughter fall for a military guy, knowing the difficulties that lay ahead. Maybe they didn't want to see their only daughter leave, after they had made a commitment to settle in Wisconsin. Most likely, they would simply be skeptical of any relationship. After all, she was their only child. Luckily, they didn't have to worry. JD loved her fully and completely and would go to great lengths to see her happy. Paul knew it. He made the mistake of questioning it once and would never do it again.

One night, during their senior year, he made the mistake of telling JD his doubts about their relationship. Paul told him that he was in too deep, and looking back, it probably was a little out of jealousy because he barely got to see his best friend anymore. But Paul was also afraid of seeing JD get hurt after his own struggles with Marie. Relationships were tough in general. Going to different colleges would make that tougher. Military life would make it tougher yet. Senior year, JD was spending every waking minute with Lynn, even quitting the sports he once loved—football and baseball—to get more time with her. Nights where JD and Paul were together like this were becoming rare. The way Paul saw it, she was his drug, the one thing he couldn't live without.

As Paul confronted him, JD stood and looked back at him with determination and a little defiance. "You don't get it, do you, Paul," he accused. "This isn't some silly relationship, that's here one day and gone the next. She's the woman of my dreams and I'm . . . I'm going to marry her. I'm in love with her. I'm sick of hearing that this isn't going to work, that it's not a good idea. You're my best friend and I need to know that I have your support, if no one else's."

Paul took a step back and averted his gaze, considering his response.

"I knew you were serious but had no idea how deeply you felt. Of course, you have my support," Paul paused and smiled, "under one condition."

A slight smile formed at the corner of JD's lips as he leaned forward. "Sure, what's your condition?"

"That I get to be the best man, of course," Paul beamed back. JD let out a short laugh.

"Of course. I wouldn't have it any other way. And I'll be yours, right?"

"Absolutely."

Paul never questioned the relationship again after that point, and never needed to. From that day forward, he took more notice of the strength and commitment of their relationship, rather than his selfishness of not getting to see JD as often. Paul simply looked at their relationship as if they'd be together forever.

Paul thought it was funny that JD fell for the daughter of a career military guy since his father had been very active in the National Guard all his life. Here they were in the middle of Wisconsin, with no active Army bases around, and JD and Lynn somehow found each other. Maybe it was fate that they were together. As much as JD had sacrificed to be with her during high school, you'd never know it now. He was a natural leader that was quickly climbing the unofficial ranks of ROTC. The ROTC cadre absolutely loved him and he was already friends with nearly every cadet. He was by far the most squared away — knew what was going on, had everything together all the time, knew the answers, and always looked sharp — cadet that they had seen, but unlike many of the other cadets of military parents, he was also modest.

JD also knew exactly what he wanted to do unlike most cadets at this point in their short Army career. Everyone expected he would get exactly what he wanted, too. JD wanted to be in the infantry and wanted to be an Airborne Ranger. He didn't say it often but you could tell it in everything that he did. His uniform was a little crisper than the rest, his boots were a little shinier, nothing was ever out of place. He excelled at every task from marksmanship and land navigation to understanding tactics and leadership. Just as quickly as he would master a task, he'd turn around and mentor others.

Paul thought that he probably got a lot of that from his father, who was now the commander of the Wisconsin Army National Guard Brigade. He was a Ranger as well and served in the Illinois National Guard in a Special Forces unit when he was younger, deploying to remote countries around the globe, most likely assisting in some of the numerous conflicts that they had been discussing in Global Perspectives. For his day job, JD's dad was the CEO of one of the large insurance companies in Stevens Point. That's what led them to the Merrill area, where his father got his start at Church Mutual, years ago. After assuming the helm at Sentry Insurance three years earlier, he now made the almost hour-long commute down to Stevens Point each day. In JD's eyes, his father had done everything that you could in the Army and as a businessman. JD absolutely worshipped him. At least, he did when he didn't despise him. Even though they were both the nicest people and always agreeable with others, they fought about absolutely everything imaginable.

Paul remembered two times when he thought JD's dad would disown him. Both times JD spent multiple nights at Paul's house. The first was when he quit the football team. The second was when his father found a condom in the toilet that apparently JD forgot to flush. Naïve until that moment at the level of his involvement with Lynn, JD's father panicked and kicked him out of the house. Later, he acknowledged that he was happy that JD was using protection, but the damage was done. JD avoided going home and their fighting only escalated. Even though it scared the hell out of him at the time, Paul knew that JD thought it was hilarious now. Most of their fights were about silly things. JD was aloof about his future to his father, only revealing his plan late his senior year. His dad wanted him to be successful, to have a plan, which is likely why JD rebelled. Both were stubborn. Both were set in their ways. The inevitable conflict was the result.

As Paul lay in his bunk thinking of JD and Lynn, he was restless. Despite the late hour and his lack of sleep the night before, his thoughts kept drifting back to the bittersweet ending with Marie. Paul was excited by the prospect of his relationship with Dawn, but she wasn't Marie. There was just something about Marie. During their freshman year of high school, they dated for several months, a long time at that age. Their love quickly grew and their friendship flourished. They had so much fun and made so many memories in a short time. However, like a fast burning candle, it burnt out and neither could explain why. Maybe their relationship moved too fast or maybe there was too much physical distance between them during the summer.

By their senior year of high school, they were both involved in very serious relationships with other people. Despite that, their friendship continued to grow. Nearly every week, they would talk on the phone and still passed notes from time to time at school. Every interaction in class or the hallway left Paul with an overwhelming feeling of happiness. Despite dating someone else, he couldn't deny his feelings for Marie. He was pretty sure she felt the same way. He could see it in her genuine smile and her unexpected gazes, plus the way her voice lit up when they talked on the phone. His mind would always drift back to her. With their continued friendship, it was quite natural that they would turn to each other if they ever had problems in their current relationships.

Lo and behold, relationship problems came for both. Perhaps it was the realization of leaving for college and wondering if their relationships would last through the big move or maybe things were just too comfortable and it was time for a change. Whatever the reason, both of their relationships dissolved during the spring of their senior year, mere months before they both left for college. They began to talk a little bit more, both in school and on the phone.

Finally, it was senior skip day. Marie had invited Paul up to her family's cottage. He remembered going up there with her family when they were dating. Her mother had taken a picture of them, feet dangling off the dock, with the beautiful lake in the background. Paul thought of it often. Wanting to go so badly, he never gave her a final answer, simply said he would try to make it. Unfortunately, he had to go to class in the morning or he wouldn't be able to play in the next baseball game, the following night. *Lucky JD*, he thought, since JD was no longer on the team. *Probably enjoying his senior skip day with Lynn.* As the clock slowly ticked along on the wall, Paul was undecided as to what to do after class let out. He had the afternoon free and Marie's invite was lingering. He did the math. *Four hours until baseball practice, forty-minute drive each way. Oh heck, who I am kidding.*

Marie invited him and he still loved her. Of course, he was going. *Maybe this will be the spark, the moment we get back together.* Nervously, he made the drive up there and surprisingly found it with little difficulty. *That's a good sign.* It was tucked away in a secluded location. As he pulled into the driveway, doubt swept over him. Staring at the familiar cottage he thought, *What am I doing? Why am I here?*

He pushed the thought aside. Walking up, he saw her and that excited, nervous, fluttery feeling rushed over him. *Get it together, Paul.* Wearing a black bikini, she was relaxing with some of her friends on lawn chairs.

Wow. She's beautiful.

"Hey, Marie," Paul said quietly, short of breath, trying to control his emotions and not wanting to make a scene.

Marie turned and smiled widely. "Oh, hey, Paul! I'm so glad you could make it." She got up from her chair, and gave him a big hug. *Definitely more than friends*, he thought. "I wasn't sure after we talked last night. Guess I'm worth the trip," she whispered and smiled again, looking into his eyes, but then quickly turning away. "But, I'm guessing you're still heading back for practice."

"You are definitely worth it and yes, I am heading back for practice," he confessed. "But until then, we can have some fun."

"It's a deal," she said, smiling again. Turning, they joined the rest of the group, still lounging on the lawn chairs. Throughout the afternoon, they laughed and joked. One brave soul even dove into the frigid May water only to retreat under several towels. Everyone laughed but no one followed.

Every time Paul looked at Marie, she was already looking at him. She'd smile and then turn back to the conversation. He was completely infatuated. *I want to be with her so bad.* Losing track of time, he glanced at his watch and saw that hours had slipped by.

"Sorry, everyone, gotta run. Already late for practice," Paul said as he stood. He noticed Marie sigh, almost imperceptibly. "Have a good time, everybody."

"Can I walk you out?" Marie asked, starting to get up and then hesitating.

"Of course. I'm never in that big of a hurry."

And she smiled that smile again. *Maybe I should just skip practice.*

"What are you up to this weekend?" he asked as they reached his car, trying to sound confident and hide all the mixed emotions that were running through his mind.

"Well . . . I was planning on going to this sorta concert thing in town," she answered hesitantly. The connection that had been forming over the course of the afternoon was missing in her response. *Maybe I'm making this into something it's not.*

"Would you mind if I came along with you—I mean, I'd really like to see you again?" Paul said hopefully, trying not to sound desperate.

"Yeah, I think that would be fun. Why don't you come over to my house about seven o'clock on Saturday and we'll head over there together?" she asked with some growing enthusiasm and her smile returned. "Just friends though, right?"

Paul's heart sank.

"Sure, yeah. Just friends," Paul replied, trying to act like he meant it and hoping the disappointment he felt wasn't showing on his face. *Now what?*

"OK, see you then. Hope that you're not too late for practice."

Then he was off, more confused than ever, but still anticipating the weekend.

Deciding to try to woo her, Paul showed up with flowers.

"Oh my God, Paul, they're beautiful," she said with obvious surprise, her cheeks flushed, grabbing the flowers and hugging him again simultaneously. *Good start to the evening.* "You didn't have to do that, really. But I like them. Thank you."

Paul started talking to her parents as if he was over every other day. They left and headed to a concert in the basement of some guy's house, whose parents were either out of town or didn't care. Neither knew him. Marie had heard about the concert from her friends. Their conversation was comfortable, but seemed a little forced, with some awkward moments of silence. *I wonder what her hesitation is?* When they arrived, they went their separate ways, meeting up with friends.

Paul kept trying to catch a glimpse of her, to catch her eye. Marie appeared to be having a great time and he was pretending to as well. *Should I just go over by her? But, I don't want to push her away.* He couldn't fool himself. He was disappointed not to be next to her, disappointed in her lack of interest.

Here she comes! "Hey stranger, how's everything going?" she asked casually.

"Honestly, it's fun, but I'm just here for you," Paul said, hoping to get a better read on her intentions.

"I kind of figured that. Why don't we go outside and talk? Actually, let's just head back to my parents' house and talk on the way. I'm kind of sick of this party anyway."

For the first few moments, they sat in relative silence, listening to the radio play a better brand of music than they had just heard. The highway was mostly empty, with only a few late-night cars travelling. Marie broke the silence.

"I'm having a hard time getting over him. I just don't even know what went wrong."

So that was the problem.

"I know, I'm struggling too. It's never easy, but sometimes things happen for a reason. That's why I think it's happening now. We're starting to question everything since we're leaving soon."

"Yeah . . . that's another reason that I'm confused."

Paul glanced over at her quickly. "What is?"

"Paul, there's no denying we have a certain connection. We always have. I really like you, but that also scares me. One minute I think, yeah, this could work and the next I feel like I should distance myself, like tonight."

I really like you.

Paul tried to focus. He nodded. "I know, I noticed, but I didn't know what it meant. I really like you too, you know that, and you really like me. To me, that is all there is to it."

Marie sighed and shook her head. "I wish it was that easy. So, let's say the summer goes great, we fall in love again, have lots of fun. Then what? Then, we're off to separate colleges, hundreds of miles apart."

Paul hesitated at the anxiety in her tone. "Then, that would be great and we'd find a way to make it work. Love conquers all, right?"

Marie bit her lip, looking out the window. "Paul, why did we break up in the first place, sophomore year?" she asked quietly.

"Honestly, I don't even remember now. Why?"

Marie didn't answer for a few moments. "It was just so . . . great. And then my heart was broken."

He felt horrible amid the renewed silence.

"It was great and it could be even better this time," he said finally as they pulled into her parents' driveway. She looked at him and he could see the tears filling her eyes.

"I know."

"So, why don't we give it a try?" he said, placing his hand on her leg, hoping to provide comfort. She didn't push him away.

Marie was shaking her head again. "I don't know. I'm just so confused."

"Maybe this will help," and he leaned into kiss her. For a moment, she froze, then turned her head.

"I can't, Paul. It's just not the right time. I'm sorry."

Embarrassed and hurt, he was consumed by emotions. Deep down, he was mostly disappointed. There was no hope after that. They said a quick goodbye and he got in his car and drove off.

And that was kind of where it ended, Paul thought as he pulled the pillow over his head. He was here, off on his own for the first time, and he should be thrilled. He was, but something was still missing. He still loved her and wanted to just talk to her, especially after things had ended so awkwardly. Like most students, Paul didn't have a personal computer, so he climbed out of bed to go to the computer lab. JD was still chatting with Lynn, and Paul knew he really wanted to be alone. Dorm rooms were generally not very conducive to that.

When he arrived, he checked his email and found a forward from his cousin about Taps and how it was first played in the Civil War. It was a heartwarming story that turned out to be only partly true, but it reminded him of Marie. One of the many things he loved about her was that she loved playing trumpet in high school and had played Taps at several military ceremonies. It was something unique that made her even more special in his eyes. He decided to forward it along with a little note.

Marie,

I hope you're enjoying college as much as I am so far. Knowing you, I'm sure you are. I know we haven't talked since the night of the basement band party, so I just wanted to say hi. I think about you all the time and hope that I get to see you soon. Until then, I'll be missing you.

Paul

He never heard back. Perhaps if he would have realized he wouldn't talk to her again for almost four years, he would have written something more thoughtful and profound. However, he knew from the moment she turned her head away, that it wouldn't work to pursue her. Time would be the only cure if there was one at all.

CHAPTER 3

The sun was rising over the mountains to the east when Nasir woke up. He started with his morning prayer and faced more to the east since no one was around, instead of directly west toward Mecca. He just couldn't help it, he loved watching the sunrise every morning. Salat, the ritual Islamic prayer, was the most important part of his life each day and Fajr, the dawn prayer, was his favorite for this reason. Like many teenagers, Nasir had recently begun questioning the things he saw around him every day. He never voiced these questions openly, of course. There was no place for that now that the Taliban occupied his homeland and one slip-up could result in death.

I've seen it too many times, Nasir thought. Images of the woman with the missing eye and shattered leg living on the outskirts of their village appeared in his mind. As did the child he saw torn from his parents' home and murdered. A punishment to his mother and father for not following Taliban customs and laws. There were more unexplained disappearances. People spoke about them but didn't understand. The stories from the young men from the village, now fully part of the Taliban, haunted him the most. He couldn't forget them no matter how hard he prayed.

"We lined them up and shot the men," one of the older boys, no more than eighteen, explained in a casual conversational tone when he returned from a Taliban operation last summer. "Then we took what we wanted and burned their homes. All their crops were destroyed, but best of all was watching the women and children scramble about. We knew we could have any one of them that we wanted and we did. Grabbing the children, we'd simply threaten to kill them unless the women submitted. We took turns on one after another until we were satisfied, then left. They were lucky we let them live. That should teach them to question our authority."

Others told similar stories, many worse. Murder, rape, torture, and abuse were common atrocities on their quest for power. He saw no remorse during their tales. His stomach churned at the thought of the inhumanity and violence. Given Nasir's propensity to vomit following these accounts, the other boys had begun calling him "sewage stomach" and "daddy's boy." That didn't bother him, but thoughts of the violence continued to haunt him during every prayer. He wondered how long it would be before he'd be forced to fight.

What does my future hold?

There were only three options where he lived. Either join the Taliban, pretend you supported them, or leave. Each one carried its own risk, but the safest, by far, was to join the Taliban. He wasn't sure how many people lived in Zhari, his district, but he knew that most of them supported the Taliban. He vaguely remembered a time when it wasn't like that, but he was too young to remember it well. Now the Taliban were interwoven in every aspect of their daily lives. Even before the Taliban, there was recurring violence among and between tribes. Only the protection of his father kept him safe from both, but he wondered if that would change one day.

What will I do then? What if my father's influence changes?

Maybe this daily debate was fitting, considering a proverb Nasir remembered from his youth. Their prayers were founded on the daily cycle of the sun based on Abraham's search for Allah. The story goes that as Abraham searched for Allah, he first worshiped a bright star that shone at night, thinking it was his Lord. When the star set, he realized he was in error, and turned his prayer focus to the moon. When that too set, his focus of worship became the sun. With the setting sun, Abraham concluded that neither the stars, the moon, the sun, nor any other created thing could be his Lord. He vowed to worship the unseen Lord, just as Nasir did every morning. And every morning at dawn, the interior debate raged as to what his future might hold.

Nasir had just turned thirteen last week. His mother told him that he was born just before the weather began to turn colder for the year. She was pretty certain of the year, but couldn't recall the exact date. Like Nasir, most of his friends would just pick random days to celebrate their birthdays. There wasn't much to celebrate anyways. For Nasir, the day came and went without much celebration. Still, he enjoyed it. It was something different, breaking up his mundane routine.

Shortly after prayer, with his family still preoccupied, Nasir prepared to leave their family compound to tend to his daily responsibilities.

He lived in Siah Choy, a small village named after a village elder and former malik who had recently passed away. Most of the buildings in the area were similar to his house. Single story mud structures that were simple but provided the necessary shelter from the elements and a place to share life as a family. However, his family was fortunate to live in a *kala*, an intricate compound that held many houses and much of his extended family. There was a large open area in the center where the children played and the elders discussed important matters. It served as a community center, dining room during warm weather, and a place to pray. Trees were scattered throughout the compound giving it a relaxing feeling. Surrounding the open square were the rooms where his family lived and outside of that the mud wall that surrounded the compound. He loved their kala and the fact that they had one of the largest in the area. Nasir's room had a dirt floor with a large open area built into the wall for the fire that would keep the room warm in the winter. The ceiling rose well above his head in an arch nearly ten feet tall. Built into the far wall was a mud shelf. At one time he shared it with all three of his sisters, before they were old enough to be called women. Now, he lived in the room by himself, but it was often used as a guest room for traveling visitors.

They were very fortunate to live in the foothills of a small mountain, with fertile cropland and a small stream running next to his family's home. That stream was the lifeblood of the area, supplying their drinking water and all the wadis that irrigated the fields before eventually flowing into the Arghandab River to the south. Drought dominated the entire country over the last several years, causing many to flee their region. However, his village was fortunate. Their water supply never disappeared. Many passed through the area in their quest for water. Some stayed, some continued on. His family had been here for generations and all of his living relatives lived close by with the exception of his older sisters and some aunts that had been married and moved away. His family would stay no matter what the conditions.

Dressed in ragged, cotton trousers that hung off his thin frame and an equally unkempt cotton shirt that was once white, but now more closely resembled the colors of the field dirt, Nasir departed. Following the narrow, winding road that contoured the field near their home, he first checked on his flock. Behind a makeshift fence, abutting the backside of their compound on one side and grape fields on the other, two dozen sheep and a handful of lambs, grazed. Later, he'd return and allow them to search for greener pastures, before again returning them to their nighttime safety. For now, he leashed his donkey and loaded his cart. Today he was heading to market.

The landscape was a maze of trails lined with thick vegetation. Massive trees were common. The trails were the perfect size for a cart but not much more. Each path led to another in a network that connected the entire district. Eventually, they all led to the only paved road in the country, Highway 1. Several markets lined the highway. This was Nasir's destination today. From there, crops were sold in the adjacent districts or moved to the larger population centers near Kandahar City.

Entire families, fathers and sons working alongside mothers and young daughters, were continuing to harvest their fields, as Nasir rode a small cart full of vegetables, fruit, naan or foot bread, and some lamb, pulled by his trusty donkey. Together with one of the village boys, Batoor, they would gather goods from their fellow villagers and trek to the markets of the north. Nasir had always considered Batoor, who was a year older, a friend. In fact, he was his only remaining childhood friend. Many friends from his youth already fled, while those that remained grew weary of his growing skepticism toward the Taliban. His relationship with Batoor had also become strained.

"Salaam Alaikum, Nasir," Batoor shouted as Nasir approached. He was leaning against one of the many grape huts that dotted the landscape. Batoor's short stature and scrawny frame was further diminished in the shadows of the nearly thirty-foot-tall grape huts. At the structure's center was a large door and there were nearly one hundred equally-spaced slits throughout the rest of the structure, built in to allow the air to move freely to naturally dry the grapes.

"Salaam Alaikum," Nasir replied, using the common Afghan greeting meaning peace be upon you. "Are you ready for our adventure?"

"You know that I'm always ready," he said, already climbing aboard. The donkey jumped at the extra weight.

"He must not like you, Batoor. He does that every time you are around," Nasir joked, then climbed down to soothe the donkey, deciding to walk alongside him for a while. The path narrowed up ahead with towering grape fields on each side. Acres of grape fields surrounded the many grape huts as they travelled. Huge mounds of earth, nearly as tall as a person, made up the grape fields and gave the trails the feel of a maze. They were difficult, if not nearly impossible, to climb over.

"Do you think we'll run into any trouble today?" Batoor, named for bravery, usually didn't wait for too long to bring up his favorite topic. "I hear that the Taliban are anxious to get these crops sold, so they can make some money for their upcoming offensive." The Taliban took a portion of most things from the villagers to support their continuing battle against the Northern Alliance. Sometimes it was the goods themselves, other times the money, but always something. They never knew exactly how much that might be or when they would come to claim their share.

"You have nothing to fear when you're with me," Nasir claimed, but his confidence did not reflect his true feelings. In fact, he was terrified of any encounter, especially the checkpoints.

"Sure, sure, we'll see, sewer stomach. Must be nice to have

a father with so much power. Me, I can't wait to get out of here and join them. That will be a real adventure. What about you, are you still avoiding it as long as you can?"

"I'm not avoiding anything; I just like being here." Again, his answer avoided his true feelings. He wanted nothing to do with the Taliban.

"Sure, sure. I just think you're afraid."

"I'm not afraid of anything," Nasir declared, hopping back on the cart. "Just don't like all the stories."

"We'll see about that soon, won't we?"

Up ahead, they could see Highway 1. Motorcycles screamed around the traffic that was stopped up ahead. Dozens of cars of all varieties were lined up. Bongo trucks strapped down with crops. A bus had a mattress fastened on top with several kids enjoying the ride. Semi-trucks mixed in with small pick-up trucks. Carts pulled by donkeys, some hand-drawn carts, and pedestrians passed on the side, moving much faster than the stalled traffic. They couldn't see it but knew it must be a checkpoint. Exactly in the direction they needed to go.

"Last week, I heard that they shot a boy, just older than us, for refusing to give them his cart," Batoor said, knowing that it heightened Nasir's fear. "But they didn't kill him, just shot him in both knees so he couldn't pull the cart anymore."

"Why do you seem to enjoy stories like that?" Nasir asked.

"Why do you seem to hate them? We're some of the chosen ones. My father is off fighting for the Taliban and yours is a malik in charge of the village where Mullah Omar came from. They won't mess with us. We're part of the Taliban, the ones with the real power in Afghanistan. We control the country now."

Nasir didn't know what to say. They walked on in silence.

Their tribe, the Alizai, had been very supportive of the Taliban from the beginning. The few that weren't were quickly killed and the rest followed suit. Some, like Batoor and Batoor's father, loved being connected to power. Others may not have agreed with the Taliban, but they weren't dumb. For them, it was purely for survival. Nasir was one of them and learned it from his father. His father despised the Taliban in private, but offered overwhelming support in public.

Nasir remembered when Mullah Omar came to, or rather returned to, Sangesar, named for the abandoned British stone fort from the 1800s, after the Soviets were defeated. Omar came and started a madrasa, where older children were educated in the proper Islamic ways. Nasir never attended because he was still too young, being only five at the time. Omar's views were extremist and after a few years he had enough recruits to take the next step. It all started when Omar heard that two local girls had been kidnapped and raped. He killed the warlord responsible and hung him from the barrel of an old Russian tank as a sign to anyone that wanted to oppose him. From there, Omar armed fifty students, or Taliban, the Pashtun word for student, who believed in his cause and together they fought local warlords that were feuding as part of the struggle for power in the Soviet's absence. That was about six years ago now. His cause gained momentum and before the end of 1994 his Taliban forces claimed the entire Kandahar area. Two years later, they overthrew the capital of Kabul. President Najibullah was castrated and dragged around the palace behind a jeep, before being shot to death. His brother suffered a similar fate. From that moment on, the Taliban essentially ruled Afghanistan with Mullah Omar as their president, with only small pockets of resistance in the north.

Many loved him for what they saw as his righteousness and for eliminating local conflict. They called him their savior. Soon, however, they discovered they must live by Allah's word under the harshest interpretation of Islam in the world.

"I guess the part I struggle with is all the rules. They just don't make sense to me," Nasir said, breaking the silence. "Have you ever heard about the laws that the Taliban government passed?"

"I'm not part of the government so why would I care? If they passed them, they must be Allah's will," Batoor retorted.

"You should care because it affects you every day. Women's veils must cover their whole body, can't be decorated or colorful. No perfume, no talking to other men, no leaving the house without their husband's permission. Forbidden from working outside the house. Forbidden from studying in schools. Forbidden from virtually any recreation their entire life. For violating these or any of the dozens of other laws, they can be whipped, beat, stoned, whatever. No questions asked. Remember the woman who was running a school in her house? When the Taliban discovered her, they beat the children and then threw her down the steps. They continued to torture her when she couldn't move with her broken leg. Who knows what else they broke. You have to remember that. I know that I can't forget it. After throwing her in jail for months, they stoned her to death for the entire village to see." His stomach turned queasy remembering.

"Of course, I remember. What do you care though? You are not a woman."

"But my mother is, my sisters, my aunts, and someday hopefully a wife. I don't want any of them to live like that. And it's not just the women. They just have it the worst. It's illegal to watch television, not that it would matter, we don't have electricity. Men must abide by their own dress codes too and can't even shave or trim their beards. Remember flying a kite as a boy? Can't do that anymore. Read books they don't like and you could be executed. That is for the fortunate ones that can read. Allah forbid you changed religions. You'd be killed on the spot."

"What, you don't want to be Muslim anymore? You're right, they'd probably kill you just for saying that. What are you thinking, Nasir? Where is this nonsense coming from?"

Nasir took a deep breath, thinking of how he could help Batoor understand. "I don't know. I just started questioning things lately, wondering if there is a better way. How do you know this is what Allah wants? Have you ever read the Quran?"

"Of course not," Batoor said, looking at Nasir quizzically. "And neither have you. Neither have most people. That's why we have mullahs. They can recite every word verbatim."

"True, but how do we know?" Nasir's anger was rising again. He took another deep breath, hoping for calm. It didn't work, only made his heart and words race faster. His stomach continued to churn. "How do we know what it says and what it means if no one we know can read the Quran? We don't. We trust the mullahs like you said. But why didn't the mullahs five years ago, ten years ago, or longer ago have these rules? How are we just now discovering Allah's words? It doesn't make sense."

"Nasir, you are treading on dangerous ground. Stop. You're going to get yourself killed." Batoor glanced around, though there wasn't anyone near, and then continued, "It wasn't exactly a wonderful place before the Taliban came to power. Don't you remember?"

It was true. Most thought that their current conditions were better than constant war and they were probably right. *What if I had been one of those children that were kidnapped, beaten, raped?* Nasir thought. He knew that he might think differently, but the truth was that his family was lucky and had managed to avoid the violence by being smart and playing along. Even before the Taliban, they gave passive support to the most powerful warlords, just as they were doing now with the Taliban. That's how Afghanistan worked. They protected their village by catering to the powerful. If someone disgraced them, they did likewise. On and on the cycle continued.

"I do remember, just wish it was different. Wish it was better."

"You've always been a dreamer, Nasir, a daddy's boy. What does your father think of all your ideas?"

"I'd be crazy to tell him and you know that. I only confide it in you, my friend," Nasir said sincerely, changing his tone. He knew that he was indeed in dangerous territory. Approaching a Taliban checkpoint was certainly no place for this conversation. If the wrong person overheard, it would surely mean his end, even with his father's protection.

Clutching AK-47 Kalashnikovs, a half dozen Taliban fighters manned the checkpoint. Another half dozen could be seen on the perimeter, providing security. Dressed in loose pants and long shirts, that looked like flowing robes, their gray robes blended into the mountainous backdrop. Each wore a white turban and the customary beard. Earth toned scarves were wrapped around each. They didn't look hardened or even cruel, rather just like a bunch of boys having fun. Nasir knew from experience that was just a deception. Evil lurked behind their smiles.

Most vehicles were passing without issue. They'd stop, pay their expected charge of either Afghanis, their local currency, or a portion of the goods they were trading. The problem came if they couldn't pay the toll or they resisted. Worse was if they were found in violation of some law. Although sometimes fighters seemed to just enjoy having fun at someone else's expense. The unpredictability terrified him.

As a colorful van, painted a combination of red and yellow, with what appeared to be a busload of children approached, Nasir could see that their demeanor changed. He and Batoor were close enough to overhear as they halted the van.

"Everyone out!" yelled the guard and shot a rapid burst from his AK-47 into the air. The children started screaming and the driver panicked. Throwing the bus in reverse, he tried to flee.

A single bullet shattered the windshield and the driver slumped over the steering wheel. He was instantly dead. Still in reverse the vehicle continued to roll backwards. Vehicles to the rear scattered in chaos, both at the shots and vehicle rolling toward them. Again, the same checkpoint guard fired, and then again, with a series of ten rapid shots. This time he aimed at the engine block.

Nasir and Batoor instinctually dropped, arms thrown over their heads in a protective pose, like many others in the crowd.

The car stopped as it began to smoke. Oil began to spew to the ground. The guards were smiling.

"Why are they shooting at them?" Nasir whispered to Batoor. "They didn't do anything. Hadn't even gotten out yet."

"I have no idea," Batoor replied in disbelief, holding his breath, hoping they wouldn't look their way. "Maybe they've been looking for this vehicle."

Two guards approached, pointing their weapons at the children. "Out, now!"

Screaming had subsided and tears replaced their cries. One by one, they exited the vehicle.

"Line up over there and face the mountains. I don't want

to see your faces," the Taliban fighter shouted with a scowl on his face. "Who's your elder? Who's leading this van?"

Nobody moved. This time the shot came right over their heads, exploding into a nearby building.

Without thinking, they hit the ground.

"Get up, get up now! I asked you a question. Who's in charge here?"

A boy, just younger than Nasir, pointed toward the driver.

"Well, that solves our first problem. What about you?" He turned his attention toward a man about twenty years old. "You look to be the oldest living person here now." He paused to let that reality sink in. "Do you think we don't know what you are doing? I'm going to ask you a question. If you lie, I'll shoot the children one by one, killing you last. Do you understand?"

He slowly nodded.

"Where are you going?"

"Kandahar City," he replied without hesitation.

Bang. The child on the far left slumped to the ground.

"No!" the man screamed and hit his knees.

"I don't believe that for one second. You are trying to escape from Taliban controlled areas to the north, where you think you'll be safe. Am I correct?"

The man made no sound and didn't dare look at the perpetrator.

Bang. Another child slumped to the ground next to the first.

The man began sobbing now. "Please stop. What do you want from us?"

"I told you. All I want is for you to answer my questions truthfully and immediately. If you do that, perhaps no one else will die at your hand."

"At my hand!" the man said defiantly, starting to stand.

The butt stock of the rifle immediately knocked him back to the ground. The guard laughed.

"Now, I believe I have your attention. I'll ask you one more time. Were you trying to flee?"

He didn't hesitate this time.

"Yes, we were leaving, searching for some place to enter

absolutely into peace as Mohammed directed."

"I see we have a mullah here," he said pointing to his companion who was still pointing his weapon at the line of children. "What else can you tell us, mullah?"

"I can tell you that I worship Allah with all my heart just like you. Please let us pass and search for that peace."

"I will let you pass on one condition."

"Please. Anything."

"If there are no Hazaras with you, you can pass freely. If there are, you will all die."

The man began to cry again and softly spoke. "Please, no. We have no Hazaras. We want no trouble, only peace."

"Somehow I think you are lying to me. Let's have a look at all these children."

Nasir's heart sank. Hazaras and Pashtuns have a history of conflict dating back generations. Most Hazaras are Shi'a, while most Pashtuns are Sunni. Now that the primarily-Pashtun Taliban ruled Afghanistan, Hazaras had essentially become a target of extermination.

The guard grabbed the child and moved the scarf aside. He smiled before turning back to the man in a sarcastic tone.

"Indeed, you are correct. I must have been mistaken. Those narrow, slanting eyes, flat ugly nose, and enormous cheeks certainly can't be Hazaras. They must be Pashtuns. Aren't they?"

Tears continued to roll down the man's cheek. Looking only at the ground, his face fell lower, knowing he was only being chastised and the inevitable was coming. "Yes, they are all Pashtuns. May we now pass."

"Certainly."

"Let them pass!" he shouted to the rest of the guards.

"Children, follow me now!" he said beginning to walk away from their disable vehicle with renewed hope, yet an urgent tone. Just as he reached the first child, the guard raised his gun and pointed it directly between his eyes.

"Do you think I'm stupid?" he whispered. "I know what you are. I know what all of you are." Turning to the other guards he said, "Kill them all and hang their bodies from the tallest buildings."

"Let this be a warning to all of you. Harbor the enemy and you become the enemy," he shouted, turning to the assembled crowd, now diminished but still plentiful, waiting to cross through the checkpoint. As he did, shots rang out.

When he turned around, they were all dead.

"Let's keep this line moving," he bellowed, prompting his fellow guards to begin funneling people and traffic through the checkpoint.

Nasir and Batoor rose and proceeded as if nothing had happened. Neither said a word. Conversation resumed in the amassed crowd, but not a word was mentioned about the murder. At the checkpoint, the Taliban scrutinized their goods and took what they wanted. The boys passed through unscathed and continued to the market.

"I can't believe that just happened," Batoor whispered after they had cleared the checkpoint.

"I know," Nasir solemnly acknowledged, his eyes never leaving the ground in front of him. "This is what I was talking about. This is what I don't understand."

"But it wasn't us. We're not Hazaras."

"I know, Batoor. We're not women. We're not Hazaras. We're the chosen ones. But, it could be us next time, or our family. Plenty of Pashtuns have died at their hand and even more Afghans that stand in their way. Don't you understand?"

Batoor had no immediate reply and walked in silence for a moment. "Maybe I don't understand. You are the only one I know that ever talks like this. Everyone else supports the Taliban with no thought. My family fights for them, shelters them, gives support. Maybe I don't want to think differently."

As he said this, two nearby men with full beards and weapons, stopped mid-step and stared at them. No doubt Taliban. They were the only ones with weapons in this part of Afghanistan. As Nasir and Batoor walked past, the men began to follow them.

"Perhaps, we should discuss this later."

"That is a good idea. Should we meet at our favorite place later this afternoon?" Nasir asked with his eyes straight ahead. As he did, the men turned and walked down an alley, out of sight. The boys spoke very little the rest of the journey.

Arriving back at his family's compound, Nasir was relieved. This had always been his sanctuary, but even more so after trips like today. He wished he never had to leave.

"Hello, Nasir," his father, Daulat, called as he arrived. Daulat was a fairly imposing man, standing nearly six feet tall and rather skinny like his son. His face looked like a wrinkled canvas. Hard years had taken their toll on his body and he walked like a man that was much older. Despite the fact that he tried to carry himself proudly, he always walked with a limp. Nasir never knew why. "How did everything go today?"

"Fine, Father," Nasir replied, "but we're a little short on supplies."

"I see and can I guess the reason?"

"Yes, Father."

Although his father did not support the Taliban behind closed doors, he was one of their biggest advocates in public. "Just as any good Pashtun would do," he often declared. As the village leaders, maliks were involved in all aspects of the local leadership and organization. His father took special pleasure in his role as village malik. His influence was helped by his large family, nice compound, and expansive cropland, but he knew his power only went as far as his support for the Taliban. Initially, he supported Mullah Omar with no questions. The warlord that Omar killed had dishonored the entire district along with Daulat's tribe. Daulat thought that he rightfully deserved to die a dishonorable death. More importantly, he wanted to protect the thing that he held most dear—his family. He sensed Omar's power from their first meeting. Resistance would be foolish and futile, whereas, an alliance would not only benefit his family, but the entire village. His assessment was correct, but over the preceding years, he began to despise the Taliban for their harsh interpretation of Islam and their cruelty.

"You made it back safely and that is what is important," Daulat said, cupping his hand around Nasir's head with affection. "Now show me what you have."

Nasir ran back to the cart and brought the best melons back first, never saying a word about the incident.

"Ah, my favorite!" Daulat exclaimed, with a smile as wide as his face. "I knew you'd get some of them."

"It was the first thing I found, Father, but there is more." He returned with two varieties of cheese.

"From the nomads?" his father asked, surprised. Nomads were once very common in Afghanistan, but decades of conflict limited their movement. Now they were a novelty. "I thought I recognized that as cheese from the Kuchis."

"You have a good eye, Father, or perhaps a good nose. We met them along the highway, just before we got to the market. And of course, I have all the essentials, tea, rice, fruits, vegetables—"

"Of course, you do, so what are we waiting for? Let's feast! Bring those to your mother. After we eat and have Dhuhr, I would like you to join me at the village shura." Usually, the prospect of a feast would excite Nasir. Not today. He tried not to show his feelings.

"Yes, Father. I'll deliver those to mother right away." Nasir turned to go, but his father grabbed his shoulder.

"What is bothering you, my son?"

"Nothing, Father."

"I've known you since you were born and I know you now. Something is bothering you. Please tell me." And Nasir did. He told him the entire story, leaving nothing out as his father simply listened. Only when Nasir was done did his father speak.

"Nasir, in times like these we must enjoy every moment we can. Feasts like these, moments with our family, sharing afternoon prayer. There has been war nearly my entire life, but I hope that you one day find peace. One of my favorite quotes from the Quran, one that I heard when I was a young boy: *O You who believe! Enter absolutely into peace. Do not follow in the footsteps of Satan. He is an outright enemy of you.* I've dreamed of that peace, but don't think I'll see it in my lifetime. I hope that one day you can have that peace."

Nasir stared at him blankly. It was the same phrase he had heard at the checkpoint earlier today. *Enter absolutely into peace.* He had never heard him talk about his own immortality, nor heard that verse. It scared him. *What I am going to do if that ever happens? If I ever lose him?*

The answer came to him without consideration. *All I can do is enjoy this day, just like Father said. Perhaps one day we'll all enter absolutely into peace.*

"I hope we all can, Father."

"Me, too. Perhaps your experience from today will help in our decision making at the shura and everyone will surely want to hear about the markets, although they are likely preparing their own feasts."

Nasir's mother, Mina, was named for love, and she lived her life just as she was named through the kindness she showed every person she met and the devotion to her family. Despite the austere conditions of their lives, Nasir had never heard her complain. In fact, she always taught him and his siblings gratitude. At the age of thirty she had four children, Storai, the youngest at eight, and Palwasha, the oldest at sixteen. She had lost four others, two during childbirth and two as infants. Even for this she told Nasir she was grateful. Many mothers were lost during childbirth without proper medical care and no doctors. She was grateful just to be alive. Like most mothers, her children meant the world to her. With dark black hair and piercing green eyes, she had a quiet beauty. Her smile was her defining feature. With full lips turned upwards and no teeth showing, it made her entire face light up. This was how Nasir found her when he delivered the food.

He ran up and wrapped his arms around her.

"You haven't hugged me like that since you were a young boy," Mina beamed. "Come over here and give me another one. I was caught off guard on that first one." This time she hugged him back with the same zeal. It was just what Nasir needed with all the uncertainty. "Now, tell me why you are hurting."

"Maybe I just wanted to show you how much I love you," he replied sheepishly, avoiding her gaze.

"Well, I appreciate that. I love you, too, Nasir. Now, please tell me. You can't fool your mother."

"What was it like before the Taliban took over?"

She pondered for a moment, not expecting the question. She rarely traveled outside their compound anymore. When she did, it wasn't very far and she was covered head to toe with a black burka. She despised wearing it but Daulat insisted that she did to keep her safe. As much as she loathed what it represented, she knew he was right. Through the stories of visitors and friends, she knew how other less fortunate woman were treated. Beaten, harassed, and even killed for lesser violations than not wearing a burka.

"It wasn't good, Nasir," she said, unsure of how to answer. "Things haven't been good for quite some time in our land. But we're very fortunate. Look at our life, especially compared to our neighbors. We have a beautiful compound, running water in our backyard that sustained us through years of drought, abundant cropland, and we have each other."

"I'm grateful for all that. I really am. I just want to hear about peace. I want to imagine it."

"Well, before the Russians came and all the tribal feuds that followed, before the Taliban meant more than just a student, I remember wandering around my village as a little girl." At this she smiled, remembering. "We were so free. Free to do what we wanted. I remember playing games with my friends. And I remember sitting and talking for hours with no cares. We came and went and didn't worry. Now, I'm sure there was crime, and maybe even conflict, but I didn't see it. But, the thing I liked best was going to school. Learning to read, learning to write, math, learning about the world. That's what I miss most, and what I miss most for my girls. They never had that opportunity, which is why I teach them everything I know. It isn't much, but at least it's something. Why are you wondering?"

"I've just never seen that and have never known that. I want to find that picture you describe."

"I hope you do, too, and I pray that you find peace. But, it won't come easy, Nasir. And you must be careful. Whatever you do, just know that I support you." Perhaps she was thinking he would leave to find that peace or perhaps she thought he would stand up to the Taliban. She could stop him but sensed that would only strengthen his resolve. Love and support was what he needed. "You are a man now and a good man. I'm sure you'll do what is right by Allah."

"Thanks, mother." And he hugged her again, not fervently as before, but gently and held her embrace.

"How is that feast coming?" His father limped through the door. Nasir had the feeling he had been listening.

"Just getting started, Father."

"Since we haven't started yet, perhaps we'll have our afternoon prayer early. I think we could all use that and it's getting late. Then we can take our time and feast. Will you join me, Nasir?"

"Of course, Father."

Sun shone bright on their faces as they entered the center of their compound. With structures all around, this was a large open dirt area, where they commonly prayed.

"Today, we say a special prayer for peace," Daulat said, looking to the sky as he placed his prayer mat on the ground. Nasir placed his next to his father's. Standing tall, they raised their arms in unison.

"Allahu Akbar." With hands folded over their chests, Daulat recited his verse from earlier. *"O You who believe! Enter absolutely into peace. Do not follow in the footsteps of Satan. He is an outright enemy of you."* They raised their arms again. "Allahu Akbar." Bowing at the waist, they recited, "Glory be to my Lord Almighty." Standing tall again, they called out in unison. "God hears those who call Him. Our Lord, praise be to You."

Together, they knelt and rocked forward until they nearly kissed the earth. "Glory be to my Lord, the Most High." Rocking back, Nasir assumed the prostrate position with his legs touching the ground from his knees down and the rest of his legs gathered on top. "Allahu Akbar." Then, he rocked forward again. His father rocked in unison reciting the solemn words. Together they prayed. Father and son, side by side.

Nasir was his father's pride and joy. Moments like this proved it. Increasingly, he found himself managing all aspects of the cropland and homestead. He loved this time with his father and had an immense amount of respect for the man. It was clear that he was being groomed to take over the household as the eldest son of his well-regarded father. Years ago, Nasir would have been excited about staying and protecting the homeland that he loved so much, but now he wasn't so sure. For a while now, he had known he was different and he knew he would have difficulties supporting the Taliban like his father did in order to protect their family. Today firmed his resolve. Of the three options for those that lived in Zhari, leaving seemed more and more like the best option, although he had no idea when or where he would go. Allah would dictate the time.

With Storai by her side, Mina thought of her children as she prayed. Her other two daughters had been married since they were fourteen, just like her. Diwa, who was two years older than Nasir, lived in the same compound. She would be joining them for the feast. Traditionally, the wife leaves her home and lives with the husband's family or the couple will venture out on their own. Diwa's husband, Sarbaz, tragically lost his family the year before they were married. His father died fighting for the Taliban in their pursuit of Kabul and his mother had been violently raped and beaten by an opposing warlord in his absence. Neither incident was ever discussed openly. The pain was simply too great. An uncle had taken him in and arranged the marriage. Her other daughter, Palwasha, had married several years earlier and was rarely seen. Both marriages had been arranged according to local traditions to up and coming soldiers of the Taliban movement. Daulat had relatively little choice since most young men were supporting the Taliban and he obliged "like any good Pashtun would." To say no to an eligible suitor because he happened to be a member of the Taliban was a sure death sentence. Their husbands and their families paid the necessary fee and he grudgingly let them go.

Mina remembered mourning for days. As she thought about it, she never really stopped. She felt so fortunate to have Diwa and her husband nearby. Mina and Diwa spent most of their free time together, along with Storai. She had been able to shelter Storai for her entire life and enjoyed her company. She already dreaded the day she had to leave. She hoped by then there would be peace. Nasir was her only surviving son and today she especially prayed for his protection. From Daulat, she heard stories and understood they were very fortunate. Most young men, those not much older than Nasir, were already fighting for the Taliban or being sent to training camps like the nearby Al Farouq for al Qaeda. Her husband spoke of them more often now and always with disgust. She couldn't bear the thought. Today, she prayed for peace. Peace for her children.

Shortly after prayer, Diwa arrived to prepare the feast. Storai eagerly helped them both. Daulat and Nasir were still talking in the courtyard. Sarbaz arrived a short time later and joined the men. Before long, the tablecloth was spread across the courtyard ground with their feast.

When they were all assembled, Daulat rose. "This is quite the feast that you have prepared. Thanks be to Allah for this food. Thanks to my son for harvesting and trading at the market and thanks to my wife and daughters for preparation. Together our family is strong. Now, we eat!"

Naan, a traditional flatbread, was used to scoop the rice, beans, and lamb. Everyone shared freely from the food in the center and the conversation was lively. Water was boiled from their nearby stream, for the freshly brewed green tea that was poured in every cup. Daulat savored his melons and cheese from the nomads. Pomegranate and grapes rounded out the dinner. Most days, their meals weren't this hardy, but today with the harvest and trading, they could indulge.

"Nasir, I've changed my mind," Daulat announced just as they finished eating. "You will not be attending the shura. I believe I have everything I need and want you to enjoy the afternoon," Daulat stated as he finished. "Sarbaz, what are you hearing in the village? You've been awful quiet today."

"Thank you, Father," Nasir said before Sarbaz spoke. The slightest smile showed at the corner of his mouth. He'd been hoping for that.

"There have been some concerns about the share of the harvest that we are taking. But, I always hesitate to bring up issues like this in front of the women," Sarbaz stated.

"Very well, we will depart," Daulat acknowledged. "Thank you for the wonderful meal," directing the comment toward his wife. "We are truly fortunate for this harvest and must remember this feast. Nasir, will you please join us?"

Nasir's smile faded, knowing his departure had been delayed.

"Tell me their concerns," Daulat directed.

"Many are afraid they'll starve, that our cause is taking too much," Sarbaz said, always speaking from the Taliban viewpoint that he fervently supported. "They will come to you, asking for help, asking for you to speak with us, but there is no other way. Our cause is growing and the fight must continue," he paused, "and I will be leaving again soon to continue our fight in the north. We've nearly captured the entire county and with the help of Osama bin Laden and his fighters, we can finish what we started and establish Pashtun dominance throughout the country. That is the message I need you to tell them," he said with a certain finality that was unaccustomed when speaking with elders, particularly a malik. However, Sarbaz understood Daulat's unsaid, private reservations and he understood his position of dominance. He leveraged that at every opportunity. He sneered as he looked toward Nasir. They had never seen eye to eye. Nasir kept his distance and dared not cross him.

"I understand your concern, but I don't like your tone. We took you into our family and I demand your respect," Daulat scolded, not for the first time. "We may not see things the same way, but you know that I will, and always have, given my support to the Taliban cause, just as I have to you. I, however, always have to look out for our village as well. Something that you don't understand."

"I'm sorry, Father. Forgive me."

"Of course. You know that I have concerns about this growing relationship with bin Laden and these training camps. We're attracting attention that we don't want, and it may harm us all."

Nasir's interest grew at this. He had only recently heard about these training camps.

"It does not concern either one of us since we have no control. They are helping our cause and in turn we provide them refuge in our country. It's that simple."

"Nothing is ever that simple," Daulat declared, ending the conversation.

After bringing in more water from the stream for his mother and tending to the flock, Nasir took his afternoon prayer, Asr, in solitude. He was happy of his reprieve from the shura. Today, his father had greater concerns than preparing his son to one day lead the village. Daulat was again caught in the balancing act. Away from the family compound and the eyes of Sarbaz, Nasir again pondered his future. More and more, he saw it wasn't here. Where, he wasn't sure, but somewhere that offered peace.

Batoor was waiting where the small stream by Nasir's house met the Arghandab River. Both enjoyed the soothing water and the closest village was just out of sight. Diwa had showed him this place when they were both children, when she was free to roam. They'd play in the river on warm days and search for fish and crabs on other days. Now, like her mother, Diwa spent nearly all of her time in the compound. Under Sarbaz's watchful eye, Nasir now rarely talked to his sister. Even though she lived in the same compound, he missed her greatly. Storai joined him here occasionally and helped out with the flock and crops, but he was always afraid for her. Afraid something terrible would happen that Nasir could not stop. He sensed his mother was worried, too, and let her out less and less.

One thing that changed since Diwa and Nasir came here years ago were the poppies and marijuana fields that now dotted the landscape. All the land that didn't grow grapes, or crops for food and trade, was cultivated with either marijuana or poppies to fuel the lucrative drug trade for the Taliban. Each year more and more cropland went into this effort. One of the largest fields, with marijuana plants that towered over Nasir's head, was located at this juncture. Nasir loved to sneak off and smoke hashish whenever he got a chance and Batoor was usually in his company. It allowed him to escape the reality that he lived in, if only just for a moment.

"My brother leaves to fight with the Taliban in the north

soon," Batoor said. "I've decided to join him and will be going to training tomorrow."

For a moment the boys just looked at each other. Both knew they had drifted apart. Their conversation today foreshadowed what was to come and Batoor's proclamation confirmed it. Both knew that their lives would go down separate paths. Their childhood was ending.

Nasir was speechless, but all he could think about was Batoor doing the evil things they had seen today. He couldn't imagine his childhood friend ever doing that. "Even after—"

"Before you start, Nasir," Batoor interrupted with fiery passion, already breathing hard. "I know you don't understand and I realized today that you never will. We see the world differently. Our family isn't rich like yours. We don't have a large compound with fields everywhere. My father isn't a malik. Our lives are better now. Better with the Taliban in charge. Better with Pashtuns in charge of our land. There has always been death and violence our whole lives. I want to be on the winning side of that. Sacrifices have to be made, just like today. I know that you will never understand."

Nasir looked at his friend, not knowing what to say, not wanting to fight. "Sarbaz is leaving to fight, too. He's not sure when he'll return but he carries the same passion as you. Maybe I'm the one who doesn't belong. All I want is peace and it's clear this isn't the place for that."

"That's what I want too, Nasir. That's why I'm going. We just have different means to accomplish peace."

Nasir wasn't convinced, but reluctantly agreed. "Maybe, I just have a hard time accepting that peace can come through more killing."

"That's 'cause you're a dreamer. You don't see reality. As I said, we will never agree. But, I hope we will always be friends."

"Of course, more than friends. We'll always be brothers."

At that Batoor parted and Nasir remained, deep in thought once again. Confused at the future, yet certain it wasn't here. *But where? And when?*

At sunset, the family was again together in their kala for their sunset prayer, maghrib. Everyone together for a moment of peace. There were no visitors tonight. Lately, it had become routine for visitors to stay for days, no doubt there to communicate with the leader of the Taliban, who grew up just down the road, or his influential lieutenants who frequently travelled between his former home, Kandahar, and the frontlines of their latest conflict. The harmony continued into the evening. Cool autumn air forced them inside shortly after dusk, and without electricity they gathered around a small earth fireplace for warmth and light.

Nasir would always try to recall moments like these as he pushed out the horrors he had witnessed in his young life. Today at the checkpoint was one of those times he would always try to, but never could, forget. *Every passenger massacred, just because they thought they were Hazaras. Just because they were different.*

Nasir's day ended as it began with Isha'a, his night prayer. Only one verse came to mind tonight. *"O You who believe! Enter absolutely into peace. Do not follow in the footsteps of Satan. He is an outright enemy of you,"* Nasir whispered, just as his father had earlier that day. From his prayer mat, Nasir saw his father do something he had never done before. Breaking his prayer rhythm, he turned, and smiled at Nasir.

CHAPTER 4

With his last final exam complete, Paul was done for the school year. The first year of college had been an absolute blur and now it was coming to an end. All in all, it had been a good year. Coming back after Christmas break, the myths turned out to be true as they arrived to find a ghost town. Of the eight guys they called neighbors, only four returned. Three had failed out and one decided to move after his buddy wasn't coming back. That left an empty room next to the trio and Paul jumped at the chance for a room to himself. He loved JD and Chad had become a great friend, but Paul was an introvert through and through, and needed a little more space. That way he could hang out with them, watch movies, play Mario Kart, but then disappear into his sanctuary. It worked like a charm.

It worked especially well when Lynn came to visit, which was often. The four of them had fun together during the day, exploring the city, but every night as the sun got lower on the horizon, JD's hands started to get lower as well. Then it was time to escape. Chad would usually follow him over, needing a sanctuary as well.

They partied a little, made some good friends, and took advantage of everything they possibly could on campus. There was a club for everything under the sun from the Art Club to the Pistol Shooting Club. Campus had dozens of intramural sports and they played in a few. The winner received a coveted t-shirt that students would proudly wear around campus declaring their victory. They somehow managed to win one, for being the Intertube Water Polo champions, a sport they didn't know existed until they went to college. They lost every game during the regular season and then won every game during the playoffs by forfeit. It wasn't pretty, but they wore that t-shirt with pride everywhere they went.

They went to watch the Badgers—football, basketball, volleyball, it didn't matter—every chance they got. Camp Randall Stadium was a sea of red every home game and a madhouse, especially in the student area of Section O and P. Students chanted back and forth throughout the game to fire up the crowd. It didn't take much to get the Badger faithful going. Those that didn't like it could leave. This was football after all and this was their school. They belted On Wisconsin and jumped around every time the song declared they should. Paul was pretty sure that Madison was the only college where you learned how to cheer at football games during the freshman Welcome Week. They did waves of all sorts—super-slow, super-fast, backwards, forward. And they always stayed for the band after the game. Most would get tanked before and after the games and that only added to the excitement. Plus, they always had some drunk passed out close to them to make fun of, write on, or do whatever other funny things came to mind. It never failed. Badger basketball was another favorite, although they suffered a huge let down when Coach Bennett up and left after only three games into the season. The year prior they were in the Final Four for the first time in almost sixty years and then he just up and left. No one could figure it out. Brad Soderberg tried his best but he was in a tough position and was quickly let go at the end of the year. Nothing short of a long March Madness run would have saved his position. They tried to make it to every sporting event, but it just wasn't possible. There was simply too much going on and they loved it. Most of their conversations revolved around sports, girls around campus, and the Army. Rarely did they talk about school and even less so about anything that was going on in the world around them, despite Dr. Hamm's appeals and Major Suter's warnings. They simply wanted to enjoy life now, not worry about the future.

Soon, JD and Paul would be finished loading his car and ready to head for home. First, though, he had a hard goodbye. Paul and Dawn were meeting in fifteen minutes at their favorite café. Looking at the time, Paul hurried out the door. As he exited the building, Paul noticed Dr. Hamm across the street, waiting for the light to change so he could cross. Without a doubt, he was Paul's favorite instructor and they conversed frequently after class ended. He waited, wanting to say good-bye.

The class truly lived up to the name, Global Perspectives, and Paul had a new awareness of the world around him, even if he tried not to think of the future. He partly avoided it because it made him uneasy. One incident could alter his entire life, and the lives of all the military service members, and their families. The men and women he would soon lead. Those that he called friends, his ROTC buddies, would be the ones serving alongside him. That fact was always in the back of his mind now, no longer oblivious to the violence and hatred that existed in the world.

"Dr. Hamm," Paul said, smiling as he approached.

"Paul, good to see you," he replied, firmly shaking his hand and looking him square in the eyes. "Off for the summer yet?"

"Just finished, grabbing lunch, and then packing up."

"Good, that's always exciting. Heading home, right?"

"Yep, heading home this summer. Maybe something a little more exciting next summer." As fun as the year had been, Paul was excited to get home. Paul valued his independence but wasn't ready to leave the comforts of home during the summer just yet. He also missed his siblings badly. Being away from them had been the hardest part of the first year.

Dr. Hamm smiled. "You'll have plenty of time for excitement. For now, enjoy time with your family and friends. You'll miss these days once you're in the Army. I know I still think back to them all the time. We discussed a lot of eye-opening, important events in class, but I hope you don't lose sight of enjoying the moments. So many people say goodbye with a naïve spirit, thinking they will see each other again soon, saying they will keep in touch, and then offering a simple good-bye. They truly believe or maybe hope, that they will meet again soon, but the truth is many moments like this are fleeting. They are only there in the moment and you can never return to them. Not just college or summer friendships, but the feelings of playing when you're a child, the feeling of your first kiss, holding your child for the first time. We all hope that we'll return to those feelings, but we rarely do. The only remedy is enjoying the moments while you are there." He seemed lost in his own thoughts, then refocused as he looked at Paul. He laughed. "Look at me, once you're a professor you can never stop teaching. Doesn't matter if you are in the class or not."

Paul didn't mind. In fact, he had grown to appreciate his guidance. Like many Vietnam veterans, Professor Hamm didn't discuss his time there much. Paul got the sense that he had seen some horrible things by the way his eyes misted over, and how he stared blankly into the distance at times. The thousand-yard stare Paul had heard it called. No doubt he was envisioning those that were no longer there, wishing he could bring them back.

"No, I really appreciate all the advice. Even if it is over my head right now, it will probably all make sense someday. I really enjoyed the class, actually it was my favorite all year," Paul confessed, happy to see the pleased look on his mentor's face. "It definitely makes me think more about the world, but in a way I think I'll enjoy this summer more than any others. Different perspective, I guess, just like you were saying, you know?"

"I do indeed, Paul, and you sound like you are wise beyond your years. Perhaps, we have a future professor here?"

"Me?" Paul replied, surprised at the suggestion. "I've never thought about that before. Actually, never thought about anything else once I decided to go into the Army."

"Well, you'd make a good one."

A professor. Hmmm, never considered that. Paul looked down and smiled, taken back by the compliment. "Thanks," he finally managed.

"Well, enjoy your vacation, Paul, and I'll see you next year."

"Sounds good, you too." Paul started to walk away but turned back. "Dr. Hamm, do you have another minute?"

"Sure, I'm not in any hurry. You're the one heading home. I've still got a few more days before the semester ends for me."

"I'm just still shocked that you were able to predict the election," Paul admitted. Professor Hamm had revealed the note predicting George W. Bush would win in a close election a few days after the 2000 election. His prophecy of a tight election was almost surreal after George W. Bush won the electoral college by a 271 to 266 margin, and Al Gore won the popular vote by a 50,999,897 to 50,456,002 margin. It all came down to Florida where fewer than 600 votes changed the course of the election. Recounts confirmed President Bush as the winner. "When you had me come up to the front to verify for the class, I was shocked as I'm sure you saw. But there was something else written there that I saw, but you never talked about it. Not directly anyway."

For the first time that Paul could remember, Professor Hamm looked noticeably uncomfortable. His eyes looked past Paul and he was uncharacteristically shuffling his feet. "You weren't supposed to see that, Paul, but you're probably not surprised now that you did. When I was an advisor to President Reagan's staff, I would often make these predictions and then check in to see if they came true. Most didn't, but some did, and I found I got better as I studied history more and stayed up with current events around the world. Teaching this class and learning more about some of these extremists, I fear that America will get attacked again, similar to some of the embassy bombings. It will likely be small scale, but our response is unpredictable. I hope I'm wrong."

"I hope so, too, but if not, I'll be ready."

Professor Hamm looked uncomfortable again. "I know you will, Paul, but I truly hope that it doesn't come to that. Just remember what I said and enjoy the moments while you're in them."

"I will, and thanks for everything this semester."

"It's my pleasure Paul and you take care. Enjoy your summer."

America getting attacked. It's hard to fathom. What would my life be like now that I'm in the military? Well, it didn't change after the Oklahoma City bombing or after Osama bin Laden's plots. Why would it change this time? But he knew the answer. He raised his right hand and swore an oath. Caught up in thought, Paul was now standing awkwardly on the curb as people raced by him in all directions and traffic rushed by. *Dawn!* He would certainly be late at this point. Paul didn't want her to leave, especially without saying goodbye.

"And here I thought standing me up was your way of breaking it off for the summer," Dawn said with a hint of spite in her voice as Paul approached the table. Before he could answer, she stood, smiled, and kissed him. She had a way of easing the tension quickly. "Did you run over here?"

"Yeah, sorry I'm late," he replied sheepishly and kissed her on the cheek before sitting down. "I ran into Dr. Hamm on the way here. That's where it all began, right there in his class, remember? Did you really think I wouldn't make it?"

"Of course I knew you'd make it, but there was a twinge of doubt. But I know I've got you hooked and it's going to be a long summer apart, so I figured you'd show. Promise you'll write and visit?"

"Every chance I get. Maybe I'll even convince my family that it would be a good vacation spot."

"That would be nice, but I really just want to see you, if you know what I mean." And Paul did. The blush hue rising in his cheeks indicated just that.

"And I want to see you, too, of course, and don't worry, I know exactly what you mean," and he winked. After meeting in Dr. Hamm's class, their relationship had progressed quickly. It didn't take long before Paul was spending all his time with her. Then, it was him instead of JD that was gone all the time with his girlfriend. JD didn't mind though. In fact, he completely understood.

They both ordered their usual: club sandwich for Dawn and a Reuben for Paul.

"Besides visiting me this summer, what do you have planned?" Dawn asked as they waited.

"I'm really excited about seeing my siblings. Can't believe how much I miss them," Paul said, but could tell by the distant look on Dawn's face that she didn't understand, being an only child. Paul's siblings had met Dawn earlier this year when they visited, but the visit was brief. She never asked about them again. Paul decided to change directions in the conversation. "And my Mom and Dad, although it's going to be tough living at home again after a year of freedom."

Dawn didn't reply and her distant look lingered. "Why does this always have to happen?" she finally began. "We've been hanging out almost every day, loving every minute, and now we have to go home and not see each other for a month, maybe more, who knows? Reminds me of my childhood."

Dawn had told Paul how she was from a small town in the northern part of Wisconsin, a little vacation community called Delta. Her parents owned a resort on the lake and she loved everything in the outdoors. In fact, she loved most things about growing up on a lake—the fishing, swimming, hiking trails, sledding in the winter—but the thing she didn't like was the fact that people were constantly coming and going.

Each week, new families arrived. It was great having lots of friends to play with until she was about thirteen. That's when she became interested in boys. It seemed that every week during the summer she had a different boyfriend, and every time they broke her heart. Each year the relationships got more serious. They promised to write, call, stay connected. She held her end of the promise and would sometimes get a letter or two in return. Her heart would break. Then, it was over until they showed up next year. More heartbreak. So, she got used to the routine.

They had this conversation several times, usually at the end of a heated argument. Dawn's insecurities came out often and drove Paul nuts. She wanted to know who he was with and what he was doing at all times. Paul loved his independence. There was bound to be conflict, but each time they got over it and seemed stronger. Both loved to make up. The last few weeks had been especially difficult, with summer break looming.

"I know, it sucks. Really sucks, but you have to be excited to see your family."

"Of course, and I miss the lake, too, but I want to be with you. Promise you'll visit as soon as you can?"

"You know I will. How could I not, just look at you?" he

said, raising his eyebrows and smiling.

"Paul, I'm serious. I'm worried you'll find someone else, get bored, not want to do the distance thing over the summer, whatever, just because I'm not there."

"Dawn, you're being silly. We've talked about this before. I'm not going to find someone else or get bored," Paul said, yet an image of Marie flashed in his mind as he spoke those words. "I want to be with you and I will definitely come to visit every chance I get."

"Promise?"

"I promise. Now, let's enjoy our food and talk about all the fun things we'll do when I come up there."

"OK," she acquiesced, smiling reluctantly.

Conversation was light during the meal, but the tension remained. *How will we ever make it through Army life if we can't even make it through a summer?* Paul thought, and not for the first time. Dawn's insecurities ran deep, but the moment came when they had to part. Hand in hand, they walked back to campus, back to her dorm. Arriving at her room, she burst into tears and hugged him. "I don't want to let go."

"I know, baby, me neither," and he kissed her.

"Kiss me again," she said as soon as the first kiss ended. When that kiss ended, she wrapped her arms around him again. Her eyes were pleading for him not to go. Paul returned the embrace, looked into her eyes, and kissed her on the cheek. Then he left.

Paul would definitely miss her, but he vowed to take Dr. Hamm's comments to heart. *Enjoy every moment.* With that in mind, he strolled back to his dorm room, free and unburdened.

JD and Chad's door was wide open when he walked past. The window was open too, allowing the cool May breeze to flow through. He couldn't help recalling with a smile, the time they had tried to barbeque on Paul's little tailgate grill in their room last fall, thinking that an open window and small fan would push the smoke out. Unfortunately, the fire alarm gave them away. The RA didn't find it funny either and confiscated their grill. They'd get it back today. Moments like those were some that Paul would never forget. Half packed boxes and bags were scattered throughout the room as Paul peered in.

"You're not going to believe this," JD said close to his ear as Paul walked past him, entering the room. JD was heading out in the opposite direction. Judging by his short tone and quick exit, Paul got the sense that he was flustered. Maybe just shocked. He couldn't put his finger on it, but it wasn't typical.

"What?" he asked, but his question went unanswered. JD was already halfway down the hall.

"There you are," Chad said, appearing uneasy himself. "How was your lunch with Dawn?"

"Not bad," Paul responded. "What's going on around here? You two are acting funny. Should I be watching my back, expecting a joke?"

"No, nothing like that. JD and I were just," he paused, avoiding Paul's gaze. "Well . . . just talking, and he thinks I'm making a mistake."

"About what?" Paul asked, growing short himself at the confusion.

"I'm not coming back next year. Already let the cadre know that I'm done."

Paul opened his mouth to speak but didn't know what to say. Just yesterday they were playing Mario Kart after lunch and talking about their summers. Chad had given no indication, but he continued now.

"Shocker, huh?"

"You can say that. Wow! What are you going to do?"

"Not too sure yet. I like Madison, but want something more, I guess. I want to feel like I'm making a difference now, not waiting until after graduation. Plus, I want the big city, bigger city I should say. You know, people from all over the world, at all hours. My heart is set on New York City, but we'll see what happens."

"I don't what to say, Chad. That is a shocker."

"College was never really for me either. I need more action and excitement." Chad was smarter than both of JD and Paul, probably both combined, but he worked just hard enough to get by and it had cost him in the grade department. This was a guy who didn't study for one of the biggest Calculus 2 exams of the semester, got a 100%, which was just unheard of, and still managed to almost fail the class. He assumed that he did well without studying for one exam, so he wouldn't study for the others. Not surprisingly, that turned out to be a bad idea. The semester wasn't a complete failure for Chad. He did win the Stanley Cup on his NHL 2000 hockey game for his computer, as he always boasted.

"Well, that doesn't shock anyone," Paul said, smiling now. Finally, the tension was broken. "I'm excited for you. Wow, what an adventure. Right now, it's hard to even imagine. New York City. Twin Towers. Manhattan. All the different sports teams, food, people. Crazy. Yeah, that is definitely going to be exciting. Not for me, of course. Way too big for me. Heck, Madison is way too big for me. But it will definitely be exciting for you."

"Thanks, Paul. JD wasn't quite so excited. He says that I'm making a big mistake not finishing ROTC and going into the Army. Maybe he's right, but I've got to follow my gut."

At that moment JD walked back in, clearly in a better state of mind, with his wide grin. "Just the words I wanted to hear: 'maybe he's right.' Just kidding, Chad. Sorry I was a jerk, just realized that I'm going to miss you. This has been our freshman family here, now it's over."

So many people say goodbye with a naïve spirit. The words of Dr. Hamm were back in Paul's head. *Thinking they will see each other again soon, saying they will keep in touch, and then offering a simple goodbye.*

"Yeah, we'll definitely miss you," Paul said, walking over and giving him a hug, holding back emotions that were consuming him inside. "It's been a great year. Lots of good memories."

"You guys are going to make me cry over here," Chad tried to joke, smiling through his emotions. "It's not like it's the last time we'll see each other. I'm sure I'll be back in Madison and you guys can road trip and visit."

The only remedy is enjoying the moments while you are there.

"Absolutely, you can show us around the big city," JD concurred.

"I've always wanted to see New York. I'm sure it's a far cry from small town Wisconsin," Paul said.

"That's for sure, although I'll have to let you know. It was definitely a great year though. I'll miss you guys, too. More than you know," Chad said, trailing off as if he was already imagining the future. "But, I'm not gone yet and looking around we could both use some help packing up. What do you say, Paul?"

"Now, how can I say no to that? At least I can supervise, and we can make fun of JD while we pack," Paul responded.

"I would expect nothing less," JD said.

They planned their road trip and pried more at Chad's plans as they packed. If he had any details figured out, he sure wasn't saying. Finally, the bed and desk were clear. The closet was empty. Their loft had been torn down earlier, and they took the lumber out to the dumpster. It looked so bare. In one of those bittersweet moments, they all realized it was time to go.

"Lots of memories, gents, lots of memories," JD began, then lost his train of thought before continuing. "You take care of yourself out there, Chad."

"Yeah, and stay in touch," Paul added.

"Definitely, you guys too," Chad said. "Alright, I'm off. See you guys."

One more round of hugs and he was gone. It was just Paul and JD.

Paul and JD packed up Paul's little car with all their stuff and there wasn't a single bit of space to be found. They shoved things in the back window, piled the back seat to the ceiling, and barely got the trunk closed. Only when JD jumped on it did it finally shut. JD's parents had brought him to school but weren't making the trip to pick him up, so JD and Paul had to make it work. They threw out some other junk they had accumulated and were extremely happy to get rid of all their school supplies. Next year was another year and they'd worry about it then. For now, they were ready to go.

They felt even better than that first day of freedom at the beginning of the school year. They were heading home after a long absence and both were excited—no more school and no more Army all summer long.

CHAPTER 5

Chad's decision not to return to college had certain con-sequences. Some of them he was fully aware of when he decided to leave college and move halfway across the county. Others were a surprise along the way. His so-called "plan" to relocate from Wisconsin to New York City left him living from moment to moment, just trying to survive, and hoping to eventually thrive.

That's exactly what he wanted. His parents offered to help him, but he declined. Chad wanted that sense of adventure and wanted to prove to himself that he could endure any hard-ships. He had very little money, no place to live, and no way to support himself. Spending the first several nights sleeping in his car, always in well-lit areas that he hoped were safe, made the first item on his agenda became quickly apparent.

I need to find a place to live, and quick, he thought on the first sleepless night. Luckily, he had relocated during the early part of summer, when the night time temperature was ideal. Looking at some apartment advertisements, he quickly confirmed New York City's reputation of being an expensive place to live. *With these rates, I'm going to have to find a stranger willing to share an apartment.*

After night two in his car, he went to one of the only free places that he could think of—the public library. The New York Public Library was not like his local library back home. It was enormous, with a focus on aesthetics, rather than just purpose. It was more than books. The library was a symbol to Chad. Approaching the library, Chad realized that it was moments like these that he knew he made the right decision to leave Madison. Most people would never see this or be in awe of the beauty.

Although Chad had never been to Europe, he imagined

that this was how the ancient, historic buildings of Europe would look. Massive columns greeted him as he approached, with the reverent lions keeping watch of the stairs leading to the front entrance.

Entering, he was captivated by the expansiveness. High, vaulted ceilings arched over his head in what seemed like a football field sized room. Intricate artwork lined the ceiling. Large, arched windows filled the expanse with light. For a moment, Chad forget why he was here and where he was. The feeling was overwhelming at first, then fascination quickly took over.

Wandering around, he realized he failed to notice how many books there were lining the numerous shelves. Never a reader, he thought maybe he would soon become one. Finally, he stumbled upon the public computers. Needing a library card to access them, he continued his exploration until he found the correct counter. Library card in hand, he found an available computer and went to an increasingly popular website, Craigslist, to search for a roommate in an area of the city that he could afford. His vision of newfound freedom didn't have a roommate in the picture, but it was only a place to sleep. He could disappear into his room and would likely, *hopefully*, be working or exploring the city most nights. After an exhaustive Internet search for apartments and a few tangents to search for other attractions in the city, Chad narrowed it down to three options.

All the options were in the $500–$800 per month range. While he could pay for a nice house back home with that amount, it was just an opening bid in New York City, with a roommate no less. Anything less than that was too far out of the city, looked nasty and unpredictable, or he'd be living with more people than he could handle. The two most promising options were uptown, in Harlem, and a third was downtown closer to Brooklyn. He had dreamed of Manhattan but realized shortly after beginning his search that affordable in Manhattan did not mean the same thing as affordable in Wisconsin. With reservations made, he would begin his search tomorrow. With any luck it would be the last night he needed to spend in his vehicle.

The first and best option was in Harlem. Peggy was an older woman that appeared to be widowed. From the sounds of it, one of her grandchildren was trying to help her find someone to keep her company. The apartment was beautiful and huge compared to the other ones he looked at. Chad would get his own room and have space to spread out. As far as keeping a little old lady company, he thought it would be fun and maybe he could learn about the city in the process.

At nine in the morning, he arrived for the tour. Opening the door, the nauseating aroma of cats—hair, urine, and feces—came rushing to him. Gulping down breaths during the tour was the only way he could get through without suffocating or vomiting. He'd never seen so many cats and couldn't imagine how they kept them away from the camera long enough to take a picture.

Good luck trying to lure in a roommate, Chad thought, *Jud Crandall from Pet Cemetery might be the only perfect fit for this cat lover.*

Early afternoon brought him to his next option, also in Harlem, and it was even worse than the first. Daniel, not Dan or Danny, was a slob and could have had his own show as a hoarder. Again, the aroma was overwhelming, but this time it was overflowing garbage and uneaten food rather than cats. The laundry that was piling up didn't help matters either. Tunnels through boxes full of random unknowns wound throughout the apartment. More boxes covered what would have been Chad's room. Chad wasn't sure Daniel would be able to find an area to put them anywhere else considering the complexity of his current box formations.

The most baffling thing was that this mess occurred under the watchful eye of his mother. She was there for the tour and made it very clear that Chad would be seeing a lot of her if he moved in. She talked of home-cooked meals and movie nights. The prospect scared the hell out of Chad as he could only imagine what her apartment must have looked like. Losing faith, not only in humanity, but also in ever finding a place to stay, Chad said goodbye and went to option number three.

Apartment number three was downtown in Brooklyn on Lawrence Street. Instead of one roommate, there would be two. Charlie Donovan and his buddy Todd were attending the NYU Polytechnic School of Engineering right down the road and wanted to make a little money by renting out their third room. They greeted Chad at the door.

"Welcome to our humble abode, Chad," Charlie said with a welcoming smile. Dressed in gray sweatpants and a purple NYU POLY t-shirt, his look didn't match his imposing figure. At just over six-foot with a clean haircut, he was built like a football player. However, his handshake was gentle. "Soon to be your humble abode as well."

"I sure hope so," Chad confided, "because my last two visits have been a disaster."

"You mean we're your third visit of the day? There's your problem right there, my friend. Should have started here," Todd added playfully. Chad had a feeling he would fit in here just fine and thought of meeting Paul and JD for the first time. He sure missed them. "Unlike this slacker, I have class today, so I have to run. Hope to see you later, Chad."

"Yeah, nice meeting you," Chad said, shaking Todd's hand before he turned to leave.

"Ready for the grand tour?" Charlie asked.

"You bet," Chad responded as Charlie walked into the kitchen.

"This apartment was my dad's idea. He has some money and is always looking for an investment opportunity, so he decided to just buy an apartment while I was going to college. He figured it was easier than living in dorms or looking for apartments, and probably cheaper once he figured in the fact that he'd sell it in a few years. Who knows, he might even make some money. Plus, he hated moving all my crap and dreaded the fact that he would have to move me from place to place a couple of times a year. He doesn't come by much and, luckily, I get to reap the reward and have my own place. We share the kitchen, everyone buys their own stuff, washes their own dishes, you know the drill."

"Sounds easy enough," Chad said, already liking what he heard and saw. There was nothing special about the place.

Painted beige, really nothing on the walls, it was rather simplistic. One small, round wooden table sat in the middle of the kitchen with four matching chairs. Dirty dishes sat in the sink. There was a refrigerator, oven, and a dishwasher that looked like it had seen better days.

"Dishwasher isn't working now, but we're working on getting that fixed before that dishes pile gets too tall. This area is all the common area. Couch, TV, stereo, DVD player, are all mine, but you're welcome to use them. The only time that is off limit is when the Giants are playing," Charlie explained, again with that easy-going smile. A dozen empty beer cans sat on the small coffee table and a half empty Jim Beam bottle next to those. "You got a football team there, Chad?"

"I'm from Wisconsin, need I say more?" Chad said, enlightening him.

"Ah, a Cheesehead. We'll look forward to taking you down this year. Looks like we play you the last game of the season here in New York. Maybe we'll have to try to score some tickets."

"That would be awesome. I haven't been to a game since I was a kid."

"Well, it's a deal. That's my room. That's Todd's room. Over there is what you saw in the ad. We put up a wall in the common area and figured we could make a few extra bucks renting it out. It's probably not legit but it's almost the same size as our rooms, a little smaller, and that's why we're charging a little bit less. That's about it. Any questions?"

"I like what I see so far—"

Charlie cut him off. "I almost forgot one thing. This complex has a common area, too," Charlie continued as he walked out the door and down the hall. Chad followed. "Up two floors, so we'll take the elevator. I think it was designed for college students, being close to campus like this. There is an area just to hang out, something like you'd see in a college dorm room. Games, TVs—definitely a fun place to watch football, although they frown on getting too crazy—couches, chairs, work desks, the whole works. Plus, wait until you see the view."

Arriving, Chad could see all the big players on the New

York skyline. The Empire State Building and the iconic Twin Towers that he'd seen in so many movies, including one of his favorites—Ghostbusters—dominated the view. He was fascinated by the World Trade Center and although he wouldn't have a lot of extra time on his hands once he started working, he would take in the view every moment he got.

"You ain't kidding. That's absolutely beautiful." Chad thought for a moment. He could quickly see that Charlie didn't need the money. It would all go back in his pocket and probably meant that he could party a little more. Chad didn't really care where it went. Charlie seemed like a great guy and easy to get along with. Plus, Chad's main concern was money and from what he had seen from his last two visits, $500 a month was a steal. He was tired of looking at apartments after the failed attempts, and more so, he was tired of sleeping in his car. He finally found the place he would call home until he could make some money and get a place of his own. "This place is perfect, Charlie. When can I move in?"

At that Charlie smiled and the two shook hands. Chad would begin moving his stuff immediately.

Settled into his makeshift room, Chad laid down on his futon. *Now that I have an apartment*, Chad thought, *next up is the job. The search begins first thing tomorrow.*

He wanted to be at the center of it all and that meant working as close to the World Trade Center as possible. What he was looking for was right there in the title—World. He imagined meeting people from across the globe, learning new languages, and exploring the similarities and differences in cultures. There were really seven distinct buildings, but to New Yorkers, and everyone else in the world, the focus was on the two 110-story buildings that were affectionately known as the Twin Towers. The other buildings had offices and a hotel, but when you looked at the skyline, it was the Twin Towers that identified your location. Without them, you could have been anywhere. There was a quiet kind of technological beauty to them. They were full of businesses conducting global transactions and Chad wanted to be there. Chad decided he would don the hat of a tourist to investigate and take a tour of the World Trade Center. There, he would ask some questions and with a little luck, set out on a course toward landing a job.

Since he was nearly out of money and living one credit card swipe at a time, he decided to walk. Taxis were too expensive and the old beat up Dodge Aries station wagon, ol' Baby Blue, his very first car, the one he drove all the way from Wisconsin, was running on fumes. Plus, it was stored in a parking garage and he didn't want to fight traffic. Maintenance problems were adding up and Chad knew it was only a matter of time before the car would be more trouble than it was worth. *I'm going to miss you, old car*, Chad pondered last night in bed, *but New York City is no place for a poor kid with a vehicle*. Selling it would pay the first month's rent, buy some groceries, and leave a little spending money for getting around on his job search. Plus, he wouldn't have to pay for parking, or worse yet, look for parking.

What a nightmare. How do people do that every day? he thought every time he saw the expansive traffic jams.

It was a nice morning and Chad was excited to continue his exploration. The warm June air felt refreshing and had yet to reach the eighty-degree forecast. He'd get a chance to explore the Brooklyn Bridge up close and personal for the first time since arriving. Finished in 1883, after fourteen years of construction, the Brooklyn Bridge was another iconic New York City landmark. Connecting Brooklyn to Manhattan, it crossed the East River and was the first steel-wire suspension bridge ever constructed. Crossing the 1,595-foot bridge made Chad's legs turn to jelly as he snuck quick glances at the water flowing over a hundred thirty feet below.

I didn't think I was afraid of heights.

Heavy traffic flowed in all six lanes. After getting to the Manhattan side of the bridge, his legs relaxed. Chad decided to take a short cut and go through a small tunnel underneath.

Here he saw the ugly side of the city up close for the first time. Homeless people lined the tunnel, covered with garbage. They didn't ask for money or beg, but rather had a distant look. Most didn't even notice he was passing through. In a city with this many people, there was bound to be some people that were less fortunate, but it was still hard for Chad to witness. He noticed many people walk right by the home-less, likely having become immune to the sight after having lived in the city for so long.

I hope that never happens to me.

He had known that there would be dirty streets, unfriend-ly people, and crime but this quick shortcut showed Chad just how naïve he had been. Gone were the days where he could leave his doors unlocked, like he did in his small hometown, or walk around without worry. Mentally, he made a note that he would watch things a little closer. Aware, but not afraid, would be how he would take care of himself while he was in the city. He paused for a moment at the end of the tunnel and said a quick prayer for all the homeless and thanked God for all the great things that he had. Although it wasn't much at the moment, he was confident that would change soon and continued on his journey.

On the walk, he saw different types of food options—fast food dives, delis, food trucks, sidewalk vendors—not to men-tion dozens of different ethnic food restaurants. It was a far cry from dormitory food back in Madison. With his funds dwin-dling, he decided he better keep eating cheap and stopped at a hot dog stand to get a token Coney Island dog for breakfast. Covered in all meat chili, with diced onions and a strip of mustard right down the middle, he was satisfied.

Now it's time for some investigating.

He went to a nearby street vendor that was displaying one of the I heart NY shirts that he remembered Kramer wearing in Seinfeld when Kramer went to visit his girlfriend across town. Although he had little money, he had always wanted one of those shirts.

Alright, I'm going to do it. It's a fair trade for having to sell my car, he thought, laughing to himself.

If I can't live in Manhattan, at least I can work here, Chad thought as he arrived at the World Trade Center, straining his neck to see the top. The hum of business reverberated through the walls as soon as he walked in. Now he could see what they meant by a New York minute as people rushed by in all directions.

Tours beginning every hour, Chad read, shortly after entering the South Tower through the revolving doors. On the Concourse Level, there was a lobby with a sign in one corner. He read it a little closer. For $13.50, he could visit the Observatory Deck and for a little less than double that price he could be part of a guided tour that visited the Observatory Deck. He didn't even hesitate. He wanted the whole experience despite his limited resources.

Another gift to myself.

His watch showed 10:45 and people were already beginning to gather. Several men in black suits, white undershirts, and ties monitored the counter with what looked like a massive directory behind them.

That's an unbelievable number of companies.

Inside, people continued to scurry. The sound of the express elevators hurrying people from all walks of life up and down, just as he hoped, were all part of the building's rhythm. Men and women, mostly walking alone, but some in small groups, went from the elevators to the doors without so much as looking up. They were entranced with business. Nearly all of them wore professional attire, many held briefcases, and everyone seemed to be in a hurry. Chad couldn't help but smile, knowing soon that would be him, if he was lucky.

"Everyone that is taking the tour, please gather over here," the young woman yelled above the growing crowd. She had long dark hair, dark brown eyes, and was just a couple inches shorter than Chad. "Welcome everyone! My name is Ali and I'll be your tour guide today. For those of you in New York City for the first time, welcome to my city. The best city in the world." Smiling the entire time, she was bubbly as she spoke. Chad instantly liked her.

"Right now, you are in the South Tower, one of the buildings that is affectionately known as the Twin Towers. The North Tower is the matching twin," she began. "Although the Twin Towers dominate the landscape, the World Trade Center is actually part of a seven-building complex. They were designed by architect Minoru Yamasaki, which you'll need to remember for the quiz afterwards," she joked. Two older ladies next to Chad both had a momentary look of panic before relaxing and letting out a little laugh. Judging by the long vowels he heard when they talked and the occasional eh, he guessed they were from Canada. "They were initially designed to be eighty stories high, but later extended to one hundred and ten stories, which we'll be discussing shortly. If you'll follow me, our tour is actually going to begin outside in the Austin J. Tobin Plaza."

Walking out to the large open expense, Chad saw a monument. A copper-colored sphere that looked like a massive basketball or volleyball was being hoisted up by what looked like an abstract bronzed person. The plaza was filled with flat pink benches, and huge garden bowls between them filled with red, orange, and yellow flowers. More gardens encircled the sculpture. Families, students, and tourists roamed about in a much more relaxed setting. Buildings rose up in all directions.

"I'm sure by now you can see why I like to start here. For one, the buildings are much more impressive from the outside." As she said this everyone gazed upwards. "Second, is this beautiful sculpture. It's called the Sphere and was designed and built by German artist Fritz Koenig. Standing twenty-five feet, it's made of bronze and consists of over fifty segments. It's meant to symbolize world peace through world trade. Perfect for the World Trade Center." She gave everyone a moment to admire the sculpture. "The World Trade Center opened in 1973 and was the brainchild of the Port Authority. Their goal was to beat the Empire State Building for the claim to the tallest building in the world. And that is just what they did. That's why eighty stories just wouldn't do. Ironically, the Sears Tower in Chicago passed the Twin Towers shortly after it was built. The tallest building is the world now is the Petronas Towers, which follow a similar concept with twin towers. They're located in Kuala Lumpur, Malaysia, but I still like ours better," she added, smiling for the group. Nearly everyone chuckled. "Now back to the Twin Towers. Just in the Twin Towers alone there are ten million square feet of office space. Any guess as to how many employees that could hold?" she asked the crowd, which Chad guessed numbered somewhere around thirty.

"Ten thousand," an older gentleman said from the front.
"Quite a bit higher."

"One hundred thousand," the woman with him replied.

"OK, maybe not quite that high. Let's try somewhere in the middle. How about you? What's your guess, mister tourist with the I Love New York shirt?" She looked at Chad and smiled.

"Somewhere in the middle would be fifty-five thousand. How about that?"

"OK, so it wasn't literally in the middle, but you're close enough. The two buildings have capacity for somewhere between thirty-five and fifty thousand people, depending how you divide it. That's why it has its own zip code. Pretty amazing, huh?"

That's five times the size of my hometown, Chad thought.

"Most New York skyscrapers were what they call stacked glass and steel box construction. The designer, with the name that you're all supposed to remember," and she paused, "Minoru Yamasaki, right? Well, he came up with something revolutionary using two hollow tubes supported by steel columns encased in aluminum. The floor trusses then connected the exterior to the central steel core. The idea is that the outside provided more strength, without relying on the internal columns as much. Pretty neat, huh? Here are some quick statistics for you. The Twin Towers consist of more than 200,000 pieces of steel, 3,000 miles of electrical wiring, over 400,000 cubic yards of concrete, 40,000 doors, and over 40,000 windows."

"Alright, let's keep moving on. We're going to make our way over to the North Tower, and then back to the South Tower to head to the Observatory Deck, with a detour or two of course, but before we do, I want you to look up." Everyone obeyed her command. "Now imagine a tightrope between the Twin Towers. Anyone have the guts enough to do that? Well, shortly after it was built, Phillipe Petit did, and walked from one tower to the next. Several people have parachuted off the top and mountain climbers have scaled the outside. Think about that for a minute and while you do, follow me."

The Brooklyn Bridge was enough for me, thought Chad.

Now on the sidewalk next to the North Tower, Ali stopped

again. This time she had a forlorn look on her face. Everyone became silent as they noticed her changed appearance. "The World Trade Center is not without tragedy. Of the 10,000 workers that it took to build the Twin Towers, sixty of those workers lost their lives during construction. Right here below us is a parking garage and the very same one where terrorists placed explosives and tried to topple the building in 1993. There is a reason you are all here today and a reason it was attacked. The Twin Towers are a very symbolic structure and one recognized throughout the world. Luckily, they did not topple the building, but six people were killed and over a thousand were wounded. The blast tore a hole five levels up but now you couldn't even tell where the damage was unless you knew what you were looking for."

Osama bin Laden.

She never mentioned that name, but it popped in Chad's head at that moment.

I remember Paul talking about this attack and how he's still out there somewhere. They never officially connected him to this, but Paul's professor was sure he was behind it.

She continued to discuss facts about the building and construction, but Chad was momentarily lost in thought. Chad remembered the USS Cole attack as well and their physical training the following morning was still etched in his mind. They never caught him after that either. *If he's still out there, what's next? A maniac like that is not going to stop until he's dead.* An eerie feeling came over him as he imagined over one thousand pounds of explosives ripping through this area, yet he marveled at the durability of the construction.

Now on the first floor of the North Tower, the group stopped when Ali did. "The World Trade Center is more than meets the eye. While everyone can see the buildings that soar above the ground, there are actually seven levels below us as well. Besides the subway station, there are several stores and other companies. The complex was actually built on an old landfill. Quite the improvement, huh?" Moving to the elevators, she pointed to them as she spoke. "If you take this to the 107th floor, you'll get to the Windows on the World restaurant. Although I've never eaten there, I've heard it's delicious and as you can imagine has great views. Speaking of views, our next stop is the Observatory Deck and some trivia when we get up there."

Arriving on the 107th floor of the South Tower, Chad could see the expansive city below. Although he didn't know many of the buildings now, he had a feeling that would soon change.

"Alright, who wants to play a quick trivia game and then we'll go see what you all came here to see? Try to guess the one fact about the World Trade Center that is false," Ali said, reading off a sheet for the first time. "A) It cost four hundred million dollars to build the entire World Trade Center Complex. The 1973 value of course. B) Rudy Giuliani has a bunker in 7 World Trade Center. C) There have been seventeen babies born on the complex. D) There is an estimated one hundred million dollars in gold bars stored in the basement of the complex. E) Over eighty tons of food are delivered on a daily basis. F) There is an art museum on one of the floors that houses some of the rarest pieces of artwork in the world. G) The World Trade Center gets approximately 200,000 visitors per day."

"OK, I'm going to say them one more time and then we'll take a vote on which one you think is false."

She listed them off again, then proceeded to the voting. No hands went up for A, a couple for B. A quarter of the hands went up for C, more than half for D. "There's no way they hide gold here with so many people," a man wearing khaki pants and a beige collared shirt whispered to his friend as he put his hand down. E and F both had a few hands, and none for G.

"And the winner is . . . F. There is valuable art on the premises at any given time, but no museum. There are works by Picasso, Lichtenstein, and Le Corbusier and, of course, the sculpture you saw, and another called *The Three Shades*. I guess they are rare since they are one of a kind, and there may be rare pieces in private collections, so I guess you're all correct. I'm a huge art buff, which is one reason I love this place. That's what I'm going to school for at the School of Visual Arts, which I must thank you for helping me pay for with this tour. So, yes that means that hidden beneath us all is a lot of gold, and the chances of a baby being born are slim, but it does happen. Although, if you think about it, 200,000 people a day, every day for that many years and the odds of someone having a baby are pretty good. Well, I'm done talking for now and I'll let this amazing view speak for itself. As part of your tour you get to experience a virtual helicopter ride around the city."

Chad had forgotten about the helicopter ride when he purchased his ticket. Now in the virtual world, they sped out over the Verrazano Bridge, through Central Park, and on to Times Square. All places that Chad had on his list to visit. The aerial view was spectacular and the sense of being in an actual helicopter was intensely realistic. Finally, they arrived back at the World Trade Center and back to reality, although this reality still seemed unreal to Chad.

"Now we'll take a few minutes to just look around," Ali said quietly as they finished the virtual portion of the tour. "Anyone that wants to go to the rooftop can just take the escalator up to the 110th floor and look around there."

Looking out, Chad was in awe of the extent of the great city. It just kept going. Miles and miles of buildings extended in all directions. Surprisingly, the landscape was greener than he thought, too. Parks were scattered throughout the neighborhoods. The East River and the Hudson River were both prominent as they converged nearby. Boats sped along both. There was his old pal the Brooklyn Bridge. And Battery Park. Ellis Island. Governor's Island. All places that were also on his list to visit. Traffic rushed in all directions.

"Pretty impressive, right?" Ali said quietly as she came up behind him. "I like to save the best for last."

"You sure did," Chad replied, surprised that she approached him. She was even more beautiful up close. "Impressive is an understatement."

"Yeah, I could stay up here all day. Sometimes I come up here to paint or just think. Anyway, we're wrapping up the tour if you want to join us over there."

"Sure, I'm right behind you." At this she smiled at him, then turned to lead the way.

I have to find a way to talk to her more.

"That pretty much wraps up the tour. I hope you enjoyed and learned a thing or two about the World Trade Center. If anyone has any questions, I'll hang out up here for a couple of minutes, then on the first floor where our journey began for a while. If not, you're free to look around here some more or continue your exploration of the city. Either way, I hope you enjoy."

Everyone burst into a round of applause. Ali's cheeks turned blush.

Boy, is she beautiful, thought Chad. *If I had any courage, I'd go ask her out after this. Maybe I will.*

Back down on the first floor, people were taking turns asking questions and thanking her for the tour. Finally, she was all alone and surveying the crowd to see if anyone else was approaching. She smiled as Chad advanced.

"That was really a good tour. Can't believe you knew all that without notes," Chad said with a shy smile, hoping he didn't sound too silly.

"Thanks, after the first dozen times it just rolls off your tongue," she responded casually. "What brings you to New York City?"

"Actually, I just moved here. Pretty much down to my last penny, but it's been a dream of mine."

That was dumb. Why did you tell her that you're broke?

"That's really cool, although I wouldn't have guessed by the shirt," she responded with growing interest, pointing and giggling at his shirt. "I wish I had the guts to just leave like that. Since you're down to your last penny, I'm guessing you're in search of a job, huh? Or school?"

"No more school for me, at least not yet. I'm looking for a job to make a few bucks, hoping to get to know the city better, and then go from there. Judging by your comment, I'm guessing you grew up here."

"Yep, born and raised in Harlem, but love Manhattan."

"Maybe you could show me around the city sometime. I can even buy you lunch, once I get a job, that is." Just like that, he had done it.

She didn't even hesitate. "Yeah, I'd really like that."

"Great, how do I get ahold of you?"

"I'll give you my number, but you can find me here most days during the summer."

"Sounds great and it will give me some incentive to find a job faster." At that, she blushed again, and Chad couldn't wait to call her. "By the way, if you can take groups on tours like this, you definitely have the guts to go anywhere you want. I'd never be able to do this."

"We'll see," she said, and cast her gaze away. "Nice to meet you . . . Wait, I don't even know your name!"

"Chad."

"Well, nice to meet you Chad. I'll look forward to seeing you again."

"Me too, Ali."

Chad began walking away, then glanced over his shoulder. Ali was staring at him as he walked away. She smiled and turned around to pack up.

Is it too soon to call her now? Chad had an instant crush. *Now I need to find a job.*

Having one year of college under his belt did not make Chad qualified for much as far as employment possibilities, but he did see something that intrigued him on his jaunt as a tourist. Twice, he saw people delivering packages to the World Trade Center on foot and just after he said goodbye to Ali and left the building, he saw a guy roughly his age deliver another package using his bicycle.

What a great idea, Chad thought as he saw him lock his bike. *I'm going to watch what happens.*

With a job like that, he'd be at the center of everything here at the World Trade Center, make some connections, and it might even lead to a better opportunity. Plus, he'd learn his way around the city and have his transportation issue resolved. Getting the chance to see Ali on a regular basis was a bonus. The delivery man must have had a delivery at one of the upper floors because he was gone awhile. When he finally came down, Chad went over and spoke to him.

"That looks like an interesting gig you got there, delivering packages all around the city. You must run into all kinds of people," Chad started.

The young man was surprised and obviously in a hurry when he responded. "Yeah. I love it. I can make some cash and it gives me time to write my book." Chad had the college part wrong but was glad to hear that he enjoyed the job. "Hey man, I've got to run. Got another package to deliver before I can go home for the day," he said as he climbed on his bike.

"You too, take care. Wait a minute. What company do you work for?" Chad waved, tried to get his attention as he rode away.

"Quik Trak Messenger Service. They're almost always hiring, too. See you!" he replied as he disappeared around the corner.

It was settled. He was going to sell his car, buy a bike, and stop by to see if Quik Trak needed a hand. Right now, he would head home.

Home, Chad thought, smiling to himself. *It felt good to have a home. And maybe I'll give Ali a call.*

So many people he met over the years seemed to have big dreams that they never followed. Chad could look in the mirror tonight and know that he'd never be one of those. He was living his dream in New York City.

CHAPTER 6

Paul and JD had been back at school for three weeks now. Within days, they had quickly settled back into a routine. They were roommates again, although they had upgraded this semester to a suite. With that, they shared a bathroom with two other cadets. Jeremy Schuler and Roy Williams. One was supposed to be Chad, but he was living his dream out in New York City. Instead, they were stuck with Roy. No one wanted to be his roommate and he jumped at the opportunity after Chad left. Jeremy was alright, but most times they stayed to themselves, and JD and Paul were just fine with that. Both had other priorities. Dawn and Lynn.

Lynn had stayed with JD for a few days while they were getting moved in. Every weekend so far this semester, JD had travelled to stay with her. Paul noticed something different about their relationship. Over the summer, it had progressed. They were still as lovey-dovey and frisky as always, but there was now a certain maturity to the couple. They were more confident, more comfortable with each other in general. It was hard to describe, but Paul was envious. He had quickly rushed back to Dawn the day they both returned. However, their summer was filled with jealousy and arguing, and the awkwardness lingered. Still, they were trying to make it work. Being together again definitely helped.

For some reason, Paul thought of Chad as he snuggled under the blanket on their couch/bed combo for his daily ritual of taking a nap after their early morning physical training session. Luckily, he avoided the early morning classes this semester.

Way too big for me, he knew as he considered what it would be like living in New York City. They had only spoken once over the summer and the road trip never came to fruition.

When they spoke, Chad was infatuated with this girl he met, Ali, and they were spending a lot of time together.

How many times had he made fun of JD and me for being "in love" and now we can't even return the favor? Chad smiled, wishing he could make fun of him again. Still getting settled with a new job, which sounded pretty cool, and a new apartment, Chad wasn't quite up for guests yet. They had their sights set on spring break.

"Hope you're not getting too comfortable there," JD yelled as he rushed out of the bathroom, grabbed his backpack, and rushed out the door, leaving it wide open, on purpose. Paul just laughed out loud, although he doubted JD heard him, as he stood up to close the door. Every day, JD ran back from physical training, showered quickly, or didn't, depending on how much time he had, and then barely made it to his 8:00 class. And every day, he had some antics for Paul. Sometimes JD threw things at him, other times he'd put stuff on him, but his favorite thing was to leave the door wide open for anyone to wander in.

What are buddies for, right?

Paul's first class wasn't until eleven, and with any luck, he'd never have an early morning class again. Getting up before the sun was up every morning for his morning physical training was already enough, without having to rush to another class right afterwards. With three hours to spare, it was the perfect amount of time for a nice nap. Before long, he was fast asleep.

"Oh crap, I forgot something," JD yelled again, rushing in and rushing out. Paul didn't even twitch as JD turned the TV on and slammed the door, hoping to wake him up. No luck today. Paul was gone to the world.

At some point, Paul rolled over and had this disturbing image in a dream. He saw the Twin Towers in New York City. Smoke was billowing up into a sunny sky. Apparently, an airplane crashed into the side. An accident? What are the chances that a plane would accidentally hit the tallest buildings in New York City? Not very likely. His dreams transfixed on that image, dreaming that he was on the plane as it pummeled into the side of the building. Dreaming that he was just going about his daily life, showing up to an office that was now in flames. Dreaming that he was in combat in some far-away land.

Like millions of other travelers, Mohammed Atta and Abdulaziz al-Omari boarded a plane at Portland International Jetport in the small town of Portland, Maine on September 11th, 2001. Unlike other travelers, their intent was different. They landed at Logan International Airport in the early hours of the day. At seven thirty-five, they boarded American Airlines Flight 11 after a brief phone call between the two confirmed that their mission was ready. Instead of the expected destination of Los Angeles, the eighty-one passengers aboard were thrown into chaos when two flight attendants were stabbed, and the plane was taken over. Mohammed Atta now controlled the plane.

At almost the same time, United Airlines Flight 175, carrying fifty-six passengers and nine crew members, took off from Logan as well, also headed for Los Angeles.

Five minutes later, American Airlines Flight 77, carrying fifty-eight passengers and six crew members, took off from Washington Dulles International in Virginia, heading for the same location.

Hijackers were aboard both flights waiting for the right moment.

Flight 11 banked sharply, heading toward New York City. The hijackers assured the passengers, "Just stay quiet and you'll be OK. We are returning to the airport."

The Northeast Air Defense Sector, responsible for air security, specifically in the form of detecting danger and air defense in that region, was notified by airport authorities.

Two F-15 pilots began suiting up.

After a forty-minute delay, United Airlines Flight 93 departed Newark International with thirty-seven passengers and seven crew members. The time was eight forty-two EST when flight attendant Amy Sweeney reported the Flight 11 hijacking to her ground manager in Boston. "We are in rapid descent," she declared.

At the very same time, Flight 175 was hijacked.

Amy continued, "I see water. I see buildings. We are flying low. We are flying very, very low. We are flying way too low." After a brief pause she said, "Oh my God, we are way too low," and then there was static. Travelling at a speed of almost five hundred miles per hour, Mohammed Atta led Flight 11 directly into the north face of the North Tower of the World Trade Center just below the one hundredth floor.

The two F-15s ordered to intercept Flight 11 never got the opportunity.

Pandemonium was everywhere within the building. Those below the crash tried to evacuate. Those above were left with no good options. Flames and smoke were everywhere, and dozens of people took their chances and jumped. None of the jumpers survived. The 1st Battalion Chief of the New York City Fire Department made the call to his first responders and firefighters and they began rushing to the scene.

Within two minutes, a New York City news crew was reporting and within three minutes network television picked up the story.

As millions tuned in and tried to figure out what was happening, Flight 77 was hijacked.

Chad had several packages to deliver that day and he was already exhausted. Ali and he had been up until almost two in the morning playing dominoes, drinking wine, and talking. She didn't have class until the afternoon on Tuesday and her first tour was at nine that morning. That left them plenty of time to hang out during the night. They had been doing that more and more lately. Chad loved every minute of it.

Chad reported in for his morning deliveries shortly before eight. The New York Stock Exchange was the first stop, followed by a financial company on Fulton Street, and then over to the South Tower. *Maybe I'll get to see Ali*, he thought happily, even though they had just parted ways. *I love surprising her and seeing that huge smile.* After that, he'd be heading up to Fifth Avenue in Midtown Manhattan for several other deliveries.

Chad never delivered the most packages, nor did he try. He loved exploring along the way and engaging in conversations. Deadlines were always met, but rarely was he early. Today, he would have to fly to meet his aim to be at the South Tower by eight-fifty. That's when Ali would arrive. Luckily, he was quickly learning all the streets, traffic, and shortcuts. The first two deliveries went well, and he was only a couple minutes behind schedule. Flying down Fulton Street, he came to Broadway. There he froze. Smoke was rising from the North Tower. People were staring up from the street. Drivers in cars were trying to get a better look. Several taxis unexpectedly stopped, letting out their passengers. Sirens blared as emergency vehicles navigated traffic, heading in that direction. Everyone seemed to be frozen in place, contemplating what was happening. Chad was among them, momentarily unsure of what to do. *What could have happened? An accident? Oh no! Ali!*

Flight 77 made a turn from its pre-designated course as the intercom in the South Tower announced that their building was secure, and everyone should return to their offices. Some did, while others continued to evacuate, but many were in common areas watching the scene unfold to the north. Moments later, Port Authority officials changed course and ordered the evacuation of both towers through the public address system.

The two F-15s were now airborne but unaware that Flight 11 had crashed. They were still without a destination.

Peter Hanson called his father from Flight 175 warning that, "They've taken over the cockpit. An attendant has been stabbed and someone else up front may have been killed. The plane is making strange moves. Call United Airlines."

There was pandemonium at the Federal Aviation Administration's (FAA) New York Center as the air traffic control manager realizes that it was not just the one plane that crashed. Several more had been hijacked.

Franticly, the FAA sent a message to the Air Traffic Control System Command Center in Herndon, Virginia as they tried to locate Flight 175. "We have several situations going on here. It's escalating big, big time. We need to get the military involved with us. We're involved with something else; we may have other aircraft that may have a similar situation going on here."

But it was too late.

They couldn't find Flight 175.

Just as the phone call ended, it struck the South Tower, near the 80th floor, travelling almost six hundred miles per hour and instantly killing all sixty-five people on board and hundreds of onlookers on the south side of the building. Jet fuel exploded into flames.

What the hell? This can't be happening, he thought as he watched the second plane hit the South Tower. Chad couldn't believe his eyes. Not knowing what happened after initially seeing smoke, he was now certain this was an attack. He just couldn't figure out why. And who. And how.

Just like millions of Americans, Chad was trying to make sense of it all in his head. Confused thoughts disappeared as Chad picked up his pace, heading to the ground floor of the South Tower.

Oh my God! I have to get ahold of Ali. Why didn't I listen when she told me to get a cell phone? Now, he had no way to reach her. *I must find her.*

Smoke billowed from both buildings. *What! Did someone just jump? What a horrible way to die,* he thought, *but I guess it sure beats burning to death.* Chad couldn't imagine what it was like to face such a difficult decision. *Jump,* he thought, knowing that at the time your brain is probably in overdrive and you don't have the luxury to ponder. *You just do what instinctually feels right.*

Venturing closer now, he saw a wave of people rushing away from the buildings. *Maybe I should follow. Ali must be with them.*

"Ali! Ali!" he screamed over and over again. It was hopeless amid the chaos, so he turned back toward the towers. Despite his pleas they wouldn't allow him in the South Tower.

"No one goes in. We're under evacuation orders," one of

the fire fighters explained, trying to bring control to the pandemonium.

"But my girlfriend is in there!" Chad yelled in response. "She was on the first floor."

"She's probably evacuated already if she was on the first floor. Now follow that group," he ordered, then turned to help an older man in a suit who tripped on the sidewalk outside the South Tower.

Running now in the opposite direction, Chad was looking for the first pay phone he could find. Or at least a lobby that looked inviting. His thought process was beginning to jump from making a plan, to panicking, and back. A middle-aged lady on the street was crying as she hung up her cell phone.

"Ma'am, I'm sorry to bother you but it's urgent. Can I use your phone for a moment? My girlfriend was in that building."

Understanding, she wiped her tears and handed Chad her phone.

He quickly dialed Ali's number.

No answer.

He tried again.

No answer.

Ali, where are you? How do I find you?

Disturbed by the dream, Paul opened his eyes and looked around.

He was still in his dorm, still in his second year of college, and he was safe. He probably just had the dream because Chad was in New York City right now. Relieved, he heard that the TV was on. *Another one of JD's shenanigans*, he thought.

Paul turned over and saw the image from his dream on the TV and froze.

It wasn't a dream. It was a nightmare.

Somehow, he must have woken for just a moment, long enough to subconsciously cement that image in his mind, and then drifted back to sleep.

Instead of just one tower smoking, both were now smoking.

JD returned just then, and they sat motionless on the couch for a moment, glued to the TV. The television showed the planes hitting the towers over and over again, then shifted between press conferences, and scenes of first responders rushing in to save lives.

"What the hell is happening?" JD began. "Someone was talking about it when I got done with class, but I didn't believe them. I ran back here as fast as I could."

"I have no idea, but I don't think this was an accident. One maybe, but not two. I hope Chad is alright."

"Me, too. Let's give him a call," JD said but Paul was already picking up the phone. He dialed the number to Chad's apartment.

"Hey, is Chad there?"

"No," an unknown voice responded. "This is his roommate. Can I take a message?"

"Do you know if he's safe?"

There was silence on the other end of the line.

"I'm not sure, bro. I sure hope so."

"Me too. Please tell him Paul and JD called when he gets back," Paul asked, then paused. "Are you guys alright over there?"

Another pause.

"Yeah, we're good. Just in shock. Everyone here is . . . just trying to figure out what is going on. They just closed off everything in the New York City area. Scary stuff, man."

"That's for sure. You take care and please have Chad give us a call right away."

"Will do."

"Thanks," Paul whispered and hung up.

"No word, huh?" JD asked.

"Nothing, yet," Paul confirmed.

"I'm going to give Lynn a call," JD said, standing to take the phone from Paul. "I don't want her to worry any more than I'm sure she already is."

Paul tried not to listen, but it was hard not to, being in the same room. JD was calm and reassuring of her concerns and tried to comfort her as much as he could through the phone. Lynn sounded understanding and supportive.

Wow, they have such an amazing relationship, Paul thought. *I wish Dawn and I had the same thing.*

Finally, JD and Lynn made plans to see each other during the upcoming weekend and to talk again tonight.

"I love you, baby. Can't wait to talk to you again soon," JD whispered, then hung up. Without saying anything, he sat down next to Paul.

Their eyes returned to the television. The scenes that were caught on live television earlier continued to play, broken only by new developments. Millions continued to tune in from around the world.

"I can't believe some of these news anchors are still claiming this was an accident," JD declared. "What more information do they need? This is an attack, plain and simple."

Paul was deep in reflection, thinking about Dr. Hamm's Global Perspectives class, the USS Cole, and Major Suter's warnings. They all came back to the same thing. Or rather the same person. *Osama bin Laden.*

"You're right, JD. Things like this don't accidentally happen. They are coordinated by evil people. Those that think otherwise either are not real intelligent or don't understand how the world really works. Whoever coordinated this attack got exactly the reaction they wanted, and I think I know who was behind it."

Survivors were scrambling to find their way to freedom, either in the last remaining unblocked stairwell, or heading to the roof in hopes of an evacuation that never came because of the smoke.

President George W. Bush was reading *The Pet Goat* to a group of elementary students when he was alerted that "America is under attack" by his Chief of Staff. A short while later he was surrounded by members of the Secret Service and shuttled to Air Force One.

The FAA grounded flights throughout New York's airspace. All bridges and tunnels to Manhattan were closed in hopes of preventing further attacks and getting a handle on the situation.

Meanwhile, authorities attempted to establish communications with Flight 77 just as hijackers stormed the cockpit of their fourth flight of the day, Flight 93.

Moments later, flight controllers overheard communications from Flight 93, "Ladies and gentlemen here . . . is the captain please sit down . . . keep remaining sitting. We have a bomb on board."

Secret Service was preparing to evacuate the White House as Flight 77 approached the presidential dwelling.

Instead they targeted the Pentagon.

A few brief minutes later Flight 77 impacted its destination, hitting the west side of the Pentagon at over five hundred miles per hour. Everyone on board was killed, along with one hundred and twenty-five Pentagon employees.

Flight 93 changed direction and began heading east.

FAA ordered fighter jets to intercept the rogue plane.

For the first unplanned time in history, the United States airspace was completely shut down and all major facilities in Washington DC were evacuated.

Shockingly, groups began making false claims that they were the ones behind the attacks as authorities scrambled to figure out the culprit.

After learning about the other crashes from frantic family members and friends, Flight 93 suspected something worse than a hijacked plane. They suspected their plane would soon be used as a weapon to target innocent Americans at another iconic destination.

They decided to fight back.

Eventually, they overtook the cockpit. Their heroism saved the lives of countless as they catastrophically crashed in a Pennsylvania field. The likely destination would have been the White House or the Capitol Building.

For nearly an hour, but what felt like an eternity, Chad ran from group to group shouting for Ali. It was no use. There were too many people, too much disorder, and too much confusion. Again and again he called her, whenever he was able to find a phone. The result was always the same. No answer.

Paramedics, fire fighters, and police officers in uniforms were rushing in, trying to rescue those that were trapped. Other concerned citizens joined them. Their bravery made Chad want to do something, but he wasn't sure what could be done.

Then, it happened.

In an instant, the South Tower began to collapse and then it came crashing down. Everything was smoke and dust. The noise was unbearable. As the dust began to settle, Chad looked up, and there was emptiness on the New York skyline. Thinking only of the brave men and women he had just been watching, he knew he'd just witnessed many of them die trying to save others.

It was in this moment that he sprang to action. Something came to life inside of him.

Chad saw an ambulance stop about a block away and ran in their direction. A man about twenty years his senior hopped out, eyeing Chad.

"I just saw the tower go down. Can I help you guys out?" Chad pleaded.

"Do you have any medical training?" he questioned.

"No."

"Then, you can help us find bodies and bring them here. The dead over there, seriously injured there, and those with minor injuries here." The man pointed to makeshift buildings that were quickly becoming triage locations. "Can you do that, son?"

"Absolutely."

"Remember, these people have just been through hell. Treat them well and try to comfort them any way you can." And then he turned around to lead a small group, heading directly toward the collapsed buildings. Without hesitation, Chad followed.

Luckily, the first person Chad found had only minor wounds, but was having trouble walking. Sprained or maybe a broken bone in his ankle was Chad's quick diagnosis. Chad wrapped his arm around his shoulders to steady him. Dressed in what was once a nice-looking suit, the man looked to be about forty years old. Together, they hobbled back to the waiting first responders.

As they approached, Chad saw the man who got him started. He had already delivered a woman to the triage location and was heading back to the rubble. As their paths crossed, he hollered, "Thanks, kid, for the help. The name's Steve by the way and I look forward to having you buy me a beer after all of this." Even amid the chaos and death, he was able to find humor.

Chad, always quick to answer wisecracks, hollered, "Chad's the name and that sounds like a plan. I'll buy you one right after I drink your first two." Even the man Chad was helping, who up to that point hadn't said anything, was eased by the exchange.

"That does sound good right about now, doesn't it?" he declared. "Do you have any idea what happened back there? I'm in town from California and next thing you know I'm staring at a hole in the Twin Towers just before it collapses. I'm just happy I was far enough away that I didn't get crushed." The man held out a hand. "Thanks, Chad. The name's Mel."

Chad shook Mel's hand as you would shake your grandfather's hand when you went to see him in the hospital. "I'm happy to help, but I'm not really sure what happened." Chad paused, then added, "But, I'm pretty sure it was an attack. That second plane looked like it was heading right for the tower and there is no way there could be two accidents so similar. No one is really saying much yet. Everyone's trying to either get to safety or help out. I don't think anyone has processed it yet."

They talked for a while longer, and Chad learned that Mel had served four years in the Army back in the 1980s. Mel said, "The world has been relatively quiet and peaceful for a while now up to this point if you're right about those attacks."

Chad's mind drifted to his old college roommates—JD and Paul.

Where would this attack take them? And the others? Who was behind it? Were there more attacks coming?

Trying to distract himself, he looked around for Steve as Mel continued to make small talk. Knowing he should return to help, since there would certainly be more that needed care, he began to stand up. Just then, another earth-shattering noise ripped through the city.

What now? Chad thought. *What else could possibly happen today?*

It only took a moment for someone to coming running up with the news that the other tower collapsed. Somehow Chad knew Steve was likely dead. The news hit him hard.

This can't be happening.

There would be more people wounded and more dead bodies now. Chad couldn't make small talk any longer. "Mel, it's been great talking to you, but I've got to go. More people out there need my help."

"I understand, Chad, and thanks again for everything. Stay safe out there, okay?" Mel said, with obvious concern, taking Chad's hand between both of his as he shook it.

"You've got it," Chad said, rounding the corner, heading toward the dust and debris. After each person he helped to safety, he would call Ali.

No answer.

I have to find her.

Knowing she wouldn't be able to find him either, she would likely go to his apartment or wait back at her place. After another failed attempt, he called his apartment.

"Charlie, good to hear your voice. Are you and Todd alright?" Chad began. They had turned out to be excellent roommates, and were starting to become friends, showing Chad how to let loose and have a great time.

"Yeah, we're good here, just wondering about you. Where are you, man? You okay?"

"I'm over here, right next to the towers. I'm okay, but that's not why I'm calling. Have you seen Ali?"

"No, but she called earlier."

Thank God, Chad thought. She's alive.

"She's going home to be with her parents tonight. Ali said she lost her cell phone in the chaos and to tell you to call this number immediately," and he rattled off her parents' phone number. "She was pretty shook up, just like the rest of us."

"Thanks, Charlie. You have no idea how good it feels to hear that."

"I can imagine, buddy. You stay safe over there."

"I will. Don't wait up for me, OK?"

"You know we'll be up all night, just like everyone else in America right now. Still can't believe this is happening."

"Yeah, I know what you mean. I'll see you soon, Charlie." He hung up the phone and instantly dialed the number Ali gave him.

Events of the day were being revealed on every TV station as authorities begin piecing everything together. The carnage was unimaginable.

Paul's eleven o'clock class came and went. Neither JD or Paul moved. Moments later Dawn came rushing in. "Oh my God, Paul. It's so terrible!" she cried as she wrapped her arms around Paul. "You're not going to have to leave, will you?"

"Of course not," Paul replied without hesitation, though he was unsure of the future.

I wish I could though and make them pay for what they did.

"Good, I don't know what I'd do without you."

Paul didn't reply, just sat back down and watched the footage again. He patted the seat next to him and Dawn quickly joined him, sidling up as close as she could. Paul put his arm around her.

"I love you," she whispered, close to his ear. "I was so scared when I saw the towers this morning after class. It really made me realize how strongly I feel for you and how much I don't want to lose you."

He pulled her closer. "You don't have to worry about that." Again, he doubted his words. All he wanted to do was kill those responsible. A switch had flipped inside of him.

Lunch came and went and the three of them remained glued to the television. No one had an appetite. Dawn tried to make conversation, but Paul's replies were simplistic. He had turned inward, deep in thought. Paul figured JD felt the same, pondering their future. The little conversation they had was limited to new developments, and each new development seemed to be worse. Projected death tolls were rolling in from all four crash sites. Analysts were discussing who was behind the attack, though Paul already had a good guess.

Shortly after noon, Paul received a frantic call from his mother. Just as he did with Dawn, he reassured his mother, yet doubted his own words.

How do you tell your mother that this changes everything?

"Ali?" Chad asked, thinking he recognized her voice.

"Chad! Thank God you are alright," she said, letting out a big sigh amid the sniffles. Chad had never heard or seen her cry. "Where are you? I want to see you so bad."

"I'm OK, just glad to hear your voice. I've been trying so hard to find you, but Charlie said you lost your phone."

"Yeah, I have no clue where it is. Everything has been a blur since I got to work. One minute it was all clear, the next we were being evacuated. Wait, where are you?"

"I'm still here, just on the outside of the debris. There are a lot of people that need help here and I'm going to stay and do whatever I can."

"I would expect nothing less, Chad. Just promise me you'll be safe."

"I will, and I'll come see you the minute I'm done."

"You'd better because I think I'm falling in love with you."

Chad had never heard that from a woman, nor said it to anyone other than his family. After three months together, he definitely had strong feelings, but wasn't sure he was in love. Maybe it was the emotions of the day that got to Chad as he whispered. "I love you, too, Ali, and I'll see you soon."

After a quick call to reassure his parents he was safe, he rushed back toward the destruction. Mayor Rudy Giuliani ordered the evacuation of all residents in Lower Manhattan south of Canal Street, so people were fleeing in all directions.

Chad chose to stay.

All night he searched for survivors and helped the wounded. Steve's memory kept him going. He finally collapsed on an empty cot the following evening. He'd never been so tired, so miserable, and so disappointed in all his life. Chad hated those that caused this destruction. Yet at the same time, he felt so empowered by helping others and seeing heroes rush into action. Knowing he had been searching for his true passion when he came to New York, he now knew what he wanted to do for the rest of his life. Chad wanted to help, serve, and protect others.

"Freedom, itself, was attacked this morning by a faceless coward, and freedom will be defended. I want to reassure the American people that the full resources of the Federal Government are working to assist local authorities to save lives and to help the victims of these attacks. Make no mistake: The United States will hunt down and punish those responsible for these cowardly acts," President George W. Bush declared from Barksdale Air Force Base in Louisiana, aiming to reassure the American people.

"I've been in regular contact with the Vice President, the Secretary of Defense, the national security team, and my Cabinet. We have taken all appropriate security precautions to protect the American people. Our military at home and around the world is on high-alert status, and we have taken the necessary security precautions to continue the functions of your Government.

"We have been in touch with the leaders of Congress and with world leaders to assure them that we will do whatever is necessary to protect America and Americans. I ask the American people to join me in saying a thanks for all the folks who have been fighting hard to rescue our fellow citizens and to join me in saying a prayer for the victims and their families.

"The resolve of our great Nation is being tested. But make no mistake: We will show the world that we will pass this test.

"God bless."

Shortly after his statement, President Bush was ushered to an underground bunker, one that could withstand a nuclear blast, with a tough decision to make. How would the United States approach this act of war?

JD and Paul had their second year ROTC class at two and they certainly didn't want to miss it. Word quickly made it to them that Major Suter still wanted to meet. Of course, they knew they wouldn't be covering their previously assigned topics, but rather focusing on the events of the day.

They arrived just before the class was starting and the room was silent. Major Suter walked in and started by telling them the one thing that they'd all been thinking since it was first confirmed a terrorist attack. "This moment, this act of war, just changed your lives forever."

Major Suter was a combat veteran from Grenada and the innocent nineteen-year-old cadets looked to him as if he knew the answer to everything, not just in this moment, but always.

"Think about this," he continued. "The last time there was an attack of this magnitude on the United States, millions of Americans were called up and sent to fight across the globe in Europe, Africa, and Asia."

Paul thought that most of them had probably considered this at some time, when they decided to join, but never really thought it would actually happen to them. In their eyes, the world had been safe their whole lives. They never thought that would change.

"There is no doubt in my mind that we have already identified who did this and our military leadership is planning our counterattack at this very moment."

As they analyzed the day's events and discussed the possibilities for future courses of action, each of them considered what the uncertain future would bring. For most, including Paul, JD, Chad, and many across the country, it was the worst day they ever experienced.

Paul and JD naturally turned on the TV as soon as they returned. Reporters were continuing to analyze who was behind the attacks. Just as Paul suspected, it all pointed to the same man he had learned about during his very first week of class freshman year with Dr. Hamm. All evidence pointed to Osama bin Laden.

If we knew about him then, how could we let this happen?

CHAPTER 7

For Nasir and other Afghans, September 11th came and went just like every other day. Millions saw the airplanes crash into the World Trade Center, but Nasir was not one of them. They received no world news most days and today was no different. Televisions were forbidden and even if they weren't, the average Afghan wouldn't care about the United States. The US had no influence on their day-to-day life. They didn't help them survive. Most of Afghanistan was illiterate, and their knowledge of world geography was equally dismal. Furthermore, they have never interacted with an American. In their world, it was almost like the United States didn't exist, just like most other countries around the world. Their focus was on what they could see in front of them. And survival.

The exception was the highest level of the Taliban leadership and their associates al Qaeda, specifically their leader, Osama bin Laden. He closely monitored the events of the day from his stronghold in Afghanistan.

Early on September 11th, the U.S. Central Intelligence Agency (CIA) intercepted a call from Osama bin Laden to an associate in the Republic of Georgia. In the call, bin Laden declared that he had heard good news and there was more to come. Bin Laden had become the official leader of the al Qaeda movement with deep pockets and an uncompromising commitment to Allah. There was nothing he wouldn't do to sabotage westerners, but he particularly hated Americans for meddling in Muslim regions. Time and time again, he had shown this by coordinating attacks on the US embassies in Kenya and Tanzania, along with the bombing of the USS Cole. His six-foot-plus stature made him an authoritarian figure in the Muslim community. His radical ideas made him a prophet, savior, and king to many and a liability and nuisance to

111

others. His madness made them fear him. It was this clout that led him to Mullah Omar, now the leader of Afghanistan, and his Taliban forces. By the time bin Laden and Omar met in Kandahar late in 1996, Omar was furthering his control of Afghanistan each day. Battles were still raging against the Northern Alliance in the north and Omar welcomed a partnership. Bin Laden requested Taliban protection in exchange for Omar's unconditional support and financial backing. Marriage sealed the bond between the families and the path to future evil was laid. Osama bin Laden's vision was to have training camps scattered throughout Afghanistan to train fighters for future attacks on Americans. It was here that the September 11th hijackers were first trained under his watchful eye.

The CIA was well aware of these events and monitored them closely. On several occasions, they had eyes on key al Qaeda leaders and their terrorist training camps, just waiting for authorization to destroy them and their training camps. This type of action needed to come directly from the top, President Bill Clinton. Authorization came in the form of covert operations to capture Osama bin Laden. Cruise missions were launched in response to the embassy bombings. However, further commitment by the government or military was not a viable option for the president. He feared civilian casualties and collateral damage. Instead, US authorities told the Taliban to banish Osama bin Laden from Afghanistan and worked closely with the Pakistani government. The Taliban never complied. There were some successes as the CIA arrested a terrorist on the US-Canadian border and broke up a cell forming in Jordan. Another time, they almost caught two of the operatives from September 11th, but lost them in the madness of Bangkok. Unfortunately, none of the strategies led to Osama bin Laden. After September 11th, it was relatively easy for the CIA to pinpoint the culprit and his location.

On September 11th, Afghans throughout the countryside tended their fields and followed their prayer rituals. Just as they did any other day. Nasir's family ate rice and lamb which

Mina had prepared over the fire. Storai and Diwa were at her side during preparations and the entire family now convened for the midday meal. Coolness was coming to the air and Nasir looked forward to getting past the hot weather for the year. Working in the fields was much more bearable as the temperature fell and he always enjoyed the fall harvest. Nasir had spent the morning assessing the croplands throughout the region.

"How are the crops looking, Nasir?" Daulat asked his son, still sweating heavily despite the cooling air. Responsibility was coming to Nasir more each day as his father was becoming more involved with the Taliban movement. Any prior reservations, even silent ones, were now gone, and his father was fully committed to the Taliban cause. After all, his father was the malik and a cleric from Mullah Omar's homeland. As a result, he was recently promoted as one of the leaders in the Taliban movement.

"Fine, Father," Nasir started.

"I need more than just fine, give me details, boy."

Nasir had gotten use to the new harshness in his tone, but he was still not use to his father's long absences. For his entire life, his father had always been home. Now it seemed that he was gone more than he was home. And Nasir didn't really understand where he went.

Why does he keep it from me? Why does he still shelter me and treat me like a child?

Yet, Nasir never stood up to him, never defied him. He always obeyed. Their talks were more business than counsel now, and he missed his father's wisdom. Still, Nasir dutifully gave his reports on the crops.

"Very good. For us and the cause," Daulat announced to his family following Nasir's accounts. Sarbaz, Diwa's husband, was still noticeably absent. He continued the fight against the Northern Alliance in Kapisa Province. "I have good news from the front. We have taken control of the Shokhi and Khan Aqa districts after several days of hard fighting, but the best news is we have finally killed the Northern Alliance leader, Ahmad Shah Massoud. Let's give thanks to Allah and pray safe return to Sarbaz and all of our fighters." Diwa's usually pleasant face showed her concern, especially her sad eyes, as she bowed her head low in prayer.

After several moments, he continued. "Our crops will be used to support this ongoing effort and Allah willing, we will control the entire country soon."

They ate in silence.

Finally, Nasir spoke up. "Father, I know you are leaving again tomorrow. Can I come with you?" He had never made this request before and Daulat seemed to ponder it for a moment.

"I'm afraid not, my son. You are needed here to look after our family, our house, and our land. Your day will come soon."

"OK, Father. I'll be ready when that day comes."

"I know you will be, Nasir. After this, let's take a walk. I have a visit to make and perhaps you will understand more."

At this Mina looked at her husband, trying to comprehend, but quickly turned away after catching his eye. Nasir didn't miss the exchange. Nor did he understand it.

What am I missing?

Though she had obvious concern, Mina didn't say anything. Daulat had become more cross with her lately as well, particularly when it came to conversations about the Taliban. Although it was unsaid, criticism of the Taliban was forbidden both inside and outside the walls of their compound. Taliban factions had been in control for nearly five years and everyone around them was a supporter.

After finishing their meal, Daulat and Nasir departed, leaving the women to clear the remaining food and utensils.

"Nasir, I have taught you a great many things but there is something we have not really discussed openly," Daulat began as they strolled down the path that led to a small creek nearby. Lush fields of marijuana lined both sides of the path. "We've never discussed the Taliban."

Nasir was interested, but remained silent, as his father continued.

"It's no surprise that you've had your doubts, although I trust very few outside of our family know of them. I once felt the way you did but have always supported them. That's how things work in our country. We support the powerful or we perish. But we can not only support them with words, we must support them with action. That's what I've done, and it's protected our family from the brutality that comes to others. That's why I travel, recruit, collect and distribute crops and funds, whatever it takes. I do it for our family. Do you understand?"

"I think I do, Father," Nasir replied, although he wasn't sure he understood completely. "I see that in you, but I'm not sure . . ." Nasir stopped, feeling uncomfortable revealing his true feelings to his father for the first time.

"Go on, Nasir. Like I said, we have never talked about this, but I want to today. I want you to discuss it freely and openly. After that, we will shut the door on this conversation. Both of us know it is too dangerous to recount."

"OK, Father. I'm just not sure I can do that. I'm not sure that I can support something that I don't agree with."

"I understand, but what if the alternative is death? Or extreme hardship? Or torture?"

"Father, I feel I would rather die than live that way. I can't kill innocent people like they do."

"I see," Daulat began, looking around to see if any other people were nearby. "But what if it is your family that will be killed, tortured, or left to suffer? What then? What if it is the people you love most in this world? What if it is your only son?"

Nasir looked up, confused, but touched by his father's emotional openness. He paused, considering his next words carefully. "I would do anything to keep them safe."

"Exactly," Daulat smiled, sensing his son was beginning to understand. "Just as I would."

They walked in silence, pondering their conversation, as the path now wound along the stream. Soon, they would be close to the place where he said goodbye to Batoor. Nasir had not seen him since that day and missed him greatly. Accounts from other Taliban soldiers said he was fighting the Northern Alliance, moving along the front as the war progressed. Nasir had no other friends and mostly kept to himself. In fact, many young men his age had already joined the Taliban cause, leading to his next question.

"Is there a reason you are telling me this now?"

"You've always been quick on your feet, Nasir. And you've always made me proud," Daulat expressed, looking at his son. "There is very little room to demand with the Taliban, but my one request has always been to leave you and my family alone. I will do whatever is required, if they accept that plea. So far, they have. But I'm not sure how much longer I can protect you."

"I'm not sure that I understand."

"Nasir, I'm not a young man and have outlived many of our people. There is a reason that they've come to me, both as a malik, cleric, and as one of the village elders. I must start to consider what will happen when I'm gone. I will no longer be able to protect you and our family. That responsibility will fall on you."

Nasir had considered this several times, but it still came as a shock to hear his father discuss it so openly. Nasir knew he was sheltered and feared that would be changing soon.

It looks like that time has come.

"What do you ask of me, Father?"

"You have already been doing so much, watching over the animals and crops, collecting goods from the village and taking them to market. Assessing the village croplands for me just like you did this morning. Everything I've asked, you have done. Yet, I ask one more thing. Put your doubts aside, Nasir. Embrace the Taliban. After I am gone it will be your responsibility to protect our family, to protect the land that has been in our family for generations. The Taliban is the only way to do that," Daulat professed. "You must protect our legacy. Can I count on you to do that for me?"

Nasir considered. *Perhaps my father is correct. Maybe it is the only way.*

"Of course, Father," he said, although his reservations continued as he uttered those words. "But I have one question. Last year during harvest, you told me these words. '*O You who believe! Enter absolutely into peace. Do not follow in the footsteps of Satan. He is an outright enemy of you.*' They have stayed with me since that day and I always thought you were referring to the Taliban. What am I to think?"

"That is a good question, but a difficult one to answer. You must never utter the words I am about to tell you to another person. Do you understand, Nasir? Do I have your word?"

"Yes, Father."

"Good. I too have always had my doubts, just like you. I have this vision of what it was like here when I was a child, before the Russians, before the wars after they left, and before the Taliban. There was still conflict, but villages were left alone if they stuck together. People didn't have to worry so much and watch their every move. They were free to live life. I dream of that peace and pray for that peace. That is why I always come back to that quote. Now, I must acknowledge that I will only see that when I die and arrive in paradise. For now, I must live in our reality . . ."

"And that reality is the Taliban," Nasir said, finishing his sentence for the first time.

"Now you understand, just like I knew you would. And you will continue my legacy after I'm gone. Protect our family, protect our land, and protect our village. Do what you must to survive. Promise me you will do that, Nasir. Promise me." Daulat had stopped now and grabbed his son by both shoulders, squeezing them as he fervently said these words.

"I will do it for you and Allah," Nasir replied with confidence.

"Good. Thank you, Nasir. Our family is in good hands and I am at peace knowing that."

Caught up in conversation, Nasir hadn't noticed they had wondered away from the creek to a small mud hut on the edge of a narrow poppy field until they stopped. Dingy-looking clothes hung from a line connected from the house to a nearby tree. Garbage surrounded the meager home.

"In this house lives a woman whose husband died fighting for the Taliban nearly a year ago. She refuses to remarry and has no more family in the area. She repeatedly violates our codes. Going in public alone without an escort or the proper attire. Speaking for all to hear. Refusing to marry. Refusing to give her daughter away to marriage. And there are rumors that she doesn't follow our traditional prayers. Teaching her children filth. The list could go on and on. Today is her last warning. She brings disrespect to our village."

Nasir watched as his father entered without warning. The instant recognition and fear in the woman's eyes indicated that Daulat had visited before.

"I've warned you before and you continue to defy me," Daulat scolded as he picked the woman up and brought her to her feet. She did not make eye contact, but rather stared at her children. There were two boys, one several years older than Nasir and one several years younger, and a girl about Nasir's age. He recognized all of them from his journeys around the countryside but had never had a conversation with any of them before. Fear also showed in their eyes, as they avoided Daulat's gaze and cowered in the corner. "We have selected a suitor for you, and you will be married before the sun sets tomorrow. Your new husband will arrange a proper marriage for your daughter. If you don't, your children will be ripped from your arms and you will never see them again. Your sons will be made suicide bombers to forgive your evil ways, and your daughter will be sent far away to the most brutal of husbands. As for you, you will be publicly flogged as an example to the rest of the district. Sunset tomorrow or you will see me in the night."

He threw the woman aside and left. Nasir was shocked. He had never seen his father threaten anyone, let alone threaten violence. Daulat could have a harsh tone, but generally treated Nasir's mother with respect. He showed care and compassion for the people he led. Yet, here he was, carrying out the evils that Nasir hated. To see his father act this way scared him and confused him.

After what we just discussed about protecting me and our family. How can I carry on this legacy?

Still, Nasir knew he must. He had given his word to his father. Furthermore, he knew he would be on the receiving end of these threats if he disobeyed.

Perhaps peace is only for the promised land.

Before he turned to follow his father, he glanced back at the terrified family. They eased slightly as he peered around, then met his gaze, pleading. Nasir's eyes locked with the young woman's eyes for a moment. Although it was dark in the small hut, he could see that her eyes were a bright, deep green.

They're beautiful.

Instantly conflicted, yet knowing his father was waiting, he turned and slammed the door.

They walked home in silence. Daulat never looked in his son's direction, knowing he was grappling with his confusion. Just before they arrived, Daulat stopped. "When we left our house earlier, I encouraged you to be open and honest. I enjoyed our conversation, but the time for talking is done. We must never speak of this again. We both know what we must do."

Nasir nodded, knowing this realization was what his mother feared with her earlier expression.

My father is right. I must do what I need to protect our family, protect our land, and protect our village.

He vowed to keep his promise.

A few days later, they received an unexpected guest from Kandahar in the early morning hours. Mullah Mohammed Omar himself was standing at their entrance. His face was worn and harsh. His eyes blazed with passion and they were especially forceful today. The beard that he proudly displayed was dark black, sprinkled with gray, matching the black and gray turban that adorned his head. What stood out to Nasir most was the scar that adorned his right eye. It was closed in a squint even as his left was wide open. Injured fighting the Russians was the rumor, but Nasir didn't dare ask to confirm. Like most Afghans, Nasir feared yet admired the leader. Mullah Omar had been at their home before, but never unexpectedly, and never looking frazzled as he did now.

Before he was even through the gate, he sputtered, "I told him not to do it and look what has happened now."

"I'm sorry, but I don't follow you Mullah. Who? What did they do?"

"Don't be foolish, Daulat," Omar replied sharply. "You've known all along about our agreement with bin Laden."

"Of course, and I know that you two do not always see eye to eye, but I know of no plan other than the refuge we provide him here in our country in exchange for his financial support."

"Yes, that is how it began. But it has escalated quickly. Yesterday he attacked the United States of America. The United States of America. The most powerful nation in the world. He gave the order and just toppled two of the tallest, most iconic buildings in America," Omar raged. After a moment, he caught his breath before continuing. "Come Daulat, let us sit. We have much to discuss."

"Of course," Daulat said, knowing that his worst fears just became worse. Instead of pondering his own death, or what would become of his son, his family, and his land after he was gone, he now was worried about preparing for a greater battle than they had ever seen. Daulat called for Mina, and she appeared in the courtyard, her face veiled.

"Prepare us some tea. Now," he ordered.

Mina bowed and left. Nasir wondered what his mother's expression was as she left without a word. Was she glad of the veil, that no one could see her face as her husband ordered her around like a servant? Or had she become numb to it, simply accepted it, as Nasir accepted his fate?

"Nasir, check the sheep and allow us to talk," his father interrupted his thoughts.

"No," Omar said, overruling. "This concerns him, and the time of protection is over. We'll need him now more than ever. We'll need every able-bodied Muslim for this fight."

Sitting, Nasir saw that his father's face was grave.

"I'm going to give you the quick version and then I want you to inform all the leaders in the area that we will be meeting tomorrow in Kandahar to discuss our next course of action. The Grand Islamic Council will meet in Kabul following that to prepare our response. You will be at both of them. I have a lot more people to talk with today and planning needs to be done immediately. You are one of my key leaders and just like Nasir, I will need you more than ever," Mullah Omar confessed and then continued. "As I said, a few days ago bin Laden gave approval to conduct a plane operation against

America. This happened after I specifically requested that he not go forward with the plan. We agree on a great many things, but I fear that he gotten us involved in something that he cannot handle and that will ultimately hurt our cause for many years. As I mentioned, he attacked several sites including the two large towers and the US military headquarters, killing thousands of Americans. Now, I've been given an ultimatum by the president of the United States, that if I don't produce Osama bin Laden, that America will attack." He trailed off, seeing Nasir's mother returning with tea.

Daulat quickly injected a question as she was pouring. "How were they able to do that?" he asked in disbelief, having never flown on a plane before. "And what are we going to do with bin Laden? Should we prepare for war?"

"We've been at war, Daulat."

"Not like this," Daulat quickly interjected, unconcerned that he had just interrupted the leader of their country. He wanted to shake Omar, wanted to shout at him, *how could you let this happen?* This wasn't a matter of defeating warlords or unifying the country under a brutal fist. This could destroy his homeland and his family.

"I know that," Omar replied, his angry tone matching Daulat's. "What's done is done. We must now make a plan. You ask about bin Laden, but you know my answer. We will not turn him in. I've been threatened by the US before and didn't bow to their demands. That will not change. He's Muslim and this is greater than one man. This is a fight for Islam."

Nasir didn't believe what he was hearing. America. Osama bin Laden. Airplane. Attack. Thousands of dead. *Surely, this must be a dream. This can't be true.* He had rarely heard of America, only recent heard the name Osama bin Laden, never been near an airplane, and now the combination would change his life forever. Judging by his father's heavy breathing, erratic questioning and interruptions, he knew his father was completely overwhelmed.

Omar continued, "Islam says that when a Muslim asks for shelter, give him shelter and never hand him over to an enemy. That is what our traditions tell us as well. He has helped us with our fight here in Afghanistan and we will not betray our guest. I'm willing to give my life and everything we've built."

He spoke the words with such finality that Daulat was left speechless. Nasir was equally shocked. Mullah Omar, sensing their uneasiness, just smiled. "You asked about how they could do it, how they could plan an attack of this magnitude, well, it took a while, Daulat. A long time. Several years ago, Khalid Sheikh Mohammed, one of bin Laden's top men, brought him the idea of a plane operation. The original plan was for ten planes and to hit both US coasts simultaneously. I didn't like it then, but I didn't think they could or would do it. I was wrong. Mohammed Atef, bin Laden's Chief of Operations, convinced me to wait and see and I went along with it. Honestly, I had forgotten about it, until they told me that they were nearly ready. I urged him not to do it, saying it would only hurt our cause. The problem was that it would only help his cause," Omar added, smiling again. "It was pretty amazing though and I would have loved to watch all the infidels suffer. They had al Qaeda operatives living and training all over the United States, in places you've never heard of, but believe me, they covered that vast land. They even had back-up pilots ready if one faltered or were not allowed to enter. It was a well-coordinated operation and the US never saw it coming. They kept thinking bin Laden was up to something overseas, but they were all completely wrong and paid the price." Letting that set in before continuing, he could see that it still didn't put Daulat or Nasir at ease as they remained expressionless.

"And that is why I'm here, my old friend. Our leaders will meet tomorrow and I want you there. Please gather the others on your journey. I will not be making the trip but will go into hiding tomorrow. They have targeted me before and I'm a target more than ever now. I will disappear for a long time, but I will still be in communication. I needed to visit the place where it all started and my homeland one last time before I leave." Omar paused and looked around at the countryside, as if memorizing the fields that his movement had started among.

He turned back with something like a sigh. "Daulat, one

last thing. Brace yourself for war. The Americans have threatened us before, but this time they will have the motive. However, remember the Americans will be vulnerable when they arrive because we have control of the people. Our people. We must keep it that way, through support or fear, whatever it takes. Everyone is needed for us to win this battle." Omar looked right at Nasir as he stood to go, and his words seemed to twist Nasir's feeling of dread more sharply.

The next day, Daulat departed for Kandahar. From there, he would continue his journey to the Grand Islamic Council assembly in Kabul. After travelling for two days, winding his way through rural villages, spreading Mullah Omar's message, and gathering fellow clerics, he arrived. The Grand Islamic Council was an impressive collection of more than six hundred influential clerics throughout the Taliban controlled area. Daulat was proud to be one of them. Together, they passed laws and debated political matters for the Taliban government. Every time Daulat was here, it made a deep impression and strengthened his fervor for their cause.

Nasir must see this one day, he thought with a smile, but quickly dismissed it, remembering the inevitable conflict and uncertain future. *Sadly, this Council may not exist in the open for much longer.*

Mullah Mohammed Omar had always had the last word on any decision, yet today he was not in attendance. Still, his guidance had been given. The mood was tense, bordering on hostility. Each instinctively knew the inevitable but debated the approach.

"Let's focus on the main issue at hand here. Whether to turn in Osama bin Laden or not?" one of the clerics with the closest ties to Mullah Omar declared from the front of the room. "We have our guidance from Mullah Omar. He has vowed to protect bin Laden yet has asked us to consider this matter and prepare a response."

"I think I speak for most, that we really don't care for the man but have only tolerated him because of his money," one replied.

"Most maybe, but not all. What signal would that send to our people though? If we turned our back on a fellow Muslim because of a threat by America. Plus, Mullah Omar had vowed to protect him. Don't forget your honor," another chastised.

"Even if we wanted to, we couldn't find Osama bin Laden at this point. I'm positive he's in hiding like our leader and his network is vast. We all know the border is very porous between Pakistan. Escape would be inevitable," a cleric from the northern district announced.

"This is our country. Give me ten men and I'd find him within a week," an arrogant cleric quickly countered.

"You're correct, but how would we keep a mission to capture bin Laden secretive and still appease the Americans? I see no good solution."

"My biggest fear is that if we don't do something and soon, we will lose our country that we've fought so hard to build. Is Osama bin Laden worth that?"

No one had an immediate answer.

"We should ask bin Laden to leave by a certain day. Perhaps that would satisfy the Americans," one compromising cleric resolved.

"You heard the ultimatum. That will not do," another responded. "Plus, we'd still be turning our back on a fellow Muslim for a country that we have no connection to and has continually threatened us."

"What proof do we have anyway?" a prominent cleric from the rear shouted. "There has not been any evidence provided to us to say this attack is connected to Osama bin Laden or that it was planned here. From what I understand, the attackers trained in America. Perhaps they should launch the attack in their own backyard."

"I agree, but why are we even afraid of war? This is our country. We know the land and the people better than any of them. We will defeat them on the battlefield."

"Yes, you are correct. Remember what we did to the last superpower that came in here? Russia left with their tail between their legs and we emerged from the ashes. Great Britain suffered the same fate before any of us were on this earth. Now America. They should be the ones fearing a conflict. Allah will make us even stronger because of this and we will once again rise after we have defeated America," a hardy veteran of the Russian conflict declared. The crowd murmured in agreement and their resolve strengthened.

Intimidated, Daulat remained silent, simply listening. He knew his region of Afghanistan better than anyone, but clearly didn't have the vast knowledge of their relationship to bin Laden or America that some of these long-time clerics had. Daulat simply wanted to avoid conflict in his homeland. The conflict against the Northern Alliance was waged primarily in the northern districts, keeping his land safe. *I'd like to keep it that way.* Before that Russian tanks frequented their fields and roads and the result was dismal. Many people died. He wanted to prevent that from happening again. Still, he remained silent.

"Of course, we can defeat America but why stop our current momentum? I suggest that the United Nations or the Organisation of Islamic Conference investigate the attacks and provide recommendations. That way it is out of our hands," a usually quiet cleric suggested.

"You know that will not work. America is just like us in this respect. Their land was attacked, and thousands are dead. What would we do? What would any country do for that matter? What would each one of you do if your district or village was attacked on that magnitude? You would seek your revenge. Their people are demanding action now and that is what they will give them. We are the target and that will not change. All we can do is delay."

This message set in as silence encompassed the group for the first time. Each was pondering the questions that were asked and knew that the wise cleric was correct. They would each take an eye for an eye and seek revenge. The Council knew they must delay and agreed on the following message to the world.

"The clerics of Afghanistan voice their sadness over the deaths in America and hope that America does not attack Afghanistan, exerts complete patience and accuracy, and investigates the issue in its totality.

"We recommend calling on the United Nations and the

Organisation of Islamic Cooperation to conduct an independent investigation of the recent events to clarify the reality and prevent harassment of innocent people.

"We have no intention of surrendering Osama bin Laden to the United States. He is a free man and can move to any place that he wishes, but we are not going to expel him.

"To avoid the current tumult, and also to allay future suspicions, the Supreme Council of Islamic clergy recommends to the Islamic Emirate of Afghanistan to persuade Osama bin Laden to leave Afghanistan whenever possible.

"If infidels invade an Islamic country and that country does not have the ability to defend itself, it becomes a binding obligation of all the world's Muslims to declare a holy war. Any Muslim that cooperates with the infidels is punishable by death.

"If the United States does not agree with this decision and invades Afghanistan, then jihad becomes an order for all Muslims."

Mullah Omar approved the message, insisting that bin Laden did not use Afghanistan as a base to attack, but rather that the training was done in the United States. Omar demanded evidence and he didn't want any trouble with the United States. Their message was delivered and now they would wait for the response.

CHAPTER 8

Response came swiftly. It was exactly what the Taliban feared, yet expected. Shortly after the Grand Islamic Council issued their response, the United States Congress declared war on Afghanistan.

President George W. Bush signed it and the stage was set. More than a declaration of war, this was a broad stroke allowing the US to go after anyone that they deemed responsible for the September 11th attacks.

The Grand Islamic Council quickly changed their stalling tactic once the declaration was signed. They were now willing to try Osama bin Laden in an Islamic court. Pakistan served as a go-between for negotiations, but like the previous discussions, these also faltered. Taliban leadership was unable to quickly produce what the US demanded. Each Taliban counteroffer was rejected. Negotiations were done and bombs began to fall.

Airstrikes hit all major strongholds in Kabul, Jalalabad, Kunduz, Mazar-e-Sharif, and of course Kandahar, the home of Mullah Omar. The US response had overwhelming international support and it was swift and deadly. Taliban leadership braced for a fight. The Grand Islamic Council scattered across the country, returning to their home districts, blending in with local populations. Others went into hiding like their leader.

With broken negotiations and the declaration of war, US ground forces were launched shortly after the initial bombing campaign.

However, the Taliban sent the US a warning.

By invading Afghanistan, the United States would share in the same fate that befell Great Britain in the 1800s and the Soviet Union in the 1980s.

Americans laughed at the thought. Any lingering doubts from Vietnam had long since dissipated, replaced with confidence from Desert Storm.

How could one of the poorest, most illiterate, oppressed countries in the world possibly defeat the world's superpower? That was the sentiment shared by most.

With that, Paul's uncle, Rick, received his orders and was heading to Afghanistan. Rick knew from the moment the first plane hit the World Trade Center that he would be going somewhere overseas. Predicting either Afghanistan this time or Iraq again, he was correct when he got his marching orders. In fact, his bags were already packed when he received the call. Always on top of the latest intelligence, his unit remained in a constant state of readiness. They continuously monitored oppressive regimes throughout the world, and other countries that may interfere with US interests. Rick had been in Desert Storm in 1991 and Somalia in 1993, among other hostile locations around the world. After eight years without major conflict, he was excited to get back in the action. With four years left until retirement, he knew this would probably be his last chance.

Rick was assigned to 5th Special Forces Group—the Green Berets—at Fort Campbell, Kentucky and had been there for most of his career. They were generally the first response to any conflict along with other members of the special operation community—Delta Force, Navy Seals, Marine Recon, Army Rangers. Aiding matters was the fact that 5th Group's area of expertise was the Middle East.

Unconventional warfare was their specialty. That could include covert operations, reconnaissance, training foreign militaries, or tracking down criminals, like Osama bin Laden. Whatever was asked of them, they'd find a way to get it done. Most members of the military have thoughts of joining the special operations community at some point in their career, but the truth is that most people can't handle the rigorous training, physical strain on the body, or have the mental capacity to continuously perform during high level of stress. It takes more than dedication. It's a mindset. It's a culture. It's a lifestyle. That's the only way to be successful. It's already difficult to be a member of the military—physically, mentally, and emotionally—but special operations takes everything to a whole new level.

After saying goodbye to his family in what had almost become a routine, he loaded up and headed to the hangar. His family wouldn't know his exact location or when he would return. Deployments, training, and maneuver exercises created a never-ending cycle of absences. Families got used to this way of life. Still, it was never easy. Especially when it was war.

By design, their flight path took them directly over what had been the World Trade Center. Weeks later, Rick could still see the smoke rising amid the massive hole in New York City and the carnage below. It was a reminder of what they needed to do and why. Of course, none of them needed the reminder, but it only strengthened their resolve. The images of those two towers collapsing would always be with him and the others, and now the image of the rubble below would forever be etched in his memory. As defenders of freedom, military personnel took it even more personally than the average citizens. Memories of those towers crumbling, and thousands of dead innocent people would sustain them when the bullets started flying.

Desert Storm, Somalia, and all those other small conflicts around the world were one thing but this is different, thought Rick. *This time it is personal.*

Less than a month after September 11th, Rick arrived in Afghanistan as the US launched ground forces. CIA operatives, along with special operations from every branch of military service, and several key allies were among the first on the ground with two primary missions. First, partner with the Northern Alliance and other factions opposing the Taliban to defeat al Qaeda and Taliban forces. Second, capture or kill Osama bin Laden.

Within days, Rick found himself on the Afghan countryside, in the small little village outside of Charikar. Only twenty to thirty miles away from the capital, Kabul, it was a crucial location. Northern Alliance factions controlled the area to the north, and the Taliban controlled the area to the south and east, essentially making it the front line. Rick's team had a mission to link up with a Northern Alliance reconnaissance element and push toward Kabul. Abdullah Khalili would serve as the guide.

"Assalamu alaykum," he said holding out his hand to Rick.

Without hesitation, Rick replied, "Waalaikum as-salaam," and gently shook his hand. Just as Rick's team prepared for the culture of Afghanistan, the Northern Alliance must have done likewise. Handshakes generally weren't a custom in Afghanistan. Knowing this was a good sign, Rick smiled. "I'm Rick, and that's our commander over there, Billy. That's Tom there, Jeremy, Dylan, Marco, and Bobby Sue. The rest of the guys are around here some place."

They each took turns shaking hands. Unlike conventional military forces, there were no ranks and last names were seldom used. Nicknames were common, otherwise they used first names. Rick was the longest tenured member of the team and the only warrant officer. His team consisted of eleven men, each with a unique specialty, ranging from foreign weapons to explosives, and medical to radio communications. All of them knew a second language and were experts at calling in close air support to rain down bombs on the enemy.

"Very nice to meet you," Abdullah replied in broken English. "My team is getting ready for the mission, but you will be working mostly with me. I'm their leader."

His team consisted of only six Afghans whose primary mission was to provide the on-ground experience to the Americans. Collectively, they would relay intelligence to their respective headquarters. From there, the higher echelons of command could maneuver forces as needed to defeat the enemy and take control of Kabul. With simple introductions complete, they wasted no time departing for their first mission. Time was crucial as al Qaeda fighters were no doubt trying to get Osama bin Laden to safety or a stronghold.

Avoiding main roads, they were to advance through the rugged mountains and set up an observation post east of Kabul in a Taliban controlled area. From there they could guide close air support and Abdullah could position the thousand-strong Northern Alliance element for maximum effectiveness in their efforts to take control of Kabul. Heavy enemy resistance was expected.

"We're glad to have your support, Rick," Abdullah confided as they departed. "We've fought this battle for many years now and we're confident that with American help we can finally defeat them."

"We have mutual interest in that regard, my friend. It's no secret what al Qaeda did to our nation with the help of the Taliban," Rick replied. "Like you, we are experienced fighters and there will be situations where we have to count on and trust one another. Can we count on you and your men?"

"Absolutely, Rick. The situation has caused us to skip our normal formalities, but make no mistake, those that fight beside us are called our brothers," Abdullah boldly stated. Rick knew full well of the Afghan culture of sharing tea and building trust, but also knew time was crucial. He also struggled with the concept of working with wicked people to defeat even more malicious people. Northern Alliance factions were basically warlords trying to gain their own power. Human rights were not high on their agenda. Rick pushed those thoughts aside and focused only on the mission.

"Tonight, when we are settled in camp, we will be sure to share tea and talk more," Rick replied, placing his hand on Abdullah's shoulder as they moved back toward the group. Despite their intense physical training, the weight of their equipment combined with the speed in which they needed to move would make it nearly impossible to travel by foot. Four wheelers weren't really a possibility here with the treacherous mountains. Instead, they turned to something the United States military hadn't used for generations. Horses.

"All of the fancy machines that you have—helicopters, tanks, and armored vehicles—but here you are riding . . . or *trying* to ride horses," Abdullah laughed. "You had better be able to keep up."

"Don't worry about that," Rick said, matching his smile. "Just show us the way."

Although most of his team had never rode a horse, they

quickly learned. Desperate situations called for any necessary measures. Luckily, adaptability and flexibility were defining traits of the special operations community.

Abdullah led them down a winding path where they could only travel two wide. After nearly four hours, they arrived at their designated rest point for the night. Mountain spurs provided the perfect lookout for security.

"Hey Tom, let's set up our patrol base here," Billy said, surveying the landscape. "That valley looks pretty empty down there." Stars were just showing in the sky and from their location they could see miles across the valley to the other mountain range. At first glance, the valley appeared empty, but smoke could be seen at several locations indicating that there were some houses or small villages.

"Good call," Tom replied and left to prepare.

"Looks like a couple of people down there anyway," Rick said, joining the conversation. "Friendly or enemy, what do you think?"

"For now, I'm going to guess enemy, but we'll see tomorrow," Billy said. "Either way, we'll be ready."

"Yes, we will. Ready for anything, right? But for now, I'm preparing some hot water for tea with our guests. Should I pour you a cup?"

"When in Rome my friend, when in Rome."

"Billy, everything looks secure, especially with these thick trees all around us," Tom reported, returning to the group. "But we can't see very far to the rear. What are your thoughts? Send a couple of the guys over there?"

"I've already sent two of my men over there to set up an observation post," Abdullah replied, overhearing the conversation. Tom, Billy, and Rick exchanged concerned glances. Reading their minds, Abdullah continued. "Don't worry, they will switch halfway through the night to get some sleep. They know the consequences if they should fail and we never fail our brothers. Trust me."

"That'll work just fine," Billy replied. Settled in for the night, they discussed their strategy for the next day over a cup of tea.

Pulling out a map, Billy showed them their destination on

a ridge just outside of Kabul. From there, they could oversee the approach to the capital and provide intelligence accordingly for the assault.

"What do you think is the best path to get there?" he asked, looking at Abdullah.

"It's best to avoid any villages and stay high in the mountains to give us good fields of observation," Abdullah replied tracing his finger along the proposed route on a map.

"I agree, but I'm concerned about this valley here. From the route you just showed us we'll be very exposed at this location when we cross between these two points," Rick pondered, pointing to the map. His years of experience gave him an intuition about potential ambush locations and this location was prime for a surprise attack. The rest of the group echoed his concern.

"I've been in that region many times and the people there are friendly. The Taliban generally leaves them alone because they do what they ask and don't ask questions. We'll be safe," Abdullah reassured the group.

"Alright my friend, let's get some sleep and digest the plan overnight. We'll confirm in the morning after everyone has had a chance to think it over," Billy said, putting an end to the conversation, reaching for his sleeping bag. "I'll see if I can get the latest intelligence from headquarters. Maybe the CIA guys have been there recently."

Adventure was something Rick craved, and it was tough getting any more adventurous that this. Sleeping in the mountains on the eve of war. He missed his family and missed home, like always, but he was among his brothers here. Misery bonds a team and he was with some of the toughest men that America had to offer. They were more than colleagues, they were brothers. Training and missions had taken them to all corners of the world, from the hottest deserts to the coldest mountains, across war torn countries, with little sleep and even less food. Yet, each time they grew closer as friends, and emerged stronger as a team. Without knowing what the future had in store here in this far away nation, that was a reassuring thought. They would be ready for anything, ready for any challenge. Quietly laying under the stars, not knowing what the next day would bring, was one of the feelings he loved most. Breathing in the cold air, satisfied, he closed his eyes and drifted off to sleep.

"Good morning, my friend," Rick started as he approached Abdullah with his morning coffee already in hand. "I needed something a little stronger than tea this morning to get me started. The more I think about your plan, the more I feel we don't have any choice. The alternate routes take us too far out of the way, and we need to be set up before dusk. Knowing that the valley is a likely ambush location, we can ensure that we have air support as we approach."

"I agree, but I do not think we will face resistance," Abdullah replied, smiling. "Plus, we came to fight. If they should choose to face us there, then that is where they will die."

"I guess that sums it up," Billy said, just finishing making the rounds and talking to each member of the team. "Everyone is ready to go. They know what we're up against and they know why we're here. Never thought I'd be able to actually say this to its literal meaning . . . Let's saddle up and head out!"

Travelling the ridges with their horses, they maintained the high ground. Travel was relatively easy. Villagers they encountered went about their normal days, essentially ignoring them. Only a few were openly happy to see them, but caution was certainly in the air. Rick had the feeling that the enemy was among them, watching. Rick looked back and made eye contact with each member of his team, a silent sign to get ready.

They paused with the questionable valley in sight.

Something about it just still doesn't sit right, his intuition told him.

Deep down in his gut he knew that the enemy would use this location. *Maybe not today though,* he hoped. *There is really no good way around it,* Rick reminded himself, *if we want to get to our objective on time. Let's do it,* he thought.

He was never afraid of a fight but didn't necessarily go looking for them either if he could avoid it and still accomplish his mission. Being smart got him this far.

Descending and entering the valley, there were very few

people and most huts looked abandoned. One uncertain look from Abdullah said it all, but to confirm he whispered, "This is not the place I remember." Of the few people in the village, no one made eye contact with them. Heavy beards adorned every individual. There were no women and children that they could see. Several men on the outskirts appeared to be carefully monitoring their movements, glancing in their direction, and then quickly looking away.

"Act natural, like you don't suspect anything," Billy relayed down the line. "We're continuing on our same path." They had planned a rally point on the opposite side of the village to give them good visibility. Getting there was the next goal. Without picking up their pace, they moved forward. Rock outcroppings lined the mountain incline with some sparse trees intermittent throughout the slope. Luckily, more trees were found outside of the village on the valley floor, but there was a large open area before the mountain began to rise again.

That's where they're going to hit us, Rick thought, scanning his surroundings. To the west, there were three mud huts and a row of trees.

A shot rang out, interrupting his thoughts.

Within seconds, gunfire came from every direction. Without thinking, they dismounted the horses and instinctually took cover, returning fire.

Muzzle flashes blazed from the rock bluffs, but enemy fighters were nowhere to be seen. They were clearly entrenched in the mountainside.

Suddenly, there was more gunfire in the opposite direction. Taliban fighters emerged, clearly visible, and advancing.

Rick instantly recognized one of the villagers that he suspected was a lookout. Just as quickly, he pulled the trigger and the man toppled over. *I hate when my hunch is correct*, he thought, reaching for his radio.

"Sierra Kilo 2, this is Renegade 3, we have fifty enemy fighters in fortified positions located at TG56834927. Request close air support, over," Rick requested, not knowing the actual number of fighters, but experience told him to give them something. Estimating the muzzle flashes, he had to be in the ballpark.

"Roger Renegade, enroute to your location. Expected time on target is five mikes. What is your method of marking?" the assault helicopter pilot responded. They had coordinated air support prior to departure and Rick was glad they did. They were called Silent Killers for a reason. They would appear over the mountains without warning, surprising the enemy, and they were extremely deadly. *We can hold them off for five minutes,* Rick thought, rising to fire at another adversary. The ragged fighter never saw Rick and quickly fell to the ground. He never twitched.

"Marking target with smoke, over."

"Roger, we are inbound. Time on target now four minutes. Standby for target marking, over."

"Roger, standing by for marking."

Tom Ridge, the ranking non-commissioned officer of the team, assessed the security situation and saw that nearly all of his men were facing the contact on the mountain, leaving them ill-prepared for the assault coming from behind.

Only two men faced that direction.

"Mac, lay down some grenades on that hill on my command," Tom shouted over the gunfire. "Chuck, hit that assault from the village with everything you got."

"Roger, ready," Mac replied.

"You got it, boss," Chuck shouted.

"Go!"

Weapon specialist Jeremy McDaniels rained down grenades from his grenade launcher as Chuck Levin's automatic rifle cut down the assaulting enemy. Tom quickly worked to arrange his special operations fighters into a 360-degree perimeter, focusing efforts both at the mountain and the approaching Taliban opposite the mountain.

Connecting on the first assault from the village, Tom saw the automatic machine gun hit its mark, decimating their initial assault. At least five lay dead between the two huts.

Mac was limiting their ability to aim effectively from the mountain. Together, they allowed Tom to finish off his perimeter.

Facing the mountain was Rick, in charge of that element,

along with five other operators and four Northern Alliance fighters. Toward the village, their team leader, Billy, was leading, with three operators and two Alliance soldiers. Tom joined this group. They now had 360-degree security with heavy cover from trees and mud huts and enough concealment to make them difficult to find.

"Renegade 3, this is Sierra Kilo 2, over."

"Roger Sierra Kilo 2, Renegade 3 here."

"Two minutes from your location, over."

"Roger, marking target now," Rick calmly replied, loading a yellow smoke canister into the grenade launcher attached to his machine gun.

Bullets continued to shower down from the mountains even though the assault from the rear had been slowed. Silhouettes from the mountain remained elusive, leaving their firepower relatively ineffective. They continued to focus their fire on the muzzle flashes. Clearly, the enemy was deeply entrenched in the rocks and waiting for them. Maneuvering toward the mountains would be suicide. Maneuvering toward the rear they stood a chance, but they maintained their position, hoping the incoming close air support would push them from their hideouts.

"Renegade 3, I see yellow smoke. I say again, I identify yellow smoke, over."

"Roger Sierra Kilo, yellow smoke is affirmative. Target is located one hundred meters north of yellow smoke, entrenched in mountains, over."

"Approaching from the east. Will drop payload at requested location on first pass and hit them with the thirties on the second pass, over."

"Roger," Rick replied, seeing the two helicopters approaching from his left. Apparently, the Taliban also noticed as their tracer rounds began to light the sky.

They were ineffective and too late.

"How's everyone looking on ammo?" Tom yelled, but his voice was silenced as the helicopters unleased their payload.

Bombs peppered the mountainside. Rocks sprayed with every impact as the firing from the mountain momentarily ceased. Ordnance covered what appeared to be every inch of the location where the Taliban fire was coming from.

How can anyone possibly live through that? Rick wasn't sure, but they always did. It seemed that no matter how many bombs were dropped, some managed to escape. *This will certainly dampen their efforts though.*

The M230 Chain Gun unleashed thirty-millimeter highly explosive rounds into the mountain side on the final pass. At a rate of over six hundred rounds per minute, it was an impressive display of firepower, but it was short-lived.

Eerie stillness consumed the battlefield as the helicopters departed. But only for a moment. Seconds later, the violence resumed.

Only sporadic potshots came from the mountainside now, but the force from the rear had grown in number. And they were close. Too close for air support.

Every special forces operator facing that direction fired simultaneously. Rapid bursts suppressed the enemy assault, and quickly transitioned to controlled fire. Taliban fighters dropped after each shot. Afraid to reveal themselves, the remaining fighters began to point their weapons around the corner of the abandoned buildings and spray erratic bullets.

With this ineffective fire, Billy's squad could wait them out and pick them off one by one, if they were foolish enough to show themselves. However, this village wasn't their primary mission and they knew a whole lot more depended on getting to their designated location by nightfall. Maneuvering now would expose them to the remaining shooters on the mountain.

Gunfire from the mountainside was increasing in intensity again. Rick estimated maybe a dozen fighters remained. *One more round of bombs should put an end to that,* he thought, getting on the radio. Knowing the helicopters were still rearming, he changed frequencies and reach out to his headquarters. Luckily, an AC-130 gunship was ready for action.

Within a matter of minutes, an assortment of ordnance again peppered the mountain.

Two enemy combatants tried to escape the destruction. Dylan Boucher, one of Rick's best shots, picked them off, one after the other. Realizing that bombs would rain down on them until they were dead, six more came rushing at them from the west. Clearly disoriented, they performed a poorly executed frontal assault. They were quickly mowed down by Alliance soldiers covering that sector.

Another pair came rushing down from the other side, but the operators had it covered perfectly. They fell like the rest. Another pass from the gunship and the mountainside was silent.

This was the moment to capitalize.

Leaving four guys in place, under the watch of Tom, overlooking the mountainside, Billy ordered the rest to assault the village. Estimating approximately twenty remaining enemy fighters, they were fairly confident of their locations based on their spray and pray shooting.

The team quickly divided into two squads. One group would provide cover fire while the other assaulted. Once that element was in place, they would provide suppressive fire, while the other maneuvered. Back and forth they would maneuver and close the distance with the enemy. The basic infantry tactic of bounding overwatch was simple, effective, and most importantly—deadly. Together, they had rehearsed this battle drill so often that it was second nature.

Rick's commander, Billy, led the first group. They assaulted while Rick's squad laid down a wall of fire. Enemy combatants didn't dare poke their heads out. It had the desired effect.

With Billy's squad in place, Rick's squad stopped firing, getting ready to reposition. Enemy heads began to appear during the momentary calm. Billy's crew opened up a deadly barrage instantly killing several. With the enemy suppressed, Rick's team moved into place.

The pattern was repeated as they methodically cleared the village.

Arriving on the other side of the village, the gunfire ceased. The chaos that consumed them moments earlier, had been transformed to tranquility.

Over their internal radios, Billy asked for a situation report from each element.

"Low on ammunition, check. What about casualties?" Rick

overheard Billy reply to Tom on the radio. Afterward, Billy turned to Rick who was now standing next to him. "How are we looking? Mind checking on all the guys while I call up the situation to higher?"

"No problem," Rick replied, and moved to assess the team. Everyone was maintaining their security positions, as Rick and Tom conducted their assessments.

"Of the four guys with me, we're green," Tom replied over the radio, indicated that they didn't have any casualties. "We've only had one stubborn shooter since you left. Marco dumped some grenades on him, and he quieted down real quick. We're good to go. Let us know when you're ready to move out."

"Roger, good to hear. We're getting a status check here and will let you know when we're ready to move. Standby," Billy responded, jumping between internal communication and reporting to their higher headquarters.

Rick returned and said, "Boss, two minor casualties. Bobby Sue took a round through the calf muscle. Minor, and he's already patched up and ready to go. One of the Alliance guys took a shot through the side of the neck. Close call, but no arteries. Other than that, we're low on ammo like you said but have plenty of everything else. Oh yeah, and we lost three horses. I bet those sons of bitches were trying to pick them off. We'll have to leave them here and double up."

"Thanks, Rick. Got our horses, huh? Damn. Let's sweep through this village one more time before we go take a look at that mountainside. Then we need to get moving. We have a long way to go yet and less than four hours to get there. The terrain looks rough and now we're down some horses."

"Roger," Rick replied while gathering his gear and moving out. After assessing the village, they found nearly one hundred dead enemy fighters, mostly what appeared to be Afghan Taliban but Abdullah identified several as Chechens and Arabs.

"Those Arabs are al Qaeda. They are scum," Abdullah uttered with disgust. "They come to our country from all over—Iraq, Syria, Yemen, Saudi Arabia—just to cause trouble. You wouldn't be here right now if it wasn't for them and the Taliban would be weaker. I sent my men to the mountainside to clean up."

Rick knew what that meant. "If you find any alive, make sure we treat them according to the Geneva Convention."

"Of course, Rick. What do you think I am?" Abdullah just smiled.

No shots rang out and they returned.

"How many did you find?" Abdullah asked his men impatiently.

"More than one hundred for sure. They were everywhere on that mountain. Most were scorched. No survivors that we found. I'm sure we would have seen them try to escape if there were any," came the hurried reply.

"Good. So, there you have it, Rick. We had two minor casualties and killed almost two hundred of their fighters. You have teams all over the countries partnered with us and if all of them are doing the same thing, how much longer can this war really last?" Abdullah summed it up but received no reply. The Americans were already packing up and moving out.

CHAPTER 9

Two months after September 11th, JD and Paul still thought of little else. Judging by their conversations with the other cadets, they felt the same way. It was Saturday night, and there was a party out at Tau Nu Tau or TNT as it was known by the Army guys. It wasn't a chartered fraternity, like others on campus, and there was no rushing to join; membership was only granted to those that were willing to serve their country.

TNT was symbolic more than anything. Instead of an organized club, it was a loosely arranged group of cadets that partied together and hung out every weekend. The location changed each time. Upperclassmen secretly vetted the membership, leading underclassmen to vie for their approval. No one knew their system, but they tended to avoid cadets like Roy Williams. Annoying only began to describe the kid who thought that he could carry his father's rank into ROTC. A military brat, Roy had not managed to make any close friends after nearly three semesters. Roy was scrawny and a little shorter than average. What stood out most was his huge head, both physically and figuratively. His demeanor indicated he was better than everyone, even though his performance was generally substandard. Roy tended to go his own way and that usually conflicted with the way everyone else was going.

Walking down State Street, JD and Paul could see their breath in the frigid November air. They had left early, hoping to sneak out and not alert Roy that there was a party tonight. Somehow, despite not being invited, he managed to find his way to the TNT parties from time to time.

"Do you think we were sneaky enough?" Paul asked, tucking his bare hands in his pockets to stay warm as they strolled.

"I hope so. I can't stand that little punk," JD replied.

"I know. He's so creepy. Especially the way he hits on all the female cadets. I wish one would just slap him."

"That would be hilarious. Wish I could slap him, too. The dude is just so lazy, it drives me absolutely nuts."

"Of course it would, JD, but not everyone is a super stud like you."

"Funny, Paul. But you know what I'm talking about, right? Remember freshman year, he was doing just fine. Then, all of a sudden he was conveniently injured so the rest of us freshman had to carry his equipment."

"Yeah, I remember. There is no doubt that he's a royal piece of shit. Let's just hope he isn't there tonight."

"I'll drink to that when we get there," JD concluded, and they picked up the pace.

"Have you heard from Chad lately?" Paul asked a moment later.

"No, not since he called us back that day after September 11th. I left a message with his roommate the other day, but never heard back. Sounds like he's pretty busy helping out. Even quit his job."

"I imagine he's still pretty rattled. Could you imagine being that close to everything? Scary stuff."

"You ain't kidding, but our day is coming," JD reminded him, trailing off. They took a few steps in unison, now seeing the house a couple of blocks away. "How are you feeling with everything?"

Paul looked at JD briefly, saw that he was serious, and stopped on the sidewalk.

"Remember that day on the river, when I was torn on what to do with my future?" Paul asked.

"Of course," JD replied. "I think I outfished you that day, didn't I?

"Very funny. I'm serious."

"Me, too. Sorry, I just couldn't resist," JD smiled. "No, I remember it well. One of those days that I'll never forget actually."

"Yeah, me too. You've always known what you wanted to do and that's shown ever since we got here. I've been more uncertain, I guess, just going through the motions both with school and ROTC."

JD nodded as Paul spoke.

"When I saw those towers go down though," Paul stopped, trying to find the correct words.

"I know," JD said, putting his hand on Paul's shoulder. "I know exactly how you feel."

"It changed me, JD," Paul explained, looking up at his best friend. "All I want to do is be in Afghanistan right now, hunting down bad guys. I can't think of anything else."

"Me neither. I know it sucks, just sitting here preparing and training, when others are out there living it and taking care of business, protecting our country. I'd give anything to be there right now."

"Yeah, me too."

"But, there is nothing else we can do tonight. Come on, I'm getting thirsty," JD said, ending the conversation. "It's boys' night out tonight and we need to take advantage!"

Dawn was at home visiting her parents and Lynn stayed at school to work on a big project. Despite being roommates, it was the first time Paul and JD went to a party together, just the two of them, since they arrived at school that fall. The night was long overdue for both.

Tonight, the TNT party and festivities were in a house rented by two of the older cadets—Folley and Waylon. Paul and JD tended to refer to upperclassmen by their last names and their peers by their first names. It was something nobody really questioned. Houses on State Street were generally party houses, and besides the location, it was nothing special. The house was two stories and had mundane tan siding with reddish shingles, maybe in honor of the Badgers or maybe just a coincidence. Inside revealed an interesting combination of what had once been an impressive home but was now dingy and rundown after many years of neglect by college students. The view from their sidewalk offered an impressive contrast. Looking to the east, the Wisconsin State Capitol stood prominently in the distance. The large dome rose above the other nearby buildings and appeared to be glowing in the night.

"Pretty cool, huh?" Paul said, admiring the recently designated national historic landmark as they arrived at the house.

"Yes indeed, my friend. Just think, someday I'll be sitting in there and you can come and visit," JD replied with his usual witty response.

"Sure, JD. Whenever you do a tour next, I'll be happy to join you," Paul returned his joke. "Ready?"

"Oh yeah, I was born ready."

Walking in they quickly made their way to the keg, then made the rounds to see who was there. Classic rock music blared, but no one was dancing. A large group was cheering on the beer pong teams. A game of flippy cup was just ending. Others were playing video games on the television, but most were talking in small groups. Empty cups were already on most tables with a half dozen bottles of hard liquor scattered around. It was mostly the ROTC TNT group, but there were several faces that neither JD, nor Paul recognized.

They made their way back over to their fellow second-year classmates, who had now all congregated around the keg.

"Shit, look who just walked in," JD whispered to Paul. Somehow, Roy found out about the party and here he was filling up his red Solo cup. He didn't waste any time making his presence known.

"I can't wait to go over there and kill some of those motherfuckers," he declared, even though no one had been discussing the war in Afghanistan. As much as everyone disliked him, they all murmured their agreement. Everyone except JD. He had been growing more and more irritated with Roy lately.

"Roy, you wouldn't know what to do if you saw one of those Taliban bastards anyways. You're just all talk, *Roy*," JD scoffed, making sure to emphasize the first name that Roy himself hated.

Moving closer, so they were nearly face-to-face, Roy sprayed back, "Shut your face you little kiss ass. Everyone can see how you suck up to all the cadre. You're their little favorite, aren't you? Don't worry about me. I'd show them all how we do things in America."

"Sure, you would," JD chided, inching closer. "Just like

you did when Winchell was carrying your weapon because your little toe hurt. You wouldn't last one day over there."

"Anytime you want to go, JD!"

"I'm right here, *Roy*," JD said calmly, standing his ground.

"Well, that sure didn't take long, did it?" Folley said, stepping in between the escalating duel. "You can both get the fuck out of my house if you're going to be little pussies about it. Look, we're all fired up right now. We all want to be heading over there instead of sitting here. Our time will come soon enough. Just enjoy the beer while you can, you soups." Soups was the affectionate name that the upperclassmen gave to the freshmen. Each had their own variety. JD was chicken noodle and Paul was cream of broccoli, although he wasn't sure why. Paul couldn't remember what Roy's was. Probably something nasty, like pea soup. Now that they were sophomores, being called "soups" was even worse.

Taking advantage of Folley's intervention, Paul grabbed JD's arm and went to refill their cups, standing away from the group.

"What the hell was that all about?" Paul said casually. "What a dick, huh?"

"Yeah," JD agreed. "But I shouldn't have said anything to him anyway. He's fun to pick on but can't take a damn joke."

Some of the other cadets joined them. Roy was not with them. Exercising good judgment, he must have decided to go a different direction.

"Well, it's nice to see you guys out for once," the tall, lanky Jeremiah Schuler said, looking at JD and Paul as he entered the cluster. "I can't remember the last time I talked to either one of you outside of our ROTC classes and I live right next door to you."

"If you didn't have that little punk for a roommate, that might be different," JD replied. "I don't know how you stand him."

"He's harmless. Just all talk, like you said. Mostly, he just sits and plays video games day and night when he's not in class. And you know where I am whenever there is a party," Jeremy said, raising his glass. "So, what do you guys really think?" he asked, turning to the group.

"About what?" Ryan Houghton, one of the more outgoing freshmen asked.

"What else, Houghton? The only thing all of us have been thinking about the last two months. I was never one for school, but now I can't focus at all. All I want to do is go fight. That's probably why JD is all jacked up, too. More than usual, that is," Jeremy said, continuing to carry the conversation.

"I'm tempted to get out right now and go enlist so I can get in on the action," Ryan quickly replied.

"Me, too," Andy, one of the second-year cadets slurred, obviously ahead of everyone in the drink department. "Everyone says the war is going to be over in a matter of months. Heck, look what we did to the Iraqis in Desert Storm. If you weren't there at the beginning, you missed the entire fight."

"This may be our only chance to see combat and I don't want to miss it," Ryan agreed. "I even heard there were some famous people thinking about joining, I think I heard something about that with Pat Tillman after the football season is over. Can you believe that shit? He wants to give up a multi-million-dollar NFL contract to go to war. As much as I want to go, I'm not sure I could do that."

"A modern-day Ted Williams," Paul said. Judging by the blank looks from about half the group, he saw they didn't understand the reference. "You know, Ted Williams. He was one of the greatest hitters in Major League Baseball history even while serving in World War II and Korea. Ted just kept on playing baseball in between the two wars and after, racking up some huge career numbers."

"I'm not a baseball guy, Paul, but that is exactly what should happen when our nation goes to war. You've all heard 'Fortunate Son' by CCR, right? It shouldn't be those that have no choice. Everyone should be volunteering and ready to go," Ryan declared.

"What about the people that don't agree with the war?" Dan Friske questioned, getting in on the action.

"Don't agree!" Ryan shot back. "Is that even a thing? They should be the first ones to go then. I don't agree that we should have to wait until we're twenty-one to drink, oh wait." He laughed, looking at the beer in his hand.

"No, I agree with you, Ryan. There are a lot of stupid rules, but once Congress declares war, everyone should get on board or get out of the country in my opinion," Andy agreed, spilling beer as he made his argument.

"You're not a big First Amendment fan, I see," Dan, the political science major laughed, but was the only one. "That's one of the things that makes our country great and one of the reasons that I raised my right hand. Even if it means protecting and defending those that disagree with what I'm doing."

Ryan agreed in a roundabout way, "I'm glad there isn't going to be a draft though, like Vietnam, serving with a bunch of people that don't want to be there. Look at all of us, just waiting on the word. That's the kind of group that I want to be a part of."

"What do you think, JD? It's not like you to be so quiet," Roy said loudly, rejoining the group. JD guessed Roy was hoping that he was the reason that JD wasn't saying anything.

Everyone turned to JD who paused, considering his response. "Look, I want to be over there as much as anyone, believe me. This is exactly what I signed up for. Our country was just attacked, really for the first time since 1941, and I'm pissed. I want revenge. I want to kill the guys that did this, but most importantly I want to protect my family and this country that I love, so this never happens again. I've never really considered it this much until the last month or so, but that is why I truly joined."

Paul nodded and smiled as JD looked around at the listening faces. Even Roy was paying attention now. JD continued, "Enlisting right now is definitely an option, but I want to lead soldiers in battle, and to do that we need to stay on our current course. They say it will be a short war, but I'm not convinced. Afghanistan has been at war for decades, centuries really, and we're not going to change that overnight. It will still be there when we graduate. This is more than a job or a career, it's a lifestyle and when we do get our chance it will change our lives forever. Some of us may not make it back."

JD's gaze dropped to his cup. "Plus, I've got a lot of beer to drink," he added, raising his cup. JD always tried ending things with a little bit of humor, but it didn't have the desired outcome this time. Ever since the World Trade Center fell and killed thousands, each of them had questioned their reason for joining. Paul agreed with JD; it was more than a job. It would be their life. Dealing with that reality was difficult. Even more difficult was the fact that they knew they could get killed. They all had heard this quote more than once: "The average life expectancy for a lieutenant in a hot LZ in Vietnam was two minutes, five minutes, or sixteen minutes," depending on who you talked to. Whatever the exact time was, it wasn't much, but the point hit home.

Was it worth the cost? Unanimously they all agreed that the United States needed to resolve the situation and hold those responsible accountable for this great atrocity. What that resolution would be, they had no clue. Even with the dismal outcome in Vietnam, the young cadets were completely confident that the leaders of their great nation and the military would lead them to victory. Of all the things they questioned, that was certainly not one of them. They trusted their leaders, but they still had trouble deciding whether it was worth the possible cost for them personally. College had been their focus and the military their future, but most dreamed of more than just the military. They dreamed of getting married, having kids, getting their first house, seeing the world, adventures, getting that dream job after the military, and living a long, successful, happy life. There was just so much life ahead. What if some radical jihadist cut it short? Was it worth it?

Noticing that he had obviously soured the mood, JD tried a different approach. "Look, I'm sorry. I shouldn't have said that. It's just been on my mind a lot the last couple of weeks and I know that you are all feeling the same way. It's more than just hunting down and killing bad guys. The reality is that bad things can happen to us, too, and I've decided that there is only one way to counter it. We need to live our lives like this is our last day—drink as much as we can, get laid as much as we can, and just have a great time. As much as humanly possible, we can't worry about what tomorrow holds."

Just like Dr. Hamm said, Paul thought. *The only remedy is enjoying the moments while you are there.*

"JD is right. Sitting here and wishing we were there or lingering on all the bad is just going to drive us all crazy. Let's fill up our glasses and have a great night," Paul agreed with the spirit of Dr. Hamm's words in his head. "Just like you guys said, it's not often we all get together like this. We better enjoy the moments that we do get."

"I'll drink to that," one shouted and the others joined in. The others departed, but Paul grabbed JD's arm as they left.

"First, I have a little something that I was saving for later," Paul said pulling out his custom flask, filled with Jim Beam, from his coat, "but this seems like a good moment."

He passed it to JD.

"It's not often that we get a night out together like this anymore," JD responded after his drink. "It feels good, like the old days when we hung out every weekend in high school. I miss those days. Nothing to worry about, really."

"That's for sure, but we've got tonight. Let's just enjoy that and take it from there."

"Yes, indeed," JD acknowledged.

"That was pretty impressive what you said back there. Maybe you'll be in that Governor's chair one day after all. How come you never told me any of that? About being afraid of dying and all."

JD seemed to consider, looking back toward the party.

"I'm not sure to be honest. Maybe it's the alcohol talking. I guess when I'm with you, I'm carefree and don't usually consider things like that much. We just joke around. It's simple and fun, you know?"

"Yeah, I get that," Paul said, considering. "I guess I'm the same way. But it's something that has been on my mind, too. I just don't want you to be afraid to tell me anything."

"I appreciate that and the same goes for you. I just keep thinking about getting married to Lynn, starting a family, and all that. Not now, but that's what I ultimately want someday. What if I never get the chance? It's such a weird feeling, such a contradiction. I want to go to war so badly, just drop everything I'm doing right now, and go. But there is this little voice in the back of my head, blinking, warning me that it's not going to be all roses. It's war."

"I think that, too, JD, maybe without the blinking in my head, but definitely with the mixed emotions. But, it's like you said and Dr. Hamm told me last year. All we can do is enjoy the moments when we're in them. It's not going to do us any good to overthink the future."

"You're right," JD said, looking at Paul and taking another swig from the flask. "You're absolutely right." Before long, they were dancing to the music and enjoying the night on their journey to enjoy each moment before they graduated and faced the inevitable.

CHAPTER 10

Citizens of Kabul celebrated as Rick and his team passed through. Men were shaving their beards, no longer a requirement of living under Taliban rule. Bicycles were everywhere ringing their bells, kites were flying, and woman threw away their burqas. Music was blaring around every corner. For many, it was the first time they heard their favorite song in years. Rick had seen these types of celebrations before only to watch the euphoria of victory fade to reality. Many thought that winning this battle meant that the war was over. He knew that was far from the truth. The Taliban, al Qaeda, and other extremists would regroup, formulate a new strategy, maybe even recruit other terrorist organizations, and return with a vengeance. Saying something wouldn't help anything. Instead, he just smiled, thinking that it sure beat the alternative.

It is nice to see the oppressed celebrate for a change.

That smile quickly turned to a scowl as he saw the bodies from the earlier fighting still lined the streets. The Northern Alliance was still searching for holdouts. Taliban fighters that didn't escape were taken prisoner and beaten; Arabs were brutally beaten worse or killed.

Random gunshots could be heard around the city well after it had been liberated. Many were celebrations. Others were no doubt executions, although Rick couldn't prove that fact. He hoped that he wouldn't see any, otherwise he'd be forced to confront the perpetrators, who only minutes earlier had likely been their allies. In many ways, he sympathized. The Taliban had killed at random, ruling through a strict, misguided code of religion. It seemed like anything that brought joy—music, flying kites, dancing, television, reading certain books, and the list could go on—were removed from society. Women couldn't even get medical attention, nor walk alone in public. Education was outlawed. They controlled every aspect of people's lives.

How could people live like that, he thought, even while knowing that it happened to millions around the world each day. This was certainly one of the vilest and strictest regimes he had seen. *They really didn't have much of a choice. Escape was nearly impossible at best and a death sentence at worst.* He was happy to see it end, or at least see the beginning of the end for this brutal regime. That's why he volunteered for the Special Forces—to free the oppressed.

Three days earlier they had arrived at their designated location on the mountainside and quickly set up a patrol base for observation overlooking the city of Kabul. Blending into the natural environment, they set up base camp, knowing they would be there for several days. The selected location had a perfect view of the capital and offered breathtaking views of the surrounding mountains.

It's illogical, Rick thought, *but even in combat and among this horrible oppression, there are still scenes like this that make me appreciate the greatness of the world.* He thought of his family, longing to share this beauty with them. Rick was here so his family would never have to live under the subjugation of this evil.

Their top notched optical devices allowed them to nearly peer inside the houses of the residents of Kabul from an extreme distance. Residents had no idea they were being watched right now by dozens of special operations teams tucked into the surrounding mountainside. As exciting as Rick's missions appeared to people outside the military, much of his time was spent hunkered down in observation. Learning the enemy and preparing for battle was one of the keys to success.

Twenty-four hours passed.

They monitored everything. Movement, suspected Taliban positions, mosques, areas that needed protection, clothing, weapons, vehicles, numbers of people, any key locations. No piece of information was overlooked. They were looking for anything that would give the Northern Alliance and embedded American operators the edge once they assaulted.

Another day passed. Their observation continued.

The assault would begin the following morning.

Abdullah sent two of his soldiers to link up with the main Northern Alliance element. Intelligence was delivered to their top commanders, who were encamped nearby. At this point, there seemed to be some contradicting reports. One objective was to determine the readiness of the Taliban forces. Initial assessments indicated that Taliban forces knew they were coming. The United States had declared war over a month earlier and there had been fighting all around the city. Plus, there had been an intense bombing campaign. However, if the Taliban knew the US was coming, they didn't give a lot of indications.

Or, they are arrogant and defiant. Rick couldn't figure it out. They weren't dug in or making preparations. In fact, it seemed that everything was completely normal, just everyday life in Afghanistan.

Taliban checkpoints were still set up on all major roads entering the city, no doubt demanding payment of some kind for travelling. Similar to the Chicago tollways in that sense, only a person would be beaten if they didn't have the required fees, instead of just fined. Not only would the Taliban beat or harass those that didn't comply at the checkpoints, but they'd take what they wanted anyways, creating a system of injustice and fear. Either way they got what they wanted, so why fight. Rick observed that the locals seemed to conform or tried to avoid the areas all together. He hadn't seen any violence yet today and the streets were rather quiet.

Perhaps the people know more than their actions indicate, Rick thought.

Civilians had most likely gotten use to the Taliban routine. Women all wore burqas and men all wore long beards. Distinguishing friend from foe was relatively easy though as most of the suspected Taliban activity centered on areas that were patrolled by men with weapons. Essentially anyone that had a weapon was an enemy since the Taliban government also controlled the weapons. There was no Second Amendment here nor any of the other Bill of Rights for that matter.

Controlling the weapons made it easy to exert their barbaric will on the population without the risk of resistance.

The special operations observation posts monitored suspected enemies over long time periods to reveal where they travelled and linked locations that should be targeted. Preparation like this was essential for victory, but more often than not, the information was forgotten once the bullets started flying. However, it would certainly help with staging forces and planning the initial operation. The biggest advantage from these observation posts would come in targeting locations with the American's superior airpower. Most of the key locations would be destroyed long before any soldiers arrived. That was typical United States strategy and it usually worked extremely well during the initial phases of a conflict. Third world countries like Afghanistan didn't stand a chance. The problems came later when the enemies blended into the population and created an insurgency. Americans didn't live among the people and would leave one day. That's when things got tricky.

As planned, American aircrafts leveled all the key locations on the morning of the assault. Precision missiles were directed right to the locations that Rick and his team sent up to their higher headquarters.

I love when a good plan comes together, he thought, as he watched the firework show from afar. If the enemy wasn't worried before, their tune quickly changed. Enemy forces were now scrambling to regroup. Some retreated.

Moments after the bombing campaign ended, Northern Alliance soldiers came along all major roads leading into the city. Others assaulted through the open areas where there were no roads. Special operations accompanied most of the Alliance elements. There was no place to escape.

It was a haggard looking assault. Old tanks, worn out tracked troop carriers, recoilless rifles mounted in the back of pick-up trucks, and other random military and civilian vehicles filled with personnel. Some were still on horseback, others arrived by foot. AK-47s were carried by nearly all the Northern Alliance soldiers. Most of their teams had one or two soldiers with Rocket Propelled Grenades (RPGs) slung on their backs, as well. It was a true motley crew with whatever weapons they had collected over the years of fighting.

But it worked.

After the bombing campaign had the Taliban on the run, Northern Alliance elements quickly broke through the initial line of resistance. It took less than an hour of fighting for them to arrive at the city limits.

House by house, they went through suspected locations, searching for any hidden enemy fighters. Any enemy resistance within the city was quickly met with fierce Northern Alliance opposition.

The liberation of Kabul was at hand.

After enjoying the victory and reconsolidating, it was time to say goodbye to Abdullah and his men. The next day Rick's team would begin patrolling the mountains to the east. Abdullah would regroup his main element. With the Taliban on the run, the Americans would focus their efforts on bin Laden. Northern Alliance leaders would follow the Taliban to thoroughly shatter their resistance.

Meeting in front of the abandoned building where Rick's team made their temporary home, Abdullah was the first to speak, "Rick, my friend, thank you for helping rid our country of these vermin. As we said in the beginning, you will always be our brothers. With your continued support we will rule this country soon."

"Remember, my friend, the Taliban failed to rule with responsibility and justice, but we know that you will succeed. We will always remember you as brothers in arms," Rick spoke the words with confidence but inside doubted that they would succeed in governing Afghanistan. The thought saddened him.

"And now we must pursue the Taliban until there are none left. We hope that you find your target as well but be warned that he is deceitful. Although we crushed their spirits in this battle, many will remain faithful and protect him until death," Abdullah cautioned.

"Thank you for your advice and good luck in your pursuits. I hope we meet again."

"You can count on it, Rick. If not now, then when Allah

calls us home."

Rick smiled and waved, although Abdullah did not see. He was already moving out looking for the next fight.

We might live with them for days, fight next to each other and run the risk of dying side by side, then we part ways, likely to never see each other again, Rick mused. Over his career, this had happened repeatedly. Although, he'd miss meeting people from all over the world, he wouldn't miss the chance of dying for their cause. Retirement was looking more inviting each passing day as he longed for his family, home, and normalcy.

For three weeks after saying goodbye to Abdullah, they patrolled the mountains east of Kabul. Resistance was still strong, but it was no longer always direct. It was becoming more unpredictable. Taliban and al Qaeda factions had already lost thousands from their ranks, killed in action. Even more were wounded or captured. Seriously damaged, they were in no way defeated, but they began to alter their strategy.

Ambushes were becoming more common and generally in smaller elements. Instead of fighting to the death, they would surprise the Americans and retreat. Suicide bombers were emerging. Rick didn't like this kind of fighting because there were no preparations that could be made. Everything was reactive. The odds of getting hit greatly increased. His team became more methodical with their movements, avoiding predictability and moving more at night. Their night vision optics gave them superiority once the sun went down. During the day they would rotate shifts, half would sleep while the others provided security and observed. However, sometimes they had no choice. They moved when the mission dictated.

Rick was just waking up and getting ready to take his rotation as lookout, when Bobby Sue, their communication specialist, skeptically questioned, "Hey Rick, did you hear that?" He had been monitoring specialized communication equipment that allowed them to intercept messages on enemy communication devices. This was one key area their foreign language proficiency greatly aided them. Teams all over Afghanistan were monitoring enemy communications, gathering intelligence, and hoping to determine their objective's location.

"I sure did," Rick said quickly, instantly understanding what he was listening for and recognizing the voice. "That's a creepy voice to wake up to in the morning, but I think you're correct. It certainly sounded like bin Laden's voice, but I'm not 100%, since I don't speak the language as well as you." Their team had been briefed on key words to listen for and had heard recordings of bin Laden's voice. They played the recordings daily to make sure they didn't miss an opportunity like this. Of course, it was hard to distinguish after intercepting hundreds of voices over the past few weeks. They weren't certain, but all signs pointed to the voice belonging to the reason they were in this country.

"Let's relay the information to the CIA team and have them listen. They've been tracking this guy for years and should know his voice."

"Good idea. I'll reach out to them now. You keep listening and taking notes," Rick advised.

It didn't take long for the confirmation. CIA officials were already monitoring the conversation and quickly confirmed. His message pointed to one fortress—Tora Bora. That's where Osama bin Laden was hiding. It was early December now and their objective was in sight. Located high in the White Mountains, not far from the Khyber Pass, Tora Bora was said to be an immense cave complex. Rumor and intelligence were sometimes the same, but in this case, they weren't sure what to expect. Either way, indications were that Tora Bora contained a mansion among caves. Rick and his team would prepare for that worst-case scenario: power from mountain streams, weapon stockpiles and hotel-like accommodations for up to one thousand people. This complex network was said to be impenetrable.

CHAPTER 11

With Osama bin Laden's likely refuge identified, Rick's team received their new marching orders and wasted no time moving out. They were heading to Tora Bora. Located just north of Mitariam, they planned to depart for Jalalabad. Here, they would briefly rendezvous with the rest of Task Force Dagger and determine the best approach to capture or kill Osama bin Laden.

"We've got to move," Billy said to the group. "I'm sure he's plotting his escape into Pakistan right now. Rick, what's the status on that helicopter pick-up?"

"Request is approved, and we have a pick-up location about a mile to the south," Rick quickly replied. They loved to joke around, but when it was time for a mission, they were all business.

"Perfect," Billy acknowledged. "Tom, how long before everyone is ready to move out?"

"Nearly ready to go, five minutes," Tom responded as he walked through their makeshift camp, checking everyone's status.

"Alright, we're moving in five, everyone," Billy shouted. "Rick, get me the best route to get there."

"Already done."

Four minutes later, they were on the move.

The pick-up location was in a small valley, outside of a remote village that was now under the control of the Northern Alliance. Approaching, they could see smoke rising from several of the mud huts. The cool December air was perfect for descending the mountainside, but too cold for comfortable living, forcing everyone inside next to their fires.

"Looks like the village is quiet," Rick overheard Marco whisper to Dylan as they approached. "I'm OK with that today. Let's just hitch a ride and get the guy we're after."

"Yeah, I want to be the one that takes that bastard out," Dylan professed, then stopped, raising his hand. "Hey, do you see that cart approaching?"

The entire team saw Dylan raise his hand, and quickly saw the donkey pulling a cart blocking their path. Billy motioned to the left and they began moving around a small complex.

As they rounded the corner, a young man approached, asking for food.

They halted again. Telling him they had no food, and deeming him harmless, they continued.

The cart that was blocking their path, had now turned in their direction. No weapons, but the cart was filled with something that was covered with a gray blanket.

"Let's keep moving," Billy shouted. "Let's keep our eyes on our objective."

They picked up the pace.

Another young man approached asking for food.

This time they continued moving. The cart was still approaching from the rear, although the distance between them was now increasing. The man accompanying the cart continued to look toward the ground.

"We're not messing around anymore. Let's move back up the mountain and skirt this village," Billy ordered. "Marco, keep your eye on that cart."

They left the village, navigating through the foothills of the mountains, bypassing the village. The cart had stopped when they departed. The man never looked up.

With their objective in sight, now past the village, they began to descend.

"Rick, what's the ETA on that bird?" Billy asked.

"Thirty minutes," Rick replied.

"Roger, let's set up a perimeter at the LZ and hunker down," Billy said.

"Already on it, boss," Tom acknowledged.

With security facing the mountains and the village, they waited. Everything was quiet.

As they heard the rotors of the helicopter approaching, they began collecting their belongings, their eyes never leaving their assigned security sector.

Two helicopters approached. The assault helicopter remained stationary, providing security, as the Blackhawk began descending. The team quickly loaded the helicopter, while still providing security. The Apache attack helicopter began to circle.

With everyone onboard, the Blackhawk ascended.

Boom!

Seemingly out of nowhere, a figure rose from a rock outcropping, lined with thick vegetation, and launched an RPG at the Blackhawk as it rose.

Maneuvering to avoid the incoming RPG round, the Blackhawk pilot rotated quickly to the left, away from the launch site, then nearly vertical, rising quickly.

The evasive maneuver worked as the RPG narrowly missed the tail rotor. Had it connected, it would have likely been a death sentence for everyone on board.

The Apache's chain gun opened up on the launch position, but the rounds came up empty.

Two men on a motorcycle were departing, weaving on a small trail that followed the mountain's ridge.

The attack helicopter pursued, but soon lost the assailants in the thick vegetation.

They all knew the most wanted man in the world was waiting, so they gave up pursuit and departed for Jalalabad.

Coordination in Jalalabad was brief. They'd be going in light. Really light. CIA, Delta Force, British commandos, and only a handful of other special operations teams. Green Berets would be limited. They would rely on the Northern Alliance again and other forces opposing the Taliban without conventional forces at this point.

Rick and his team were again set up in a remote location, overlooking the cave complex. From there, they used their laser markers to coordinate air strikes for the laser guided bombs and missiles that the Air Force dropped. From their vantage point, they watched as bombs poured down on the suspected hideout. Later reports would indicate over 700,000 pounds of ordinance was dropped on Tora Bora in a four-day period.

"How could anyone still be alive after all that?" Rick said to Billy and Tom as they sat observing and waiting for the assault.

"It always baffles me, too, but you guys have seen it before. It always looks bad and blows up lots of stuff, but I'm always amazed at how many people walk out alive," Billy responded.

"Especially with the caves they're talking about," Tom added. "Yeah, they're probably watching Paris Hilton right now, drinking a whisky and coke, and eating Cheetos in their lazy boys while sending out messages that the Americans are evil for their western ways."

They all laughed.

The team had quickly learned about the twofaced nature of the Taliban and al Qaeda. According to religion they said one thing, but did as they pleased in private, in addition to openly growing marijuana and poppies to fuel the drug trade.

Nothing like hypocritical purity in the name of religion, Rick and the team had all thought at one time or another. *As long as everyone else followed the rules.* Most oppressive regimes they observed over the years had the tendency to follow the same pattern.

"What they really need to use are the GATOR mines we used back in Desert Storm," Tom said with a reminiscent smile. Dropped from aircrafts, GATOR mines essentially create a minefield. Anti-tank and anti-personnel are the two options, and both are effective at controlling movement. "Just drop them at every possible exit and no one will get out of that cave alive. I'm still not sure why that request was denied. Someone making decisions who's probably never been on the ground anywhere. They're certainly not here right now. It's already one of the most heavily mined nations in the world. What's a few more?"

"Yeah," Rick agreed. "Caves can protect from ordinary bombs, but it's hard to move knowing that every step could be your last."

Another bomb lit up the night sky. They were far enough

away that they would see the explosion and then moments later they would hear and feel the concussion. Rick had learned to enjoy times like these, because he was never sure when he'd be rushing in with the bombs going off right next to him. Following the bombardment, Northern Alliance fighters and other Afghan forces would lead the assault just as they did in Kabul. Special forces operatives would again serve as advisors and continue to target enemy forces with precision bombs.

"What I can't figure out is why there aren't more of our troops around here?" Billy questioned. "It's been bothering me ever since we left Jalalabad. As much as we all hate working with regular units, I'd sure feel better if we had some more around here now."

"Never thought I'd hear you say that," Rick joked.

"I know, we must be desperate, right?" Billy replied, looking at Rick and then Tom before dropping his head to continue. "I get it. It worked in Kabul. That's what they are thinking, I'm guessing. But we have bin Laden here, at least that's what everyone is saying. If it were up to me, I'd have everyone in the military surrounding this mountain right now, even the Coast Guard."

"Shit, we are desperate," Tom agreed. "I'm not sure I agree with that, but at least some more SF teams. Seals. Rangers. Maybe a division or two blocking the escape routes. Marines. Heck, Pakistan is right over there," Tom continued, now pointing toward the east. "What, a few miles at best. Have the Marines link arms and block the border. I hope they are not counting on the Pakistani military to do that."

"Any idea why there aren't more troops here, Billy?" Rick asked.

"I honestly have no idea. We've got a lot of space to cover and not very many of us, but this is it. Kill him now and maybe this whole thing ends. Lose him here and who knows what happens. No, I can't explain it."

"Yeah, me neither," Rick agreed. "But then again, we've been in plenty of places with a lot less support than we needed. Nothing like this though. The most wanted man in the world was never within our grasp like this with so few of us."

"Not to mention the fact that we're in one of the most rugged countries on earth," Tom added. "Guess we just have to end it here."

As the Northern Alliance assault began, Rick noted the fighting pattern of the enemy. As the bombs were dropped, they would run into the cave complexes. Then, they would quickly emerge in fortified fighting positions once the bombing stopped, just as the Northern Alliance forces assaulted. As expected, the bombs did damage but produced limited casualties with the protection of the caves.

Throughout the day, Alliance fighters poured down the valley and up to the enemy positions in fierce fighting. Slowly, they advanced with US ordnance helping every step of the way.

With dusk approaching, Northern Alliance fighters appeared to be leaving the positions they had fought so hard to obtain. All day long they had fasted with no food and water while fighting. Now was their time to recover and feast. Ramadan was the most sacred month in the Islamic calendar because it commemorated when their savior, Muhammad, received the words of God during that holy month centuries earlier. Their traditions demanded fasting during daylight hours, causing them to become weak and dehydrated during the physical exertion of combat. Not even war or possible death allowed them to deviate from this sacred ritual.

As they retreated from their positions for the evening feast, Rick wondered if the enemy was doing the same.

Most likely not.

More hypocritical ways.

No doubt they would eat, but they would also use this valuable time to regroup, rearm, and refortify. That would make the Northern Alliance assault the follow day that much more difficult. Since Afghan forces made up a bulk of the assault element, there was not much that could be done at this point without them.

Although they had managed to trap Osama bin Laden here, Rick began to get a bad feeling they weren't going to find him. He was likely using this sacred time to plot his escape.

We must put the pressure on him now.

Anyone who has ever hiked through the mountains knows that there is more ground to cover than meets the eyes. Nearby, the Afghanistan-Pakistan border was porous, with escape routes everywhere. Pakistan was supposedly guarding the border, but Rick had his doubts on their effectiveness. Cutting off the likely escape routes was one thing, but it would be impossible to block them all. Particularly since the request for additional troops had been denied.

Who would deny additional troops on the manhunt for the world's most wanted criminal when there were hundreds of thousands itching to help back in the States? Rick wondered, not for the first or last time.

The fighting raged for days. Casualties mounted among the Northern Alliance forces. The US aerial bombardment was nonstop, both day and night. However, little was known at this point about enemy casualties. Each day they continued to fight, and they were gaining ground. Soon, they would overtake the impenetrable complex.

On the seventh day of the assault, Rick's team intercepted a radio communication. This time they recognized the voice immediately.

"Our prayers were not answered. Times are dire and bad. We did not get support from the nations who call themselves our Muslim brothers. Things might have been different."

Rick could hear the defeat in the voice of bin Laden. He and his fighters must be desperate.

"This is the time to strike, finish them off, and use their weakness to our advantage," Billy declared, relaying the message to all of their team.

Rick pointed wordlessly up the mountain in disbelief. Instead of capitalizing on the moment, their *partners* were coming down earlier than usual to start their Ramadan festivities.

"Wait, one minute. So, you're telling me that we just intercepted a dire message from the enemy, and the next minute all of our *allies* are walking down the mountain with no prisoners?" Rick questioned Billy. "Does that sound right to you?

"Of course not, Rick," Billy responded bluntly. "Nothing about it sounds right. Just talked to higher and they are ordering all teams to assault without Alliance assistance. We're supposed to finish them off."

"What are we waiting for? Let's move out," Rick barked, grabbing his gear.

He turned to find one of the Alliance leaders pointing an AK-47 at him.

"What are you doing?" Rick shouted in disbelief. "If you're not going to get them, then we'll get them."

"Don't move, my friend," he responded. "This is our country and our war. They said they surrendered, and we'll get them tomorrow. After our evening Ramadan festivities."

"What if they get away? What if he gets away?"

"That will not happen. We have them surrounded and we have their word."

"Their words don't mean anything. They are the enemy. They are the ones that are trying to kill us."

"They are fellow Muslims and we will honor their words during this sacred time."

Rick had a million thoughts running through his head and a million others he wanted to say, but instead he bit his tongue. One look at Billy, now shaking his head, told him that the situation was happening throughout their operational command. That's why they got their orders to assault.

We could turn our weapons on them as well, but what would that help? There would be a war within a war. Plus, we are vastly outnumbered.

"This is bullshit," Rick muttered, when he concluded the situation was hopeless.

"I know," Billy whispered. "But what the hell are we supposed to do?"

"Nothing, not a damn thing," Tom said, joining the conversation, spitting in disgust. "How many other hopeless situations have we been a part of over the years? But, this one, yeah, this one sucks the worst. You can only lead a horse to water, can't make them shoot bin Laden."

At this, they gave a short chuckle. They had learned to control what they could control and try not to worry about the rest. As they looked around, it was clear there was nothing they could do.

So, they waited for dawn.

Instead of a surrender the following morning, fighting erupted in an unusual location. It happened away from all the previous week's fighting. All Northern Alliance fighters focused on that location as US bombs continued to rain down throughout the cave complex.

The familiar voice of Osama bin Laden was once again intercepted, this time with desperation in his voice.

"I'm sorry for getting you involved in this battle. If you can no longer resist, you may surrender with my blessing."

But for bin Laden, surrender would not be an option. During the hoax surrender, or as some were calling it—truce, he had slipped safely into Pakistan.

There was nothing that Rick's team or any of the other American elements could do to prevent the escape. They simply didn't have the resources.

Quickly losing their will now that their leader had abandoned them, the enemy was quickly overrun. Less than two weeks after the initial bombing, the Battle of Tora Bora was over. Even though weapons had been pulled, Alliance fighters and the Americans once again worked side by side to clear the caves. Although they found scores of al Qaeda fighters dead, no sign of bin Laden or his leadership was found. It was a clean escape. Instead of a mansion among caves, the accommodations were paltry. Small natural caves were all that had been used and there were barely enough supplies to support the two hundred-strong enemy fighting force that they projected had been there.

Disappointed in the caves and disappointed in the escape, Rick's team turned their attention to the inevitable next battle. With bin Laden gone and likely in Pakistan, they had no idea what that would be. All they knew is that they had a feeling that there was no end in sight for this war now that Osama bin Laden had escaped.

CHAPTER 12

Paul hesitated as he picked up the phone. He hadn't spoken to his uncle for years, since he was a child really. Yet, he had thought of him often, especially while he was in Afghanistan. In many ways, he had been the inspiration for Paul joining the military. That and a little prompt from JD.

"Hey, Paul, how are you, buddy?" Rick said. He had just returned to Fort Campbell, within the last couple of days. Now, he was calling everyone in the family, letting them know that he was safely back in the United States. Paul was getting ready to return to college and start his third year.

"I'm good, getting ready to go back to college next week. The real question is, how are you?"

"Happy to be back, Paul, that's for sure. How are you liking Madison?"

"I'm really enjoying it, but I'm itching to graduate so I can go over to Afghanistan, too. What's it like over there?" Paul inquired, feeling nervous about asking but interested in gaining any insight he could.

There was silence on the other end of the line.

"It's tough to describe, Paul. It's like a whole different world over there. Imagine life here, then imagine the opposite. If you do that, you'll be close."

Paul tried, and had some ideas, but couldn't really comprehend. He imagined nobody could completely understand unless they saw it firsthand.

I hope I get that chance.

He wanted to ask so many more questions. Did you kill anyone? Shoot at anyone? See anyone get killed? Were you there when they were after Osama bin Laden? He decided better.

"It's tough to imagine. Almost like one of those movies

that take place in an alternate reality, I guess. We are all just glad that you're home."

"Thanks. It's good to be home, that's for sure," Rick said again. "Yeah, it's a lot like one of those movies. You're still in ROTC from the sounds of it."

"Yep, I'm planning on sticking with ROTC and going in when I graduate. I just hope the war isn't over by the time I graduate."

"Glad that you are sticking with it, Paul. It's a tough life though and even tougher during a war. I know the movies make it look cool, but it's probably not what you are imagining right now."

"I know. We hear that all the time, but I just want to do my part."

"That's good and it will be a great experience. Just enjoy the time you have now. Enjoy being in college and try not to think about war. Your day will come soon enough and then you'll wish you could be back in college."

"I'll try, Uncle Rick, but it's hard. Anyway, I'll look forward to seeing you again next time you are in Wisconsin. Everyone is waiting to talk to you here, so I better pass the phone."

"Sounds good. Good talking to you, Paul, and good luck. Remember, just enjoy the moment."

There it was again. Enjoy the moment. Why has everyone been telling me that?

A year later, the dust had finally settled from the horrific scene of the World Trade Center. Media coverage of the attack and operations in Afghanistan were now minimal. Emotions that had once run high were calm again. Stock markets had recovered. A sense of normalcy had returned, but the memory was always just under the surface. The same held true for the UW-Madison cadets. They knew their time would come, but JD's words stayed with them. Enjoying every moment was the best thing they could do. Some didn't feel the same way. In fact, two cadets dropped out and enlisted over the summer. They just couldn't wait to get in on the action.

On September 11, 2002, the UW-Madison cadets, along

with several of their classmates, climbed Bascom Hill and placed almost three thousand flags to commemorate those that had lost their lives in the tragedy. The moment of silence brought them back to that moment, just as they would return to that moment often during their daily lives. Simple things would remind them of that day. Each time they were reminded, they could see the towers falling, imagine all the people trapped inside, and thought of those trying to bring Osama bin Laden and his associates to justice.

Afghanistan was rarely mentioned in the media after the one-year remembrance. It was overshadowed by another looming conflict that had emerged and captured every headline.

Iraq.

Unlike Afghanistan, there were more skeptics for US involvement in Iraq. The United Nations Security Council was torn. National support was wavering. French fries became freedom fries after France was unwilling to support the military intervention. The possibility of weapons of mass destruction was the primary justification for war, and Saddam Hussein's arrogance of denying international inspectors into the country only strengthened US resolve. Many were convinced that military intervention was the correct path with the lingering memories of September 11th. Possible connections between Iraq and al Qaeda fueled that speculation.

Saddam Hussein continued to defy the United States and the international community, and it appeared that all diplomacy had failed. The US decided it was time to overthrow Saddam Hussein and eliminate any possibility of him using weapons of mass destruction. President George W. Bush made the connection between Iraq and September 11th as he pledged to use a preemptive strike against any nation that he thought threatened America's national security.

The cadets at UW-Madison couldn't understand the delay. Evil people who resisted the United States deserved to die was their philosophy. Their minds were not molded for diplomacy. Not yet, anyways. They were molded for combat, and each wanted in on the action just like a vast majority of the United States military. In their minds, they existed for this reason and they were getting impatient. The United States was now going to be at war on two fronts and they were sitting here in college learning about combat, rather than being there.

On March 20, 2003, the United States military advanced on Baghdad after a several day bombardment. Operation Iraqi Freedom dominated the headlines. After only a short break at home from Afghanistan, Uncle Rick was back in Iraq. Paul thought of him often as he religiously followed the news coverage, hoping it wouldn't end as quickly as they thought.

He didn't want to miss out on this war either.

In the morning, he would check the news, captivated by the fighting.

After class, he would check the news again, smiling at all the Iraqis as they pushed over statutes of Saddam and hugged American soldiers.

Before bed, he would check the news again, nearly in tears as Americans were ambushed and killed.

And so, the routine would go every day, just like following his favorite baseball team, the Milwaukee Brewers. Paul was obsessed. JD was just as bad, throwing himself into ROTC even more than usual. They discussed little else when they were together. Every UW-Madison cadet was eager for combat.

Together for nearly two years now, Paul and Dawn were officially a couple. The summers had been rocky, Christmas break as well, but now that school was back in session, all was well. Each time they were apart, Dawn pleaded for Paul to come to her. Most times he came running. When he couldn't, she found ways to make him jealous—giving an old boyfriend a call or worse, meeting up with them. More than once it went too far. She always came back crying and apologetic. Although Paul couldn't quite explain it, for some reason he always forgave her. Now, that was in the past. When they were together, it was like those bad times never happened.

Dawn was becoming more serious, not only about Paul, but life in general. Maybe, it was there before but Paul had never noticed. Marriage was never mentioned but future plans now included we, us, and ours. She wanted to escape her small town as much as she loved it, knowing that she would probably return one day. And she wanted Paul with her. Reveling in her vision of the future, Paul enjoyed the moment, but had his doubts on what it might hold for them as a couple. None of her goals revolved around Paul's likely future—war. Relationships were difficult. Long distance relationships were even more challenging. Paul wondered if she knew that long distance relationships, with the stress of combat and the inevitable changes afterwards, were next to impossible. Last summer and her constant need for companionship didn't bode well for this difficult future.

Afghanistan was demanding more troops as they turned to rebuilding the nation and who knew what the future of Iraq held now that fighting was escalating. Fighting two fronts was going to be a challenge for the US military and Paul knew that they would need every soldier. Deep down, Paul thought that Dawn knew this fact, as well, but they had only skated over the topic in the past.

Paul decided that he would talk to her tonight. He would be leaving for his summer training camp at Fort Lewis, Washington after the school year was over. This camp is where he would be tested on everything he learned in ROTC the last three years—leadership, planning and executing missions, physical training, marksmanship, land navigation, and generally how he would perform as an officer. All the cadets would be ranked, and that ranking would directly relate to their future assignment. It was similar to basic training, but more of a test and focused on their leadership potential. Cadets were expected to know nearly everything when they arrived, rather than being taught while they were there. It was already April now and that meant they only had a little over a month to spend together. Any type of communication would be limited, and he couldn't drive up every time she had doubts.

Tonight, they would go out to their favorite place to eat, Mariner's Inn, a picturesque restaurant not too far from campus overlooking Lake Mendota. It was expensive for college students which meant they didn't go often, but they splurged once in a while. With Paul leaving soon, it was the perfect opportunity.

After that they'd go to another one of their favorite places—a dead end road in the middle of farm country. Driving one day, Paul found it by happenstance and couldn't pass up the opportunity to show Dawn. Naturally, she loved it. Surrounded by woods it offered the seclusion that the young couple craved and gave them a chance to be alone. The short drive was always memorable. They'd make love and then talk for hours. Not once did they see another person.

Paul picked her up just after five.

"Well, hello there, handsome," she said when Paul opened the door.

"Hello. Wow, you look absolutely great," Paul said, raising his eyebrows and taking in her body. She was wearing her hair short this year and her dark blue jeans were tight. Her black heels matched her flowy black shirt. "Are you sure we can't just skip dinner?"

She appreciated the attention and leaned in to give him a kiss.

Keeping the conversation light during dinner, Paul decided to save the deep conversation for their secret spot. Dinner was superb as always, and they quickly headed to their vehicle when they were done eating.

"What are your plans while I'm out at camp this summer?" Paul said as they drove, sensing it was finally the right moment.

"Nothing really, just heading home to see my parents for a week or so and then I plan to stay around here now that I've got that good job on campus," Dawn remarked casually.

Paul had forgotten about her new job on campus doing research at the library and was momentarily relieved. He really didn't want her to go home. Too many old friends.

"That sounds like a great plan, especially since I'll be coming back later this summer and then we can enjoy the rest of the summer together. Just think, we can visit this spot all the time," Paul smiled.

"I'm not going to have a roommate, so we won't need to go anywhere, remember?" She teased.

He had forgotten that, too, probably absorbed by the footage of Iraq while talking to her on the phone.

"That's right, how can I forget that? But you forgot that you'll probably have a summer roomie because I'm not going to want to leave when I get back."

"That will be perfect. Don't worry, I'm going to work like crazy when you're gone and stay out of trouble. Heck, I don't even know any guys around here anyway," Dawn said as if reading his mind.

Feeling good about where they stood as a couple, he smiled, seeing their turn-off ahead.

Seconds after hitting the dirt road, her shirt was off.

Immediately after that, Dawn dangled her bra over the steering wheel and reached for his belt.

It's a good thing we're in the middle of nowhere, Paul thought, remembering he should at least glance at the road once in a while.

Moments after stopping, they were in the backseat.

When they were done, they rolled down the windows to enjoy a little of the cool air.

Looking down, Paul instantly saw that two things were wrong.

First, lights were coming up in the rear-view mirror.

Second, his usually reliable condom had somehow broken. Coming from a devout Catholic family, Dawn refused to take birth control, and always insisted on using condoms. So far, they had worked extremely well.

Dawn didn't notice the condom in her scramble to get her clothes and Paul didn't have time to say anything as he did the same.

An elderly couple pulled up beside them. "Nice spring night out here, don't you think?" asked the woman.

Dawn smiled and replied, "Yeah, we love coming out here to talk. It's so nice and quiet."

With a knowing smile, the old lady said, "Oh, that's what you two were up to. Bill and I were wondering because we usually don't see too many people out this way." Then added with a wink, "Well, you kids have a good night . . . talking."

Dawn broke out laughing as they drove off. After Paul

didn't join her, she asked, "What's wrong, Paul? They didn't care that we were out here. I think they thought it was funny."

"It's not that. I think it was hilarious and really don't care what they think anyway, but just as they pulled up I noticed something and got a little worried."

"What is it?" she asked, eyebrows drawing together with concern.

"The condom broke," he replied bluntly and looked at her, waiting for a reaction. Her face went blank and for a few moments she said nothing.

"Oh my God! What should I do? This has never happened to me. I can't get pregnant with school. I'm too young and you are, too. Plus, my parents would kill me! We're both too young and not ready for this. How did it happen? Didn't you feel it? You should have stopped. We can't handle this, we—"

Paul interrupted her ramble, "It's going to be OK."

"No, it's not Paul. This could ruin everything. We don't all live in your little fantasy world where everything just always works out."

"Ouch! Let's not make this personal. Let's at least think through this. What can we do?"

"I have no clue, Paul. You seem to have all the answers. What do you think?"

"First off, I don't think it's the end of the world. The chances are slim that you'll actually get pregnant. But, if by some small chance you are, then I think we'd make good parents. You know I've always wanted to be a father."

"How can you even think like that? I'm just not ready, Paul." Dawn covered her mouth with her hand as tears started forming in her eyes.

"I know. I'm not either." Paul gently gathered her into his arms. "But we'll get through this together."

She leaned against him and started crying. For several minutes Dawn's crying was the only sound and Paul looked out at the stars as he gently stroked her back. Then she picked up her head, wiped her eyes, and looked at Paul.

"You're right," she said. "We will get through this together. The likelihood is slim, and we've come a long way, got through some rough patches, and here we are."

Dawn turned away from him, staring out at the moonlit fields around them. "Growing up I became convinced that I'd never meet someone that saw a future with me. I always had these big dreams of getting married, having a family, and growing old with someone, too. Those dreams were crushed time and time again and pretty soon I forgot them." She turned back to Paul, her eyes still bright with tears but smiling now. "Thanks for bringing them back."

Smiling, Paul felt a deeper connection than he had ever felt to Dawn in that moment. "I never knew you felt like that, but I'm glad I could bring those feelings back." He leaned over to kiss her deeply, but tenderly. In that moment, all his doubts were gone. Facing a difficult situation, they were growing stronger together.

All night, they talked. The future. The possible baby. The Army. Dawn's future career. Travelling the world. The wars that Paul would find himself in soon. That night they felt they could make it through anything the world threw at them. He never loved her more.

CHAPTER 13

Fort Lewis, Washington was a beautiful place, with Mount Rainier dominating the landscape and majestic evergreen trees growing in every direction. Paul could understand why so many travelled to the area just to see the countryside, but he knew he wouldn't have time to enjoy the scenery. Training would take up all his time. Obstacle courses, rappelling, physical training, leadership reaction courses, land navigation, water survival, marksmanship, the grenade course, road marches, medical screenings, and of course the situational training lanes where they would be evaluated on their leadership abilities.

Those were just a few of the many skills that cadets would be evaluated on during their month of field training. With each event, they would be ranked against their peers. Rankings added pressure since they were a key factor in determining a cadet's future duty location and branch assignment. The more coveted the assignment you were after, the more importance on the rankings. Training wasn't the real reason Paul wouldn't be able to enjoy Washington though. Paul wanted to do well and had his sights set on being an Engineer with the 101st Airborne Division at Fort Campbell, Kentucky, but at the moment all he could think about was Dawn.

And the baby.

Two days before he left, Dawn told him she was pregnant.

After the condom broke the month before he left, he hoped and prayed that she wasn't pregnant. Now a new reality was upon them both. Their parents wouldn't find out until he was finished with training. Dawn didn't figure she'd be showing until a few weeks after he returned. Then, they'd tell them together, they decided.

Or had I decided?

The conversations were all a blur now and he longed to talk with her face-to-face, to hold and comfort her.

Dreading that future day of telling their parents didn't help his outlook. Once his training was complete, they could really sit down and talk and figure out their future.

Then, we'll get back on track.

Living in open barracks wasn't an ideal situation, but Paul made do like he always did and snuck out every chance he got to use the phone. Free time was rare, but there was at least a limited amount—sometimes ten, sometimes fifteen minutes—most days.

Dawn was a wreck.

Paul tried to remain strong, but it was all a show.

Their conversations went nowhere. Dawn was hysterical, talking more to herself than Paul most days. She clearly needed comfort more than ever and Paul wasn't there to provide it. He often wondered where she would go to get it and when.

Another haunting distraction.

How are we ever going to make it through this now or in the future?

After a particularly difficult conversation, Paul thought, *I have to talk to the one person who would understand. The one person who has always been there for me.*

Even though they were in the same general vicinity on Fort Lewis, it was harder than he thought to find JD; Paul stopped at more than ten different barracks before locating him. JD was nearly done with training and heading home soon, whereas Paul was just beginning. The seasoned cadets were told not to provide any information to the newly arrived cadets. Knowing JD would comply and not say anything about camp, Paul pried.

Paul got some tips, vague ones at best, but found out that JD was ranked in the top two of his class. Paul wasn't surprised; JD was a stud.

"JD, I'm disappointed. Really disappointed," Paul said with a sly smile. "I thought you were number one material."

"We'll see where you come in, smartass," JD replied quickly as he generally did.

"I'm going for top third and that's it. I'm not a super stud like you." Paul hesitated, then took a deep breath. "I've got something serious to talk to you about. I know we don't have much time, so I'll just say it. Dawn is pregnant."

"Wow . . . I wasn't expecting that." JD hesitated as his eyes widened and he blew out a deep breath. His eyebrows were now raised in surprise. "I don't even know what to say. What are you going to do?"

"I have no idea," Paul said quietly, blinking back sudden tears. "It's miserable here. I can't focus, and I just want to be with her to figure this all out."

"I wouldn't be able to focus either. Wow," he said again, still in disbelief. "What can I do to help? What have you guys discussed at this point? Do your parents know? Wow, Paul. That's all I can keep thinking. Wow. Did not expect this."

"Me neither. No, neither one of our parents know at this point. To me there's only one option at this point—get married and raise our child. I'll still go in the Army and all that. Lots of people have families in the Army. It's nothing new."

"And how does Dawn feel?" JD inquired.

"She's not sure and really hasn't said much about the options. She mostly cries when we talk, dreads telling her parents, and keeps saying, 'This can't be happening,' repeatedly. Guess she's still in denial. Marriage doesn't seem like an option for her, at least I don't think, even though we just talked about it on that fateful night. Weird how it changed things. I can't explain it. Every time, I bring it up, she says, 'It would be stupid for us to get married, just because I'm pregnant.' I don't know," Paul stopped and put his head in his hands. "She hasn't said anything yet, probably because she knows my thoughts on it, but I know she's thinking about something that makes me sick just to mention."

"Obviously, you're against that option," JD asked for clarification, concern evident in his voice.

"I've always been against abortion, and thought she was too, being Catholic and all. Heck, she never even wanted to take birth control, yet she's contemplating something even worse now. It's a living creature we created. Our own flesh and blood. I'm not sure I could ever do that. If Dawn doesn't want the baby, I want to raise it on my own." Paul looked up, tears bright in his eyes. "The worst thing is that, I really don't even have a choice. She doesn't need my blessing. In fact, she could do it today and never tell me. It's my baby, too, and I don't even have a say." Paul let out a breath, tears rolling down his cheeks now. He had finally said all the things he had on his mind. This was the reason he had found JD. Paul knew that if Dawn was going to do something, she'd simply tell him after it was done. Being in Washington, he couldn't even talk to her face-to-face.

"I don't know what to say, Paul, only that I'm here for you, whatever you need, you know that," he said, as he wrapped his arms around Paul in a rare embrace. "Do you want me to talk to her when I get back? Try to see what she's thinking, how she's doing, and see if I can help in any way?"

"I appreciate that, but it won't help. If anything, she might become more adamant. Just being able to talk to you helped. Shit!" Paul swore, looking at his watch. "I've got to get back. We had formation two minutes ago." Pausing, he looked over his shoulder. "Thanks, JD."

"Anytime, Paul, anytime at all."

The next few days were more miserable than the rest. Overnights in the field prevented Paul from calling. As soon as they returned to the barracks, he called. Voicemail. Cold shoulder, no doubt.

Hopefully, this doesn't represent the future, Paul thought. One month in Fort Lewis was nothing compared to what was coming. Soon, they would be apart for a year, maybe more, and he would be in some of the worst conditions in the world. He may not be able to call for weeks. *Maybe she just doesn't want to tell me,* he thought with a shiver. The terrifying thought kept creeping into his head. *I'll never get to meet my child.*

Dawn hated that she couldn't get ahold of Paul. Only he could call. She had no control. Even though she had been extremely lonely and longed to hear his voice, she ignored the call as the phone rang, knowing it was him.

"I just can't be with someone that's always going to be gone," she said aloud to the empty apartment. And then she screamed loud and hard. Confusion, fear, and uncertainty ran through her and she couldn't take it anymore. It was the only option. Knowing it would end things with Paul and likely haunt her for the rest of her life, she picked up the phone. The appointment was set. Next time Paul called she would answer and get it over with. Quick like a Band-Aid. Then, she'd try to move on.

His call came the next day.

"Dawn. Is that really you? I'm so sorry I couldn't call earlier. I had training and then I couldn't get ahold of you. How are you feeling?" Paul said in one breath, trying to say everything at once.

For a moment she hesitated, so happy to hear his voice, and lost her strength. In that moment, she wanted to go to Washington, wrap her arms around him, and run off to get married. They could have a hundred kids if that's what he wanted. She'd give him anything he wanted if they could just be together. She was momentarily overcome with love yet brought back to reality quickly as she realized it would be weeks before they would be able to embrace once again.

I just can't do it.

Knowing what she needed to tell him and what was already scheduled, she cried instead. Words couldn't be found. Nothing she could say would change the facts. Rushing off to Washington wouldn't change his inevitable absences. She just couldn't handle it.

Why am I such a mess? Dawn thought, feeling helpless, which only made her cry harder.

"Dawn, please don't cry. I just want to talk to you. I've missed you so much and would do anything right now to be with you," Paul pleaded for something, anything.

"I know, Paul. I know you would and that's why I love you so very much," she said, gaining strength and courage.

Paul began, "It's so great to hear your—"

"Paul, please let me finish what I need to say," Dawn interrupted and then hesitated. Taking a deep breath, she fought back the tears.

I must do this now, she thought. "What I was saying is that I know you love me, and I love you. We've had so many great times. Ones that I'll never forget."

Paul's heart sank. He had expected to talk about the baby, figure out their future. Not this, not whatever was coming next. Breaking up was always hard, but Paul had never felt so much pain with the inevitable words that he knew were coming.

Continuing, Dawn said, "Paul, I can't handle this lifestyle. I know that now, after only a couple of weeks, and it breaks my heart. The future we planned in the back of your car was beautiful. I wish that it could come true, but it can't. Having you so far away is miserable. I scream to myself in this empty apartment. I feel like I'm going crazy. You are the man I want to be with, but I also know that I need someone around. I can't imagine a whole year with the chance that you may not come back." Not knowing what to say next, she simply whispered, "I'm sorry, Paul."

Crushed, Paul scrabbled for anything that might fix the situation. "Dawn, what can I do? Is there anything I can say to change your mind? What if I left today? Just ran out of here, hopped on a plane, and came back."

"Oh, Paul, how did I know you would say something like that? Of course, I would love it, but even if we patched things up now it would create more pain in the end. You'd have to leave again eventually and the more time that goes by, the harder it will be."

Paul knew that was true and the constant dread he had been feeling returned even stronger now. He asked the question, fearing the answer.

"What about the baby, Dawn?"

There was a brief pause and then she sighed, "We can't bring a child into this world, Paul. Look at us, we're not even together."

"Dawn, think about what you're doing. It's a child we're talking about, not a breakup. If you don't want our kid, then I'll raise it."

She cried again, not expecting that response. Guilt overwhelmed her. "You can't raise a child by yourself, Paul. You're crazy! Plus, it's my body and I'm not ready to be a mother. If I carry this child for nine months, I'm not going to want to let it go. I've already decided and scheduled the appointment."

Paul's heart sank deeper.

"Dawn, I'm begging you not to do this. I understand our relationship is over, but don't do this to the baby. It already has a beating heart, think about that."

But she couldn't think about it or continue the conversation. Gently hanging up the phone, she vowed not to talk to Paul again until they could see each other face-to-face.

CHAPTER 14

Buildings collapsed in the distance and this time he could see the face of a young child. Beautiful, innocent, and screaming louder than he'd ever heard anyone scream before. Yelling "Mommy, Mommy, Mommy," repeatedly.

Each time was louder and more frantic. The side of her face was all mashed in, but that didn't seem to bother her. All she wanted was her mommy. Chad tried to take her hand to comfort her, but realized it was missing. A mangled stub of sinuous flesh was all that remained. Jagged bones tore at the deformed surface.

Chad gagged, and vomit rose in his throat. Although Chad couldn't bear it, her missing arm didn't bother her either. The only thing that would satisfy her was mommy.

"Get a tourniquet on that now!" Chad heard one of the paramedics yell at him as he passed by. Shock was setting in and the world seemed to spin.

Too much blood, too much screaming. Blackness was almost upon him. He was frozen, unable to move, unable to help, and then there was nothing. The screaming had stopped.

The little girl was dead.

Chad woke up covered in sweat, reaching for the little girl. Nightmares again. Each time was worse than the last. He had seen the little girl in real life on September 11th, walking with her mother earlier in the day. Chad stood next to them as they all waited to cross the street. It was still early, maybe she was heading to school.

Or a day out on the town with mommy, Chad thought, wondering what they were doing in New York City that day. Holding hands, they both smiled at him, and the little girl hollered, "I like your bike."

The light changed, and they were gone.

Now, they were always there. The little girl haunted him each night as he drifted off to sleep. Initially, he thought they were probably fine after the attacks, but they were the last people he interacted with before the planes hit the towers. Somehow that memory was implanted. Chad knew that impressions like this are sometimes embedded deeply in the brain but couldn't quite figure out why.

Then, one day it became clear to him. During all of his months in New York, very few people ever said anything to him, let alone smiled.

The mother and child weren't New Yorkers, he concluded. Chad begin looking for pictures of the deceased or missing, desperate to find out who they were, and what happened.

He didn't know quite why, but he was driven to find the answers. Obsessed, really. Every day after volunteering, he would search using the computers at the library, scanning picture boards that had popped up around the city. And then one day he found them and instantly wished he hadn't.

Posted on the internet by the little girl's father, back in Fort Calhoun, Nebraska, were the pictures of Vanessa and Allison Bradshaw, missing since September 11, 2001. Vanessa had never left her small town, not until that vacation, and was bound and determined to take her only daughter to New York City.

It was the only trip both would ever take.

Shortly after finding the pictures, Chad moved home to Wisconsin. There were simply too many bad memories in New York City now. Amid all the destruction and death following September 11th, Ali and Chad confessed their love for each other and their relationship escalated quickly. Following her dream, just as Chad had done to come to New York City, she was now studying in Europe. Unfortunately, that meant they were apart. He longed for her companionship. They talked often but the future of their relationship was uncertain.

Nothing seemed to matter anymore. Delivering packages

seemed useless. He never went back to work after September 11th and didn't bother to call or go for his last check. For all they knew, he could have been killed as well, although he was pleasantly surprised to get his last check in the mail a couple of weeks later. Chad did feel bad for not at least telling them he was leaving; they were probably in turmoil, too, just like all the other local businesses. He wanted to do more. Chad wanted to prevent terrible things like this from happening, but knowing that was impossible, wanted to help others when disaster struck.

Something was holding him back though. He couldn't quite place it, but he knew it had something to do with the haunting memory of Vanessa and Allison Bradshaw. It didn't make sense. He thought he knew what he wanted to do with his life, yet after helping for months following the tragedy, he still ended up sitting in his parents' basement. When was he going to take action? After quitting his job, he had no money. Saying goodbye to his roommates was easy since he was hardly ever there anyway. Charlie turned out to be a saint, letting him stay for free the last three months because he knew he was out there helping the victims and later with the cleanup. Chad would always remember that generosity. Kindness like that seemed bountiful following the attacks. America was united, and it was a beautiful thing.

What other options did he have? College really wasn't his forte either, he had learned after a year of misery. Maybe a change of major would help. Helping people was one thing he really enjoyed. The military was another. Although he hated classes and did the bare minimum to get by, he had enjoyed ROTC and always had a small regret that he never finished the program. Maybe that was his answer, not ROTC but the military, doing something that helped people. But Chad knew there was something else, someone holding him back. The nightmares and guilt he felt would not go away if he went in the military. Perhaps, it would make it worse.

He must clear his head, get some closure. Road tripping across America and visiting Fort Calhoun, Nebraska was the only thing that he thought could possibly help. After that, he would decide what the future would hold.

CHAPTER 15

True to her resolve, Dawn didn't talk to Paul again while he was at camp. Paul left countless messages, pleading for her to just answer the phone. She never picked up and Paul couldn't know if she even listened to them. The distance between them had never seemed so absolute. Paul knew their relationship was finished but he couldn't help hoping that she had changed her mind about the baby.

Paul couldn't focus during his last two weeks of training. His heart simply wasn't in it. Everything was a blur and his focus was single-minded on getting home and figuring out what happened to the baby. He was anxiously awaiting his results to find out where he ranked, then he would finally be able to go home.

"Cadet Foster," the call echoed through the barracks. Instantly, Paul started moving toward his commander's office.

"Have a seat," his commander announced once he arrived. Paul obliged. "My duty here is two-fold as I'm sure you realized by now. My primary objective is to evaluate you, determine how you rank among your peers, and where you'll find success after you commission. Secondary, is to help guide and mentor you, plus answer any questions you have. That's the part I enjoy most about the job and I hope I've been able to do that for you this summer. Do you have any other questions before we go over your evaluation?"

"No, I'm just anxious to find out the results and get home," Paul responded.

"Most are at this point," he said, then his face relaxed and he took on a gentler approach, speaking more personably instead of matter-of-factly, "but, you have seemed more distracted than most while you were here. Is there any truth to that?"

More than you know, Paul thought, but kept his reply short. "Probably a little bit, just some family stuff going on back home." It seemed like an easier explanation that would garner less questions.

"I'm sorry to hear that, but if you'd like to talk with a chaplain at any time, please let me know. Otherwise, I'm sure it will just be nice to get things figured out once you get home."

"Yes, that will definitely be good."

"And now to the real reason we are here," his commander said with the serious tone resuming once again. "Of all the cadets here, just shy of one hundred that I rate, I'd say that you have the most unrealized potential. There is no reason that you shouldn't be in the top ten. However, whatever has been distracting you has definitely hurt your ranking. Even with that, I think you'll be pleasantly surprised, and want you to know that you did a nice job this summer. I hope you can resolve whatever is on your mind and reach your true potential. Here is your evaluation. Review it and let me know if you have any questions. This is your copy and another one will go into your cadet file and be sent back to your university."

At this he stood and held out his hand. Paul stood and shook it as firmly as he could. The report, complete with the results from all the events over the past month, was placed in his other hand. Near the bottom was a written evaluation, mostly positive, and below that his ranking. Somehow, he made it into the top third. Paul was ecstatic.

Reality quickly returned, but at least the agony of waiting was over. The night Paul returned, JD was there to pick him up from the airport. They rushed to Dawn's apartment in silence. Paul was hoping there was still a chance.

JD had some news he was dying to share with his best friend, but knew the time wasn't right.

When will it be, though? he wondered, glancing over to Paul, staring sightlessly out the window. Intuition told him Paul was going to be crushed in a matter of minutes. The glimmer of hope Paul still had only made it worse.

"Here we are, buddy. Are you sure you don't want me to

wait?" JD said, more pleading than asking.

"Yeah, it's OK." Paul stared at the house. "Whatever happens, I could use a good walk back to my place. Hey, I appreciate the ride and sorry I'm so out of it. Really, I just can't think about anything else. How about we get together in a few days and catch up?" Paul said, glancing away from the house toward JD.

JD nodded. "Sounds like a plan. Good luck."

For a moment, Paul didn't move, just stared out the window. Slowly, he opened the door and gave JD a quick wave before he slammed the door. Hesitantly, he strode up her sidewalk. Before he could even knock, she opened the door.

Paul hated her.

Hated that she was still able to take his breath away.

"Paul," she said warily.

"Is it too late?" Paul asked, harsh with hope.

Dawn wouldn't look at him.

"Dawn, is it too late?" he asked, his voice rising.

"Yes," she said softly.

Paul couldn't speak. The small glimmer of hope flickered out. Hearing it before had been crushing, but this reality was far worse.

Dawn started to reach out to him but caught herself, drawing back.

"It's for the best," she said quietly, with the echo of words she had told herself over and over.

Paul's fists clenched. "How can you say that to me? Maybe the best for you, but what about for the baby? What about me, the father? I wanted to raise our child."

Dawn didn't reply and Paul didn't expect her to.

"I guess that we've got nothing else to talk about then," Paul said, turning to go.

All hope was gone.

Paul walked, letting the tears fall silently into the evening air that was now beginning to cool. He couldn't stop imagining what the baby would look like. Whether it was a boy or a girl. He knew he would always wonder. He had casually thought about being a father before but never really considered what it would be like to be a parent. Now, he knew he wanted that above all else. That and a happy marriage. He and Dawn had been wrong from the beginning, but he kept trying to convince himself that it was right. Never again. His mind bounced back and forth during the two miles back to his place, never finding any resolution. Hoping the walk would make him feel better, he was wrong. When he arrived back at the house he was renting, he felt as if he had hit rock bottom.

As promised, JD had dropped off his gear. It could wait until another day. Brushing his teeth could wait. Changing his clothes could wait. Everything could wait. Gingerly getting into bed, though it was barely eight, he stared at the ceiling before drifting off to sleep.

Fourteen hours later he woke. The rock bottom feeling remained.

Two weeks went by and it was the same routine. Paul sat in his room and sulked. School was beginning in less than a month now. Paul never returned to his summer job as planned, even though he enjoyed it immensely. He would rarely return phone calls, even from his family though he had just been gone for a month. JD and Paul never got together as they had planned the night Paul returned. Paul justified ignoring him because he didn't want to bring him down.

Although the unborn baby was always there, the truth was there was more on his mind than just that. He was alone now. Self-loathing and depression replaced his usually optimist perspective. Nothing in the world would ever feel right again. He was helpless and hated himself that he had not been able to save the baby and make Dawn love him. Knowing that it was the last year of college and then he was off to the Army scared him. What if he was killed and never got the chance to fall in love, get married, or have the family that he wanted so badly? The prospect scared the hell out of him. Most of the guys would rather go in the Army living the single life, but not Paul. Family was always first and foremost, and he couldn't imagine waiting. Or worse, never getting that opportunity. Meeting someone while he was in the Army and away to war would be next to impossible. Relationships in the military rarely worked out, he already knew. Only those built on a strong foundation were able to weather the difficulties. It was already too late for that.

Plus, what would he do in the Army? Would he even like it? Besides the fact that he wasn't in a relationship, he would be away from his family for at least four years. Being in college was one thing, but being across the country, or on the other side of the world, was another.

Then, the baby's face was there again. Always forefront of his mind. Right next to his anger toward Dawn. Even with everything that happened, he still wanted to go to her, be with her, and take her away. Common sense told him that was foolish, but he couldn't deny his true thoughts. He didn't want to be alone, especially not now.

His head was spinning in a never-ending circle of thoughts that led nowhere. The depression continued to get stronger and linger longer. He couldn't explain why, and the more he contemplated, the worse it got.

Relentlessly, JD kept calling. Paul ignored him, but continually felt guiltier. Tonight, his message was simple. It was Thursday and school was starting soon. A couple of their buddies had come back early and wanted to head down to their favorite bar. Paul should come so they could catch up.

Ever since they turned twenty-one earlier that year, they had one bar in particular that they would go to every Thursday. Cheap beer, five-dollar pitchers of Long Island iced tea, and twenty-five-cent buffalo chicken wings always did the trick. It was usually packed with patrons and one of their favorite activities was people watching. There were always interesting characters and the girls that they talked about but were always afraid to approach. Tonight, it would be quiet, generally only locals, since most students were still enjoying their summer break.

Hesitant at first, Paul decided it was time to face the world again. Sulking the summer away had been miserable. Plus, he really wanted to see JD, so he dialed his number.

"Hello," JD answered.

"JD, I got your message and I'll be there tonight," Paul said.

"Wait, who is this? I think you have the wrong number. I used to have a good friend that sounded a lot like you, but I haven't talked to him in forever. I think he might have joined the Peace Corps," JD said with a big smile on the other end.

"Very funny. All right, I've been a dick and I know it. I'm sorry, but thanks for bugging me."

"He's back!" he shouted into the phone. "Tonight will be glorious, my friend. We're going to celebrate your rebirth into the world. Meet me there earlier than normal though. There is something I've been waiting to tell you, but I want to do it before the other guys get there."

"Sounds like a plan. It feels good to be alive again," Paul confessed.

Excitement began to fill Paul; a feeling that he hadn't had for months. Before too long, a little before six, he was approaching their favorite haunt. This time he was out of breath. During his absence from the world, he didn't really do much for physical activity. He could certainly feel that now.

JD was already waiting outside.

"There he is!" JD shouted, throwing his arms around him in an unusually affectionate embrace. "My best man!"

Paul hugged him back, then quickly withdrew with surprise, and interrogated him with a smile, "What do you mean, 'best man'?"

"That's right, my friend, just like it sounds. Lynn and I are getting married as soon as we graduate! Can you believe that shit? It was a thing of beauty when I proposed, and she actually said yes," JD said, grinning from ear to ear. "I've been trying to tell you since you got back but, well, you know. It just wasn't a good time."

"Unbelievable. Congratulations! I always knew you would, but it's still shocking to hear. You should have told me even if I was being a little bitch. Come on, I want to hear the story."

"You know how I like to play tricks, right?"

Paul nodded. Of course, he knew; Paul had been the victim of many of them over the years. The one he always remembers best is when they were fishing with kayaks on the river. Paul was reeling in a big fish and instead of coming to help him with the fish, JD stole his paddle instead. Without noticing, Paul reached for his paddle after the fish broke his line, only to find JD heading to shore full speed with his paddle in hand. There was no doubt that Paul was a funny sight, splashing with his arms while trying not to let the swift current take him too far downstream. Paul wasn't too happy when he finally reached shore all soaked and wet. JD never stopped laughing the entire time.

"Of course, how could I forget?" Paul muttered, making a paddling motion with his arms.

"That was hilarious, wasn't it?" JD smiled fondly at the kayak memory. "You know how we love Seinfeld, too?"

"Of course, now tell me the story," Paul said, pleading in suspense.

"Shortly after I got back from camp, we were watching a movie and I took out two Pez dispensers that I saved. One was filled with Pez, so I offered it to Lynn. She took one. The other Pez had the ring attached to the top. When I offered it to her again, she took it without looking. Slowly, she turned her head to look at the unexpected object in her hand and there was this massive rock. OK, massive for me, but probably small as far as most engagement rings go. Without saying anything, she wrapped her arms around me and said yes. I'll spare you the rest of the details."

"That's hilarious! Congratulations again, buddy. I'm really happy for you. Now let's go in so I can buy you a drink to celebrate. Then, I'm going to get drunk and call your fiancé, so I can say something stupid that we'll both regret," Paul said, wrapping his arm around JD's shoulders and pulling him toward the bar.

JD just smiled and walked through the door. Things were finally back to normal.

Beer wasn't the drink of choice tonight. Instead, they were drinking pitchers of Long Island iced teas as fast as they could. Since Paul hadn't had a drop to drink since shortly before his training, it didn't take him long before he was beyond the point of control. After pissing under the table on

the back deck, it was time to go, according to the bartend-
ers-turned-bouncers.

Getting thrown out of a bar was a first for the guys.

Laughing the whole way out, they just couldn't stop. It
was already turning into a good night as they were trying to
make up for the entire summer in one night.

Paul forgot about his planned drunken phone call to Lynn.
He also forgot how to walk. Weaving all over, he couldn't
stand up straight. JD wasn't much better, so he wasn't able to
help. Suddenly, they ran into each other and both fell down.
Again, they laughed and laughed as if they hadn't laughed in
years.

It felt good.

"Alright buddy, let's get you home," JD said, knowing it
was time for the night to end.

Slurring, Paul responded, "I'm good, I'll walk like I always
do."

Wanting to argue, but knowing it was no use and the fact
that Paul was only a few blocks away, JD relented. "OK boss
but give me a call when you get there."

"It's a deal. Congrats again, JD. I'm so happy for you,"
Paul said, sounding sincere and almost sober. "Thanks for tonight. It's just what I needed."

The next day, Paul woke up with a different outlook and
remembered back to JD's message from the party that night.
And the message from Dr. Hamm and his Uncle Rick. Soon,
very soon now, with graduation nearing, they would be at
war. As much as they desired combat, deep down they also
knew the reality.

It was time to climb out of his hole, start living again, and
enjoy every moment.

CHAPTER 16

Leaving with his parents' car, Chad decided not to listen to the radio or do anything else relaxing or productive. Instead, he would remember 9/11 and dedicate his trip to Vanessa and Allison Bradshaw. He would take in the scenery. He would watch the people. Most importantly, he would decide what he would do for the future. No more sitting around, being a slug. Chad knew he had so much to offer the world and now he must pursue that future. The drive south would be a commemoration and driving back would be a celebration of the future. By the time he left Fort Calhoun, Nebraska, he would have a plan.

Driving down for most people would have been considered boring. From Illinois down to Nebraska was mostly just fields, but for Chad it was perfect. Appreciating the vastness of the country, the bountiful food supply that the fields produced, and all the happy little towns he passed was refreshing. He knew it was not like this for many around the world. Many struggled just to survive. On the other hand, most Americans had everything they could ever want. Plenty of food. Clean water. Safety and security. Access to healthcare. Entertainment around every corner. Of course, there were exceptions, but for the vast majority this was true. The most important aspect, Chad realized, was that no one dictated the future. It wasn't stories of fortune and fame that made America great. Most never wanted that. They just wanted to be left alone to live their life. Many just wanted to make a living, buy a house, raise a family, and find their happiness. That future was out there for nearly everyone that pursued it.

It bothered Chad that this was not the case for much of the world. Water and food were often in short demand, millions lived on less than two dollars a day, and corrupt warlords or controlling governments often dictated the life their people lived. Evil people wanted power and wealth and fed on those that were less fortunate, those that didn't have enough to eat, and those that would never have a chance to find true happiness. They were vulnerable to misinformation and misdirection.

Just as those that carried out the evil acts of September 11th were manipulated, Chad thought sadly.

Chad considered how the US used its influence on other nations, most of the time with overwhelmingly positive results. However, sometimes it ended poorly for those that the United States supported. He knew that Afghanistan was one of those examples. The US had supported the Mujahideen against the Russians, ultimately driving the Russians out of Afghanistan. Then, instead of staying, helping them rebuild, and building a partnership, Afghanistan was essentially abandoned. Cost was no doubt the justification, but how did that compare to the cost of 9/11 and the war that continued in Afghanistan?

Chad was mostly idle when he moved home, but the energy that he did display was directed toward gaining an understanding of 9/11 and the war in Afghanistan.

He didn't like what he found.

Much of the environment that allowed Mullah Omar to take control was created in the vacuum following the Russian departure. US government support, a military partnership, and helping to rebuild their infrastructure and schools may have prevented this entire conflict.

Or maybe not.

Perhaps Osama bin Laden would have just gone elsewhere to carry out the attacks. Maybe he was a madman that would stop at nothing to attack the United States. The problem was that there were a lot of what-ifs and not a lot of concrete answers. Generally, answers were clearer in retrospect, but Chad was quickly finding out the truth; that was not always the case.

International relations are complicated, and the path to war is even more complicated. Chad pondered these and other thoughts as he silently drove across the country. These were the feelings that had consumed him as he tried to pick himself up after September 11th. He was trying to explain why. Why would someone attack America? He hoped this trip would bring clarity and understanding, but the more he pondered, the more he realized he may never understand.

Even though his thoughts often conflicted, Chad could never explain why someone would kill innocent people like Allison and Vanessa. He tried to put himself in the shoes of the perpetrators to understand. It was difficult to think like a mad man. What would possess someone to commit the premeditated murder of thousands?

To create fear, perhaps? That may have been temporarily true, but what he had seen in the aftermath was a country emboldened by September 11th, rather than afraid.

To promote Islam, maybe? Why through hatred though? Nearly all of the Muslims around the world, except for those small terrorist factions, were peaceful and condemned their actions. Alienation was inevitable.

Payback? This was certainly true in their eyes. Payback for the US relationship with Israel. Payback for sanctions in Iraq and other Middle Eastern countries. Payback for our relationship with oil-rich countries like Saudi Arabia. And just our general involvement in Muslim countries and the Middle East.

Power?

Control?

Misguided ideology?

All of these were reasons cited by intelligent people around the globe, but it all centered on payback for decades of US meddling in the Muslim world. With the state of affairs around the world, like extreme poverty and hopelessness, it was easy to understand how Osama bin Laden created a culture of hatred against the powerful United States. Events as important as these must be analyzed, both by experts and by everyone affected, but it must not be allowed to consume.

For if it does consume people, then they've succeeded.

Chad paused at that last thought, knowing that he had been defeated the moment he'd been faced with the death of Allison, Vanessa, Mel, and the other victims of 9/11.

Defeat would end with this trip.

Arriving in the late afternoon, Chad decided to drive through town. Quaint only began to describe the place that Vanessa Bradshaw had never left before her trip to New York City. Chad imagined pioneers arriving here generations earlier, itching to move west. With roots as Fort Atkinson, the first fort built west of the Missouri River, the city has continued to modernize, but the simple way of life could be found everywhere.

Chad drove by the school that Allison had likely attended. It was a grade school, middle school, and high school all in one. He guessed the graduating classes numbered only a couple of dozen people, maybe thirty at most.

She'll never get that chance now, Chad thought sadly, stopping on the street momentarily before continuing.

Main Street contained the usual assortment of small-town shops and cafes, he noticed as he drove.

Not much different than every small town I drove through, but to Vanessa it was her world.

Two blocks off Main Street, he noticed a park, and turned in that direction.

Whereas the surrounding landscape was generally void of large trees, rather covered by vast fields and prairies, this park contained expansive trees. Local residents gravitated to this shade and Chad saw several lazily loitering nearby, enjoying their warm evening. Chad walked to a foot bridge spanning a small stream and paused in the middle, soothed by the flowing water. Small fish darted in all directions as he stared down. The central feature of the park was a large hill, bright green with perfectly mowed grass. Chad climbed the gentle slope and took a seat once he reached the top. A few families were just finishing their picnics and one young couple laid on a blanket, holding hands, and staring up at the sky. He had no doubt that Allison had played here many times just as Vanessa had done in her youth.

Never again will they feel the grass beneath their feet, Chad thought as he slipped off his shoes and laid down.

With no particular place to go, he laid there for a while, contemplating. Despite the hours in the car, he was amazed that the thoughts continued to bounce around his head. He would always question the reason for September 11th, how to stop something like that from happening again, and realized he would never quite find the answers that he was seeking.

Maybe that's OK, as long as I do my part to help.

Chad was beginning to discover what that was.

Leaving the park, he turned at the sound of a little girl screaming with joy. Her mother smiled happily as she rolled down the hill and stood up in a dizzying spin. Chad smiled when the mother glanced toward him. She returned the smile.

After leaving, Chad continued to drive, then noticed another hill just outside of town. On top was a cemetery and he drove in that direction next. Pausing before getting out of his vehicle, he saw that the cemetery crested in the middle and formed a barely noticeable ridge. Not knowing how, Chad instinctively knew that was where he'd find their gravestone.

He approached slowly and there it was, covered with several bouquets of flowers. Tears instantly formed in his eyes.

Both stones were dark gray with white etching. Allison's gravestone had a heart spanning the entire stone with flowers in the corner and her picture in the center. It was a picture that Chad had seen in his mind every day since that horrible day. Underneath her picture it simply said *Beloved Daughter*. Vanessa's was similar except without the picture or heart, but with matching flowers. Her gravestone read *Beloved Mother, Wife, Daughter, Sister, and Friend*. Both had September 11, 2001 as the day of death.

Anger again rose in him. The terrorists wanted to make a point, striking the heart of Western culture. Payback.

But what if Mohammed Atta had the opportunity to look Allison Bradshaw in the eyes? Would he still fly that plane into the side of the building?

Chad thought that, unfortunately, he still would. The thought sickened him.

Not knowing why and not being able to control his thoughts, Chad reflected back to the most painful time in his life before 9/11. The pain was real at the time and left unconscious scars that made him think about it at moments that he didn't want to, like now.

Just before high school graduation, he had been blind-sided by an unexpected breakup with his high school crush. After dating for over a year, she simply broke up with him over the phone right before graduation. No explanation. No reason. Three weeks earlier they had been talking about marriage and going to college together.

Then, it was over.

For weeks he looked and found no answers. Lost afterwards, he fell into a state of depression. Like many high school break-ups, it was short-lived. It had been horrible, something that he didn't think he would make it through at the time, but he did. Looking back, it had been silly, but he realized it was all part of growing up. It was the toughest thing he ever faced, until the next toughest challenge came along. Whatever pain and confusion he experienced then, didn't compare to this. Innocent death for no reason was something he couldn't comprehend.

How could someone hate someone else that much—enough to look them in the eyes and kill them? Chad knew that he would never know the answer to that question. *I couldn't help them, but maybe I can help others.*

Chad didn't know how long he sat by their gravestones, fighting his anger, searching for answers, and wishing he could meet them, but when he looked up the sun was setting. A host of colors covered the sky. Bright orange, streaking yellow, against the darkening blue sky, all mixed with a variety of purple-colored clouds in a breathtaking display, celebrating the day's end. His eyes rarely left the sunset as he strolled back to his car.

Address in hand, Chad paused on the road by Vanessa and Allison's house, before heading back to his hotel. It was a blue, two-story bungalow, with an impressive-looking tree house in the backyard. The gardens were grown over but showed signs of past beauty. Chad wondered if the father and husband still lived there. Tomorrow, he would stop and find out.

Chad knocked on the door and waited. Inside, he heard foot-steps and dread filled him. What would he say? Why was he here? Would this man even want to see him, or would he kick him out?

It was too late now; the door opened. Who Chad thought must be Allison's grandma answered the door. Behind her stood the man Chad was searching for. His face was haggard with sorrow, even though two years had passed since their death.

"Good morning, ma'am. I'm sorry for intruding but was hoping to talk to you," Chad began, then looked toward the man. "Sir, I know this sounds strange, but I'd like to talk with you a moment about your wife and daughter," Chad said, then instantly regretted mentioning his family right away. Anger showed in his eyes but quickly faded to pain.

"Who are you?" The man's voice was hoarse as he replied. The older lady gave him a sad look, patted his shoulder lovingly, and left the room.

"My name is Chad Snow and I was in New York City on September 11th. I saw your wife and daughter the morning of the attacks and they've been on my mind ever since that day. Yesterday, I arrived from Wisconsin and explored your town. I'm not sure why. Trying to find answers, I guess. If it's a bother, I'll leave, but I'd like to talk with you."

Softening a bit, the man approached, and motioned him in. Around the corner was the living room and Chad was asked if he wanted to sit down. Reluctance was still in the air, Chad realized, as he sat there. During his search for answers he had learned the man's name, but he had still not offered it.

He had the look of a tough old farm boy, nearly six feet tall, muscular, with calloused hands. Chad doubted he had ever cried much before that day, yet now tears formed in the man's eyes, but never fell, as he asked, "Where did you see them that morning?"

Chad told him everything he could remember. What street they had been on, what they had been wearing, and why they made such an impression on him.

As he began to tell him the thing that stuck with him most, Allison yelling out, "I like your bike," Chad broke down. More than tears rolling down his cheeks, his chest was heaving. He had never cried like that before and two things caught him by surprise as the sobs subsided.

First, he felt horrible but also relieved at the same time. After all that holding back, the pain was slowly released with each sob. It would never go away completely, he knew, but he no longer felt imprisoned by the pain.

The other surprise was that Vanessa's husband was now sitting next to him instead of across the room. As Chad looked up, he saw the understanding in the man's eyes as he placed an arm around him in a gentle embrace.

"Thanks for telling me all of that. I know it wasn't easy for you and it certainly isn't easy for me to hear, but stories like that help them live on. My name is Mark by the way, although I'm guessing if you found my house all the way from Wisconsin, you probably already knew that."

Mark openly talked about Vanessa and Allison as if he'd been waiting to for years. Talking about painful experiences is difficult for most and especially in a small town like this, where pride and hard work reign and emotions are often suppressed. It was clear that he never moved on to another relationship. His love showed through every time he showed a different picture of Vanessa and Allison. Chad had the feeling that he had made a lifelong friend. The bond of misery often ties people closer together than any other emotion besides the one that Mark displayed so freely—love.

That night, Chad couldn't sleep, imagining losing the two people that he loved most on this earth. Chad couldn't comprehend the pain and suffering, the needless murder. However, even with the lack of sleep, he was surprisingly energized in the morning and had a new outlook on life.

Driving back, he made a new plan, to honor Vanessa and Allison, and live his life to the fullest. The life that they would never have. He would not allow evil to defeat him, but rather he would take the fight to the wicked. Not only would he seek to avenge Vanessa and Allison's murders and prevent them from ever happening again, but he would help others in the process. Chad was going to return to his original desire to join the military, but this time he was going to join as a combat medic.

CHAPTER 17

There was no way to avoid the fact that a new phase of his life was starting as Paul packed everything in his room. He was a college graduate and an Army officer now.

Soon, he'd be leaving for training.

Over the past year the hopelessness ended, the drunkenness had passed, but his desire to go to war never faded. He had enjoyed the moments, the best that he could, just like the advice so many had suggested. But now it was time to focus on that inevitable future and mentally prepare himself. He had his assignment and it was just what he wanted. Paul would be an Engineer Officer with the 101st Airborne Division at Fort Campbell, Kentucky.

Paul took his time, packing one thing at a time, reminiscing about all the good times, all the rough times, and how different a person he was today compared to when he started four years ago. Four years ago, his life centered around JD and Chad, living their simple life in the college dorms. Then, it was Dawn. And the baby. Tears still welled up in his eyes each time he thought about that moment. Now, all his focus was on joining the military and going to war.

JD and Lynn were putting the final touches on their wedding this summer. He had never seen them so in love, so in sync with everything. JD's future was inevitable as well and they embraced it with ease. Infantry was his assignment and he'd been chosen for the exclusive 173rd Airborne Brigade in Vicenza, Italy. No one was surprised. Lynn screamed with joy at the prospect of spending four years in Europe. She was optimistic, focused on that positive, rather than the fact that JD would likely see some of the toughest combat that the wars in Iraq and Afghanistan had to offer. It was highly selective for a reason. They only wanted the best because they would be sent on those difficult missions. She knew that was what he wanted and supported it whole-heartedly.

Chad, on the other hand, had been on a roller coaster ride since he left college after freshman year. Living his dream in New York City, he had been right there when the planes hit the towers. For months he stayed and helped with the clean-up efforts, then essentially disappeared and no one heard from him. All of a sudden, out of the blue last fall, they got a call from him. He had just returned from a road trip. On a whim, he decided to see the entire country, all fifty states, by himself. Sounding re-energized and full of life, he had decided to enlist in the Army as a Combat Medic. Ali was still in the picture, but just as she returned to New York, he was enlisting. They rarely found themselves in the same zip code, but they made it work, according to Chad.

Paul didn't pry.

In Alaska now, Chad was heading to Iraq soon.

It's crazy how things change, Paul thought.

As he packed, a book caught his attention, one that stood out more than the rest. *The Fishing Dictionary* made him laugh out loud. Wow. It had been nearly four years.

I wonder what Marie is doing now. Probably engaged or even married. She was such an amazing person. *There was no way she could still be single,* he thought, half kicking himself and half smiling thinking about all the fun they had together.

Well, it wouldn't hurt to give her a call and see how she is doing. They had been good friends in the past and it would be nice to catch up. Settled, he decided to give her a call.

Settled into his temporary home located in the attic of his buddy's house, a couple of days later, he finally dialed her old number hoping to catch her at home.

"Hello," a familiar voice answered. It had to be her mother. Trying to sound sure of himself, Paul asked if Marie was around.

"No, she isn't. She's living in Green Bay," her mother replied cautiously.

"Oh, well, I was just hoping to catch her at home or get

her number. I haven't talked to her in years and I just wanted to see how she was doing," he uttered, aware of the awkward situation.

"Who is this calling?" questioned her mother.

"I'm not sure if you remember me," he said as he gave his name.

"Oh sure, I remember you. How are you doing?" He told her that he just graduated college and was heading into the Army. After talking for a minute or two she gave him Marie's cell phone number in Green Bay. Wow. He had dialed her home phone number without really thinking but now he had her cell phone number and her voice was only ten little numbers away. Without realizing it, his hands began shaking and his heart was pounding.

This was the girl, he thought, remembering all the great times they shared and the amazing relationship they had even though they were only fifteen. Looking back, he remembered the first time they met.

He confidently strolled into the classroom and took his usual seat right behind her. Why that seat? To everyone else the seat selection may have gone unnoticed, but it was no mistake. Paul loved to watch her, and she always smelled amazing, but most of all he loved to flirt with her during the short time they were together. Advanced math was the subject but hardly the object that was accounting for most of his brain power.

What was it about this girl? How do I ask her out? Paul always asked himself.

Flirting was one thing but taking that leap to "going out" was incredibly difficult for a fifteen-year-old boy. Finally, after weeks of pondering the question, he just blurted it out one moment when they were alone.

The proposition was nothing romantic or special but to his surprise she excitedly said yes, and they were officially a couple.

Weeks later they strolled down by the river, hand in hand, an image of teenage love. As young lovers do, they dreamed of and talked about forever as they strolled toward his favorite spot on the river.

He didn't take just anyone here. No, this place was special to him. It was here that he would go when the world was too crazy, and he just needed to escape. The river soothed him and put him at ease. Any time a big decision was at hand, he would contemplate while sitting on a large rock off a peninsula point. Marie naturally loved it, too. They continued to talk of the future and being together forever. It made Paul's favorite destination even more special. This favorite spot of his wasn't far from the place where they shared another memorable moment that day.

The tennis game had started innocently enough. Both being competitive, they made a small bet. The loser would have to kiss the winner. Not really much of a bet, and no real loser, but they had fun with it. They played on, trading kisses, when it started to rain. They couldn't stop now though and continued to play despite the elements. Rain from above combined with the splatter of the ball hitting the court; soon, they were completely drenched from head to toe. Of course, for her this was a great strategy because he couldn't help himself and stared at her body as the damp clothing clung to her figure and emphasized every curve. A game that he was once winning quickly turned into her victory. That was fine with him though because that meant that as the loser, he would still get his kiss. Little did she know he was thinking about nothing else as they played. Finally, Marie won after hitting an ace right by him. They both made their way to the net and their lips quickly met. As they kissed there on the tennis court in the falling rain, neither wanted to break the moment of passion. And neither did for quite some time. Each time they stopped, they would start again, unable to resist each other.

Eventually, they ended the kiss and stared at each other lovingly. Everything was perfect. Slowly, they began the walk back to his house, holding hands, laughing, and joking the whole way.

Marie was just a naturally fun person. She was down to earth and easy to get along with. Paul doubted a more perfect girl existed anywhere as he was brought back to another one of his favorite memories.

One night after baseball practice, they arranged a date.

All day long she told him that she had something to tell him before their date. He barely paid attention during practice, hurried to the shower, quickly changed, and ran out to meet her at her locker.

"What is it that you wanted to tell me?" he asked excitedly.

"Well, nice to see you, too," she teased as she gave him a quick kiss. They continued to talk as she finished packing some items into her locker. "What I wanted to tell you is that I love you," she declared as she closed her locker and put her arms around him.

Paul was speechless. He felt the same way but had been unable to muster the courage to tell her. "I love you, too, Marie," he replied, simply yet perfectly for her. They stared into each other's eyes as both saw eternity with their newly confirmed love. At that perfect moment, both knew there was nothing that could stand in the way of this amazing love that was growing.

Smiling at the memory, Paul quickly jumped to another.

A few weeks later, he paced back and forth between the guests at the party and the window awaiting her arrival. Finally, her parents' car pulled into the driveway. Anticipation was mostly because he couldn't wait to see her again but also because he was nervous to introduce her to his family. This wasn't just his immediate family; this was his entire family here to celebrate his confirmation.

"Come on in," bellowed Paul's father loud enough for his entire family to hear.

Dang, I didn't manage to keep the entrance quiet, Paul thought as he walked over to Marie.

"Hey, how are you doing? I'm so glad you could make it over," he said, quietly aware of the ever-growing crowd of family that was trying to catch a peek of his girlfriend.

His family hovered like vultures looking for a fresh kill. Fortunately, her parents quickly departed, and the crowd dispersed as the couple began mingling with the people they already knew, hoping to avoid the new introductions as long as possible. After a while the inevitable came, so they nervously approached his mother.

"Mom, I'm scared."

The look of death that spread across her face showed that she had misconstrued the reason for his fear. Mothers will be mothers, but how she could think his girlfriend of only a few months was pregnant while they were still in ninth grade seemed just crazy to them.

Of course, they simply laughed and told his mother the real reason for the alarm. He was simply scared to introduce her to the family.

Awkwardly, with his mother's assistance they went to each family member with a quiet introduction and he only managed to forget one of his uncle's names. He was new to the family, so it was an understandable mistake, he told himself as they crept toward his bedroom for some alone time.

Well, alone time with the door open that is, since his parents wouldn't permit him to have a girl in his room alone. His mother, still white-faced from the earlier comment, was bound and determined not to hear anything sounding remotely close to pregnancy for another ten years. When they were as alone as they were going to get, she presented him with a small present.

The Fishing Dictionary.

It had funny quotes and definitions for fishermen and was the perfect present for the diehard fisherman. They talked awhile longer and visited with some of his family. She wasn't able to stay long and, before they knew it, another one of their limited times together was coming to an end. He walked her out and waved as she left. After he went back to his room, he read the book she gave him and couldn't help but smile. What a great present. And now here he was looking at it once again.

Wow, he thought as he suddenly jumped back to reality. They had made so many memories despite the short time they dated. Like many young loves it was not meant to last though as the summer came and they saw each other less. Perhaps it was for the best.

Best at that time, that is, but what about now?

I must be crazy, Paul thought out loud as he suddenly imagined a perfect future with this girl that he hadn't talked to for years. *No, I'm sure she's taken, and she's probably not even interested if she's not.*

He tried to bring himself back to reality. Further doubt crept in as he remembered how they broke up for a reason that he couldn't even remember now and how he tried pursuing her senior year, only to be turned away.

Their relationship ended at the beginning of the summer almost as quickly as it began during the spring of that year. No drama, just a simple phone call. He was truly heartless as he made up some thoughtless reason why they shouldn't be together anymore. Now he couldn't even remember why.

Something stupid, I'm sure. Heck, we were just kids.

The summer rolled along for both of them and soon it was back to high school. That meant they would not be able to avoid each other since they were sure to have at least one class together. Both of them were skeptical as they returned, nervous for the first meeting. Surprisingly, there was very little awkwardness and before too long they were talking just like old times. They would even occasionally chat on the phone. Sophomore year rolled along as did their junior year. With senior year at hand, Paul tried to atone for breaking up with her years earlier.

Paul recalled their date during the end of their senior year of high school with a smile instead of pain now. It was the last time they had really spoken, except for his dumb email.

Her words, "It's just not the right time," echoed in his head. Now here he was, with the phone in his hand, ready to call after all these years.

Oh, what the heck, I'll just do it and see how she is. If nothing else. It will be nice to catch up, Paul thought again.

But there is no fooling the heart. He took a couple deep breaths and slowly dialed her number. He could feel his heart in his throat and his hands trembled more with each number he dialed.

CHAPTER 18

The phone was ringing, and he couldn't help but think that maybe fate was on the other end. Pacing back and forth in his small room, he couldn't sit still.

What should I say? Should I just hang up? OK, relax. You're just talking to an old friend.

"Hello," Marie answered sweetly, yet with uncertainty in her voice.

"Hey, Marie, it's Paul," Paul replied.

"Paul, Paul Foster?" she said, surprised at the unexpected call.

"Yeah, I know it's been a long time and I just wanted to call and see how you were doing."

"Oh my God, Paul! It's so great to hear from you. It has been a long time, too long. I'm great. How are you?"

Paul gave the brief overview about graduation, the Army, and heading to training and then Kentucky soon. She seemed to hang on his every word, asking questions, and showing great interest. "But, enough about me," Paul finally said. "What about you? How are you doing?"

Marie was excited because she had just graduated as well and gotten a job in Boston. She was leaving in a few weeks, too. Then she paused for a moment, confusing Paul.

"Marie, are you still there?" he asked.

"Yeah, I'm still here. I just remembered something and now that we're on the phone talking, it's crazy to think about. It's all so strange."

Paul was intrigued.

"You're killing me with the suspense, Marie. What is it?"

"I'm not sure that I should tell you. You might think I'm crazy, too," she replied, and Paul could sense the smile in her voice.

"I already know you're crazy, so what do you have to lose?" Paul joked.

Marie laughed.

"I had a dream about you last week."

"Really?" Paul said, caught off guard. "That is strange, but I like it. What happened in your dream?"

"We were a couple again, not in high school anymore, but now. I woke up asking myself where you were now. Then lo and behold you gave me a call out of the blue. This is so bizarre."

Amazing. This can't be happening, Paul thought.

But it was. This was no dream.

Paul couldn't think of what to say, but finally managed to mutter something.

"Wow, Marie, I'm speechless. That's quite a dream. To be honest, I think about you often, too, and remember all those great times we had together. I wish we hadn't broken up all those years ago."

"Really?" she asked sweetly, with no caution in her voice now.

"Absolutely."

Then, there was a pause as both were contemplating this serendipitous conversation.

Finally, Paul broke the silence. "I'd really like to see you again. My graduation party is this weekend and I'd love it if you'd stop by."

"It would be great to see you again, too. Unfortunately, I've actually got plans that day, but I might stop over afterwards, if that's OK? If not then, we'll make a new plan. How about that?"

"That sounds great. I'll hopefully see you then."

"OK, it's a plan. It was really great to talk to you, Paul."

"You too, Marie. See you soon."

"Definitely. Bye for now."

"Bye."

As he hung up the phone, Paul collapsed in his chair.

This can't be happening. This was it. This was the girl. Unbelievable.

Now, all he had to do was wait. Paul knew exactly what he

was going to do when he saw her again.

Finally, it was the day of his graduation party. He always disliked any celebration where he was the center of attention. However, avoiding notice just wasn't possible when the party was in your honor. Today was different though. Of course, he was excited to see his family, hang out with JD and his other buddies, but he absolutely couldn't wait to see Marie for the first time in years.

If she comes, Paul thought.

When he spoke to her during their brief call, she alluded to the fact that she *might* come. She may have been flirting, she may have been scared, or she may have been just being nice. He didn't know which it was and only time would tell. Throughout the day, he played games outside and chatted with his family and friends, always keeping a close eye on the front door. As they talked, his mind never left Marie and he began to prophesize to JD and his family what he was going to do when she showed up. Of course, no one believed him. Who could believe such a crazy scheme?

Day turned to evening and they headed to the house for a game of cards. Visitors began to disappear and pretty soon almost everyone was gone. His parents said goodnight as they too went to bed. Only his siblings, JD, and a couple of other close friends from high school remained. As they played and laughed, he began to doubt whether she was going to stop by.

Well, I guess that was to be expected after all these years but now what? Paul thought. Should he take this as rejection, or should he go after her?

As he thought about the possibilities, the door rang.

This was it—she's here!

Paul rushed to the door. Instead of Marie, he found an old friend at the door.

"Hey, Nate," Paul said as excitedly as he could through the disappointment. "Come on in."

"Good to see you, dude. How's the party?" Nate replied, stepping in and closing the door behind him.

"Winding down but a few of the hardcore are still here.

Good to see you, too, been a year or so again. Crazy how that happens."

"Yeah, you're telling me, always too long. I miss the days we hung out all the time back in high school."

"Me, too, man."

"Oh yeah, I almost forgot to tell you. I just ran into Marie at the concert." Paul's heart skipped a beat, now hanging on every word, as Nate continued. "She said she's planning on stopping by tonight after the concert and told me to keep the party alive, so that's what I'm here to do."

She's stopping by any minute!

Pretty soon the card game and laughing were in full swing again as Nate joined the fold. Paul tried to focus but couldn't stop looking toward the door. Waiting and anticipation consumed him. As things often happen in life when you are anticipating something so badly, the moment Paul took his mind off the door, was the moment the knock came.

This was it.

Paul enthusiastically made his way to the door but became more nervous with every step.

Opening the door, there she was.

She was everything he remembered. Gorgeous, yet unassuming, and a smile that made his heart leap. Her light blue eyes cut straight into his. Yes, this was the girl of his dreams and he was not going to let her get away this time.

"You're here," Paul said, still in shock, staring, completely aware that he was making it awkward, but all rational thought left him at that moment. "I can't believe you're really here."

"I told you I'd come, didn't I?" Marie said smiling, then spread her arms and gave him a hug. "It's been forever. It's so good to see you."

"It's great to see you, too," he responded, finally coming down to reality but his hands were still shaking. "You look amazing as always."

"Thanks," she replied as her cheeks grew flush. "It's been a really interesting week after we talked, hasn't it?"

"That's one way to put it, me finding the book and calling you, your dream, and now here we are. I'm just glad you're here," Paul started, then sensed it was getting too deep, too soon and changed directions. "Let's head in, but promise me we'll talk more, just you and me later."

"It's a promise but answer one thing for me first."

"Sure, anything."

"What book are you talking about?"

"Oh yeah, I forgot to tell you. I found *The Fishing Dictionary*. Remember the one you gave me when we were together in high school? After that, I couldn't stop smiling and had to give you a call."

"Well, I'm glad you did," Marie said smiling as she gently brushed passed him, lingering for a moment, and then headed toward the group.

As they played cards, they stole glances at each other. Paul joked with her about having a proposition for her. Then he thought of another and finally another but had to wait for the perfect time to lay out his three propositions.

After an hour of cards, the remaining group decided to relocate to Marie's house where she would be meeting some friends soon.

"Do you mind if I ride with you?" Paul asked as the group began dispersing.

"Of course not. Then we'll finally get a chance to really catch up," Marie responded with a smile and they walked to her silver, two-door Dodge Stratus. Paul opened the door for her.

"What a gentleman you are," she said as she got inside.

Driving, Marie was the first to speak. "So, you have me alone now. Do I finally get to hear the propositions?"

"I'm glad I've got you thinking about them, but to answer your question . . . no, you still have to wait a little bit longer. The anticipation will make it even better, I promise," Paul responded, teasing her. The truth was that he was terrified to utter the words that he was planning to say.

"You're driving me nuts," Marie said with a light, flirty touch. "But, I like it."

"Good, I'm glad you like it. Besides, this will be a good chance for us to get to know each other again."

"I agree, so you get to go first. Tell me more about going into the Army."

They were finally alone and despite not seeing each other for years, they quickly found themselves in complete comfort. They talked about their lives, reminisced about their past, and discussed what lay ahead for both of them in the future. After twenty minutes, but what seemed like only moments, they found themselves pulling into her driveway.

"Darn, we're here," Marie said, looking at Paul. Her eyes told him that she wasn't ready to go inside. "That sure went quick. How about now for those propositions?"

Paul began to speak, but before he could, the rest of the group pulled up beside them. The moment just wasn't right.

The party moved to her parents' basement and everyone was quickly having a great time. Unable to wait any longer and confident in his decision, Paul couldn't wait anymore to make his propositions. When everyone was distracted by one of JD's stories, he asked Marie if she would go outside with him. She happily agreed and up the stairs and out the door they went.

Standing on the front porch, he gently grabbed her hands and she gave a little squeeze as he did.

"You're very mysterious, you know?" Marie began. "Now what are these propositions? I'm dying to find out."

"I like to keep you on your toes," Paul said, smiling, eager to finally ask. His fear had subsided, replaced by anticipation. "Can I kiss you is the first proposition?"

"Yes," she replied simply with a smile. They kissed as if they had been waiting years. Their lips tingled as the passionate kiss ended and she asked about the next proposition.

"Can I come visit you in Boston over the 4th of July?"

She again smiled, surprise across her face now. "Of course—I would love that! You'd really drive all the way out there to see me?"

"Absolutely. It's been too long, and I don't ever want to go that long without seeing you again."

They made some simple plans for the journey as both grew more excited about the prospect of this relationship.

"I had one more thing I was going to ask you," Paul quietly whispered because he had her full attention. He hesitated a moment and then looked into her blue eyes. This was not just a simple glance. Paul looked deep into her eyes as he made his last proposition.

"Will you marry me?"

As excited as she was at the prospect of their future relationship, she was caught off guard by the question. "Are you serious?" she asked, but she already knew that his answer was yes. "Well, I don't know — I wasn't expecting this at all. I obviously can't say yes right now. We haven't seen each other for four years! Really? Are you serious? What about the Army and Boston? All those plans we just talked about."

As much as he expected this answer, Paul was still a little disappointed by her response. He wasn't going to be deterred this time and he hoped that she heard that in his response.

"I didn't figure you would say yes, but I know that I want to be with you. I'm fine with however fast or slow you want to take this but just know that I do want to marry you and I'm not going to give up."

Marie just smiled at that and the grin said it all. Although she wouldn't say yes today, she was beginning to think of them as a couple and a couple that may be married soon.

Her dream was coming true.

CHAPTER 19

Although war had ravaged much of the Afghan country-side for the past three years, Nasir's region was relative-ly unscathed. In fact, it had become a stronghold with more fighters than Nasir had ever seen in his homeland.

All of that was about to change.

Because it was becoming such an important stronghold for the Taliban and because it clearly still had influential leaders, they got the sense that NATO forces, the collective group of militaries led by the United States, were making it a priority during their summer campaign. They continued to approach closer, but Taliban scouts kept an eye on their movements. Nasir heard the term NATO occasionally when Daulat met with high level leaders, but more often they were just called infidels. Although the Americans made up the bulk of the NATO forces, dozens of countries were now in Nasir's native land. He had so many questions, but they were better left un-said. Nasir discovered that the hard way when he was young-er, with a good slap from his father. Now, he generally kept his questions to himself.

Taliban forces were dug in throughout Zhari district, heav-ily armed, and not willing to retreat. In fact, they were eager to fight. They planned to leverage the population to overpower any resistance the infidels could mount. Nasir feared it would not be that easy.

Batoor was one of the Taliban soldiers that had returned to the area. He was anxiously awaiting another fight and spoke enthusiastically of his travels across the country. Combat ex-cited him and he tried to convince Nasir to join him when-ever they spoke. Despite the fact that Batoor was now home, they spoke infrequently. Whatever closeness they shared in their youth had deteriorated. Batoor's life revolved around the Taliban and Nasir sensed repressed hostility in his body language when they spoke. Nasir knew it revolved around his reluctance to join their cause. Still, Nasir considered him a friend and always would. Childhood memories don't fade easily, and Nasir had so few friends. Plus, he carried hope that this would all end one day.

According to reports that Daulat received, the war was progressing according to the Americans' plans, although Daulat had his doubts since the war was already entering its fourth year. Nasir was becoming more familiar with military affairs, where the fighting was, and received regular updates about the war through Taliban channels that communicated with his father.

Still he did not have to fight.

His father's influence had only grown in recent years and as his only son, Nasir was protected. For how long Nasir didn't know, but he wondered often.

"Sir, we have an urgent report," the messenger said after Daulat welcomed him into their compound. Drenched with sweat with the summer heat at its peak, the man was struggling to catch his breath. "Troops have just been seen moving toward Panjwaii." Panjwaii lay just across the Arghandab River.

"How many?" Daulat responded, his expression never changing.

"Dozens of vehicles, hundreds of men."

"Americans?"

"NATO forces, but not Americans. The flag on their uniform is red with some type of leaf, according to one of the locals in the village they passed through."

"And are our fighters ready?"

At this the messenger hesitated.

"Tell me now, you fool. Time is too valuable at this moment."

"Most are ready to fight, to die for Allah if necessary, but some are not at their stations. This movement has caught them by surprise."

"I see," Daulat said, carefully weighing his options. He could send all of his fighters over there now, but that didn't feel right to him. They would have the upper hand and losses could be heavy. Setting up now likely wouldn't give him the strategic positions that he would like. Retreating would allow them time to consolidate, but then they may just continue to Zhari. Again, the enemy would have the advantage without the proper time to prepare. Finally, he had his plan. "Listen to me carefully. Tell our fighters in Panjwaii that they must put up a fierce resistance, one that will make the infidels stop in their tracks and reconsider their plan. However, they must in no circumstance get into a long battle with them. When the enemy begins to gain momentum, we must retreat across the river. We will be making preparations here. Do you understand?"

"Yes, sir."

"Then go without delay."

Daulat's face was grave when he turned back toward his family. "It is only a matter of time now before they arrive. I must call a shura to begin final preparations. Nasir, you will join me."

They left without another word. As they walked, his father kept looking toward Nasir without speaking. Finally, after nearly a dozen glances, he spoke. "I'm glad you're here with me, my son. I've dreaded the day the fight has arrived on our doorstep. For years, I've protected you from this fight. Now, I fear that I can protect you no more."

They continued in silence, both unsure what to say.

Finally, Daulat continued. "No matter what happens, promise me you will protect our family and our homeland."

"I will, Father," Nasir replied. "But I'm not sure I know how."

"You will know the best path when it comes to you. Just remember it is not always the most obviously path, nor the easiest. Sometimes it takes time, patience, but I'm confident that you will figure it out."

At the shura, his father was brief with his instructions.

"An attack is imminent," Daulat began. He relayed the messenger's words. "I was disappointed to learn that we were not ready to fight today. That will not happen again." Everyone knew what that meant. If they were not ready, they would be punished, severely punished. Daulat's ruthlessness had also grown with his power and influence. "The Loya Jirga is controlled by the Americans and their pawn Hamid Karzai. The new constitution is an anti-Islamic joke, one that Allah would reject with all of his might. We must take matters into our own hands. We will delay the infidels in Panjwaii. I've already issued orders to do so. Zhari will likely be next. When? I don't know. But, we will be prepared."

"For Allah, we are prepared to fight to the death," one faithful follower shouted.

"And you will be rewarded," Daulat replied. "All of you will. Some will die, but we are not asking for a fight to death now. We will hit them with a strong resistance and take away their steam. Only when they gain momentum will we stop. But only for a moment. Then, we will return to our homes, and hit them over and over again when they least expect it. Ambushes, IEDs, snipers, whatever it takes. Little by little we will bleed them. They will try to turn our people against us, but we will not let them. We will bleed them and eventually they will all leave just as the Russians did." They'd been preaching this tactic for years. "After enough years, casualties, and bad publicity, the infidels will just leave. There will be losses, but the cause will live as long as we continued to fight. Now, go and prepare to fight in the name of Allah. It may not be today, or tomorrow, but they are coming soon. We must be ready."

As planned, their forces put up a short but fierce resistance in Panjwaii, and then had simply molded themselves in the community on Nasir's side of the river. They would frequently launch attacks from a distance or fire recoilless rifles at known NATO locations, hoping to pin them in their location. It kept them from advancing for several weeks.

The attacks began not with soldiers charging out of the mountains, but with bombs from above. As the bombs fell and with the follow-on assault imminent, Daulat had one last opportunity to consider his options. Do they make a stand? Or retreat before the infidels show up?

Retreat was the best option in Panjwaii, but not today. Not with the number of fighters they had. Not with the value of the ground that they stood on. Today they would fight.

The bombing was ruthless. They were not protected by caves, like their brothers in the east, but rather remained in their mud huts or fled to nearby hideouts. Dozens died while they waited to fight. No hideout was better than another, so they laid low, hoping the next bomb wasn't heading for them.

Daulat flinched as a bomb hit their grape hut, approximately one hundred yards from their hideout. They didn't dare stay at their house, knowing it was a likely target. After hearing the first explosion, they had retreated to a thick area along the stream where Nasir played as a child. Multiple, protective hideouts with provisions had been prepared in the preceding years by Nasir and Daulat, anticipating this moment.

After the concussion passed from the bomb, Daulat turned to his son. "Nasir, once the bombing ends, we will go back to our compound. From there, I will go to fight. You will stay there and protect our family and the others that have joined us. Others may ask you to fight, but you are under my orders to stay. If our enemy comes, let them search our house. Do not struggle. Tell them you are simply trying to live peacefully on our land. Do you understand?"

"Of course, Father." Nasir nodded, his face steady. He knew the drill. His father had been preparing him for years on what to do when this moment inevitably came.

But it didn't feel right. These infidels were now in his homeland, no longer in some far away province. He longed for peace and didn't want to fight, but felt he must. "But Father, I'm ready to fight."

Surprise came to Daulat's face. "I have never heard you say that before."

"I know, Father, and I have never felt it, but now it's different. They are here in our homeland and I want to defend it."

"I knew this day would come, and I'm proud of you. This land means so much to our family. But I can't let you fight. Not now. My entire life I've worked to protect you and I can't risk losing you. Your chance will come, probably sooner than you think, and you'll know when the time is right."

Nasir was silent as he pondered his words.

The intense firefight a month earlier in Panjwaii had the desired effect. The infidels had delayed. Early fall had now caused the conditions to cool, and instead of enjoying it this year, Nasir was sitting in a makeshift bunker listening to bombs fall, hoping this September wouldn't be his last. He was angry at the infidels and angry at those that had created this situation, causing them to come to their country. Nasir seethed as the bombs continued to drop, his anger growing with each. He was finally ready to fight and now he couldn't. But he knew his father's words were final.

"OK, Father. I will protect our family and compound the best I can."

"I know you will, Nasir."

What seemed like hours later, the bombing seemed to cease. They waited until they were positive it was over and then made their way back to their compound. Nasir was always happy to arrive back home, but especially today. He was even more delighted to find it relatively unscathed. Their west wall was mostly destroyed, but their main house remained in one piece and all of their supplies were intact.

Others did not fare as well.

Several nearby compounds were destroyed and one of their makeshift bunkers was directly hit, killing everyone inside. However, surprisingly, as other damage reports poured in, their village fared better than expected. Now, they turned all attention to the impending fight.

Shortly after arriving back at their compound, the same messenger arrived, again out of breath. "They are coming," he said, then turned to go. This time Daulat didn't need to give instructions and the messenger knew that. Everyone already knew what to do.

Daulat turned to his family. "Nasir, protect this family," he began. Mina gazed intently at him with Storia on one side and Diwa on the other. Their face was a mix of sadness, fear, and uncertainty. Sarbaz was already manning one of the fighting positions. "I shall return soon. This is not goodbye, so I will not say goodbye. No matter what happens I want you to know that all of you are the best of me."

Daulat turned and left without saying another word. Grabbing his AK-47, which was hidden in the wall, he paused at the gate and looked around the compound slowly, seeming to take stock of his life. He looked to each of his children, then to his wife. Their eyes met, and he smiled.

Then he was gone.

Mina had seen him leave many times and had always remained strong. This time she fell to her knees and broke down, weeping. Storia and Diwa dropped to their knees as well, embracing their mother, and soon joined in her tears. Nasir continued to stare at the place his father left, feeling that his departure was different this time. He couldn't explain why, just a bad gut feeling. Slowly, he walked toward his mother and kneeled beside her. Saying nothing, he wrapped his arms around her and his two sisters.

When Daulat met up with the main body, less than a mile from the compound, they were taking stock of the full damage from the bombing. They figured almost two hundred had been killed. Nevertheless, they still had a strong force nearly ten times that number that were ready to fight. Out of breath, a runner from one of their observation posts arrived.

"My radio is down, so I ran back here. They have a small group crossing the river in vehicles. We have a small group ready to attack, but we have an opportunity to hit them hard with reinforcements."

Daulat wasted no time, grabbed his weapon, and motioned for the rest to follow. Without question, they all shadowed him. Nearly everyone had AK-47s, but they also had an arsenal of RPGs and several recoilless rifles mounted in the back of vehicles. Deadly, these would be their weapon of choice to take out the enemy vehicles.

Knowing the terrain, they quickly positioned themselves on the likely approach route. Half took positions in the grape huts that filled the area. Small slits throughout the huts allowed air to flow through and dry the grapes. These slits also made excellent fighting positions, giving them visibility along with maximum cover and concealment. Others were set up in the dense grape and pomegranate fields. Experience told them it wouldn't be long. Within minutes, the infidels approached.

With so many troops, Daulat wondered why they approached with so few.

He would fire the first shot, initiating the ambush.

Closer, closer, not yet, he thought as he waited for the perfect moment. Before he could fire, they paused. *Had they seen us?*

He doubted it as he reevaluated their position but couldn't take the chance.

The shot rang out and a rain of fire poured down from their location. The recoilless rifles hit their mark.

Instantly, two vehicles were disabled. Close now, he could see that they were Canadians, just as the reports had suggested, with the red leaf on their shoulder.

Ambush locations are difficult to find, but this one was nearly perfect. After the bombardment, it appeared that there were nearly a dozen infidels that were either killed or wounded, clearly out of the fight. Despite their firepower, none of their vehicles moved.

Daulat decided it was time to assault and finish them off, knowing there was only so much damage that they could cause from a distance.

Daulat stood to charge, then quickly realized he was exposed. Never hearing the shot, he only felt the piercing in his stomach.

He urged the rest to assault.

As they did, he turned the opposite direction. He must see his family one last time.

Nasir had climbed on top of their highest wall, concealed by the large leaves of one of the trees that rose just outside their compound. Watching the firefight from a distance, he was surprised to see a figure approaching. Hunched over and holding his stomach, he could recognize that walk through any injury. Nasir ran to his father.

"Father!" Nasir cried as his panic rose, seeing the blood soaking through the entire lower half of his father's shirt.

"Nasir, take me inside quickly. You must find the wound

and stuff some clothing in it. You must stop the bleeding," Daulat pleaded and Nasir did so without hesitation.

Back at their compound, Nasir gently placed him on his own bed, and shouted for his mother. Mina, with her daughters still at her side, came armed with cloths. Together they began to pack his injuries.

The bullet had entered his stomach two inches above his navel, creating a small hole that was easy to locate. They quickly covered it, but their cloths couldn't stop the bleeding. Turning to look at his back, Nasir knew that his father had very little time.

The wound on his back was the size of a fist with intestines protruding out.

Trying to speak, Daulat began gurgling. Nasir pleaded, "Father, don't speak, please save your energy."

Daulat persisted. "Nasir, I need you to listen. I know that I'm going to die. My whole life I've tried to protect you. Now you must do something." Nasir braced himself, ready to hear what he had been dreading for years yet was eager to do hours earlier. *It is your turn to fight.*

Mina grabbed his hand with both of hers as he spoke.

"We were wrong, Nasir," Daulat said, trailing off, having difficulty breathing, but clearly wanting to say one last thing before he had no more life. "We were wrong, my son. This cause is foolish and will never end until someone does something, until someone makes a stand . . ." Daulat trailed off and Nasir leaned closer, trying to catch the next words.

"Nasir . . . go . . . dangerous . . ." Daulat squeezed Mina's hand and with his last remaining strength he whispered, "I love you."

Nasir wept as he retreated to his childhood sanctuary. Along the stream, his tears changed from deep sorrow to confusion and then to anger.

Why would his father say go? Go and fight or leave? Why would he say the cause was foolish, yet spend his whole life supporting it? Just to protect him?

Suddenly, Nasir knew why.

I love you.

His father's dying words came back to him. Ones that he

had never heard his father utter to him until that day. Love had made Daulat support a cause that he didn't believe in. Protecting his family was more important than making a stand—one that he would surely lose—against the Taliban.

Nasir knew this fear made many follow the Taliban cause. Anger began to rise. He hated everyone. Mullah Omar created this environment, Osama bin Laden stirred the hornets' nest when he attacked America, yet neither had pulled the trigger. The infidels had pulled the trigger.

What had his father meant? He was wrong. Now was not a time to run. It was a time to fight.

CHAPTER 20

In an instant, Nasir had done what he never thought he could do. Dying, his father had left him a garbled, confusing message. Overcome with rage, Nasir grabbed his father's AK-47 and followed his blood back to the scene of the fight.

Infidel soldiers were everywhere.

Some were helping a small contingency that appeared to be disabled. Others searched the surrounding area for those who carried out the attack. After the NATO counterattack, Taliban forces quickly retreated to occupy their strongholds and wait in their next ambush location.

The route to their ambush location would not be easy for the infidels. It would be lined with booby traps and connected to tunnels filled with weapons. Nasir had little knowledge of tactics but had overheard many conversations. Right now, he was completely overwhelmed with the situation, unsure of what to do next.

He was also exposed.

Canadian soldiers quickly spotted him and began to fire at his location. Nasir didn't need to know tactics to know that he had to get down and hide, leaping to one of the nearby grape fields. Furrows as large as a man made them extremely difficult to navigate. Here, Nasir would wait and set a trap of his own. Knowing that they would eventually come to his previous location, he found a covered area fifty meters away with a clear view of the area where he was spotted.

Like clockwork, they showed up moments later.

Without hesitation, Nasir pulled the trigger and watched as one of the soldiers fell. Not dead, his body began to shake, and Nasir could hear him scream for something. Although languages differ across the globe, some things are universal, and Nasir could translate his screams.

With his last breath the soldier was calling for his parents.

What have I done? Nasir thought and began to cry. Just as Nasir had lost his father, the parents of this soldier had now lost a son. And for what reason? This wasn't who he was, this wasn't the person he wanted to be. *But what if he was the one that killed my father?* Nasir thought suddenly. He must continue the fight that his father had carried on for so long. Confusion consumed him. *No, I must leave my homeland*, the thought occurred to Nasir and he nodded to himself.

Just then, Nasir heard what could only be described as a sound of destruction from above. The whistling ceased and exploded near him. Then another. And another.

My time on this earth is through, he thought as he cowered between the grape rows. *This is my fate for killing another.*

Closing his eyes, he saw his father and longed for his childhood filled with peace. *Peace?* he thought. That was never true. Suddenly Nasir realized that his life had never been filled with peace; his land had always been at war. It was his father who had protected him, shielding him from the pain of the outside world. Even today before going to fight, he had told Nasir to stay behind, even though Nasir claimed to be ready. *What had he tried to tell me when he was dying? What did he want me to do?*

Opening his eyes, he saw more explosions, but not near him. Disbelieving, he saw bombs raining down on the infidels, the same ones that had appeared to be already disabled with multiple casualties. The horrible day for them just got much worse, but it gave Nasir an opportunity to escape. Moving in the opposite direction, he found a grove of pomegranates with an overgrown ditch running through it. Here, he hid until dark.

When he was sure that it was clear, he turned toward home. He must see it one last time.

"Mother, I've done something horrible," Nasir confessed as he wrapped his arms around his mother. "I've come to bury Father and say goodbye."

"Whatever has happened can be made right through Allah," Mina soothed and held him for a moment. Her eyes were red, and trails of tears marked her cheeks. Yet, she seemed so strong in this moment when Nasir needed her most. Finally, she continued. "We've washed his body and wrapped him in cloth. We've been waiting for you, his only son, to bury him."

His sisters looked on, silent beside their mother. Their eyes were also reddened with tears.

Muslim traditions call for burying the body as soon as possible. Together they moved Daulat's body to the edge of one of their fields, along a little stream.

With his head facing Mecca, Nasir led them in funeral prayer. Several neighbors joined them. Generally, the entire community, especially for someone as powerful as Daulat, would participate in the ceremony. However, in the distance the fight raged on, with gunshots heard in the distance. Hundreds of others were dead, and the other men were fighting or preparing to fight. There was no time to wait for a large ceremony. Nasir must go before the infidels advanced.

The infidels. They killed my father.

The village would have time to pay their respects as the family mourned.

"Here he will be able to listen to the stream flow and watch his homeland flourish," Nasir spoke after the funeral prayer concluded. "We will never forget what you have done for us today and always. Now you are with Allah in the promised land, just as he knew you would be on this day. We love you, Father." With that, Nasir lowered him in the grave they had dug. Picking up a handful of soil, he poured it on his father. Then another. Then another. Mina did the same, then his sisters. The other mourners followed in turn while Daulat's family watched in silence.

As they did, Nasir turned to his mother and whispered, "I've sworn to protect you, but the best way that I can protect you now is to leave. I promise that I will return one day, and soon, but each moment that I remain here I put all of us in danger." He didn't dare tell his mother that he had killed a man, watching him scream for his mother. That was between him and Allah.

"I don't understand why, but I trust you," Mina whispered softly. "Be safe, Nasir, and hurry back. I love you."

Nasir embraced his mother, then each of his sisters. He

turned toward their home, wanting to see before he left.

"Nasir, wait!" his mother yelled. "I must hug you one last time."

And she did, holding the embrace.

"I love you, mother, but I must go."

Just as his father had done before he left, Nasir looked around, hoping it wouldn't be the last time. *Just as it was my father's last time*, he thought as the tears welling up in his eyes finally fell.

Escaping in the moonlight, Nasir looked back one last time. His father was dead. Sarbaz was completely dedicated to the cause and never liked Nasir, but he would care for his mother and their family until Nasir could make a new plan.

Nasir had no idea what would happen to their once prosperous cropland or their home. The place he loved was a Taliban stronghold and because of that it became the target of some faraway nations. Now they had paid the price. The infidels would now try to occupy his homeland. He knew the Taliban forces would never stop. They'd only become more desperate, more vocal, and more unpredictable. Nasir didn't want to see how it ended. One day soon he'd be forced to fight again, forced to kill again, and he had to leave before that day came.

His plan was simple in theory, but difficult in execution. An able-bodied seventeen-year-old travelling alone would surely be suspicious. Nasir heard about the training camps scattered throughout the country that taught young men how to kill. He knew that the Taliban was always trying to recruit through force. Most of these camps had been disrupted by the infidels the last five years but he was sure they still existed somewhere. Where, he didn't want to find out.

By travelling at night, he hoped to avoid confrontation, either with the infidels or with the Taliban. Hiding out and sleeping during the day would be his only chance. Pakistan was his final destination, as far away from the border as possible. He'd make a new plan from there. At least he'd be out of Taliban control and away from the evil infidels who killed his father and destroyed his home.

I'll build a life for myself and then I can bring my mother and sisters to safety. That's what I'll do.

He had a plan. Now, he just needed to get to safety.

He quickly noticed the low presence of NATO forces as he travelled. He saw some at a distance, but they were easily avoidable on their patrols. Most places, the Taliban were clearly in control. Taliban checkpoints, like the one where he witnessed the Hazaras being murdered, were still common. He avoided them, opting to move through farmland and vineyards. Villages that he passed near still clearly followed the Taliban customs and laws. More than once he saw the small black flags of the Taliban cause. It only added to his caution.

The first several nights went smoothly and he was beginning to lose some of his fear and gain confidence. Walking by moonlight he travelled as far as he could each night, before his body gave up from the lack of food and exertion. Culverts or abandoned buildings in the middle of nowhere generally served as his bed during the day. He would watch a potential resting place at dawn and once confident that he wouldn't be discovered, would attempt to rest. Sleep didn't come easy with the constant fear of discovery. Mountains were soon in sight and he knew he was close. These mountains made the ones of his homeland look like anthills. Nasir found them beautiful as they towered in the distance. Confident that he'd find plenty of places to hide when he reached them, he vowed to reach them the following day.

After a long daytime rest beneath a secluded bridge, he began travelling just after sunset. The moon was bright, and he saw a Taliban checkpoint along a road leading to a mountain pass in the distance. Easily dodging it, he began his journey east.

"Where are you going, boy?" a voice asked. Nasir jumped as a man appeared from the darkness. "I don't recognize you from this area. Looks like you are sneaking off somewhere, hiding in the dark. I saw you come out from under that bridge. Where are you from? What are you doing in my village?"

Nasir had to think fast. Overwhelmed with the intense, rapid fire questions, Nasir told him the truth with one small twist.

"Zhari, my homeland was just invaded by the infidels. My father was killed, and we took heavy losses. We've been ordered to retreat, and I will be meeting my family in Pakistan soon," Nasir explained.

"I'm sorry to hear about your father. Where is your family in Pakistan?"

Nasir had expected this and had his answer ready.

"Peshawar, in the northwest. Several of my ancestors were driven there when the Russians invaded. My father spoke of them often."

"I see. May Allah bless you on your journey."

Appearing to understand, he let him pass. However, as Nasir passed the man, he didn't notice the signal that was given. Just as he was out of sight, a posse of men were on him. How many, he couldn't tell.

There was no escape.

Moonlight was gone as a bag was pulled over his head. Blows seemed to hit every part of his body at once. Suddenly, his head jolted forward, and he felt excruciating pain where his neck met his skull.

Instantly, the pain disappeared, and Nasir collapsed.

CHAPTER 21

JD and Lynn got married four weeks after graduation. It was a grand affair, perfectly coordinated by Lynn and her mother. Hundreds of people filled the church and even more came to the celebration afterwards. JD's one request was that they would have a military wedding. Lynn loved the idea.

Military sabers gleaned as they formed an arch for the bride and groom as they departed the altar. Military friends that weren't in the wedding party made up this saber team, donned in full uniform and white gloves. Matching JD, all the groomsmen wore their dress blues uniform. The bridesmaids' dresses alternated between dark blue and light blue to match the two-toned military dress blues. Lynn looked radiant in her perfectly white, yet simple wedding dress.

Boutonnieres were left off in typical military fashion and even the cake was cut using JD's father's sword from when he was commissioned. In typical JD fashion, the wedding party gifts were beer mugs etched with their name, proceeded by Second Lieutenant. *Everything military for JD,* Paul thought as he took a swig from the mug.

Smiling as he watched the couple's first dance, Paul thought that JD's love for the military was only overshadowed by one thing—his love for Lynn. From the moment they had gone on their first date, they had that iconic love. High school sweethearts, yes, but it was something more. They complemented one another perfectly, were understanding, and supportive. Like most couples, Paul had seen them go through some rough times. Yet, they always emerged closer than ever. Distance during college only made their love grow. Now they had their perfect wedding and Paul had no doubt they would weather any storm. Paul looked up to JD for so many things, but above all he hoped he and Marie could find that kind of love. Reaching out, he put his arm around her and pulled her in close. She smiled and did the same.

"Would you like to dance when they are done?" Paul asked sweetly.

"I would love to," she gleamed. "Thanks for inviting me. This is amazing, such a beautiful wedding."

"I wouldn't want to be here without you," Paul responded, then leaned over and kissed her. "You're right, even I'm impressed by the wedding. They really went all out. So, what is our wedding going to be like?"

"Aren't you getting a little ahead of yourself, mister?"

"I promised I wouldn't ask you again until the time was right, but I didn't say I wouldn't drop hints every chance I got."

"I guess I should expect that, shouldn't I?"

"Yes, you should. On a little more serious note, I think it's a great idea that you're still going to Boston while I'm training and deploying shortly after. No sense having you sit on an Army base all alone, while you could be living your dream."

"You are getting ahead of yourself, aren't you?"

"I want you in my life forever, so I'm going to keep talking like this, until you kick me out of it."

"Paul, I really like when you talk about the future, our future together. No one has ever done that before, and no one has gone to such great lengths just to be with me. It really means a lot."

"I'm glad you like it and I wouldn't have it any other way."

"Good." She smiled, then leaned to kiss him this time. "Yeah, I think it's a good idea, too, that I stay in Boston. Then, as long as you're still in the States, we can get together every weekend that it works."

"I like the sound of that. Now, are you ready to dance?"

"Of course."

And they strolled to the dance floor. With the love they showed, no one would have known that they'd only been together for three weeks.

Late in the night only close friends and a couple of JD's family members remained. Paul thought this was the perfect moment.

He went to the middle of the group and begin the speech he rehearsed in this mind. "With all of our friends and family here, I thought this would be the perfect time to show Marie how much I love her." Dropping to one knee, he pulled out a ring box. Marie had tears in her eyes awaiting his proposal. Opening the box, Paul could see her face change to confusion. "Marie, would you go to the Red Sox and Yankees game with me?"

"Stand up, you jerk! Of course, I'll go with you." Smiling, Marie wrapped her arms around Paul and whispered, "I'm going to get you back for that."

"I'll be looking forward to that," Paul whispered, his lips nearly touch her ear. Then, he whirled her around and kissed her.

All of their friends were laughing.

"Now, I'll drink to that," JD laughed, raising his custom mug. "Should have said yes the first time, Marie. Might not get another chance."

"The man knows what he's talking about," Paul said, toasting JD's mug, laughing. "He's been married almost ten hours now."

"Which reminds me," Lynn smiled, joining the conversation. Her parents had just left, and she was saying goodbye. "We should be going now, don't you think?" Then, winked at JD.

His eyebrows raised, and the token JD smile filled his face. "Yes, yes, I do, my beautiful bride. Yes, I do." Turning to his remaining guests, he turned and gave a half-hearted salute. "Ladies and gentlemen, we must retire. Please stay and enjoy the festivities until they kick you out. I'm a married man and can't stay out all night and party like I did in my younger years. Until tomorrow."

At that, he turned, put his arm around Lynn, and walked to the door. They had never looked happier.

A short month after JD and Lynn's wedding, Paul proposed to Marie again. This time he had a plan, a ring, and the confidence of the great time they spent together over the last two months behind him when he dropped to one knee and asked her to marry him.

Marie had expected his visit, but not the proposal. Paul was leaving for training the following week, so they planned on spending some quality time together. He'd be driving over to her apartment after work for a weekend together. When she opened the door, she didn't expect to find a note. Quickly she read the words. In his own poetic way, he wrote sweet words about their time together, their future, and how wonderful it would be. Everything was a blur through the tears as she read. She had to find him. Without a doubt in her mind this time, she ran to the parking lot searching for him, but found nothing.

Confused, she returned to her apartment. Standing there, uncharacteristically nervous, was the man of her dreams. She barely heard the words as he dropped to one knee and presented the ring.

"Yes, of course," was all she needed to say. They were married four months later, eight days after he finished training. Neither could wait any longer, knowing their time together would be short before Paul left for war. Their wedding was small, not what Marie had imagined as a girl, but in its simplicity it was perfect. She had dreamed of the fairy tale proposal, wedding, and life, and now her dream was coming true.

True, except for one thing, a reality that she continued to push out of her mind.

War.

After a wonderful honeymoon together following the wedding, they bought their first house together just outside of Fort Campbell, Kentucky. They'd rent it out for a year, while Paul was overseas. Marie would stay in Boston and they'd reunite in their house when he returned. That was the plan.

Paul was assigned to the 101st Airborne Division and many of their units had already deployed to Iraq. The newly reformed 4th Brigade, 506th Infantry Regiment or "Currahee" was going to be his home for the next three years. They'd be the last to join the division overseas. This was perfect for Paul. Inspired by Band of Brothers, which portrayed Easy Company of the 506th Infantry Regiment, 101st Airborne Division in World War II, he knew he wanted to come to Fort Campbell. Being in the same unit as the heroes on that show was icing on the cake. More importantly, Paul also wanted to be close to his Uncle Rick, who he idolized from afar. Paul didn't know what to expect when he showed up to in-process, nor did he know when he was leaving for Iraq, but all indications pointed to soon.

Marie had never been happier, never imagined she could love someone or be so close to another person, and soon he was leaving her. Paul would be heading to a foreign country where they wanted to kill him. Thankfully, he had two weeks of leave following his training which gave them a chance to connect and finalize their plans. She was still getting used to words like leave instead of vacation. After the wild and crazy ride of the last six months, she was expecting change around every corner.

It didn't bother her. In fact, she rather enjoyed it, mostly. Paul's departure was the one change she pushed out of her mind. Thinking about it only made it more painful. It wasn't just his departure; it was where he was going. She finally had everything she wanted at this point in her life and it could be taken from her in an instant. Six months of happiness and then what?

The man she loved ripped away before they got to live their dreams? Or, maybe he'd live, but lose an arm or leg? Or be paralyzed in some other way for the rest of his life? Marie knew they were all possibilities. She could live with that though and would do everything in her power to support him.

What scared her most was that he would be a completely different person when he returned. Marie heard this happened to other returning veterans. She worried he'd be different or wouldn't love her anymore. It was like a choose your own adventure book, only she didn't decide her fate. Paul made the choice to join, and the United States was attacked, but ultimately, evil people in some distant land would decide that fate. Marie knew she just had to have faith.

"I'm Lieutenant Foster, reporting for duty here at Fort

Campbell," Paul said to the middle-aged woman, a civilian, at the in-processing reception desk.

"Do you have a copy of the orders bringing you here?" she asked.

"Yes, here they are, for 4th Brigade."

"Alright, give me a minute to confirm." Behind her, several soldiers and several other government civilians were walking back and forth helping other soldiers in-process and out-process. It was a revolving door of soldiers in and out. Returning she said, "It looks like your orders changed. Hope you weren't too set on that assignment."

But Paul was and she could tell by his expression.

"I'm sorry. Unfortunately, this happens quite a bit," she explained. "But, there is good news. It's a brand-new unit so you won't be deploying right away like 4th Brigade. That'll give you a chance to settle in at least."

"Yeah, that's good," Paul said, trying to sound positive, knowing that he wouldn't be able to change his new assignment here. However, he was already trying to figure out how to do just that. At moments like these, Paul realized how badly he wanted to deploy. He would walk over to 4th Brigade and do some inquiring.

Finding the S-1 office, which managed personnel for the brigade, Paul found a Sergeant First Class that looked to be in the heart of the office. "My name is Lieutenant Foster and I'm looking to find out information about available assignments with the brigade."

"What do your orders say, LT?" he asked brashly.

"They were originally for here, but just got changed at in-processing. I'm hoping to find a position to get them changed back."

"Looking to get overseas, huh?" he said, his tone softening a bit. The sergeant had a 101st Airborne Division "Screaming Eagle" patch adorned on his right shoulder, indicating that he had been deployed before.

"Yeah, I've been itching to go since September 11th; now I'm going to be stuck back here while the entire division is gone."

"Look, I feel you, sir. The truth is that we have more lieutenants than we're supposed to right now. We've been can-celling orders for a couple of weeks as we're getting locked down and ready to go. Don't worry, you'll get a chance, prob-ably sooner than you think."

"Yeah, I know, just ready to go now. Do you mind if I leave my phone number with you just in case something changes?"

"Sure, no problem."

Paul scrambled to find his cell phone which he had just gotten last month. The phone was his first and he still didn't remember the number.

Leaving the building he was furious with mixed feelings. Paul didn't know what to do. He'd been dreaming of combat for the last three years now. Both he and Marie had expected it and they were prepared. Now they'd just be waiting in lim-bo. Could he even fight it and get it changed anyway? Proba-bly not, as he'd quickly learn in the military. Wanting to go to Iraq so badly, he overlooked the best part. He was a husband now and this transfer meant he would get to spend more time with Marie.

If Paul thought Marie was happy on the day he proposed, then she was in heaven when he told her the news. Back in Boston, she could barely sit still.

"Perfect, this is perfect!" she screamed in the phone. All Paul could do was smile on the other end. "I'm going to quit my job tomorrow and I'll be out there as soon as I clear out my desk, pack up, and all that. You didn't rent out the house yet, did you? I'm rambling and wish I was with you right now." Paul couldn't stop smiling until she said, "Maybe you won't have to go at all! Wouldn't that be great?"

Paul didn't answer as Marie continued talking. He couldn't. How do you explain something like that to your wife of less than a month? How do you explain that you want to go to war? That defending your country at moments like these is why you signed up? That something in your life would be missing if you didn't get this opportunity? Try as he might, Paul knew that he couldn't. Luckily, Marie was so consumed by her happiness that she didn't wait for an answer. That con-versation would happen soon enough.

CHAPTER 22

Both Paul and Marie treasured their extra time together. As promised, Marie gave her notice the day after they spoke and within three weeks they were settled into their new house. Just outside of Fort Campbell, Kentucky, their house was near the base, on the Tennessee side, in a little town called Big Rock. Despite the fact that Marie had just come from Boston, neither had wanted to live in the big city now that they were together. Their quiet country setting was ideal. Just off a little gravel road, their three-bedroom brick house was situated on almost two acres. Sitting in the backyard, under the shade of their large oak tree, they couldn't see any neighbors. Cars rarely drove down their dirt road, and deer, turkey, and other wildlife frequented their yard. It was mostly open with a few larger trees. Marie had her gardens in the front and Paul had his fire pit in the back. Downstairs was a large unfinished basement complete with a workshop. At the moment, they didn't have anything to fill the basement with, but Paul had plenty of hobbies to fill the workshop. Upstairs, the living room was long and narrow and led into the kitchen. Between the two was a small open area which they declared the dining room. They had used all the savings they had to purchase the property, but it was worth every penny. It was certainly nothing fancy, but they felt like royalty living in their first house together.

Conveniently, his Uncle Rick and Aunt Debbie lived just down the road. Although they had never spoken very much while Paul was growing up, it didn't take long before Paul and Marie were getting together with them quite often for dinner or playdates with his four young cousins that he barely knew. Always curious about what it was like overseas, Paul hung on every word as Rick spoke about his time in Iraq, Afghanistan,

Somalia, and numerous other remote locations. Although the conversations of his time overseas were rare, and there were never any specifics, rather just vague stories, Paul loved listening, nonetheless. Pride was evident in all the stories. Pride for his service to the nation, pride for the guys he served with, and pride for his mission. Beneath the pride, Paul detected reservations, as well. Paul thought that maybe his uncle put on a facade to hide his true feelings. Perhaps to shelter Paul or perhaps he was unaware. Paul had noticed the same undertones in other combat veterans he encountered. Either way, Paul enjoyed their time together.

Finally getting to be with Marie everyday was what made Paul truly happy. In fact, he was happier than he'd ever been before. Before he met Marie again, a happy relationship was his greatest desire. As a result, he tried so hard to make bad relationships work. That was all a distant memory and now his dream was a reality.

"Would you like another drink, love?" Paul asked Marie, who was comfortably sitting in the folding chairs they had set out in the backyard, her latest novel in hand. It was a Saturday and they had no plans, just lounging at home for the day.

"Of course," Marie smiled. "But first I need a kiss."

Paul leaned in and kissed her gently on the lips.

"That was sweet, but I meant a real kiss," she teased. Paul didn't hesitate as he wrapped his arms around her neck and kissed her long and passionately. "Wow, that was more like it."

"I guess my plan is working then," Paul said.

"And what plan is that, mister?"

"To keep mixing these drinks strong, so you'll want me to kiss you like that."

"You should know by now that you don't need any drinks for that."

"Just one of the many things I love about you," Paul replied, then grabbed her glass and went inside for a refill. Marie watched him leave with a completely blissful look on her face.

"Thanks," Marie said when Paul handed her the drink. "Isn't this great?"

Paul stopped and looked around, first at their house, then their yard and surrounding landscape, then back at Marie and smiled. "Yeah, it's perfect."

"I know you really wanted to get deployed right away, but I'm glad we got this time together to connect and really be a couple before you left."

"I've never really thought about that before, but this is much better. We were obviously madly in love, which is why we got married right away, but we really hadn't spent that much time together. A few weekends and lots of deep conversations on the phone."

"I loved every one of them and am glad we get to be together every day now. Well, almost every day, except for your training exercises and the funeral details. But even those are pretty minimal, especially compared to a deployment."

"That's for sure. I really think this time together will help us get through a deployment better, too. Do you ever miss Boston and working in the massive John Hancock Tower though? Nothing like that around here."

"Of course, I miss it, but this is much better. Boston was always my dream, until I met you. Now, starting a life with you is my dream. Besides, if I'm honest with myself I would have gotten bored out there and missed home after a while anyways."

"Yet another thing that I love about you."

"What's that?" Marie asked in a curious tone.

"You're always just so real, so down to earth, and seemed to know yourself better than most people. You follow your heart and find happiness wherever it takes you, no matter what the circumstances. That's pretty rare. Most people, especially our age, are trying to figure out life, questioning their decisions, working toward their dreams, and trying to find happiness. Not you, you are just . . . I don't know the word for it. Perfect, I guess."

"Oh, Paul, stop. You're going to make me cry." And he could see that her eyes were teary. "You give me too much credit. I have my doubts and worries, too, just like everyone else."

"And she's humble, yet another admirable trait to love."

She laughed at that, then stood up. Putting a hand on each arm of his chair, her face was only a foot from his. She smiled.

"Now, it's my turn to kiss you." That kiss lasted longer than the one before, as did the one that followed. "Care to join me inside?" Marie asked as her smile widened.

Paul didn't need to reply. He grabbed her hand, pulled her close, and kissed her again. Together, they walked inside.

Life was great, and they discovered happiness in each other, but the feeling of being incomplete still filled Paul. His desire to deploy continued to grow.

I wish I could be more like Marie and find happiness no matter what the circumstances, he often thought.

Fort Campbell was virtually a ghost town since the entire division was deployed to Iraq. Paul's new unit had less than twenty people, no equipment, and no real mission. Reality told him they certainly wouldn't be deploying anywhere, anytime soon. Instead, they found themselves being tasked out for random events. Barely settled in as a Platoon Leader, the typical position for new lieutenants, Paul was tasked to be the officer in charge of funerals.

Almost daily, another 101st soldier arrived from Iraq in a body bag.

It broke his heart.

Now, Paul and a team of nine other soldiers would be the ones that would lay these heroes in their final resting place.

Once notified of a casualty, his team would meet the plane at the airport and move the casket to the viewing location. Draped in an American flag, they saluted and moved with precision, ensuring the proper respect. Guards were posted around the clock to honor the fallen. Following the funeral services, before the casket was lowered into the ground, the team would fold the flag. Folds needed to be tight and it was imperative that no red was showing. Only the stars should be visible. The flag was then handed to Paul for inspection.

Presenting the flag was the most difficult part of the process. Paul tried to be professional but each time he looked into the shattered eyes of a mother who had lost her son, a wife that lost her husband, or a child who had lost a parent, tears would flow freely down his face. Many times, he could barely choke out the words of condolence. It never got easier. Images of crying spouses, distraught parents, and young children that were confused and scared would stay with Paul forever.

Rather than deter Paul from war, the funerals only strengthened his commitment. More than anything, he wanted to be part of the wars in Iraq and Afghanistan. Soldiers were dying and he wanted to be there to lead them into combat. He wanted to be there to try to save them.

Deployment for JD had also been delayed. If Paul thought he had been upset and disappointed, JD was absolutely furious. Italy was where JD was going to call home. He'd be serving with the 173rd Airborne Brigade out of Vicenza. Highly sought after by all newly commissioned officers, the 173rd only took the best. Naturally, JD was a prime candidate. Just as he stood out in ROTC, he also stood out during his Infantry Officer Basic Course and Ranger School. Not only was it in Italy but they were often the first to parachute into combat. However, when JD arrived, he found that they had just returned from Afghanistan and wouldn't be going back for a year and a half. JD wasn't sure that he could wait that long. Like Paul, he had expected to leave immediately.

After securing a calling card at the post exchange, he decided to give Paul a call to see how he was faring and if he'd managed to snag a deployment slot. Knowing Italy was five hours ahead of Kentucky, JD waited until ten p.m. to try to catch Paul before dinner. He answered on the third ring and instantly recognized JD's voice. They exchanged some light conversation about how JD's move overseas had gone and then JD dropped the bad news.

"It looks like I'm not deploying right away after all," he began.

"What? How?" Paul asked incredulously.

"Yeah, no one told me ahead of time that they had just gotten back, so now I have to wait until they get spun up again. It'll be a year and a half, looks like. I'm just sitting around like a lump on a log, wasting time, and it drives me insane," JD said, irritated. Paul grunted in response. Neither said anything for a while and then Paul broke the silence.

"So, how's Lynn taking all of this? First the move, now you're not deploying for a while. It can be a good thing though, right? I hate that I'm here in Kentucky and not over there, but on the bright side, at least I've had time with Marie. And at least you'll have time with Lynn."

JD thought about Paul's words and nodded.

"Lynn is getting along great, and I know she'll stand by me no matter what. You know her, she's such a strong person. But to be honest, she is struggling to understand my need to be in the thick of the action."

"It has to be a tough thing to understand if you've never wore the uniform. Marie and I haven't gotten that deep into that conversation yet, either, just trying to enjoy the moment. Look at me, I sound like my old professor."

"That's a good perspective, but I'm just itching to go. This is what we've been preparing for, all we've been talking about for years. Now, we just have to wait."

"I know, I'm with you, bro. Let's plan a trip together, maybe we'll come visit you and that will give us something to look forward to."

"Sounds like a plan."

Although JD would keep doing anything he could to deploy, just like Paul, he'd take this time to strengthen his marriage, enjoy Europe, and make the most of this time to prepare and hone his skills. He'd need them. The two chatted a bit more and then hung up with JD feeling a little better about his current situation.

Eventually the Division returned and with it came the normalcy of Army life for Paul—physical training, field training, maintenance, meetings, inspections, inventories, repeat.

He was soon bored.

Shortly after their return, it was announced that the 101st would be going back to either Iraq or Afghanistan in one year. It appeared this was going to be the cycle for the division— year on and year off—as long as America was fighting wars on two fronts. Paul was hoping this would be his chance.

Still impatient, he contacted units every week that he knew were deploying until he finally found one. Coincidentally, it came with the help of his Uncle Rick. The assignment was even better than his dream of serving in the 101st Airborne Division. This transfer meant that he'd be supporting the 5th Special Forces Group. If his transfer was approved, there was no doubt he would deploy, and soon, but one obstacle stood in the way. After all that searching, his request needed to be approved by Paul's current Battalion Commander. Although Paul thought he made a strong case, his request was quickly denied.

Paul couldn't believe it.

When he got home, he plopped down on the couch and stared listlessly at the blank screen of the TV. Marie peeked out of the kitchen and, wiping her hands on her pants, came to sit down next to Paul. Knowing his recent efforts and frustrations, she waited for him to speak. Eventually he shook his head and wrapped his arm around her shoulders, pulling her close.

"The commander denied me. I had an in. I could've been on my way out of here, finally doing what I've been training for, doing what I wanted," he finally said.

As usual, it hurt Marie when he mentioned how eager he was to leave. She didn't say anything because she had heard it all before. She was proud of how patriotic, committed, and unselfish Paul was, but that didn't make her feel any less sad that their time apart was coming soon.

Also, no matter how many times he explained it to her, she couldn't quite understand his need to answer the call of duty and deploy. On a logical level, it just didn't make sense for someone to want to run toward possible death. On an emotional level, she knew he felt the need to answer a higher calling. But that came at the cost of leaving her at home, alone. Marie tried not to take that fact personally. She was torn, so she said nothing. She just clung to the hope that he'd never have to leave.

"I just can't keep sitting around and doing nothing. I feel worthless in the rear while there are people fighting over there, looking for bin Laden and his associates, making those terrorists pay for 9/11." Paul moved his arm from around Marie and reached up to massage his temples.

He was beginning to realize that while it was common for people to think they knew what was best for others, that mentality was even more prevalent in the military. His goals didn't matter. Troop strength was the only thing that mattered. The rationale was that the battalion couldn't afford to lose anyone, but Paul thought it was more about control and power. He silently vowed to keep looking and changed the subject to the delicious-smelling meal Marie had been cooking for them in the kitchen.

A few weeks later, although not the immediate good news he was hoping for, Paul did find out something interesting. Their unit was on a planning document to deploy the following year. Now, fittingly, both JD and Paul would be deploying at relatively the same time to two very different places. Paul to Iraq and JD to Afghanistan.

When he broke the news to Marie over dinner, she accepted it as inevitable but tears still sprung to her eyes. Although she had hoped this day would never come, deep down she knew it would. Paul looked into her eyes, searching for the promise that she'd be there when he got back.

"I'll be back in no time at all, and besides it's still several months away. We'll make it through this," he said, knowing that communication would be the key to making it work. He reached across the table and grabbed her hands. She squeezed his hands and looked down at her plate. After a few moments, she looked back up at him and sighed.

"It just feels personal, this need that you have, to deploy. Like you *want* to be away from me. I know that's not it, but it just feels like it," she began after a long pause.

"No. That's not it at all. I love you more than I ever thought I could love anyone; how could I possibly want to be away from the woman of my dreams? I just . . . I can't explain it."

"Try," she implored him. He fiddled with his napkin and leaned back in his chair.

"I guess I just want to be part of something bigger. Bigger than you and me, bigger than just an ordinary life. After watching those towers fall, I just knew I had to do something,

I couldn't just sit around and live a normal life, taking my freedom for granted."

"And you can do all that, but why do you have to be in such a rush?" she asked. She knew she was being selfish, but she didn't care. She didn't want to lose him, even if it wasn't until next year.

"Marie, I've been waiting for this opportunity for so long. I know it sounds cliché but I was born for this. I want to help protect our freedoms, even if that means leaving you behind for a little bit. Wars aren't fought by the single and lonely, they are fought by husbands and wives, mothers and fathers, family members and friends. Everyone leaves someone or something behind, but they are doing it for those they love," he said.

"What will you even be doing over there that someone else couldn't be doing?" Marie asked.

"I'm going to be with my fellow soldiers, finding the bad guys, putting an end to our country's threats, little by little. Maybe someone else could do my job, sure, but I want it to be me making a difference, however small," Paul said.

After a moment, Marie wiped away a tear and smiled at Paul. She knew nothing would change his mind, but she had also known what she was getting into when she married him. He was a good, determined man filled with passion, and she wouldn't hold him back from what he'd been working so hard for. She reached out for his hand and once it was in her grip, she squeezed. She couldn't help but to love him for what he was.

As Paul watched the emotions scroll across Marie's face, he relaxed inwardly. Deep down, he knew that they would not only make it through the deployment, but they'd come out stronger in the end. Marie also knew that and was thankful for the time they were able to spend together. These many months had brought them closer together, especially since they had formed a life away from their family and friends. Without saying the words, both planned to enjoy their remaining days together as if they were their last.

Closer now, details of the deployment were emerging. The "surge" was why Paul was needed in Iraq. That was the term that was used for the increase in troop strength. The hope was that the additional troops would provide the presence needed to quell growing violence. It also meant that they'd be there for fifteen months, rather than the typical twelve. Paul didn't mind. He was finally getting his chance. Paul's only concern was that the mission sounded relatively boring. JD would be hiking around the mountains looking for bad guys while he'd be stuck mostly on base, managing logistical operations. Not what he pictured for a deployment while watching Band of Brothers, but at least he had his opportunity.

Plus, he really had no choice. He had tried to transfer, and his request was denied. Like always, he'd make the best of it.

One thing about the deployment was certain. Saying good-bye to each other would be the most difficult thing Paul and Marie had ever done. Despite some last-minute taskers, Paul decided to take a few weeks of leave to really focus on Marie and their marriage, to just be with her. They travelled home to visit family and friends, road tripped out west to visit Yellowstone and Glacier National Parks and spent some quiet days at home enjoying each other's company. They enjoyed the simple things together, good-naturedly fighting over what movie to watch, grocery shopping, beers at the local bar, making meals together, evenings spent cuddling on the couch, talking about everything and nothing. Always present, however, were the green duffel bags and digital camo ruck sack that sat packed away in their spare room.

Now the day had arrived. Earlier in the day, they were on base together for the departure ceremony. The battalion colors were formally cased and would not be opened again until they arrived in Iraq. These colors identified the unit and dated back to the American Revolution for the US military and even further for militaries around the world. Once, they had been used to guide troops in battle. Now, they were more symbolic. After the ceremony, everyone was told to report back at two in the morning. From there they would receive their briefings and begin manifesting for their flight overseas. Marie and Paul planned to stay up for the next ten hours, trying not to think of that moment.

Back at their house, they made a glorious meal. Marie roasted a chicken, since turkey would be too much, and they had all the fixings. Instead of pie, they made brownies together. They took a walk down their gravel road. They strolled around their yard and played games. Talking the entire time, they discussed future plans and how they would stay in touch. Never did they discuss what they would do if something terrible happened. Each knew that was a bridge they would burn if it ever came. Mostly, they just enjoyed each other's company. As the time when Paul needed to leave neared, he looked at Marie and for the first time in their marriage, began crying in front of her. Loud sobs consumed him. Marie was taken aback, but not surprised, and wrapped her arms around him in comfort. Words that Paul couldn't quite get right were explained in his emotions and Marie felt them. Together, they loaded his equipment and silently drove back to base.

CHAPTER 23

Afghanistan isn't large but it provides diverse landscapes from the deserts in the west to the rugged mountains in the east. JD found himself in the most rugged of all Afghanistan mountains in Kunar Province, located along the Pakistan border. As a rifle platoon leader, he was responsible for forty-two soldiers with the typical mission to conduct patrols designed to eliminate enemy forces and gain the support of local residents. It wasn't hard to see the difficulties when the two were often one and the same. Separating who was who was always tricky. Leadership was JD's foremost responsibility, but he was also a manager of men and equipment, a tactician in the field, and the primary trainer for his soldiers. Most importantly, he had to maintain the morale and discipline of his unit during a long and difficult deployment where they were constantly exposed to violence. Knowing each one of his soldiers was vital to success. This level of responsibility, immediately out of college, is unprecedented in the civilian world. Everything, including the lives of his soldiers, depended on JD's leadership. As always, he was up to the challenge.

Moments after arriving at their remote outpost, shots rang out. They were already being attacked. Muzzle flashes could be seen as shots came whizzing by, but no enemy fighters could be seen.

Apparently, it was always like that, JD later found out. Local fighters knew all the best hiding places and used these as common attack locations. Rarely, did they attempt to fight in the wide open, likely because they knew the results. Suppression from the Americans was focused at these muzzle flashes, but they didn't seem to slow down the incoming attack. Suddenly, they heard a whistle and with only a moment to take cover, a mortar hit less than ten yards from JD, spraying shrapnel in all directions. JD checked himself but hadn't been hit.

Looking over, he saw a soldier from the unit they were replacing lying on the ground. Blotches of blood painted the inside of his thighs and medics were already treating the wounds.

A MEDEVAC helicopter was immediately requested.

Everyone knew their role.

Some were returning fire, others treating the wounded while runners resupplied the primary fighting positions. Their commander and artillery officer were on the radio, no doubt requesting close air support and providing updates.

JD could clearly see that this was not the first time they'd been in this situation. His soldiers had already begun to shadow their counterparts and he was watching the lieutenant he was replacing closely.

Hearing the chopper in the distance, JD glanced back at the wounded soldier.

No pulse.

Medics were frantically trying to revive him, but it was hopeless. He was dead and JD didn't even know his name. In less than a week he would have been back home. Instead, he had been killed in this foreign land.

Once the gunfire settled, JD had a chance to get his bearings. The outpost was small, and he really felt like he was on top of the world—physically, not emotionally.

He could see for miles and in all directions, mountains filled the horizon. Villages were seen throughout the valleys with openings often accompanying the residential areas. Trees were predominant, but it was clear to see that logging had taken its toll. Illegal harvesting was just another trademark of the Taliban. Each side of his base was well-defended, armed with soldiers manning machine guns, grenade launchers, and mortar tubes. Defensive barriers were created from sandbags, rock, and lumber.

Emotionally, he was already a wreck although he'd never reveal it to his soldiers. They hadn't even been on an official mission, yet, and already he had watched someone get brutally killed. The soldier, Specialist Young, had been a soldier in the platoon that they were replacing. The lieutenant's eyes were uneasy and full of rage when he asked about Young. Quickly changing the subject, JD decided just to focus on the mission. Only twenty-three years old, JD knew that his counterpart would harbor the pain of combat for the rest of his life. JD hoped he wouldn't share the same fate.

Kuwait was Paul's first destination. Here they would ensure that they were acclimated to the weather and confirm that they were properly prepared for their mission. His unit was a logistics headquarters that was responsible for coordinating and transporting supplies via convoy throughout central Iraq. They'd be based out of Al-Taqaddum, west of Baghdad, and operate throughout the Sunni Triangle. Named by the media, this area was one of the most violent centers of Iraq. The triangle expanded from the Ramadi area east to Baghdad and then north past Tikrit. Unexpectedly, before they left, Paul was promoted to the position of commander of the headquarters element instead of serving in a staff position. Being able to effect change and inspire others as a leader was one of the reasons the Army appealed to Paul and now, he was going to get that opportunity. The mission still didn't thrill him, but he loved the people he was with.

Flying into their final destination in Iraq, Paul was filled with nerves even though he knew it was relatively safe. After a fairly smooth flight with the Air Force, the final approach employed defensive measures designed to make incoming aircraft more difficult to hit with indirect fire. His stomach lurched as they came in at a wild angle and everything within the aircraft was wrenched from side to side.

Better than getting hit by an RPG and crashing, Paul reasoned, as he closed his eyes and waited for the landing. Unlike JD, their base seldom received any fire. It was huge, encompassing more than forty-four square miles, and was nearly all open. No trees, no mountains, nothing but sand and some small shrubs. They were fortunate to be located on a lake, but other than that, there was really no scenery. It had once been the home of the Iraqi Air Force Academy and they'd be staying in some of the old rooms.

In just a few days, Paul had settled into a routine. Honestly, it wasn't that much different than the routine that was established back at Fort Campbell except that there were no days off, there were a lot more meetings, and there was a lot more dust and sand to contend with. Paul's battalion would receive supplies from all over the world, primarily the US, and they would then distribute those supplies to units in need throughout their area of responsibility, which covered much of central Iraq. Security was the essential piece as dozens of supply vehicles would take to the roads each night. Infantry and cavalry units, attached to the battalion, would provide this protection. Ambushes were fairly rare, but the chance of encountering Improvised Explosive Devices (IEDs) placed along the roads was always a threat. Pot shots as the convoys drove by occurred regularly but posed little danger as the rounds bounced off the armored vehicles.

Paul wasn't exposed to much of this really because he was on the supply side, not the security side. Rather, he thought of himself as the glue that held the headquarters together. People were Paul's primary concern, along with organization. Paul's objective was to ensure that the battalion had everything they needed to be successful. A large part of this was daily life on their base and he quickly assumed the role of the camp mayor. In addition to administrative duties, maintenance, and managing equipment, Paul oversaw all the buildings in camp. Work orders needed to be completed, new buildings contracted and built, living areas expanded and safety inspections completed, all so that his fellow soldiers could focus on their actual jobs. It wasn't glamorous, nor what he ever imagined doing during his time in Iraq, but it kept him busy. Yet, he longed to see combat.

Meanwhile, JD was out on patrols nearly every day. Unlike Paul's mild experience, nearly every day they were ambushed. Most of the ambushes were harassing pop shots, but others were deadly coordinated attacks. Booby traps in the form of IEDs were set along any route they travelled often.

Mortar attacks continued on their base. Being ready for any situation was important for survival, although no amount of preparation could keep everyone completely safe in a combat zone. Within the first month, nearly a quarter of his platoon had already become casualties. Most had returned to the rigors of patrolling, while others were sent home with injuries. Two soldiers, Corporal Nitten and Staff Sergeant Himmel, had already paid the ultimate sacrifice.

JD and all of his guys were in top notch condition, thanks to a challenging training regime put on by JD himself. Even with that training, their legs, feet, and backs ached at the end of every patrol during the first few weeks. Altitude, combined with rugged terrain, heavy body armor, and carrying weapons and equipment, took its toll on the body. Meetings were scheduled nearly every day to determine the needs of the local villages. Getting to these locations was often difficult and they tried to take a different route every time. Naturally, roadways were the easiest, but also the most dangerous. They focused on establishing relationships with the locals, hoping to create allies that would turn away the Taliban. The problem was that each day they had to return to their base while the Taliban forces remained among the people. Those discovered to be working with the Americans were harassed, tormented, and in some cases killed, making fear a great motivator to support the Taliban. Based on those circumstances, it was often difficult to make strong allies. Nevertheless, they tried.

Targeting was also a key part of their plan to eliminate the enemy. Using intelligence from higher headquarters and information that they gathered from village elders, patrols and ambushes, they were able to pinpoint enemy hideouts, travel routes, and ambush locations. With this information they could turn the tables and conduct their own attacks and ambushes. Lethality is one of the defining traits of an infantry platoon and they excelled when they were on the offense. All intelligence and surveillance pointed to one location where all the attacks and ambushes seemed to originate. Tucked deep in a mountainside, away from any villages, was an area that they had never explored. Operation Hammer Down was scheduled to commence at that location and this time the

Americans would control the fight.

CHAPTER 24

Nasir woke up in the back of a vehicle, bag still over his head. His hands and feet were tied. His entire body ached. He knew who had him. Those who his father had just fought and died beside. Those who wanted him to continue fighting.

Where were they taking him though? And why? What were they going to do to him? Questions raced through his head, as fear consumed him.

NATO forces, predominantly Americans, now had a presence in nearly every region of Afghanistan. With this presence, Taliban training camps were essentially eliminated. Pakistan was not a reliable location for the training camps, either, because they gave lip service to the Americans and were unpredictable about when they would come through with their promises. One location in the region remained lawless. The Federal Administered Tribal Area (FATA) title was deceiving since there was very little administration. Pakistan had withdrawn their troops to counter an expected conflict with India, thus opening it up as no man's land. Al Qaeda and Taliban forces looking for a safe haven made this their de facto headquarters. The training camps were now located there, and it was where Nasir found himself once he gained consciousness.

He had often heard his father talking about these camps, so he knew that most trainees came to these camps willingly. Young men that had nothing but anger were eager to vent their frustration. These camps provided them the instruction and training to do just that. Foreigners were even turned away at times, over worries that they might be spies. Most training was not conducted in the spirit of Western training. Time for repetition of the fundamentals was not part of their program. Instead, they focused on the essentials. Ambushes, raids, bomb-making, and suicide bombing went along with learning how to shoot a variety of weapons. Further brainwashing occurred daily. Once they had the essentials, they were turned loose to do most of their learning in the field of combat.

Almost no one came to the training camps like Nasir arrived. He awoke in a small room, aching in every part of his body and unsure of where he was or how long he had been out. Outside, he heard men yelling and weapons firing. Scared at first that they were coming for him, he soon realized that he must be at one of these training camps. Many from his tribe, like Batoor, had gone to training camps before the Americans arrived and others had left for Pakistan to do the same after they arrived. Hearing stories from his father and others, the camps did not sound that bad, if you wanted to be a soldier.

Nasir was still confused. He got his revenge and it had felt good for a moment, but something wasn't right. When the soldier Nasir had killed cried for his parents, he felt such remorse and knew he had to escape.

Now he was here.

Nasir knew from experience that most people at these camps were there by choice.

So, what do they want with me?

After the noise had settled outside, he heard the call for evening prayer. Kneeling, he assumed the ritual. Within minutes of finishing his prayer, the door opened. A young man entered, slightly younger than Nasir but with the same build.

"Hello, Nasir, my name is Malang," he said, without approaching. He had one of the biggest smiles Nasir had ever seen.

Odd as the smile struck him, Nasir was trying to remember if he knew this man. Malang obviously knew him or at least his name.

"How do you know my name?" Nasir asked without moving.

"Nasir, we know a lot about you. That is why you are here. May I sit?"

Nasir hesitated, thrown off guard by Malang's eerie smile.

He could feel that something wasn't right but decided that he had to say something. "If you can help me figure things out then by all means, sit. Do you have any water or some food? I haven't eaten anything since I was knocked out."

"Of course," Malang said, nodding. "Let me get something for you. I'm sorry about that." He spread his hands. "Some of our trainees can get a little rough but they only do it because they're passionate about Allah's cause." Still smiling, he left the room. Nasir sat back, worried and confused.

Surprisingly, what Malang brought back was more than he expected. A large portion of rice with generous chunks of lamb and even some seasoning. Nasir didn't know what to think but he was content for the moment as he ate. Watching him closely, Malang continued.

"Your father was a good man, loyal, and I'm sorry to hear about his death. Allah certainly has a special place reserved for him."

Silence followed.

A moment later he continued.

"We've been interested in you for a long time, Nasir." Mid bite, Nasir stopped and looked up. Malang was no longer smiling.

"You think differently than most and were educated well by your father. Most men your age have either joined our cause or that of our enemies, been killed, or escaped. We suspect that you were trying to get away as well. Your father has been protecting you for some time."

Nasir had lost his appetite, uneasy about where this conversation was heading. He pushed his plate away slightly and Malang smirked, seeming to enjoy his discomfort.

"Our men reported that you fought well after your father died. Was it the first time you killed a man?"

Silence.

"I know it is not easy. The first man I killed was from a rival tribe that stole from us. The revenge felt good, but there was still pain." Malang looked away, to the distance, although Nasir didn't quite believe that he was upset about it. Maybe he was trying to play him. Still, he could relate. The confusion hadn't left him, and this situation wasn't making things any clearer.

"That is why you are here, Nasir, and not dead. Some think your resistance should be dealt with, but not me. I asked to work with you, mentor you, and teach you the ways of true Islam. You don't remember me, do you?"

Nasir tried to recall but couldn't. Malang, that smile, should have been easy to remember, but there was no memory.

"I'm sorry, I don't," Nasir responded.

"That is quite alright, my friend, I don't blame you. I was quite young when I first went through one of these camps. Batoor is my brother. When I returned to Zhari, your father was my mentor. He was the one who asked me to kill and I did so. Now, I'm here to teach you everything that your father taught me."

Nasir began to speak, but Malang continued. "They call us terrorists and say we are evil, especially we, the Pashtun, but *they* are the terrorists. We wanted nothing to do with America, only to live our lives by the prophet's word. Now they are there, in our homeland, with all their allies. But it won't last forever. We've learned that before. They'll leave just like all the rest and we'll help make sure they do. It will be our country again. I'm only going to ask this once, so consider carefully. Will you join me in this fight, to continue your father's legacy and restore the glory of Islam?"

Nasir didn't hesitate. He knew what he had to do. Whether he was being played or not didn't matter. He knew there was no way out of this predicament at the moment. His father had taught him this. Your words might mean one thing out of necessity for survival, but that doesn't mean you truly have to believe. So, Nasir chose to continue the cycle of fighting.

"My father trusted you and I will also trust you. When do we get started?"

Within weeks, they received their first assignment. American infantry platoons were getting aggressive in Kunar Province. They would mix with the locals and set up ambush locations along their routes. Nasir perfected what he had learned in training. Training had focused on tactics that had worked against the Americans during previous engagements, like ambushes, because they protected you. Exposing yourself to the enemy was typically a recipe for a quick death, Nasir learned. A quick death without the benefit of inflicting casualties, like suicide bombing. Suicide bombers were given a special place with Allah, according to the leaders of the camp. There was no shortage of volunteers, but Nasir wasn't one of them.

IEDs were another specialty, designed to harass the enemy and inflict casualties without revealing yourself. Nasir soon learned that the marksmanship he displayed after his father died was no fluke. Among all the trainees, he was clearly the best shot of the group. Malang hoped to designate him as a sniper, initiating ambushes with a quick death that confused and pinned down the enemy. Throughout the training, Nasir learned more about what they were trying to accomplish. Harass the enemy and slowly wear them down. Eventually, when they finally left, their puppets would be quickly overthrown and the Afghan military they created would quickly be destroyed. Without American support, most predicted they would fold under the relentless attacks. Locals all thought the same and that was why they hesitated to support the Americans, even if they didn't like the Taliban rule. Better to live with evil than die with foreign infidels. When the collapse came, the Taliban would quickly pick up where they left off prior to the arrival of the foreigners and establish a government dedicated to carrying out Allah's will. That was the vision that was promoted constantly for the trainees.

Arriving in the little village of Mangwal they came and went as they pleased. Food, beds, personal items, it didn't matter. They used as they pleased and took as they pleased. No one said anything. They were all too afraid and most supported their Pashtun brethren. The families likely had relatives that were supporting the cause. Nasir could see why the power was so addicting. There was nothing they couldn't do—they had ultimate power. They answered to Allah and no one else and their way was Allah's will. He didn't agree with this behavior, taking advantage of their brethren for what few precious supplies they had, but there was little he could do. He was doing this for Allah and his family, to fight the infidels, so if it made them stronger for their upcoming battles, it was a small price to pay.

As promised, Malang was his mentor, teaching him the Taliban way and guiding him through training. They shared meals and prayer together, and quickly became friends, regardless of the differences in their beliefs and despite Nasir's initial misgivings. Nasir still didn't subscribe to the Taliban way of life, but it was their way or no way, and he had promised his father that he'd do what he had to do to take care of the family.

This was the only way.

Days passed, most spent scouting the surrounding area, establishing their ambush locations, and plotting escape routes. Finally, they found the perfect location. Overlooking a trail that was commonly patrolled by the Americans, there was one area that funneled approaching soldiers between a steep drop off below and rock belt above. Less than two hundred yards to the east there was a hill that protruded from the mountainside. It blended perfectly into the surroundings and created an ideal observation location. Plus, the Americans would have difficulties launching a counterattack because of the terrain. The surrounding area opened toward the small village below but the only way to get there was through the gap. Just to be sure, IED belts were placed wherever the Americans could stray.

Now, they waited.

Guards would watch the location during all daylight hours. It might take days or even weeks for the moment to arrive, but they were patient.

Allah would dictate the time.

CHAPTER 25

Marie had married the man of her dreams and now her life was inextricably connected to his, just as his was connected to hers. Before he left, they spent every moment together, not just because he was leaving, but because being together made them happy.

Now, he was gone.

With the reality of the deployment setting in, Marie was having difficulties filling that void.

Emptiness consumed her.

That loss was especially sharp when she arrived home each day to an empty house. There was a piece of her missing, and she knew she had to find a way to cope.

Everything was manageable while she was teaching, because she was busy doing something she enjoyed. After several unfulfilling jobs, she finally found an unexpected career path as a high school German teacher at Northwest High School, ten miles away just over the Kentucky-Tennessee border from Fort Campbell. Never once did she imagine teaching while going to college. Rather, she imagined a life in the business world, working in huge skyscrapers, and managing unfathomable sums of money for clients around the world. That's exactly what she was planning when she went to Boston, but life has a funny way of changing plans. Now, she couldn't imagine doing anything else. Her students made her smile most of the time, and even when they frustrated her, it was better than being lonely.

The first few weeks, she knew she couldn't stay home by herself or she would go crazy. High school was a great place to stay busy. Games, concerts, and other activities were always happening, and Marie made it a point to go to as many as possible. Volunteering at these events gave her the opportunity to meet some of the teachers and it allowed her to grow closer to the students. Cammie and Tanya were two of the teachers that she began to hang out with on a regular basis. Going to school events together, or dinner and drinks after school was just another excuse not to go home. Both single, they were always looking for an opportunity to hit the town. They were also new to the area, new to the school, and new to teaching, so the bond was natural. Their friendship helped Marie forget about the emptiness, even if for just a moment.

The Family Readiness Group (FRG) on post helped as well and being the FRG leader ensured that she was involved in all aspects of the group. Spouses and family members made up the FRG and it was natural that Marie assume the role of the FRG leader since Paul was the commander. The FRG's primary purpose was to pass on information from the soldiers overseas to their families stateside and to be a shoulder to lean on when times got tough. It was yet another aspect of life that allowed Marie to take her mind off the loneliness.

The fact that everyone was going through the same experience helped more than anything. They could relate. The common bond through shared misery and suffering was a strong bond and Marie could sense that in the relationships that formed. They understood what her family and friends could not, although Marie never once spoke of the pain. She didn't need to; rather, she listened and comforted others who were feeling the same emptiness. Many in the group had been through deployments before and were champions for the rest. Others had children that were struggling, not understanding why their mom or dad had to leave. Naturally, sometimes they lashed out, acted up and got in trouble. Or they became so withdrawn that it was hard to reach them.

On the other side of the ocean, deployed parents were mostly helpless. Drama struck frequently across the FRG channels. Stories of cheating spouses on one side of the ocean or the other was the most frequent gossip, with spouses spending all the deployment money being a close second. Luckily, most of it came from outside of Marie's FRG circle, but it always made everyone stop and think. Other times, it just made them laugh. Although Marie knew that these strong friendships would likely only last the duration of the deployment, she was grateful, anyway. Monthly meetings, Bunco club, purse parties, and invites to family functions all helped. But the thing that helped the most was simply knowing that she was not alone in this journey. She would survive the pain. They would be stronger in the end. Knowing that helped her push on, but never enough to forgot.

Thinking hobbies would help, Marie began to run. The endorphins were intoxicating and with each step she thought about something other than being heartbroken. In no time at all, she was addicted and began to run daily. With each mile, she grew mentally and physically stronger. Like her newfound career and the FRG, it helped, but only for the brief moments when her feet flew along the blacktop. Still, she ran.

Home was eleven hours away. Too far for a regular weekend, but not too far for long weekends, holiday breaks, or the long summer vacation. Of all the coping mechanisms, it was no surprise that Marie found going home to be the best medicine. In many ways, she felt like a child again. No real responsibilities and her parents tried extra hard to take her mind off the absence of Paul. They'd sit out on the porch in the evening and have drinks, stroll around the farm, go to the cottage for a swim, or venture into town to shop and eat—all the things that Marie loved doing as a child.

It was perfect, except for the one thing missing. Paul.

Every time she looked to the south, down the hill she saw the trees and knew there was a perfect spot on the other side of the woods. A perfect hideaway to build their dream house. During the long months, they exchanged ideas and had finalized the plans. Marie had dreamed of building a house at that location since she was a young girl and soon, another one of her dreams would come true.

But, like most other dreams in her life, it was now on hold.

And then, he was home. Not their Tennessee house, but home, home. The place where they both grew up and where they would soon build their life together. Paul was back for his mid-tour leave; the best vacation there ever is. Rather than take it when Marie was teaching, they decided it would be best for him to take it over summer, so they'd have two weeks of uninterrupted time together.

First, they decided to visit family. Since they had gotten married in a whirlwind and then left the state, this was one of the first times they really spent an extended amount of time with each other's families. For many couples, this could have spelled disaster. For Marie and Paul, the feelings came naturally, and the comfort level was instantaneous.

Neither of their parents had balked when the two had gotten married despite their short history together. To them, they started out as star-crossed lovers who eventually overcame and conquered their fate and found each other again. Just being in the same room with them, the love between the two was palpable, so who were they to fight it? Visits were met with hugs and laughter and love, meals shared, and stories of their pasts exchanged.

After that, they went on a road trip, just the two of them, around the Midwest. They laughed over her love of terrible gas station coffee, and his disdain for all things coffee, mused over how bad drivers were from the big city, and tried to bury their growing sadness from his inevitable, upcoming return with car songs and games as they drove.

The place Marie picked out to conclude the road trip was perfect. It was a private suite complete with their own private pool, hot tub, and massage chair. The setting was really just an added bonus since they rarely left each other's arms. For the first time, they had deep conversations about their future together. One night in particular, Marie found tears springing into her eyes as they lay facing each other, chatting about silly things.

"Marie, why are you crying? Don't cry," Paul said tenderly, reaching up to wipe away a tear.

"I know, I can't help it. I'm just scared. We have all these things planned, we have our whole lives ahead of us, but what if . . . ?" she began, suddenly wanting to voice all the concerns and worries she had held back for so long. She just didn't want to be the one to hold Paul back from his dreams.

Paul didn't say anything for a while, waiting for her continue. When it was clear that she wasn't going to, he spoke up. "Nothing's going to happen. We have too many plans for something to happen to me. It's not like I'm doing anything dangerous, I just happen to be in a place where people hate us. And not all of them, most actually want us there. It's a chance we take no matter what we do, like driving on this road trip, or strolling through Chicago," Paul said, trying to bring some reason to the conversation.

Marie shook her head. "Okay, but what if something does happen, God forbid? What am I going to do? I don't want to be alone; I can't be alone. I want a family, I want to see you be a father to my babies," she said softly. "Promise me you won't leave me alone. Promise me, Paul."

"You know I can't promise you that. But I'm going to do everything in my power to come back to you, so we can have those babies, and take road trips, and go camping, and drink wine together on the porch when we're old."

"How are you going to do that if you're deploying all the time? Do you really think this war is going to end any time soon? It'll be years of you being gone, and each time I'll spend every day wondering if someone will be coming to my front door to tell me you're gone forever," Marie responded.

"I don't know," Paul said, "but I do know we'll be together again soon."

"I'll always be strong for you and I'll always support you but it just terrifies me to lose you, Paul," she said.

"I don't know," he said again. He thought for a few moments. "Maybe . . . Maybe this career isn't for me. It hasn't been what I thought it would be, and it seems like every which way I turn, the universe doesn't really want me to deploy, or at least to deploy doing the things I want to do. I don't want to just sit around on the base, just waiting for something to happen, I want to make things happen. And every opportunity I find turns out to be a dead end."

Marie held her breath, hoping against hope that he was saying what she thought he was saying.

"I just feel unfulfilled and, sure, I'm making a small difference because of what I do out in the field, but it's not what I dreamed I'd be doing," Paul continued. Marie had never heard him talk like this before. It was always about the next step to get to where he wanted to go. Maybe being apart from her was taking its toll on him, especially since he didn't feel useful out there. She waited for him to keep going but he kissed her and then closed his eyes, signaling that the discussion was over. She hoped this feeling didn't die, but she left it alone. No matter her feelings, she'd be the supportive wife for him.

After that, they didn't talk about it again, but the sadness hung over them like a dark rain cloud. They continued making the most of every moment for the last few days. Reconfirming their love, especially with deep conversations about their future, the deployment had indeed made them closer. They could both feel it and then, just like that, Paul was gone.

Having him back was wonderful in every way and confirmed their love, but in some ways, it was more torturous than if he had stayed away. They lived, laughed, and loved, cherishing every moment. Besides the wedding, it was easily the best time that they had in their young lives. However, the pain was compounded when he had to leave again.

Together seemed so far away again now.

Again, the uncertainty that he would ever return crept over her. She avoided all news for months, not wanting to hear about other spouses who would never see their loved ones again. It was easier not to know. Living near a military base, there were enough reminders. Streets named after military heroes, stores like Storming Norm's, special advertisements for the military, and of course, the monuments remembering the dead. The reminders were everywhere, and the fact that many of her students had parents that were overseas, made it so she didn't need to watch the news.

They knew, so she knew.

They also knew the pain and uncertainty that she experienced; some were glued to the news while others swore it off. Painful situations bring out extremes.

After his conversation with Marie, Paul had decided to get out of the Army. The military certainly wasn't what he expected or anything he could do a day longer than his obligation. Marie was thrilled to hear the news. Although she knew that Paul struggled with the decision and wasn't satisfied, it helped knowing that they'd only have to go through this once. Other couples were on their third, sometimes fourth round of deployments. Each time it seemed to get harder and each time the absence just became a way of life. Marie never wanted to get to that point.

Thinking back to a strategy that Paul had told her to overcome loneliness, she decided to get a dog. Paul's parents had bought a dog shortly after he left for college as a way to fill the void with having the first sibling leave the household. It seemed to work for his siblings, so well, in fact, that they joked with him that he should have left the house years earlier so they could finally get the dog they had been asking for. Marie wasn't sure what breed she wanted, but two things stood out as she visited local shelters. Lap dogs simply wouldn't cut it and Paul had always talked about how much he loved Labradors. Growing up, his uncles always had labs and he loved how playful they were, eager to fetch sticks all day, and faithful to the core. Paul was also amazed that they did so well with children, not to mention they were excellent hunters. Her mind was made up the moment she saw the shy little chocolate lab in the corner kennel. Along with her three sisters, she'd been abandoned in the middle of a large section of county forest. Luckily, someone came along shortly afterwards and found them prancing up and down the dirt roads. They were still puppies, less than six months old. She was perfect and they'd call her Maple.

Marie loved Maple, more than she ever imagined, in fact, since she was really a cat person at heart. Knowing that Paul probably would have hopped on the next plane to go back overseas if she got a cat, she wisely opted for a puppy. Snuggling up with her on the couch and having someone to take care of helped ease her mind and gave herself something else to keep busy with. Still, it wasn't enough. If throwing herself into work, the FRG, running, and finding creative ways to keep busy didn't cure her broken heart, Maple couldn't completely heal her either. Maple was wonderful and filled a large part of the void, but only one man could fill it all. She finally faced the realization that no matter what she did, that emptiness would be there, and she would just have to wait. Like always, she'd make the best of it.

And that is exactly what she did, continuing to fill her schedule at every opportunity. However, she still had to go home every night. That's when things were the worst and reality struck. Silence. No laughing, no conversations about their future together, only waiting for the phone to ring, hoping. Silence may have consumed the house, but never her mind. Going to bed was the worst. He wasn't there to hold her, kiss her goodnight, or make love. Sleeping on the couch after a night of drinking wine and eating pizza while watching reality shows on TV and grading papers was one way to avoid the loneliness. It quickly became her routine, along with one or two nights a week when she would drop by to see Cammie and Tanya at their homes, or sometimes they would meet for happy hour.

Finally, she got the call. The mission was over, but as she listened, her hope turned to dread. Paul wouldn't be coming home. Half of his unit would be, but Paul and the rest would transfer bases and prepare operations for a new unit as part of the surge. Watching the first wave fly home wasn't even bittersweet, it was just bitter. Worst of all was the fact that when she talked to Paul, he wasn't doing anything productive. Nothing to help the cause. Some days he would watch movies all day. The mission that he already despised was now even worse. She couldn't bear it anymore.

Everything she tried helped but it was only a Band-Aid. She was always there for everyone else, always put on a smile, and tried not to worry.

But tonight was different.

Marie had reached her breaking point.

Always strong hearted, she had proved that with her faithfulness to Paul during the deployment. More than one guy had made a pass at her, only to be denied. Growing up on a farm, she was also physically, mentally, and emotionally tough, but she could only take so much. Twelve months was hard, but watching his colleagues come home and being embraced by their loved ones while Paul had to stay for two more months was too much.

She had to get away and clear her mind. Always up for a drink, Cammie offered to have a slumber party at her place. Tanya would be joining them too. Not only that, but Cammie sensed that she was struggling more than she let on and offered to drive so Marie could let loose and have a good time.

Perfect, Marie thought.

Drinks were just what she needed, and she had the responsibility of a designated driver covered, so she let loose. With each sip, the pain faded, and it felt good. She danced freely, not interested in any guys but not shying away from the contact either. Attention felt good and she loved the way all the guys looked at her body. It had been so long. In between dances, she hurried back to the bar for another drink. Tanya was keeping up with her in the drink department. Cammie was right there with her, not matching her drink for drink, but not exactly pacing herself, either. Marie was too consumed to notice that her designated driver wasn't playing the designated role too well.

All night, the dancing and drinks continued, to the point where she forgot everything for a moment. She felt like she was in college again. No cares, no worries, and no reality. Suddenly, one of the guys that had been eyeing her all night came toward her. Marie flashed her smile and together they went to the dance floor. They started to dance to the music. Just as suddenly as he came over, the guy moved in to kiss her. Immediately, she backed up and, as she did, reality came back into focus. Paul. Vomiting all over No Name Guy was the last thing she remembered until she woke up the next morning on a jail cell's floor.

Where she woke up was not the real surprise, but what transpired before they got there certainly was. Tanya and Cammie rushed to the scene after the vomit splattered all over the floor, but the bouncers got there first. Unable to control her movements, they had to carry Marie out before turning her over to Cammie. Together, Tanya and Cammie carried her out, before Tanya took a taxi home. Once seated and buckled, all they had to do was drive home. Then the night would be over. Marie had gotten her opportunity to let down her hair and Cammie hoped that would be enough to get her through the rest of the deployment.

Nearing her house, Cammie noticed she was being followed. Then she saw it was the police.

Shit, she thought, instantly knowing she was over the legal limit after having a few too many drinks. Attempting to get somewhere quick in hopes that they passed on by, she pulled into the next driveway.

Plan A didn't work, and they followed her into the unknown driveway. This time they had their lights on. She'd just tell them the situation and surely, they'd understand, being from a military community. Plan B didn't work either as they asked her to step out of the car after a few simple questions.

"You too, ma'am," the younger officer said to Marie, who clearly wasn't coherent. After some prodding, Marie also got out of the vehicle, but she wasn't happy.

"Why are you arresting me?" she screamed. "I wasn't even driving."

"Ma'am, please relax and answer these questions."

Not only was she unable to answer the questions, walk a straight line, stand on one foot, or do any of the other silly things they might ask her, but she couldn't keep quiet either because she didn't understand why she was being treated this way.

"Ladies, you have the right to remain silent, anything you say or do may be used against you in a court of law. You have the right to an attorney and to have an attorney present during questioning. If you cannot afford an attorney, one will be appointed to you. Do you understand?"

Tears confirmed Marie's understanding of the situation, not agreement of the law or how they handled the situation, and Cammie was silent in disbelief. Both being teachers, they knew this wouldn't be good. Neither had ever been arrested before, or even gotten a speeding ticket. Marie had made sure that she had a ride before letting loose. Now they were heading to the Montgomery County Jail. What Marie didn't realize was the worst was yet to come.

Marie remembered nothing as Cammie highlighted the night's events. She didn't remember being thrown out by bouncers, getting pulled over, getting taken to jail, or the fact that she called her parents for bail money. Judging by the headache and aches that encompassed her body, she had no reason to doubt.

If she had any doubt, it was gone when Cammie received a call from one of their fellow teachers. "Two drunk teachers arrested Saturday night" was the headline that flashed across the morning news.

Why did it have to be a slow news weekend? Marie thought.

Apparently, in Tennessee there is a law called where the passenger of a vehicle can get a drunk in public charge. Marie would soon find that out and more as she researched the case, hired a lawyer, and eventually got it expunged. She would discover how quickly people can change based on one little mistake. Students she didn't necessarily like supported her, while others she trusted wouldn't even look at her. Even so-called respectable teachers in the community made it clear through emails and gossip that they didn't respect her any-more. Worst of all, the administration finally asked them to leave, not because of what they did but because it made the news. Marie wasn't thinking of any of that as she replayed the events in her head. Only one thought overwhelmed her. How would she tell Paul?

CHAPTER 26

As they approached the village, their radio operator began to intercept messages on the device designed for monitoring enemy communications. The terp, or interpreter, couldn't understand the full meaning because of the dialect, but he was able to make out one important word. Ambush.

Word quickly spread from soldier to soldier in the platoon, increasing their vigilance as they moved down the path. They could certainly turn back, but that is not what infantrymen do. They finish their mission. And today, that mission was to visit Mangwal and attempt to make contact with village elders. One of the key elements was to subtly determine the village's relationship with the Taliban. Was it a Taliban stronghold? Actively supporting? Passively supporting? Or resistant to their influence? The hope was the latter, since it made establishing a relationship that much easier, among other things. JD's guess was that it was either a stronghold or actively supporting the Taliban cause just like nearly every village that they visited. Because of this, a potential ambush wouldn't be a surprise. They would be ready.

Military training teaches a great deal—from personal discipline to how to execute complex operations under fire. It also teaches how to identify danger areas, although soldiers often only need to follow their gut. Approaching the narrow pass, JD became uneasy. This would certainly be the ambush location. Nearly to the open area, he decided to take a tactical pause while they still had plenty of cover in the tree line. Quenching their thirst, JD and his platoon sergeant, Sergeant First Class Mackey, analyzed the situation.

"I don't feel good about this, Mackey," JD said.

"I don't blame you, sir, there's no way these guys aren't going to take advantage of this narrow spot. It's going to funnel us right in where they want us," Mackey agreed. JD peeked through the trees with his mini binoculars for several moments to see if he could spot any movement. He could detect nothing, but he continued on, noting which spots could be hiding insurgents or which areas could be problematic.

"Terp hear any other chatter that might warn us?" he asked, still peering through the lenses. Mackey shook his head.

"No, sir, ever since those initial comms, there's been radio silence. Like they're waiting for us."

JD knew his gut feeling would turn out to be right, but they had no choice but to keep moving forward. If he didn't come up with a plan, he and his team wouldn't come out of this alive.

Meanwhile, the message that had been intercepted was a call for Nasir and Malang to move with their team to the hill overlooking the narrow pass. Armed with AK-47 Kalashnikovs, they raced to their designated location, knowing they were concealed. From the small hill, they blended in perfectly and could see both sides of the passage. Malang would initiate as he mentored Nasir on how to initiate the ambush as the designated marksman. Approaching now, the Americans were nearly to the perfect position for Malang's team to rain down lead upon them. But then, the Americans paused. Although they were in range, it was far from effective range, and Malang knew their ambush would be a failure if they fired now. Plus, they had stopped where they were covered and concealed by the tree line.

JD and Mackey set up a three-hundred-and-sixty-degree perimeter in the small tree line and then began looking toward the pass and possible ambush positions beyond. There was one area that they couldn't see very well, and they knew if they were going to get hit, that it would come from there. Exploring their options, they could either approach that obscured position or set up an overwatch on the position in case someone did show up to fight. The approach was nearly impossible from their vantage point, up nearly vertical rock bluffs. There was an area that they noticed about a quarter mile back, where the climbing was easier. Perhaps they could sneak into a position where they could safely monitor the rest of the movement into the village. After discussing it, option two it would be, with their best squad moving back to set up an overwatch along with the attachments from the mortar platoon. Mortars were lethal in situations where you couldn't see the enemy position and couldn't hit them with direct fire. With mortars, you could lob shells their way by arcing them over obstacles.

Nervous now, Malang wasn't sure how to proceed. Instead of approaching, the Americans were just hiding in the woods. A smaller element had backtracked, and they couldn't see where they were headed. Perhaps they suspected IEDs, or maybe they had gotten updated information on the village. Surely, they couldn't have seen them and there was no way to approach them. It was Malang's turn to review his options, but he wanted to confer with Nasir first. He stealthily crept to his location about twenty meters away and laid down next to him to mirror Nasir's prone position. Nasir lifted his face away from his scope and looked at Malang expectantly.

"What do you think?" Malang asked.

"I know where they are, but I can't get a good shot. And if I shoot now, they'll know we're here and we'll lose our advantage," Nasir responded and went back to looking through his scope at the tree line.

"If we wait too long, we might lose our advantage when night falls," Malang said.

"Shooting prematurely will prove fruitless," Nasir said, not looking up from his scanning.

"I was testing you. You learn fast, Nasir. We will watch and wait," Malang decided.

Confirmation came that the overwatch squad was in position. Their reconnaissance didn't reveal any enemy activity but there was a likely ambush location that they had covered with mortars. Maneuvering would also be possible if the main element came under attack. With the mitigation measures in place, JD gave the word to move out.

Waiting was a good choice, Malang thought as the Americans began to consolidate back into their movement formations.

"Almost there," he told Nasir with a smile.

Slowly the Americans approached, skeptically and watching their every step. Malang let the first group go through the narrow pass unscathed; pretty soon they'd feel confident since they hadn't found any IEDs. They'd find them soon enough once the bullets began to fly and they began to stray. He wanted to fire when they were halfway through the pass to create mass confusion. Half would be on one side of the bottleneck and half on the other while they sat back and picked their targets.

A shot rang out and Corporal Huckabee dropped instantly.

He was one of those soldiers that was hard to find, tough as nails on the outside with a physique to match, but soft hearted and quick as a whip when it came to learning.

Everyone loved him.

The bullet had struck him in the neck, causing blood to squirt out in all directions. The medic, Sergeant Parker, rushed to cover the wound, while the rest of the platoon returned fire.

While they couldn't see anyone, they could see the muzzle flashes and focused their fire on those locations. The rear squad couldn't see well so they attempted to maneuver back, hoping for some cover and a better vantage point. Moving back while firing, Private First Class McDonald didn't see the IED until it was too late. His leg was ripped to shreds as shrapnel was thrown into his groin.

Above the chaos, Nasir was taking careful aim at some of the Americans running around below. As he was about to pull the trigger, Malang lunged for Nasir, sending him scrambling to the ground, just as a bullet struck the rock near his head.

"You saved my life, yet again," Nasir said, eyes wide in shock at the close call.

"I have a feeling that sooner or later, you'll be able to repay me," he said with a smile.

Nasir was amazed that he could still smile with all that was happening, but he did it everywhere they went. Through their training and the short time afterwards, he'd begun to think of him more as a friend and confidant than just a mentor. He was about to say something when a mortar fell fifty meters to his left.

Rocks flew but no damage was done.

There was another and then another.

They were getting closer and closer with each round.

Watching the chaos unfold, JD was horrified but knew he must act quickly. Three things needed to happen simultaneously, and he moved so fast that they almost did.

He could already see mortars raining down on the enemy position.

Good, that will keep enemy fire relatively ineffective.

On the radio, he asked if the overwatch squad could advance on the enemy's position since his squad was pinned down by enemy fire. They responded that they could but would need reinforcement to maintain the three to one guideline for attacking. Based on the enemy strength, the US Army advises not to attack unless you have a three to one advantage. Of course, that's in a perfect world. They used it as a planning factor but not a hard and fast rule.

Nevertheless, JD sent reinforcements knowing that they were pinned down and reinforcements from higher would be too late.

The Taliban had a way of disappearing.

Until reinforcements could arrive, they'd hold them down with mortars.

Next, they needed air support.

First, a MEDEVAC helicopter for their two wounded soldiers.

Second, an attack helicopter for close air support. If they were smart, they'd work in tandem since the MEDEVAC needed protection and wouldn't land under enemy fire. Send in the missiles first then drop down to get the wounded.

The problem was they all operated a little differently. Most pilots were good and willing to help even if a few bullets were flying their way.

As long as there weren't any rocket propelled grenades. RPGs will take down a chopper quick in this terrain.

Other MEDEVAC pilots needed perfect conditions to land.

JD prayed for a gutsy pilot.

The American infantry advanced on Malang's position. Still owning the upper ground, they felt they could inflict several casualties before retreating up the mountains when the helicopters showed up.

But the mortars kept them pinned down, unable to take a good shot.

Then there were reinforcements and the Americans out-numbered them.

They were used to this way of fighting, but now they had to make a decision. They certainly couldn't travel down the mountains to attack the Americans. Malang knew that they wouldn't stand a chance. They relied on sneak attacks. Up the mountain, through the pass and back down to the village was their only option. They had to move quickly. Infantry-men were gaining momentum as they bounded toward them. In the distance, Malang could hear the whoop, whoop of the helicopters coming.

Neither soldier was faring too well. Corporal Huckabee's neck was bandaged but he was unresponsive. Tourniquets covered both of Private First Class McDonald's legs and he too was unresponsive.

Everyone froze when he hit the IED, just like their training taught them to do. That had prevented further injuries and with the mortars and maneuvering their assault element, enemy fire was limited.

JD could predict that the enemy was going to retreat. His element was closing in and he could hear the helicopter in the distance.

He hoped they didn't get away.

They all deserved to die a brutal death for what they had done.

Nasir heard a single shot that stood out among the bullets raining down. One minute they had been talking, and the next moment Malang's lifeless body lay beside him. Malang was preparing to move back to the village but had stood up a little too high. One of the Americans was watching closely when Malang's head protruded and expertly placed a deadly shot to his head.

He was dead before he hit the ground.

Nasir didn't have time to say goodbye, and he couldn't help Malang.

Something flipped deep down in his core. He had lost his father to these evil men and now his confidant, mentor, and friend was dead. That spark of resistance, that hope for freedom and peace was now burnt out.

He must survive.

He must get his revenge.

He rose, amid the danger, and unleashed a volley of well-aimed shots down the mountain.

JD felt the bullet rip through his flesh. His first thought was not of the pain or the possibility of what could happen, but of his men.

Who would lead them out of this if he couldn't?

Had he passed on all the information necessary for them to eliminate the enemy?

Had anyone else been hit?

Where had the shot come from?

What about his family?

And finally of Lynn.

Lynn.
What would she do if he didn't make it back?
He couldn't imagine never seeing her again.
Then everything went black.

CHAPTER 27

Pulling out of the driveway, they paused. Neither Marie nor Paul said anything for a moment. Then, Paul leaned over to Marie and kissed her cheek as he said, "I have to get out and take one last look around."

Both were the sentimental type and hopped out of the vehicle, stopping first at the gardens in front before circling around the house. Holding hands, they climbed the slope on the north side of the house, before heading back toward their car, then noticed another vehicle coming down their usually quiet road. As it turned into the driveway, Paul and Marie exchanged a glance.

"Hope we're not bothering you folks but we're here to look at the house," a person they quickly identified as a real estate agent said.

"Of course not," Paul responded. "We were actually just pulling out to head back to Wisconsin, so it's completely by chance that you caught us."

They talked for a few minutes, answering questions for the prospective buyers. It turned out they had a lot in common. Military connection, wanting to start a family, and looking for a house in the country. They loved the place and before Paul and Marie hit the Wisconsin line, they made an offer.

Timing really is everything, Paul thought as they drove away, turning to smile at Marie.

Both were content with the life they had built but even more excited about what the future would hold. Soon, they'd be building their dream house and raising a family. But most importantly, they'd be together. The next chapter wouldn't be marred by a deployment, always wondering what might happen. They hadn't talked about it much, neither wanting to relive their separation, but rather focused on the present.

There was one exception.

Paul returned home just before New Year's, so naturally Marie planned a celebration night.

Nashville had been their weekend getaway spot from the moment they moved to Tennessee. Country music blazed from every corner and a visit to the bar was like going to a concert. The city was full of singers just trying to make it in the business and they were always impressive. Most they heard could easily be famous, just waiting for their moment. Tourist attractions were all around and with their common love of sports, Nashville didn't disappoint. The Nashville Sounds, AAA affiliates of the Milwaukee Brewers, just happened to be their favorite team and they recognized many of the players. The Green Bay Packers played the Tennessee Titans twice when they lived there, and they fell in love with the Nashville Predators.

There was always something to do.

Opryland Hotel was one of those places. It was like an enclosed city and no better destination for the holidays.

Festivities began with dinner at a fancy restaurant along one of the multiple sparkling indoor streams that ran throughout the building. Marie was dressed in her favorite black dress with red high heels.

It was a dangerous combination.

Wanting to look as beautiful as possible, she still didn't understand the power she held over Paul. The cliché "worshipping the ground she walked on" didn't quite cover the way he felt, and she didn't need any dress to prove that. Paul knew it from the first day they met again. The way he felt was only made stronger by her faithfulness and strength during the deployment.

Now, here she was again, so strong and wanting to make up for lost time, but Paul felt so weak and broken.

At this point, Paul had only been home for less than a week.

Everything was truly a blur.

While he tried to focus on the moment, his mind kept shifting back to deployment. With nowhere to drive that night, they moved on to the sports bar within Opryland and the drinks flowed steadily, helping to loosen Paul up. Soon he forgot about his long absence from the civilized world and focused only on the love of his life. They danced, they laughed, they cheered for different teams during the college football bowl games, but mostly they just talked. They relived all their adventures, discussed friends and family, made plans for the future and then the conversation turned to the gap in time that was missing between them. It was bound to come up as much as each tried to avoid it.

"I know it's hard for you, being back, but I'd love to hear about . . . over there. So, I can know how best to support you," Marie said carefully. She eyed Paul and sipped her beer. "When you're ready, of course," she added.

"I know," he said. "I just don't know what there really is to say. We were out there to make sure the good guys had what they needed, so they could go and get the bad guys, the ones who want Americans dead." Marie nodded, not wanting to interrupt him. Paul decided to focus more on the good times that he had overseas. "There were some great people there, that I worked with, and, of course, it was an opportunity to do things I'll never get to do anywhere else. Most Americans will never experience what I've been through, both good and bad." Paul paused to take a gulp of his beer. "I got to see new places, have new adventures, and experience a completely different culture from what we're used to. Those were some of the reasons I signed up in the first place. But then, at the same time, people will never understand that feeling of making a true difference in the grand scheme of things. I mean, I wasn't outside the wire, but I guess I still helped the war efforts."

"Did anything . . . bad . . . happen while you were there?" she asked softly.

"Not to me, personally, I mostly dealt with keeping everything running smooth on base and our base was pretty safe. We got the occasional IDF."

"IDF?" Marie asked hesitantly.

"Indirect fire. Getting fired at by the enemy with mortars and stuff like that," he said, with a faraway look. "Sometimes we got shot at on our convoys, but our vehicles could withstand it, no problem. I was lucky to be in Iraq where the surge appears to be working and not Afghanistan from the little I heard from JD. They got hit nearly every day and of course, well, you know. JD got hit." Paul only talked about it occasionally and like most things rarely expressed his true feelings. "Hope he's alright. We barely talk anymore. I was overseas during his recovery and by the time I got home, he just didn't seem like himself. Doesn't even want to talk anymore really. Remember when we visited them. Even JD and Lynn were different. Those two were always inseparable and lovey-dovey, made me sick back in college. But now . . ." he said, trailing off.

"Yeah, I know what you mean. I guess I never really knew the real JD, but it didn't seem like the stories you told me. You two were always so close from the sounds of it. Have you been able to chat with him about the wedding at least? He is your best man after all."

"A little, I guess, but not much."

Since they were making progress talking, Marie decided they should move to the bar and get a couple more drinks. As they took two seats at the bar, she could tell that Paul was noticeably quieter and she momentarily regretted starting the conversation. She knew it was important, though, and she wanted Paul to talk to her, to tell her everything he was feeling.

I guess there is a better time and place, she thought to herself.

Marie glanced up from the drink menu to peek at Paul, and her stomach dropped. He was staring off toward the botanical gardens, jaw clenched, silent, with tears forming in his eyes.

"What's wrong, Paul?" Marie pleaded. Paul looked like he was about to breakdown. "Come on, let's go back," Marie said quickly, and Paul nodded.

Arriving back in the room, silence filled the space between them. Finally, Marie broke the silence. "Please, Paul. What is bothering you? I want to help. I'm your wife, I love you more than life itself, and I just want to be there for you, but I can't if you don't tell me."

"I know. I just . . . I just feel so stupid."

Feeling that Paul was ready to talk, Marie firmly grabbed

Paul by the arms and guided him to the bed, where they lay down together, facing each other, like they always did.

"Paul, there is nothing stupid about how you feel. I'm here for you, no matter what it is."

Now the floodgates were open. For the next hour Paul opened up about the deployment. It wasn't that he had seen things he wished he didn't or experienced traumatic situations. The fact that he didn't experience combat is what bothered him. Of course, there were funeral services for those that had died, and he would forever see their faces. But, he wasn't connected to them and he wasn't connected to the combat, although he wanted to be, more than anything. He had begged and pleaded to go on more missions, both before and during the deployment. Even the ones he did go on were unnecessary. Yet, there was this intense amount of pressure, for what?

"I still can't figure it out. People in the military just have a tendency to push people to their limits even when there seems to be no reason for it. Not to mention, I didn't admit it to myself for so long because I had no choice, but I hated my designated assignment. I loved most of the people I worked with and loved the responsibility of being a commander, but I could never embrace the mission. It just made me feel worthless, even if I was making a difference. Nothing can compare to actual combat. And the pressure, Marie, the pressure just didn't make sense to me."

Marie reached for his hand and kneaded it gently. She was thrilled that Paul was finally opening up to her, but sad that he was experiencing so much inner turmoil. She didn't know how to make him understand that he wasn't worthless, because she'd never fully understand it herself.

"That isn't even the worst part. Over and over again, I've questioned what it was all for. What are all these Americans dying for and why is the nation going into debt when it's clear that it isn't going to work? Sure, there is less violence now, but what happens when we leave. I joined because I wanted to feel pride in the mission and to feel like I was making the world a better place. I wanted to feel like I was protecting my family and the American people. That's why I put my life on the line, that's why I put my life on hold," Paul said. He couldn't stop the words tumbling out of his mouth. "And I still can't shake the thought that the Iraq invasion was a mistake. These wars have created more damage and destruction than Saddam's evil regime. And we've failed. We've failed the American people, we've failed the people that we were trying to help, the Iraqi people. *I've* failed."

"You haven't failed! You've done your duty, you kept things running smoothly out there, you've done more than the average American does in their whole lifetime!" Marie said, trying desperately to break Paul out of this funk.

He shook his head and pressed his lips together in a line of frustration. "JD did more than the average American, and I didn't do shit. I wish I had never joined the Army."

"Paul, you should be incredibly proud of what you did."

"I know, but I'm not. I just want to forget about it, okay?"

She knew the conversation was over, and she didn't push it. Several times, she tried to re-engage him after that with no success. Now, they were headed home. She hoped he was coping alright and not bottling everything up.

As they drove back to Wisconsin, Paul turned up the radio. "Marie, have you heard this new song by Montgomery Gentry?" he asked with a knowing smile, melancholy mood suddenly lifted. She had heard it before but never really listened to the words, so she focused on the lyrics.

On the radio, the words to their hit song *Long Line of Losers* began, "Granddaddy was Irish Cherokee, ran moonshine from here to Tennessee, spent half his life in the Montgomery County jail."

Paul had to laugh out loud, though Marie still didn't think it was funny. Conversations about Marie's time in jail were also rare, although for an entirely different reason. Paul always tried to be lighthearted about major events in other people's lives. While this helped ease some situations, Marie's stint in jail wasn't one of them. Even though it was expunged, and they were moving back to Wisconsin, Marie was bitter. Bitter that the cops had arrested her for doing the right thing and not driving. Bitter that they didn't even try to understand her situation. Bitter that so many people had turned their back on her. Just bitter at the entire situation. Paul knew it would eventually fade but could tell that he should steer clear of this topic.

They talked very little about the deployment, instead focusing on the present and the future. Although silence is often a recipe for disaster, they felt avoiding it helped ease their transition since they were both content to leave the past in the past.

The next few months flew by for the couple. After arriving back home, they lived with Marie's family until their dream house was built. Both agreed to take some much-needed time off. Additionally, they, but mostly Marie, had to plan for their dream wedding. The small ceremony they had four years earlier simply wouldn't suffice.

They also took a trip, heading to the west coast to visit one of Marie's old friends, who was working in San Diego, and Paul's grandma, who had officially relocated to Arizona years earlier after several winters of being a snowbird.

Timing was perfect, just as it had been when they left Tennessee, and someone was there ready to buy. This time their house would be finished the week before the wedding. Talk about a hometown honeymoon.

Even more amazing was that they found out they were expecting their first child a month before the wedding. What better way to announce it than to all of their family and friends? As they made the announcement, even those that knew Marie was pregnant cried. Everything was coming together, just as they had hoped.

The wedding ceremony and following reception was perfect. Even JD seemed like himself again and they partied all night.

After that, real life began again and that meant job hunting. Neither was having any luck finding a job that they enjoyed at first, although they certainly hadn't searched very hard. There were some that would do for now, but they were in no hurry to settle.

House payments hadn't started, and they had a little money in the bank.

Then, just like that, they both had interviews and, before long, were established at great jobs working at the same local college.

Even with his disappointment over the last four years, Paul decided to stay in the Army Reserves. This nagging feeling still consumed him, like he hadn't accomplished what he set out to do. He hadn't seen combat. Combat engineering would be his mission in the Reserves. Just what he always wanted to do, and if everything went well, it looked like he'd be a commander for his hometown unit.

They were settled into their new house, their marriage was stronger than ever, both had great jobs and their first child would be arriving in the spring. They were finally together and living the life they had dreamed about, focused only on the future.

Everything was perfect.

CHAPTER 28

JD was not coping well. Physical recovery went relatively smoothly, but his emotional state was a wreck. Of course, JD didn't consciously realize any of this. Mentally, he was still in a different place. While JD remained lost, Lynn certainly noticed the changes.

Despite the late hour, they both lay in bed, wide awake, but facing opposite directions. Their thoughts were completely opposite as well. Lynn had tried to talk to him again, but the conversation had quickly escalated into anger. She couldn't understand why. They had always been able to talk and work out their problems. Look what they had been through—struggles of a young couple, questions from family and friends about their relationship, going to different colleges, and the rigors of military life. She wasn't prying, just concerned, and the doctor said that being open and talking about his experiences would help him heal. JD insisted he was fine, but Lynn knew he was anything but fine.

Their reunion had been a shock. Getting the call that JD was wounded shook her to the core. Dropping everything, she rushed to his side, and didn't leave until he was fully recovered.

It cost her a job, but it was worth every minute.

By the time she arrived at Walter Reed, he was already stabilized.

JD was so happy to see her. He was always happy to see her, but never like this. After she walked into his room, he hugged her, and didn't let go for a full minute.

Maybe more.

Muttering over and over again that he didn't think he'd ever see her again, tears filled his eyes. Lynn had already been crying. In fact, the tears never really stopped from the moment she got the call until this moment. Comforting him, she didn't want to break the embrace. Before long it was as if he'd never been gone.

They worked together during his physical therapy. When he was frustrated, she gave encouragement. When she was concerned, he gave her reassurance.

Just as he was growing stronger physically, they were growing as a couple. The worry she had that they might grow apart faded. After a couple of weeks of recovery, he could leave the hospital for a few hours at a time. Visiting local tourist attractions, going out to eat, and watching the sunset, they took advantage of every opportunity. Lynn knew her touch reassured him, so she rarely let her hands leave his. When they did, she ran her fingers through his hair or rubbed his back, always showing him that she was there with him every step of the way. In many ways, it was better than their short honeymoon.

She never did really learn or understand what happened. Lynn never heard that for nearly twenty-four hours he had been comatose, unaware of his surroundings, only to wake up in Germany. Only once, in the hospital, did she ask about what happened, but the look in JD's eyes pleaded with her to stop.

So, she did.

Instead, she gave updates from home and talked about their life together. That seemed to help lift his spirits.

The bullet that hit JD was inches from missing him completely. And inches from killing him instantly. Entering in between his neck and his shoulder, it shattered his clavicle. The pain should have been instantaneous and horrible, but JD didn't feel a thing initially.

Instead, he was shocked, clearly aware that he had been shot. Only when he looked at it, did the reality set in.

And the pain.

After seeing so many injuries, he couldn't believe that he was now the one bleeding. More blood than he ever could have imagined. Either the bone fragments or the bullet hit an artery. It wasn't the loss of blood or the pain, although both contributed, but the shock that caused him to collapse. Unresponsive, his wound was quickly treated by the unit medic, but they had difficulties stopping the bleeding. Finally, the quick clot material did the trick and the bleeding slowed. But JD had lost a lot of blood in a very short time. On cue, the helicopter arrived, and JD was loaded on the MEDEVAC chopper. Maybe it was the morphine, maybe it was the shock, but he didn't come back to reality until the next day. By then, he was nicely bandaged and had no pain. Clearly, the painkillers were doing their job.

Because the bone was shattered, it wasn't like the typical collarbone fracture where you put your arm in a sling for a couple of weeks or months, until it heals. With the blood loss, he needed a transfusion to restore what was lost. Bruising from the transfusion looked horrible, but he was kept heavily medicated, so he didn't feel a thing. Nor did he feel a thing as they worked on his wound. Painstakingly, the doctors examined the injury, ensuring that all the bone fragments were removed. They were extremely cautious not to allow infection to take hold. Once a great battlefield killer, infection was all but eliminated during the wars in Iraq and Afghanistan.

With the new blood surging through his body after the transfusion, it was time to fix his shattered collarbone. The bullet destroyed the center portion of the bone and there wasn't enough bone left to heal naturally. JD would need a plate and screws to regain that mobility. The surgery went smoothly, the physical healing was quick, and even the grueling physical therapy wasn't that bad. Now every time the barometric pressure made a sudden shift due to incoming weather, he could feel it. But that was the only physical pain he had left.

It was his emotional pain that haunted him every day.

The reason JD couldn't sleep had nothing to do with their conversation, or Lynn's attempt at one. Sure, it was on his mind, but didn't seem too important. Not compared to everything else that had happened. His injuries didn't consume his thoughts either. Rather, the faces of Sergeant White and Specialist Young filled his mind. Every night his mind replayed their deaths and the others that were wounded under his watch. Many other soldiers in his unit had died or been wounded after he left as well.

Could he have prevented their deaths if he had been there? If he hadn't been standing in the open, vulnerable, and gotten shot?

He'd never forget the horror of watching his soldiers die. Confusion, followed by blood, then watching the breath leave their bodies and knowing it was the end. There must have been something he could have done to prevent it and he was constantly searching for answers.

Why didn't I do more?

He hated the men who carried out this evil. He hated the country that sent him to war. He hated those that didn't understand. But, most of all, he hated himself because he let them die.

Just as their thoughts were drifting apart, JD and Lynn were drifting apart. Each day was worse than the next. Talking was only out of necessity and with a purpose now. No more discussions about life and no more discussions just to enjoy each other's company. When they did talk about something worthwhile, it usually erupted into a fight. Neither liked that, so eventually, they just avoided each other. Activities they once enjoyed together were forgotten. Even things that JD loved, like hunting and fishing, were abandoned. Instead, he watched TV and played video games most days. Going back to his job, he couldn't focus and ended up quitting. He rarely talked to his family either after having yet another blowout with his dad. They always fought growing up as well, but that was teenage rebellion.

This was something different.

This was rage.

His father encouraged him to get help and tried to talk to him about getting his life together.

"I know what you've been through son," his father pleaded. "Please, let me help you."

He doesn't know what I've been through and never will, JD thought. He couldn't understand why everyone kept prying. Instead of answering his father's plea, he finally just exploded. Blaming his father for his time in Afghanistan and even for getting shot, JD unleashed a laundry list of all the reasons he hated his father.

They hadn't talked since.

Of course, he regretted it, but he'd never take it back.

Never.

Paul called repeatedly, too. Several times he even came to visit JD, but Paul didn't get it either. He was a "fobbit" when he was in Iraq, one of those headquarter guys who just stayed on the FOB (forward operating base) while others were out there sacrificing their lives and paying the ultimate price. He hadn't seen anyone get shot, blown up, or die.

War is easy when you're not exposed to it, JD thought bitterly.

Plus, Paul was so consumed with his wedding. JD wanted nothing to do with it even though he was supposed to be the best man. Years ago, he would have lived for moments like this. Now, he couldn't wait until it was over.

JD had been absent from most of the wedding planning. There was no bachelor party, nor even the mention of one. Every few weeks, Paul would call and hint around about wedding stuff, but JD always had an excuse. Paul had even tried to plan a guys' night out, head to a ball game, or something and have a few beers, but JD never had any interest.

What is the point? he thought.

Finally, Paul stopped asking.

On the day of Paul and Marie's wedding, JD, surprisingly, showed up looking sharp. He had managed to send in his measurements for the tuxedo and appeared to be in a great state of mind. Despite his bitterness, he knew his friend was depending on him to show up, to be there for him. When Paul hugged him before the rehearsal dinner, JD could see the sense of relief on his face, followed by excitement.

It made JD feel good, for a moment.

Lynn had reluctantly come. Initially, she just wanted to give him a chance to have fun. She also hoped that it would cause him to miss her as he relived memories of their own wedding.

Perhaps we can relive them together, she thought, and flashed him a smile. Not sure if he was putting on a show for everyone, or if he really felt it, JD returned the smile.

Still smiling, he made his way to the open bar for the first time. Maybe a drink would do him some good, he convinced himself.

The first sip tasted delicious.

He quickly downed the first beer and asked for another.

Hell, this was an open bar, JD thought to himself. *Why am I wasting time on beer?*

He quickly changed to the hard stuff. Jack and Coke went down just as quick. By the time Paul made it back over to him, after talking with his family, JD was feeling pretty good.

"Paul, my buddy, come over here and have a drink!" he roared above the growing crowd at the bar.

Expecting to find a depressed JD, Paul was happy to find his best friend ready to party. Never one to turn away a drink invitation, Paul quickly joined him. Throughout the night, they never slowed down. It was just like college again, drinking, laughing, and having a good time. Paul thought his best friend had finally returned. JD was unaware of what was happening, but his body was making a disturbing discovery.

With every drink, his pain, misery, and deeply rooted depression faded and for a moment, he felt great.

He wanted to hold on to that moment.

He didn't want to return to that dark place.

So, he kept drinking.

Lynn noticed the change. She couldn't place it at first, but he was happier. A completely different person, really. Maybe this was just what he needed, she thought, and that made her happier as well. Perhaps the future was looking bright. Lynn decided to just go with it and let her guard down. She couldn't believe it—JD was the life of the party, dancing every dance, flirting with her, dancing close during the slow songs, and acting crazy during their favorite college bar songs.

With every drink, he came more alive. She hadn't felt this loved since his recovery. Lynn and JD had always been so happy, that couple that everyone hated because they were so in love. Tonight, that feeling returned, if only for a moment. For the first time in months, Lynn showed him just how much she loved him back in their room.

Perhaps there is hope for us after all, Lynn thought with a smile, waking up in his arms.

Today is a new day.

Unfortunately, their same routine quickly returned after the wedding. He did his thing, she did hers. There was no more magical love making. Talking escalated into arguments. Lynn wanted to discuss the future, kids, and their life together. JD still hadn't found a job and had no interest in anything. Anything, that is, except alcohol. Ever since the wedding, JD would be drunk by the time she got home from work. Now, when their talks escalated into arguments, JD was brutal with his words. He still withdrew but he didn't hold back with the booze in his blood.

One day Lynn couldn't take it any longer.

Shortly after walking in the door after getting home from work, she came into the living room, clearly agitated. "JD, can you turn off the TV for a second?"

He obliged without looking up but was clearly annoyed, a half empty beer can still in his hand. He sighed his disapproval loudly. "What?" JD said flatly.

"We can't keep living like this. I want to help. I want to be us again, but I don't know how."

She would never, could never understand, JD thought. Frustrated that all Lynn ever did was try to get him to talk about it, he exploded. He was tired of the questions, he just wanted to be left alone with his anger.

"What do you want to know about? Do you want to know about Corporal Huckabee?" he snarled loudly. Tears that were welled up in her eyes began to streak down her face. JD didn't wait to continue, because this was what she wanted, wasn't it? To hear every grisly detail? "The bullet ripped through his neck and blood was everywhere. Why was he standing there in the open? Why? Because of me. I led him there. He died because I'm an incompetent fool," JD roared, but with his eyes still on the TV, never looking at Lynn. "We shouldn't have been there. I should have known. It should have been me that took that bullet. What about Specialist Young? Don't you fucking want to know about him, too?" JD yelled, now turning to look at her with nothing but coldness in his eyes. "He was just lounging in an area that was supposed to be safe and protected, but there really isn't a safe place, is there? He didn't stand a chance. And you know what, I was only there for less than a day. Didn't know my ass from a hole in the ground and here is this guy getting shredded in front of me. And he would have been sitting at home in less than a week. Only nineteen years old . . ." he trailed off. "What the hell is it all for anyway, Lynn? This stupid, fucking war and the dumbass politicians that think they know what they're doing. We're never going to win over there, not unless we stay forever. Maybe not even then."

"JD, I'm proud of what you did. I'm proud that you stood up to protect our country," Lynn shakily replied. She could see that he was beginning to show his vulnerability, so she wanted to change the subject to the positive.

"I know you are, Lynn, but you just don't understand. You probably never will. Nobody seems to get it. Not you, not my family, not even my friends. I wish I would have died over there."

"Please don't say that. I don't know what I'd do without you. JD, what about a different counselor? We can go together. I'll do anything I can to help you. I hope you know that," Lynn pleaded.

"I know, Lynn, but I've seen four different counselors and they're all a crock of shit. Talk about how you feel, acknowledge your anger, replace your negative thoughts with all the positives in your life. Blah, blah, blah. The talking won't bring any of them back, not Nitten, not Himmel, not Young, not McDonald, not Huckabee, nor the thousands of others that I've never met. And it won't change what we did or the fact that we failed."

Not knowing what to say, Lynn said the one thing that came naturally to her. "I love you, JD. Please let me help."

JD clicked the TV back on, took another sip of his beer, and didn't reply.

Now, here they lay in completely different worlds. Lynn was lost but determined.

JD was just lost.

CHAPTER 29

"We must deny al Qaeda a safe haven," President Obama declared before the cadets at the US Military Academy in West Point in early December 2009. The President was announcing another surge, this time to Afghanistan. Many in the audience would be there to lead troops during this surge. Many would also die for the cause, yet they cheered the announcement.

"These are the resources that we need to seize the initiative, while building the Afghan capacity that can allow for a responsible transition of our forces out of Afghanistan," the President continued. One of the resources that the President specifically mentioned was the need for more military engineers of all varieties, including combat engineers to counter the growing IED threat. On the TV, the President was saying, "These combat engineers can target the insurgency and secure key population centers," but Paul was already in a different world. The month before, he had stood before his new soldiers, eager and excited to lead his hometown Army unit. Finally, he was an Combat Engineer just like he had dreamed about. Paul knew exactly what this proclamation meant.

It was just a matter of time before he'd be going back.

He listened to the President's words a little more closely now. "We are in Afghanistan to prevent a cancer from once again spreading through that country, but this same cancer has also taken root in the border region of Pakistan. That is why we need a strategy that works on both sides of the border. In the last few months alone, we have apprehended extremists within our borders who were sent here from the border region of Afghanistan and Pakistan to commit new acts of terror. This danger will only grow if the region slides backwards, and al Qaeda can operate with impunity."

Absolutely, Paul thought. *The Taliban must be held accountable. Our military must stop the spread of violence at all costs. We must protect our families.*

Lost in thought, Paul didn't notice his body tense as if preparing for combat. Once again, for the first time since he moved back home, Paul began thinking about war.

Refocusing his attention, he began thinking about his new job as a research assistant. Not his dream job, but a stepping-stone to it. For a long time now, he had imagined working at a college, starting anywhere, doing research like this or whatever it took, and eventually working up to a full-fledged, tenured professor. Now, in just a few short weeks, he would be starting his journey, right after the holiday season. It would be the first time they celebrated the holidays in their new house.

Excited for the new position, Paul wasted no time jumping in on the first day, learning the ropes and meeting all his colleagues. Around lunch time on his second day, he received a call. Busy, he couldn't answer. The voicemail was from his new commander with a simple but urgent message. "We need to talk as soon as you get this. I might have a mission for you. Call me back."

His commander was careful not to reveal any sensitive information, but Paul knew without returning the call that the President's proclamation had arrived at their door. Just to confirm, Paul made the call. His commander couldn't give details over the phone, but his meaning was unmistakable. Paul would be going back overseas, to Afghanistan this time, and soon. Paul hung up and reaching to close his office door, he began to weep.

After the moment passed, he wiped his eyes and knew that he must prepare his mind. Hearing the speech a month earlier was one thing, but now it was actually here.

He knew it would be different this time. More dangerous. More difficult, especially with a baby on the way. Physically, mentally, and emotionally challenging. Definitely harder for Marie.

Marie.

He struggled to fight back tears again. Everything was perfect in their life right now. It was a fresh start, back at home, new careers with Paul as a research assistant and Marie as a career counselor, a beautiful house, and the baby on the way. Paul was a wreck, and this certainly wasn't a conversation they could have over the phone. He tried to turn his attention back to work, but he couldn't stay focused.

Finally, for the first time in his life, he just left work.

Before driving home, Paul strolled around the campus. Walking slowly by himself had always helped Paul gather his thoughts and ease his mind. It helped him put everything into perspective. He couldn't help but notice that part of him was excited at the prospect. It was a new adventure. He always imagined going to Afghanistan, more so than Iraq, and the mission would certainly allow him to satisfy his itch for combat.

He worried about Marie, but she was tough. Just like last time, it would only make their marriage stronger. The deployment would be shorter since he was in the Reserves. Plus, with technology getting more advanced every day, they could now communicate much easier than in the past. He knew he'd be calling Marie through Skype every chance he got. Paul always tried to look at the positives but missing the milestones of their first child would be the hardest.

More than anything else, he wanted to make the world a better place. Freedom was something he didn't take for granted. He wanted others to get that experience, free of oppression. Paul wanted to give young women a chance to experience life, rather than be pushed to the shadows of society. He wanted children to have a chance at an education, he wanted those precious humans to have at least a glimpse of the freedom that his children would have as Americans. Above all else, he wanted to hold accountable those that caused so much pain and terror in the world, all while protecting his family, and the American people. That was something that his son would be proud of one day. The walk had helped him think through his conflicting thoughts and emotions and now he was ready to grit his teeth, drive home, and talk to Marie.

He hoped she would understand.

Marie wasn't there when he arrived, which was probably for the best. His heart was pounding, almost as if he was proposing again. It was probably not knowing how she would react that had him all knotted up in a mess.

Mostly, he dreaded the conversation.

Finally, she arrived.

Paul didn't say anything at first. Instead, he let her put everything away and get settled. He hovered in the kitchen. He knew he should say something because it was only a matter of time, usually a very short time, before she figured it out anyway.

"Honey, I love you," Paul said, as he broke their embrace. She always hated when he started discussions like that with an underlying tone that only she could detect, because he only did it when he had news that he didn't think she would like. This time it didn't matter though, because she could tell there was something wrong shortly after walking through the door. Call it intuition, or maybe it was because she knew Paul so well. Marie wasn't sure but she knew either way and it drove Paul nuts. He could never hide anything, even if it wasn't important.

Never knowing how to start difficult conversations, Paul had resorted to setting the stage by saying "I love you" in a certain tone. He knew it wasn't the best thing, but it was better than holding everything inside. Not talking usually resulted in one of them getting frustrated and that was a horrible way to start a conversation. Especially this conversation.

"Why do you always do that, Paul? You know it drives me nuts," Marie began.

"I know, I'm sorry. But I'm not good at letting you know that I need to talk. Plus, you think it's cute sometimes, don't you?" Paul said, playfully putting his arms around her again.

She returned the playfulness, swatting his hands away. "You would like to think that, wouldn't you? Now please tell me what is going on."

Paul hesitated and then said, "Let's sit down in the living room. This might take a while."

At that, the first look of genuine concern passed over her

face. A million things began running through her mind as Paul began to explain. Of all the things that went through her mind, deploying again was certainly one of the worst possibilities.

Paul told her everything he knew, leaving out only how he had broken into tears when he got the news. She couldn't believe it. This couldn't really be happening. How could it happen now that they were finally at home again, finally settled, finally living the future they dreamed about together? She didn't want to think of raising their first child alone. Would he even be there for the birth? What if he died and never met their child?

No, she thought. *It can't be true, this can't be happening. Can't be happening again.*

Paul had told her that he wouldn't be going back again, that he was done with the Army and that they rarely ever called the Reserves up.

"When?" was all she managed to say, half looking up only to catch his eyes. Always strong, now tears filled her blue eyes. Several streaks already lined her face.

Details were few at this point, but Paul responded with his best guess. "Soon. I'll probably mobilize sometime this summer. I have a meeting over at battalion this weekend and should learn a little more. I'm pretty confident that I'll be here when the baby comes though. I couldn't imagine missing the birth of our first child," Paul added as if reading one of her concerns.

Marie's disbelief was slowly fading and quickly turning to anger. Not anger at Paul necessarily, just anger at the situation, at the world. Her mind was spinning.

"Please tell me what's going through your mind," Paul gently pleaded.

She began slowly and then it was like a floodgate. Every emotion she was feeling—shock, rage, self-pity—seemed to consume her all at once and she couldn't stop. For nearly an hour, she poured out her heart, expressed her frustrations while Paul listened intently and provided what comfort he could. The questions of disbelief she had asked herself now turned to thoughts of how she was going to make it through.

"I just don't know what I'm going to do, Paul," Marie said.

"You'll do what you did last time, you'll be strong, you'll keep busy, you'll do amazing, and we'll make it through just fine. Stronger, even," Paul responded.

"Yeah, yeah, but what about our baby? It's a whole different ball game with a baby."

"You're going to be a terrific mother, Marie, and you're an incredible multi-tasker," he said.

"What about the house? What if something breaks?" Marie cried. She stood up and began pacing around the room as Paul sat helpless and sad.

"What about it? We have family and friends here, and you're just as capable as me when it comes to fixing things." Paul shook his head as Marie began to cry again.

"Well, how are we going to stay in touch? How do you know if you're going to have access to a phone, now that you're going to be in combat?" Marie sobbed, stopping her pacing.

"Marie, please, stop," Paul begged her. He stood up and grabbed her, pulling her close. He held her tightly in his arms and kissed the top of her head. "Please, stop. I know its hard, but this isn't going to make it easier. You're going to be amazing. We'll get through this together and be even stronger, just like last time."

Marie nodded into his chest and gave a muffled "I know."

As if reading her mind, Paul reminded her of one of her favorite quotes, by Francois de La Rochefoucauld, "Absence diminishes small loves and increases great ones, as the wind blows out the candle and fans the bonfire." That had been their quote throughout the deployment to Iraq.

Leaning her head back and looking up at Paul, she realized that she was really just scared. Of course, they'd get through the next year. They'd done it before, and they'd do it again. But what if something happened to Paul? She wouldn't know what to do without him. This mission was going to be different. This mission would be more dangerous. Some of the soldiers were going to get hurt, maybe even killed. She pushed that thought out of her head. But then it returned. It wasn't only Paul's physical health that she worried about;

how would he handle it mentally? Knowing Paul better than anyone, she knew how attached he got to people, how he treated his soldiers like family. Would Paul be able to get through it if one of his soldiers died or was severely wounded? Would he be scarred for the rest of his life? Would it change the man she loved? These were questions that had no answers. Marie did know that the best thing she could do, knowing all the unanswered questions hung in the air, was to be strong and support him no matter what. No matter what, just like they'd always tell each other.

She wiped her tears, looked at him, and tried to smile. Smiling was tough, until she saw the desperate look in Paul's eyes. Finally, it broke and she gave him a grin, not at the situation, never at the situation, but at how proud she was of the man she loved. She admitted to herself that she should have known this time was coming. She understood Paul and knew that this was what he'd wanted all along.

CHAPTER 30

The meeting at battalion went exactly as expected. They would be getting ramped up for the deployment soon; planning meetings were already beginning. The remaining portion of winter and spring would be busy, but relatively free. Once summer arrived, they'd be pushed to the limit trying to get everything ready. Paul wasn't looking forward to the hours of training and briefings, checking and rechecking equipment, and all the out-processing, medical checklists and paperwork that always felt so unnecessary.

In August, they would mobilize to Fort McCoy.

By October, they would be in Afghanistan.

That timeline moved by quickly, too quickly, in so many ways, but luckily it was slow enough to ensure that Paul was there for the birth of his baby boy—Paul Jr. What a roller coaster ride. Sure, he had seen many births on TV and heard all about it during the many appointments they went to together. But nothing really prepares you for that experience.

The day started out strangely. An unexpected, late March snowstorm blanketed the Midwest. Living over thirty minutes from the closest hospital already left Marie in a constant state of worry, and adding a snowstorm only exacerbated that concern. On top of everything else, a FedEx driver intent on being ahead of schedule came flying down the driveway and, after slushing through the snow for about twenty feet, came to a sudden stop, right against their twisted-looking maple tree. While Paul was sorting that out, Marie was inside, fretting about all the things that could go wrong while fixing lunch, which almost kept her from noticing the contractions. She paused with two slices of bread in her hands as she felt another clenching within. She set the makings of a sandwich down and headed to the front door.

"Paul?" she called out into the snow. He looked up from his shoveling and salting, which he had taken up promptly after the Fedex driver was finally pulled out. "I think I might be having contractions," she whimpered. "Maybe. I don't know. Maybe it's nothing."

Paul immediately tossed his shovel to the side and hustled up the sidewalk to the house. He reached down to rub her belly and ushered her into the house, pulling off all his outerwear, and kicking off his boots as he glanced at the clock on the wall.

They instantly began the timing, just like they had been taught. They were waiting for the "511"—contractions that were five minutes apart, lasting one minute at a time, for one hour—before leaving. After three hours, they were still irregular. It didn't look like today was the day. Throughout the afternoon and into the evening, they remained out of their 511 rhythm. Marie felt excited but was apprehensive that this might be false contractions. She didn't want to go to the hospital, only to be told that she wasn't even in labor in the first place. Paul skimmed through a pregnancy book to see what the experts said about how to know if you were in labor or not, but didn't find much helpful information.

For supper, they decided on fajitas, hoping the spicy flavor would force the tipping point. Paul convinced Marie to walk around while he made dinner, both to keep her occupied and to help with the contractions.

No luck, at least yet, so they decided to head to bed early, thinking they might be in for a long night. Or rather a short night of sleep. All night, Marie barely slept, tossing and turning with each contraction. But the regularity never came.

In the morning, the same pattern continued, and Marie had finally had enough. Once they arrived at the hospital, the doctor asked the routine questions and checked to see if she was dilated. Nothing yet. They recommended making a few laps around the hallway to see if anything would change. With each contraction, Marie doubled over in pain, white knuckling the rails of the hallways and sucking air through her gritted teeth. Paul looked on helplessly, rubbing her back and trying to talk her through the pain as she gasped in agony, unable to walk or even talk.

Nothing really helped. Lap after lap they walked the halls of the Birthing Suite, hoping to jumpstart active labor. To their great frustration, it simply wouldn't progress, and without progression, the doctor suggested that they go home and wait. They debated staying in town and getting a hotel but decided against it and went home.

Paul was angry that they had turned his wife away but there was nothing he could do. As he drove, he clutched the steering wheel tighter every time Marie's gasps indicated another contraction was happening. Her pain was his pain, and he was sure that their refusal to admit her had been a mistake. Shortly after arriving back home, however, the contractions subsided.

Maybe the doctors were right, Paul thought

They took the time to refocus. Marie had worked hard on her breathing and meditation for the months leading up to this moment. However, that was forgotten as soon as the pain came and that bothered Marie. Next time the contractions kicked into high gear, she resolved to be ready and stay as relaxed as possible.

Amazingly, it worked.

That night, Marie awoke with a huge gush of liquid coming from her and sat up in bed. In her groggy state, she initially thought she had peed in the bed, but as the contractions began again, panic set in. She stood up, still in denial, but sat down again as another smaller gush trickled down her leg and the contractions began to grow in duration and intensity.

They had to leave.

Now.

"Paul. Paul!" Marie cried to his sleeping form. He immediately bolted upright and looked around frantically.

"What? What happened?"

"We need to go; I think my water just broke. I think—" she began, before being interrupted by a huge contraction that brought her to her knees.

Paul immediately jumped into action, grabbing their pre-loaded bags and rushing Marie to the car. The freeway was clear, so Paul could easily do eighty or ninety without worrying. In the seat next to him, Marie was using her meditation, and some prayers, perfectly. Even though she was in extreme pain and petrified, she barely showed it. He hardly believed it was the same woman that he made laps with the previous day. There was no need to count, they were clearly within their 511 protocol now.

"Paul, how much longer do we have? I'm not sure I can make it," Marie whispered during the short breathing time in between her contractions.

"About ten minutes, baby, just hold on, I'll get us there as fast as I can," Paul replied, eyes glued to the road in front of him.

Marie prayed quietly, "God, please let me make it to the hospital, please. I don't want to have this baby in our car. I'm not sure how much longer I can hold back, but I'll try with your help."

"Five minutes, babe." Silence. Marie was so inwardly focused that Paul wasn't sure she heard him. "Getting off the exit. I think we'll make it."

Practically carrying Marie, they entered through the emergency room and Paul quickly explained the situation to the attendant.

"Does it feel like you need to push?" the attendant asked Marie.

"Yes," Marie desperately pleaded.

"OK, don't push. Not yet. I'm going to get a wheelchair to wheel you upstairs."

"But I feel like I have to! Now!" Marie said the words quickly, struggling not to scream.

The attendant didn't say anything, just focused on getting her up to the Birthing Suite. Loading Marie up as gently as possible, Paul had never moved so quickly and smoothly in his life. The doors were open, and they were ushered straight into the first room. The nurses were there to greet them but didn't bother with their usual admitting procedures. There would be no need for laps around the hallway this time.

In an instant, Marie was undressed and, on the bed, ready for delivery.

"Hello Marie, I'm Jen Howard. Does it feel like you need

to push?" spoke the first nurse as the other began the examination.

"Yes, I've felt the need to push since—" Marie was cut off, interrupted by another contraction.

"He's already crowning. The doctor is on the way," replied the other nurse, who remained nameless at this point. "Marie, let's give one big push and see if we can get your baby out."

There was no time for the doctor to arrive. By the time she did, Paul Jr. was laying on Marie's chest, skin to skin, just like nature intended. Less than two minutes after they walked through the birthing suite doors, he was born.

Paul was in shock and disbelief. And then panic struck as something didn't seem quite right. The baby wasn't making any noise. Paul's heart skipped a beat and his internal dialogue started spinning out of control in a matter of seconds.

Was this normal? In the movies, they always cried.

The look on his face must have showed his fear. The unnamed nurse turned to him and offered a reassuring message of comfort, "Isn't he beautiful? Look at how healthy and handsome he is." Just then, his son gave a squawk, and it was music to his ears.

Paul nodded, grateful for the reassurance that his son was finally here and experiencing a feeling of love he had never known. The instant connection amazed and surprised Paul. He knew he'd love the baby but hadn't realized that it would be instantaneous. For the next two days, their hospital stay was more like a vacation. Neither wanted to let Paul Jr. out of their sight. Marie enjoyed the ICEE slushy machine in the maternity ward and they took the opportunity to just enjoy some time together. Family came and went, but in the evenings they were alone. Even though Paul Jr. had only been in their lives for a couple of days, it now seemed as if he had always been there.

Leaving the hospital was tough, but they couldn't delay reality any longer. From that point forward, every instant Paul wasn't focused on the upcoming deployment, he was consumed with their new baby. He'd savor every moment as if it could be the last, because he knew that for more than one new father, heading to Iraq and Afghanistan, that tragically turned out to be true.

CHAPTER 31

Back at the drill center, the 824th Engineer Company was preparing for their mobilization. For Paul, it was no longer just a one-weekend-per-month commitment. After a few days of paternity leave, he joined in with the other key leaders who were there nearly constantly, coordinating and organizing briefings and training to ensure they could fully capitalize when they were all together on their designated weekends. Each month they were greeted by new soldiers arriving, some fresh from basic training and Advanced Individual Training (AIT), others cross-leveled from other units to augment vacancies.

They welcomed these soldiers with open arms and treated them like family. Not only was this Paul's style and the only way he would lead, but he had heard more than one horror story where these cross-leveled soldiers were treated like outcasts by other units. In Paul's opinion, they were here to serve like everyone else and it didn't matter if they were from Wisconsin, Ohio, Texas, or anywhere else. When he was on Active Duty, he served with more than a few soldiers that weren't even citizens of the United States. Many Americans would be shocked to learn that, but to Paul it made perfect sense. For those that were in the US legally and working through the immigration process, why shouldn't they be able to serve? In fact, after an executive order was signed by the president during the first Gulf War, there was now an accelerated process to citizenship for non-residents serving in the US military. Of course, there were some exceptions and special military jobs they could not hold since they were not granted security clearances.

Everyone would be a valuable member of the team here in the 824th. And even if they weren't, they were still people, still serving their country, and willing to die for it. They deserved to be treated with respect.

Part of the integration process was that every new soldier would meet with Paul. It was a perfect opportunity to get to know a little bit more about each of them and establish the expectations. Most commanders preached an open-door policy, but Paul worked to live that and stressed it to every soldier.

"Hey Sir, we've got another soldier for you to meet. What time do you want to see him?" Sergeant First Class Sullivan said as he approached Paul's makeshift office.

"Now works for me. Why don't you send him in?"

"Alright, he'll be right over."

Paul continued working, focusing on the manning roster and analyzing how close they were to full strength. Slowly, they were getting there and would be ready soon. His eyes kept coming back to one area of concern, one position that remained open.

They were missing a combat medic.

Secretly, he hoped that the next soldier coming to his office would be that missing link. That was one area they couldn't sacrifice. Sure, they could get assigned one from a different unit, but he wanted the guys to establish a connection with their combat medic from the very beginning.

"I heard you were around these parts."

Paul looked up. He recognized the voice but couldn't quite place it.

"I guess I should call you Sir around here."

Paul smiled. He couldn't see the owner of the voice yet, but now he knew exactly who it was. It was just the person that he was waiting for.

Chad came around the corner and instead of a handshake to greet him, like most soldiers, Paul wrapped him in a hug. It was the hug of two friends that had not seen each other for almost ten years. Remembering back to 9/11, Paul recalled how worried he and JD were when they couldn't reach Chad. They eventually got ahold of him and found out he was okay. Chad had clearly been shaken up when they spoke, but Paul really hadn't learned anything more. The trio reconnected briefly and then Chad just fell off the radar.

Now, here he was.

Amazing.

"It is great to see you. I still can't believe you're sitting right here in front of me and joining our company. It's a little different circumstance, but pretty close to how we imagined it would happen in college. How did you get here? I can't wait to hear the story," Paul said, still in disbelief.

"It is hard to believe, isn't it? When I heard you were the commander I just had to laugh. How about we'll save the story for another time? After all, we're going to have a year together," Chad said, smiling just how Paul remembered he always had.

"It's a plan, but I can't wait a year. How about dinner tonight at my house? You've never met my wife and I even have a kid now. Hard to believe, huh? We can catch up then and have a few drinks."

"Are you sure that's okay, now that you're my boss?" Chad teased, knowing he was going to have fun with his former roommate.

"It's okay as long as you drop the 'boss' and 'sir' shit," Paul shot back, joking like they had in their college days.

A few hours later, Paul opened his front door to find Chad standing there with a bottle of wine in his hand and a smirk on his face.

"Nice house you got here!" Chad said, giving Paul's arm a slight punch.

"Thanks. I never took you for a wine guy," Paul laughed and shook his hand, and then ushered him inside.

"Guess I'm growing up."

"I wouldn't say wine means you're grown up," Paul retorted and then introduced him to Marie, who was bouncing their son on her hip. After saying hello and engaging in some small talk, Marie took the wine from him and disappeared into the kitchen to chill it.

Paul and Chad sat down in the living room, where a game of baseball was being played on the TV screen. Marie brought in some wine glasses and joined the two friends as they chatted. Both shared their story of how they got to where they were now with the 824th, with Chad giving an abridged version and minor details, leaving out much of the past almost-decade.

"What a small world we live in that we're now working together after all these years," Paul remarked.

"It's pretty amazing how it all worked out, that's for sure," Chad said, nodding and taking a sip from his wine glass. He didn't say anything else for a bit and the three silently watched the game. Paul felt like something was off but didn't press. It had been ten years after all and he had to get to know Chad again. He decided to speak first because it was clear this wasn't the talkative fellow he had known in college.

They talked about how the training would go for them. The Secretary of Defense and Congress were trying to do the right thing for soldiers when they enacted shorter deployments. The new rule essentially said that Army Reservists could only be gone for one year, including the mobilization and training prior to actually going overseas. Mobilization is the period that all Reserve soldiers go through to bring them up to speed to their Active Duty counterparts in terms of manning, equipment, training, and readiness. Before the new rule was enacted, many would go through mobilization training for three months and then spend a year or more overseas. Twelve-month mobilization and deployment sounded good to outsiders, but it wasn't reality. The thing that was neglected in all of this was the training required before they even mobilized, something that Paul was not looking forward to, because he knew it would take away from his time with Marie and the baby.

In May, they would consolidate their remaining training days, usually reserved for weekend drills, and began their home station training, mobilization planning, equipment requests, and doing everything else they could think of to prepare.

Two weeks for that training.

In June, they were required to complete their normally scheduled annual training.

Two more weeks.

In July, they were required to attend training at their Regional Training Center that tested them on all their basic soldiering skills and marksmanship.

Three more weeks.

And this didn't even include specialty training. Some soldiers required a five-week explosives course on top of this training and others, like the medics, required advanced training prior to deployment.

In August, they would finally leave for Fort McCoy.

To add insult to injury, this training wasn't protected the same way with employers as a mandatory deployment. Employers had to deal with employees who were gone for two weeks in May, two more in June, three in July, and then left for a year in August, first to Fort McCoy and then overseas. It wreaked havoc on their schedules, just like it did on the soldiers' lives. It would've been better to have all the training done in one fell swoop, rather than split up into a few weeks here and there before mobilization even began. The back and forth was difficult for everyone.

For soldiers and their families, home life was a revolving door, constantly coming and going. Families were unable to get into routines. Children didn't know what was going on. It made finances difficult. It made everything difficult. As families were trying to get in quality time before the deployment, they were unable to find much time because of all the training requirements leading up to the actual mobilization. Plus, soldiers had a hard time focusing. Each time they put the uniform back on they would have to get back in the proper state of mind.

He didn't want to think about it now, so he changed the subject.

They laughed and joked about the old days more, but under the surface there was something subtly different. Paul couldn't place it, but he would definitely keep an eye on Chad to make sure he was alright. He'd already seen the changes in JD and worried about him constantly. Heightened awareness from watching JD made him think that maybe there was something more about that horrible September day that Chad wasn't sharing.

Ultimately though, he was happy to have a combat medic on his team that he could rely on and trust. Everyone in the company knew that, unfortunately, they would need him.

They wrapped up their night early and were back at the drill center early the next morning.

Even with the crazy back and forth schedule, there was a bond forming with all the soldiers. Previously, they had only seen each other on the weekends. After that, everyone returned to their normal lives. Now, this was their life. They saw each other more than their families and had the common bond of loneliness, misery, and the anxiety over their upcoming deployment. Training was rarely fun, but it was an adventure and soon they'd be in a foreign country together where the enemy was out for blood. They didn't take that responsibility lightly and knew the importance of what they were doing. Each and every one of them knew they would have to look out for each other.

"Formation in five minutes, Sir," First Sergeant Primer said as they met each other in the hallway. "I can do the soldiering stuff, but this admin stuff is going to kill me long before I get to Afghanistan."

Always quick with a joke, Primer knew how to lighten the mood. Every commander's right-hand man was their First Sergeant, the senior enlisted advisor. Paul was fortunate to have a great one in Primer. Although he had only recently joined the 824th Engineer Company, their connection already went beyond just professional. They quickly understood one another. At five-foot-eight-inches, what he lacked in stature he made up for in spirit. His technical expertise in the field of combat engineering was dated, having recently been a Drill Sergeant for a few years, but his rapport with the soldiers was excellent. And that was the most important part.

"Oh, and it might be a good time to introduce the new soldier at formation," he continued as he raced to get ready for formation.

"Do I really have to be at formation?"

Paul heard the voice and suppressed his sigh.

"First Sergeant has a formation every five minutes and I've got important shit I've got to get done," First Lieutenant

Sidal stepped into the room, all but rolling his eyes.

If the First Sergeant was a Commander's right-hand man, then his Executive Officer was supposed to be his left-hand man. Unfortunately, that was never the case with First Lieutenant Sidal and Paul. They were never on the same page, even from the beginning. Sidal was immature and self-centered and had never quite established that all-important rapport with the soldiers. He was friends with some, but most thought he was a joker. Paul thought no differently, but nevertheless he tried to bring out Sidal's stronger characteristics and make him part of the process. Very few organizations get to completely choose all their personnel. The military was no exception, but everyone could contribute something. Sidal excelled at planning the intricate details and would be essential in coordinating all the moving pieces. Battle rosters needed to be finalized, everyone had to be medically qualified, equipment requested, received, and issued, not to mention the hundreds of training tasks that needed to be completed, both administrative and in the field. Yes, Paul could count on him for that and, perhaps, in the midst of combat, he would mature and become the leader Paul knew he could.

Paul could see the potential of almost everyone to contribute. Everyone, that is, except for Sergeant First Class Strich. At his best, he was incompetent. At his worst, he caused extra work for everyone involved and missed out on key training opportunities due to his lack of coordination. This left everyone scrambling and uncertain to get their requirements completed. Leaving for Afghanistan, there was enough to worry about. Add in this chaos and it was too much. Something had to be done.

As fate would have it, he was one of the soldiers that came back medically non-deployable, meaning he wouldn't be setting foot in Afghanistan this time around. Several soldiers suffered this destiny for a variety of reasons—combat-related injuries from a previous deployment or medical issues that couldn't be treated properly in the obscure regions of Afghanistan. Others were non-deployable for reasons that weren't medically related. Mostly, they hadn't completed the proper training. Almost all of them really wanted to go, but Paul got the feeling that Strich wasn't one of them. Most accepted their reality, but others broke his heart. They wanted to go so badly but couldn't. One stud of the group, who had overcome a drug addiction just to join the Army, found out he had cancer during the medical screening. Another standout soldier completed basic training but hadn't completed their AIT combat engineer training. With that, he couldn't deploy. These were the ones that it hurt to watch. They wanted to go so badly. Their eagerness to serve humbled Paul and he used that as motivation, for himself, and the rest of the 824th.

"Yes, Lieutenant Sidal," Paul responded. "We're a team and everyone will be at formation, including you. There will be times you have too much on your plate, but this is not one of them. I want you out there with your team every chance you get."

With that, they walked to the motor pool where their limited supply of vehicles was stored. Just outside the large bay doors was a wide-open area perfect for a large formation.

"Fall in!" yelled Primer.

Everyone lined up in their respective platoons. First Sergeant was in front, leading the way. Headquarters platoon and the maintenance section were off to his right, followed by 1st Platoon, 2nd Platoon, and 3rd Platoon. Medics were already lining up with their respective platoons.

Just what Paul liked to see. Camaraderie.

They were now at one hundred and twenty men with a few more joining them in the next few weeks and a couple after they mobilize. Males were only able to serve as Combat Engineers, at the moment, although there were several pilot programs to have females begin serving in combat arms roles.

First Sergeant went through his usual list of notes out loud, calling out the names of people who were overdue for medical or training events and going over the week's schedule.

"Company, attention!" First Sergeant Primer barked crisply after slamming his notebook shut. Each soldier instantly came to attention, locked on his every word. Another thing Paul loved to see. They had amazing discipline, too. Then First Sergeant turned and waited for Paul to make his way to the front. Exchanging salutes, Paul took command of the formation. With that, the Lieutenants made their way to the front.

"At ease, gentlemen," Paul said casually. Like many officers, he took a more laidback approach to formations. A good NCO like Primer would never consider that approach. Different styles were what made them balance each other out so well.

Looking around, Paul began, "Our team is nearly complete, but I'm happy to say that we had a new soldier arrive today. Specialist Snow, can you come up here please?"

As Chad made his way to the front, Paul scanned the formation. These were the men that he would serve with in Afghanistan and he couldn't ask for a better group. Scanning, his eyes found Specialist King, Specialist Hill, Specialist Lopez, and the others. Bonds were forming between Paul and the soldiers but in a much different way than the bonds forming among the soldiers themselves. Paul would likely never be close friends with them, and he wouldn't be out drinking with the boys, like in college. It just wasn't professional. Where they were going it was important to keep that level of distance and respect. He would be asking them to do things that would put them in danger. His orders may even cost them their lives. Their relationship would be something deeper than friendship. It would be a brotherhood that lasted a lifetime.

Another aspect strengthened that bond. Paul knew that each one had volunteered. That was the beauty of the modern Army. All volunteers. They all wanted to be here, and for those that didn't, and there were a few, it was relatively easy to find a way out and beat the system. Medical issues, family emergencies, objections to the war, or simply not showing up. Of course, there were consequences for some of those methods, but most wouldn't be going to war. Paul was okay with that. If they didn't want to serve, neither Paul nor the rest of the guys wanted them on their team. It eroded the trust. And in combat, there is nothing more important than trust.

"I couldn't believe when I looked up from my desk and this guy was standing there," Paul said as Chad came up and stood next to him, his arms folded behind his back, disciplined and respectful. "Specialist Snow and I go way back. Now I could tell you some stories, but then he'd share some about me and we can't have that now, can we?" Paul smiled. "Yes, this guy here was my college roommate freshman year, then he disappeared looking for something bigger, and I believe he found that, but I'll let him introduce himself and tell that story."

As Chad began, Paul continued to glance out at the formation. Right in the middle of everything was Lieutenant Scarborough. He was a true warrior. In Iraq, he served as a gunner and had seen fierce fighting around Baghdad and Sadr City. Standing six-foot-four-inches with a dark complexion, he towered over most in an intimidating way, but had a gentle demeanor and was always willing to help. Plus, he was always quick with humor. Soldiers loved him. Sergeant First Class McDonald was the Platoon Sergeant for 2nd Platoon. He too was a combat veteran of Iraq and served as a firefighter in his hometown. Just two inches shorter than Scarborough, he had an amazing presence. Leaving behind his wife and four children was difficult, but he never complained. He just focused on his soldiers as if they were his children. Together, they would make a dynamic leadership team.

Then there was Lieutenant Jones. Like many, he didn't come from the local area, but unlike the others, he went out of his way to point out the difference rather than become part of the team. What he lacked in stature he tried to make up for with his approach to leadership. It was a regular Napoleon complex but without the benefit of Napoleon's tactical genius. Unfortunately, he went over the top. Because Jones wasn't like that in front of Paul, he wasn't aware of Jones' style of leadership until one night when they were out in the field for training. He walked by the large tent holding many of his enlisted soldiers on the way from the Porta-John back to his own tent, and he happened to overhear "L.T." muttered in a conversation. Against his better judgment because he was not one to eavesdrop, he paused to take a listen.

"These L.T.s, man, acting like they're better than everyone else," one voice said.

"That's just how it is, brother, even if you've been in for

fifteen years as enlisted, you're still lower than a butter bar," another voice responded, using the nickname "butter bar" for a Second Lieutenant, coined by the gold-colored bar rank insignia they wore on their collars.

"Still, I've had L.T.s that gave us respect, treated us right; we're the ones doing the dirty work, after all. Jones, though, he doesn't listen to anyone except for the C.O., and even then, he's just kissing his ass," the first voice continued.

"Yeah, I've seen him. He always gets chow first, sits first, showers first and takes up all the hot water, and never does any security patrol shifts. I've had officers take our shifts sometimes, just to give us a break, but this guy, I'd be scared to be next to him in battle. He'd use me to protect himself," a third voice joined in.

Paul had heard enough and decided to keep an eye on Jones to see if these comments rang true. Sure enough, he began to notice all the things that he had been blind to before. He watched Jones when he thought he wasn't looking, listened when he thought he was out of earshot. Frequently cutting soldiers off, he never listened to their opinions. Not even from his NCOs. He was the first to eat, first to shower, and first to bed. He was the opposite of everything an officer should stand for. Besides not building an effective team, he was simply incompetent at running operations as well. An all-around disaster. Paul knew what he had to do, yet he dreaded the conversation. Leaders like that had no place in this formation. Tonight, Lieutenant Jones would be heading back home. Paul had tried to mentor him to no avail. Enough was enough. Lives were at stake and he couldn't risk an unpredictable leader in combat, especially one that his soldiers didn't trust in battle. Luckily, Sergeant First Class Taylor was an exceptional leader. As the Platoon Sergeant for 3rd Platoon, he made up for his lieutenant's ineptitude. He was there to guide his soldiers back on track when they were derailed and always listened, yet never once spoke poorly of Lieutenant Jones. He would lead the platoon until a replacement arrived.

The 1st Platoon Leader, Lieutenant Dodge, was eager. Located on the opposite side of 2nd Platoon, he paid close attention and was excited for the adventure. Just out of college, this was his first real taste of the Army and his first time in any leadership position. Yet, his confidence came through and despite some expected missteps he persevered. He showed promise and most importantly had a natural concern for his troops. He looked so young standing out there in front of his soldiers.

Beyond their platoon formation was Sergeant First Class Sullivan. By far the most experienced leader, he was a combat veteran of Operation Iraqi Freedom and served in Desert Storm nearly two decades earlier. He was an experienced diplomat from his years as a small-town mayor and you could quickly see that in the way he talked. Easily connecting with people, he also had a knack for being persuasive. That could be extremely useful overseas. Plus, he had experience training Iraqis. That experience might also prove to be vital as their mission would certainly evolve into training the Afghans.

"I'll save the stories for a different time, because we're going to have a lot of days together in the future, where it would be nice to have a few laughs," Chad spoke with a certain maturity beyond his twenty-eight years. "Captain Foster is right that I went searching for something. What I discovered was that all I wanted to be was a Combat Medic and here I am, proud to be serving with all of you. My job here is to keep all of you alive when it matters, and you can always count on that when the time comes." Rather than humorous, Chad's words were insightful and seemed to echo the quiet professionalism that the group embodied.

Paul wanted to give a few closing remarks to leave things positive and to motivate his troops. "Here we are, the 824th Engineer Company. Each of you is unique and has your own story. I know, you have your own lives outside of the military, but now you need to set that aside. Our lives will now be intertwined forever as we embark on this journey. This unity, this brotherhood, will last a lifetime. We have one common purpose, and it needs to be built and maintained on a strong foundation of trust and excellence. Together we have to do our part and be the best to defeat the Taliban insurgency in Afghanistan and protect our nation. Be proud of what we're about to undertake."

CHAPTER 32

Finally, the day came for their departure. It was August now—the time the soldiers had looked forward to yet dreaded. Training was complete, at least the initial part, but there would certainly be more to come. Equipment was packed and staged. Each soldier had their military gear issued—weapon, NBC (nuclear, biological, and chemical) masks, and other specialty equipment—and on them at all times. Personal items that would make it feel more like home had been packed into a shipping container and sent months earlier, with the hopes it would be there when they arrived.

Each soldier grappled with his own way to face what was coming. Paul and Marie had their shares of ups and downs as they mentally prepared. One moment they celebrated their remaining time together, the next they lay sleeplessly in bed wondering, waiting. The key was that they talked and always remembered the mantra that they wanted to live by in their separation.

"Absence diminishes small loves and increases great ones, as the wind blows out the candle and fans the bonfire."

They wanted their great love to continue to grow. They would connect at every opportunity through mail, e-mail, phone, video, and anything else that allowed them to connect. They would not let their love weaken. Planning their dreams, they would give themselves something to look forward to when Paul returned and well into the future. It wouldn't be easy, but no great love is. Paul was saddened by the fact that his son would likely not know who he was when he came back, but he wanted to do everything in his power to change that fact.

Then came the inevitable celebration of support with speeches from their hometown Mayor, state representatives, and finally their military leadership. The day was beautiful, sunny with a slight wind, and the moods were still bright. Optimism and upcoming adventure filled the air with the festivities. Beneath that was the dread and uncertainty. Lieutenant Colonel Anderson was the final speech of the day and left them with something Paul would never forget.

"Gentlemen, I'm not going to sugarcoat my message to you today. Your mission will be dangerous. Most of you will see combat with the enemy, some of you may be wounded, and some may not make it home. No matter what, you will all come back changed. Some for the better—with a new perspective and appreciation for life. And some for the worse—bitter and disgruntled with life. I encourage you to let this experience change you for the better. However, that journey is not easy. I know, because I was in your shoes a few years earlier. Stay connected to family and friends, lend a helping hand to the Afghans, and your brethren here in the 824th, and keep everything in perspective. This war will end, and your time in Afghanistan will come to an end, but your experience will endure for far longer. If you don't believe me, read an obituary and it will no doubt describe someone's military service and certainly mention combat—World War II, Korea, Vietnam—if the person was there. This is one of those moments for you. To the soldiers and families, your nation is forever grateful for your sacrifice and I couldn't be prouder. I just wish I was going with you, but I know you're in good hands. God bless and God speed."

This was more than a deployment; it was something that would change each and every one of them in their own way. And that change would be permanent. Oftentimes, speeches are forgotten as soon as they end. This one lingered. Paul wanted to make a difference and make that change for the better, but he hadn't really thought that it could change him for the worse. Perhaps it was important to build that awareness. To take the time to think about the inevitable. Maybe that was the key to preventing unwanted change, the key to taking control. Or maybe it didn't matter. Time would tell, but Paul vowed that just as they physically prepared, he would be mentally prepared when the time came. Unfortunately, what

Paul didn't know was that there were some things you simply couldn't prepare for.

Formation was over. Families wrapped in one last embrace, just a little longer than usual, knowing it was the last. At least, hopefully, the last for only a little while.

Then they loaded the bus and were gone.

Fort McCoy wasn't far, according to the dots on the map, but it felt like a world away, exactly as intended. As soon as they entered the gates, they were locked down. They were there for one reason and one reason only — to prepare for war.

Realistic training was difficult to replicate. They rode around in vehicles that didn't have the proper capabilities, looking for piles of sticks or wires that were supposed to be an IED. Explosions were faked. Plus, they were lacking most of the specialty equipment that would help them find IEDs once they arrived in Afghanistan.

More than once, Paul overheard the following comments.

"This training is a joke."

"Why are we here? Just send us over and let us do our jobs."

"We should be teaching these jokers. Most of them I've seen don't even have combat patches."

Despite the fact they weren't able to train in the same environment they'd be going to or with the same equipment, they each understood their mission. No matter how many fancy gadgets the Army gave them, it would be their keen sense of observation and understanding of the local environment and people in Afghanistan that would help them find IEDs. That was their mission – to find and destroy IEDs before the devices could unleash their destruction on fellow service members, allies, and the local population. They also respected what would happen if they didn't find them. Yet, they were confident enough not to be consumed by that fact.

Even though it wasn't realistic, there were a lot of benefits that the soldiers may not have noticed, but Paul certainly did. They were beginning to work together as a team and their identity was coming through. Pride in the platoons was taking shape. They developed their battle rhythms along with who was doing what and when. Exploring their strengths and weaknesses, they found the best fit. And they were learning how to communicate. For a group that worked together once a month, with half of the soldiers being new to the platoons, this time was invaluable. It would be these intangibles that would carry them through the rigors of combat.

Once again, they would be hosting a going-away ceremony, but this time would be different. After this ceremony, the training was officially over, and they'd be bound for Afghanistan. Their 824th Engineer Company colors, their flag that guided them, and represented them would be cased. They would not be unloaded and uncased until they were on foreign soil. There they would add another piece of history to the unit's legacy. What that contribution would be was still uncertain.

Marie came down a couple of days before the ceremony and stayed at a little cabin just down the road. One of the perks of being the commander was that Paul had a government vehicle. Each night, at the end of the day, Paul would sneak out and then return before duty the next day. No one was any the wiser except First Sergeant Primer. It would be their little secret. Marie and Paul felt better when they were together for that short time, but it made it even tougher when they were apart. Goodbyes were already tortuous, and a long, strung-out goodbye made it even worse. Still, neither would change that while they cherished every moment.

Paul Jr. was a great distraction, but Marie just wanted them all to be at home. This tension was killing her and extending the anxiety of the inevitable. Paul would be leaving. And soon. Things were different this time. The reality of combat constantly weighed on her mind. People were going to get hurt, maybe killed. Lieutenant Colonel Anderson said they would all come back changed.

What would that mean for Paul?

"I'm scared, Paul," she said quietly as they lay together in bed, enjoying the last few moments of their time together.

"Of what? Nothing's going to happen to me," he said.

"Not just about getting hurt, but . . . are you going to

change? Like Anderson said?"

"He just meant we'd be changed because we have the experience, not anything bad."

"Well, no, I know that. But what about if something happens? What if your men die? You love your men, Paul. It would kill you to see them hurt. What if you have to kill someone? I feel like you won't be the same after that, that worries me, too," Marie said, nuzzling into Paul's chest.

"Nothing's going to happen. I have you to bring me back, to support me, and Paul Jr."

"Are you going to miss us?" She propped herself up on her arm and looked down at Paul.

"Are you kidding? Of course, I am! It's going to be harder this time, you and I both know that. I'm going to miss so many of Junior's firsts," Paul said sadly.

"It makes me sad," Marie responded. She wiped away a tear and then laid back down to snuggle into his embrace. "I wish you could be here, but I know how important this is."

"I wish I could be with you, too, baby. And with Junior."

Paul would miss his first steps, first words, and building that bond that he'd waited so long to have. Other than meeting the woman of his dreams and spending the rest of his life with her, nothing else mattered nearly as much as finally having his own family, his own son. Marie knew that all he ever wanted was to be a husband and a father.

Enough of that, Marie, she told herself, wiping the tears away. Right now, she needed to pack up and head to the going-away ceremony. The long, tortuous goodbyes that she would miss so much were finally coming to an end.

CHAPTER 33

Touching down at Kandahar Airfield was like arriving on another planet. Everything was drab and tan-colored, as far as the eye could see. Dust billowed around them and hung in the air, and within minutes, a thin layer of the powdery stuff had coated everything they brought with them. The distinct smell of sewer hung in the air, which a few of the veterans explained came from the famed Kandahar "Poo Pond." There was no time to investigate this landmark, however, because within the hour, they would be on helicopters heading to Forward Operating Base (FOB) Alexander, or Arghandab, as it was called by the locals.

FOB Alexander was named for a heroic Canadian who lost his life operating in the area. It was located directly along the main artery through Afghanistan—Highway 1. The highway was one of the only blacktop roads in their part of the country and spanned from Route Red Bull in the east to Route Monster in the west. Gravel roads and other dirt trails connected the many villages across the countryside. It was on these roads that the 824th would spend most of their time. Their mission was to find and destroy IEDs so other military personnel could move freely and local civilians could travel safely. At one time, most IEDs were right along Highway 1, but as security improved and the American presence expanded, IEDs were placed in more obscure locations. This made finding them even trickier but all the more important.

Training with the unit they would be replacing was quiet, at first. They found a couple IEDs, but there were no "blasts," as it was known when the IED found them first. Engagements with the enemy were nonexistent. Framework operations and their routine routes were picked up easily by the soldiers, which allowed for a bit of extra training time and conversation. The unit going out was excited to leave while Paul's unit was raring to go, which made for a positive beginning. A week after they arrived, when they were mostly settled in, they got the call to participate in a major offensive. This was something new, both to them and to the unit they were replacing. These major operations came to be known as CONOPs. Although they each had mission names, there was a concept of the operation outlined for each, hence CONOP. The name made no sense but, like many things in the Army, it stuck.

Pushing deep into an area that was long held by the Taliban, they would be clearing the way of IEDs in preparation for establishing a new outpost. Arriving at their staging base, they received their mission brief and were quickly on the road. They were linked up with a young platoon leader of a Stryker platoon, Second Lieutenant Edwards. He was probably only twenty-two or twenty-three years old and fresh out of West Point on his first assignment. Despite his inexperience, he was confident. Coincidentally, he was also from Wisconsin. Besides this instant connection, he was an all-around good guy. Paul had immediately liked him, especially upon noticing the obvious respect and adoration Edwards' troops had for him. This was no LT Jones, that was for sure. He was pleased that they would be partners for the duration of the mission, and both were excited to hit the Afghan countryside.

This was really the first time Paul got an opportunity to take everything in. "Desert wasteland" could be used to describe the entire area before they got to their staging base. However, when they got closer to the river, life emerged.

So did trouble.

Remnants of powder from an IED blast littered their path. They didn't need a reminder, but this helped make it a little more real. Huge holes littered the area where locals had dug wells. Maneuvering was difficult and more than once they had to quickly stop so they didn't disappear into one of the pits. Farmers, or men who appeared to be farmers, seemed to be everywhere they turned, both in the fields and along the roads, but rarely did they look at the Americans.

Imagine if heavy machinery operated by foreigners rolled down our street, Paul thought. *Wouldn't everyone want to take a look?*

Paul couldn't help thinking that it was odd, but then again, the people here had lived through decades of wars. He was thankful they never had to worry about that in the United States. If they had, maybe they wouldn't have watched them go by either. Although the people mostly just pretended the Americans weren't there, at the same time, they were always watching. The studied disinterest and sharp alertness made Paul feel eerie.

Children never hid their attention the way the adults did. They were always interested and always wanted something. Food, water, or the most popular—qalam. Some said having a qalam, or pen, was a sign of intelligence. Others said the small device inside pens were used for making bombs. Both ideas were probably correct. Either way, it was better not to hand pens out, for fear they would be used against them in the future.

The farmers they encountered were not like what most people would expect. Their main crop was drugs to fuel the Taliban finances. Because of that, these farmers had close ties to the insurgents whether they liked it or not. Marijuana and poppies for heroin and other drugs were the most common. Each day the soldiers would pick huge stalks of marijuana off their vehicles, caught from driving through dense patches of the crops. This would be a dream come true for many and, of course, they always joked about having a little fun with it, but never did. They were true professionals. Even as they joked, Paul thought how hypocritical it was that the Taliban claimed to live by higher values, yet here they were, fueling the drug trade at the expense of others. Not to mention abusing women and children, suppressing the local population, and routine murder to top it off. And western culture was supposedly evil, according to their fictions. No, they thrived on fear. Judging by the cold welcome they received in the area, Paul thought fear was proving effective.

Three days went by uneventfully. Combat is often like that, Paul found out. Boring, boring routine and then a few moments that you'll never forget that changes your life forever. Then the cycle repeats. Complacency is an enemy in itself during those mind-numbing moments of boredom. But, the ability to fight that complacency often meant the difference between life and death on the battlefield. On the third night, they settled outside an old British fort. The next morning, they'd be moving in to set up a new base for their forces. Nearby, there was a camel with a rope tied between its legs to keep it from getting away.

That's one way to do it, thought Paul.

He was amazed that he could still find humor in the worst situations.

Paul laid a cot under the stars that night. Security was in place, but it was pretty casual. They relied on the infantry for that, or so they assumed. Being rookies, they were still naive. Staring at the stars, Paul thought about the British in this land centuries earlier, during multiple Anglo-Afghan Wars fought alongside British-occupied India, between 1839 and 1919. After that, there were the Russians. Plus, who knew how many other countries that had an interest in Afghanistan. They weren't the only ones. Throughout history, other countries and other civilizations have been involved in Afghanistan for various reasons. It never seemed to work out well for the outsiders.

Now, here we are, trying to change that record. Paul hoped it would end up differently.

Just two generations earlier, the United States had been at war with Germany, Italy, and Japan. Now, they were some of the United States' closest partners. Marie had even studied in Germany without the least bit of concern. That's what he hoped for. He hoped that one day, Paul Jr. would be able to study at Kandahar University or in Baghdad, if he wanted to. Optimism remained high at the beginning of conflicts and each rotation brought hopefulness with them. Reality often changed that.

Time would tell for the 824th.

Drifting to sleep, he again focused on the present. Tomorrow they'd be moving forward. Waking early, he found everyone asleep, including the infantry guys that were supposed to be providing security. That wouldn't make anyone feel good in the middle of enemy territory, in arguably the most dangerous place on earth. After roughly rousing the sleeping culprits, they quickly secured the area and breathed a sigh of relief that luck was on their side and no one had ambushed them. Once everyone was awake, they all received a stern talking-to about the importance of vigilance. Lesson learned. It would be one of the many learned along the way. After finding Lieutenant Scarborough and Sergeant First Class McDonald, they got their new orders. They'd be heading back to base and nobody knew why. There wasn't much they could do. The British base would wait for another day. This was also an excellent time to swap platoons. 2nd Platoon was in need of some sleep. 3rd Platoon made the swap.

Paul decided to stay. He needed to see and learn firsthand what all the soldiers were going through. Only then could he be able to connect and motivate them throughout the deployment. And pray to God that he could keep them alive. Chad was the 3rd Platoon medic and they were paired up in the Buffalo together. Route clearance, what they called IED hunting, had some unique equipment. The Buffalo, which Paul and Chad were riding in, looked like a huge boat on wheels. The boat appearance was due to a V-shaped hull that directed an IED blast away from the occupants. These vehicles could fit as many as six people and had a huge arm that was used to dig for suspected IEDs. The arm had metallic claws that resembled a small pitchfork and extremely skilled operators could do some amazing things with them, like pick up suspected IEDs from sixteen feet of clearance, rather than just poke at them. Mounted on top of the Buffalo was a Common Remotely Operated Weapon Station (CROWS), which was essentially an unmanned gun that was controlled through a computer screen.

Up front was usually a Husky, a one-person metal detector that rode high and was designed to only expose one person to a blast, rather than an entire vehicle. The vehicles were also made to detach and keep the cab intact. Huskies could be mounted with a metal detector or Ground Penetrating Radar (GPR), although neither was very effective here in Afghanistan. The Taliban rarely used metal, instead favoring plastic jugs filled with explosives, and the GPRs were touchy at best since they needed proper conditions. The Husky was not with them today due to the tricky terrain, which was another of their weaknesses.

The remaining vehicles were gun trucks, RG-31 Mine-Resistant Ambush Protected (MRAP) vehicles, with a gunner, Truck Commander or TC, and, of course, the driver. Rollers were attached to the front of at least two of the MRAPs. Designed to compress the ground in front of the vehicles, they would initiate a pressure activated IED before the vehicle detonated it. Or worse, a dismounted soldier stepped on it. Better to risk a roller.

A minimum of four gun trucks were required on every patrol, due to the danger. That meant six vehicles on most patrols—Husky, Buffalo, and four RG-31s—seven if they were lucky to have an Explosive Ordnance Disposal (EOD) team attached. For this mission, they had Strykers join in, which weren't as effective as MRAPs but still served their purpose of carrying armed personnel. As engineers, they had the training and expertise to blow up and destroy smaller IEDs. EOD was required for larger ones. Having them saved a lot of time when there was an IED find. Today was one of those lucky days with an EOD team embedded in their patrol.

Despite all the equipment, their eyes were their greatest weapons. Routinely, their eyes and senses would outperform the machines. Slowly, always slowly—scanning the road in front of them, observing the landscape, and allowing their equipment to work properly—they worked their way along the new route. Few Americans had ever been to this specific area before, even though the United States had been operating in Afghanistan for nine years. Everyone knew what that meant. This was Taliban country. Slowly, they continued, checking anything that raised a red flag, keeping their eyes peeled. Any soldier could halt the patrol at any time.

Slowly, they continued.

Over the radio from the higher headquarters, there was a suspected IED emplacer nearby. Confirmed a few minutes later, they heard an explosion out in front of them.

No more IED emplacer.

The Predator, their eyes in the sky, had delivered its payload. Unmanned Aerial Vehicles (UAV), or drones, could be found throughout their area of operations and their use was rapidly expanding due to an initiative by Secretary of Defense Robert Gates. There were a variety of types—some were armed like this Predator, but most were not. Clearly, they were effective. UAVs gave US service members the ability to conduct surveillance and reconnaissance without being seen. In a way, they could see the future, or at least predict it, when they saw what was out in front of them. This way they could avoid deadly ambushes and target enemies remotely. Or they could gain valuable intelligence to plan their own effective attack.

Within minutes, they arrived at the site. Blood everywhere, but no body. Just as quickly as insurgents were killed, they were picked up so the Americans couldn't get them.

Cautiously, they continued.

Up ahead, there was a white van moving toward them. The CROWS gunner eyed them the whole way. Suddenly, the van stopped. Out jumped four men with shovels who began digging madly in the road.

Clearly, they were planting an IED.

Weren't they?

How do they not see us? Paul thought as they all stared in amazement. At this point, no one had fired a shot. *Can we shoot? What are the rules of engagement here?*

Things like the ROE had been drilled into their heads during training, yet now it was time to execute. Unable to reach headquarters through the radio, they made their decision. They went after them, fully planning to detain these IED emplacers. After all, they hadn't seen an actual plastic jug that indicated an IED, and they weren't carrying any weapons. They'd all heard more than one horror story about heading to Fort Leavenworth for violating the ROE. Nobody wanted that fate. If they fired on these supposedly bad guys, they'd have to be ready, with all available guns pointed at their location. Naturally, as they approached, the potential IED emplacers jumped into their vehicle, leaving only their shovels behind. By this time, the eye in the sky had them and followed them back to their hideout. After picking up the shovels for finger prints, and with darkness setting in, they were ordered back to base.

Tomorrow they'd continue. Right now, the infantrymen were planning to raid the hideout during the night.

Exhaustion was starting to set in when they woke early the next morning. After nearly six days with little sleep, Paul could barely keep his eyes open. He was thankful that his guys were able to swap. Not one to usually pound energy drinks, he was now drinking one Rip It after another. Nothing worked. They approached the area where they had encountered the white van. Wondering how the raid went the night before, they were disappointed to find out it never happened, and no one would give them an answer as to why. Paul certainly didn't know or understand how these decisions were made, but he wasn't happy. Clearly, they were Taliban fighters. What more evidence did they need?

We should have shot them when we had the chance, he thought. *Or we should have at least chased them down.*

The negative thoughts took him by surprise. Slowly but surely, his subconscious was changing. What had started out as an innocent until proven guilty mindset was shifting to seeing everyone as guilty. More and more, he was on full alert. They all were. He was starting to see everyone as the enemy, rather than as a nation of people who were oppressed. And they hadn't even been engaged by the enemy yet. These feelings, whenever he recognized them, scared him.

His lack of combat experience would soon change. As they reached the location where the four IED emplacers had been the day before, Paul was consumed by adrenaline. He never really got to experience combat in Iraq. As crazy as it sounded, he wanted that opportunity. Most soldiers did.

This might be that chance, he foolishly thought, not realizing what he was truly asking for.

As they came to a stop, Paul was baffled to see another Route Clearance company coming from the opposite direction with their infantry counterpart. He was constantly frustrated with the lack of communication and organization when it came to operations.

So much for any action today, thought Paul, almost bitterly.

He let down his guard. This was their last day of the operation and then they would switch out with another unit. They would escort their infantry partners and then head home to FOB Alexander for some much-needed rest. And a shower.

Slowly, but a little faster than before, they continued on.

Paul and Chad were in the Buffalo, third vehicle in line. Farmers were in the fields as usual, although Paul was beginning to doubt that they were farmers. The river valley was below, where the white van had disappeared the night before. Based on the fact there was no raid, they were probably still close.

Suddenly, the lead vehicle disappeared.

CHAPTER 34

Nasir was gaining quite a reputation. His accuracy was becoming legendary. Throughout the country, he would travel as a sniper, initiating deadly attacks on their enemies. Etched on the butt of his rifle were twenty-four checkmarks, one for each confirmed kill. There was actually a total of twenty-five, counting the soldier he killed after his father's death. That was with a different rifle, in a different time, when he was a different person. That was a time when he despised the Taliban. Now, he was one of them, hardened by the fire and brimstone that the infidels rained down on countless innocent people—*his* people. According to Nasir's new mantra, these infidels had no business here, yet they remained, claiming they were helping to free the Afghan people.

In the early days, he'd stick around to fight, but now he was too valuable. These days, he'd initiate hostilities and quickly exfiltrate, leaving others to fight the battle. Amazingly, he'd never come close to being captured or identified. That meant no fingerprints, nor was he input into their crazy machines. He'd seen others have their faces scanned. For what, he didn't know, but he didn't like it. That was why they always kept him moving. They didn't want him to attract unnecessary attention from their enemies.

Because he had never been captured or identified, he was selected and being groomed for an elite position. He would be going undercover and he would be going home. The very first Afghan National Army (ANA) engineers were being assembled and slated to do route clearance in his hometown. Nasir would be joining them, but first, he was off to ANA basic training in Kabul. Surprisingly, getting the assignment he wanted was fairly easy. A couple of well-placed bribes and he was in. A lieutenant, no less. For the right price, you could

Servi

get anything done in Afghanistan.

His role had continually evolved, first by starting attacks to now by planning them. Recruiting had been another one of his key roles and now he'd be trying his hand at infiltration. Once he infiltrated the ANA ranks, his mission was to befriend the Americans, gain their trust, and learn everything he could about their mission. That way they would learn how to defeat their large IED-clearing machines. Plus, the engineers had recently started using a remote controlled IED-clearing machine. They were effective at finding IEDs on foot paths and his leaders didn't like that. They wanted to keep the foot soldiers on guard and limit their mobility.

That was the other part of his mission. After learning as much as he could about these machines, he was then supposed to learn the time and place they would be employing them. Then, they'd test their tactics. Once they learned their response, Nasir would make his deadly strike. The plan was simple enough in theory. But, if all that didn't work, he'd simply figure out how to attack them where they worked, or better yet, where they slept. He knew that outcome would surely mean the end for him, but he gave that no consideration.

Anything for Allah.

Going home brought mixed feelings. Although he was excited to see his home once more, his journey had now come full circle in a way that he never expected. Reluctant to fight at first, for years he avoided getting involved. In fact, he had harbored deep hatred for conflict. Nasir had hated what the Taliban had done to his land and his people. Then, he lost his father. Everything was different after that. He fled, trying at first to escape but then finding his true calling. And his best friend. He missed Malang greatly. When he stopped to rest, he could see that smile in his mind. Always that smile, whether things were going great or it was pure misery. They had developed something closer than friendship. It was a brotherhood—something that could only be forged by constantly staring death in the face.

Nasir's heart was broken, but he pushed those feelings aside time and time again. Pushed them deep down and tried not to dwell. He didn't need any more anger in his life. He had enough to motivate him for a lifetime of revenge. Instead, he focused on his work, his cause, and his upcoming mission. Nasir was amazed at what he had become, more than he ever imagined, yet something was missing. He was more than a foot soldier; he was a vital part of Taliban operations. His life had meaning. Everywhere he went, he received respect. He felt like his father and that made him proud.

Yet, it was different. Everywhere his father went, they showed him respect, not only out of fear, but because he was admired rather than feared. He was always ready to help. Plus, he was smart, the way he cunningly helped the Taliban as little as possible, yet kept them on his side. He was a natural leader and diplomat. In this way, he protected their village. On the opposite end of the spectrum, Nasir could see the fear in the eyes of locals wherever he went. They all knew what would happen if they didn't honor his wishes.

That part made him feel less noble and more lost. These were their own people, the ones they should be protecting, not the ones they should threaten or exploit. Or even worse, harm or kill. They were fellow Muslims and worshipped the same Allah. For a second, he remembered that this was the very reason he despised the Taliban in the first place. He shook that way of thinking away angrily.

What choice do I have anyway? Either be part of the Taliban, and possibly die for their cause, or live a poor life of despair, possibly dying at their hand.

Either option was bleak. It had been months since he thought of his father and Malang, and longer since he had these feelings of guilt and self-doubt. Now was not the time. His mission was too important. This may be his greatest moment. The moment he finally met Allah.

Family that he was so close to in the past, now he hadn't seen in years. The truth was, as much as he was excited, he was also afraid. Scared of what they had become and how they were being treated. Scared of what they might think of him, though they would never say it out loud. He would know. They may not even accept him or, worse, openly despise who he had become. Of course, they could never say that either. But, he would certainly know, with their looks, their actions, and he could not bear to face that. Many families grew apart, but not like this. He only thought of them now as childhood memories. He may be going to his homeland, the place of his birth and childhood, but he would not be going home, as he vowed to avoid his family.

Basic training was rather simple for Nasir. He'd seen worse, even at his young age of twenty-three. Much worse. He didn't really get along with the other soldiers. They suspected what he was and didn't trust him. There was already distrust between many of the tribes in Afghanistan and he was Pashtun, so it was all the worse. In the eyes of many, that made him the Taliban whether he was or not. He didn't care though. That's not why he was there, and it wouldn't change his mission, or the effectiveness of it. Plus, they knew exactly what would happen to them if they said anything. There had already been talk from the Americans about their withdrawal. Everyone in Afghanistan knew exactly what that meant.

The Taliban would take over once again.

Knowing that, Nasir kept his eyes open for recruits. The outcasts, those who didn't like being in the Army, or just had a chip on their shoulder were perfect targets. He avoided the ones that had relatives that were killed by the Taliban and thus joined for revenge. His story to his fellow soldiers was simple and only half a lie. Nasir's father was a tribal leader that despised the Taliban. That eventually led to his death and Nasir fled. After having no meaning in his life, and wandering, he decided to do something. So, he joined the Army. Enough bought his story to allow him to mostly fly under the radar. Some even had similar stories that allowed them to relate to him. As a natural leader, many even began to look up to him. Nasir hadn't expected that, but he would use it to his advantage.

There was one particular American soldier that he met during their joint training sessions with the Americans: Sullivan. He was an older soldier who told of his time fighting Iraqis, not in their recent conflict, but with the US two decades earlier. He came up with the engineers. The same ones that Nasir would soon be joining.

Why not start my reconnaissance here? Nasir thought, and he quickly befriended the American.

It was easy to like him. The man had a level of energy and enthusiasm that surprised everyone around him. It was contagious. Always motivating and easy to talk to, people naturally gravitated toward him. It didn't take long before he was friends with most of the ANA soldiers. Nasir's commander loved to tell stories of fighting Russians on horseback and Sullivan loved to join in with his own stories. Back and forth they would go. Nasir just listened and smiled. His stories were better left untold.

CHAPTER 35

There was a low hum in Paul's ears, and he stopped breathing, for a lifetime, it seemed. Time stood still, objects flying through the air seemed frozen, voices—yelling and screaming—and popping noises were muffled, like someone had plugged his ears and dunked his head into molasses. Paul closed his eyes and shook his head forcefully, trying to piece together what had just happened. A sudden flash of light followed by an extremely loud bang, and a concussive force that shook their entire vehicle violently, Paul couldn't quite figure it out. Then it all came rushing back to him, along with reality. And fast. Paul peered out the windshield through billowing cloud of smoke to see that, other than the crew capsule, the lead vehicle was now in pieces, scattered all over the field next to them.

There was no response from the soldiers within.

Tink, tink, tink. Bullets sprayed the vehicles and gunners opened up from every vehicle. Frozen, Paul felt helpless. He pushed back his worst thoughts. He had to get to his guys. Were they all dead? He didn't know. Everything was a blur—he'd never been in an attack before, or an IED explosion. It seemed like he was immobile for an eternity. In reality, it was only seconds. One clear thought surfaced, and Paul stood up. MEDEVAC couldn't be called until they had their assessment. He had to act.

Chad flew by him, aid bag in hand. Chad always knew what to do, always had, since the moment Paul met him. Paul jumped up and was right behind him. Knowing that secondary IEDs surrounding the initial IED were a favorite tactic and a deadly killer, they had the driver pull up to the next vehicle. Across the roof they went, onto the next vehicle. Still no movement from inside the lead. Radio communication was obviously destroyed. Bullets continued to rain down from their vehicles, although it was now more sporadic with the enemy mostly suppressed.

Chad and Paul continued.

Almost there, they knew they had to close the gap. Paul and Chad crossed the road without hesitation.

No more explosions.

Thank God.

Clearing the wreckage, they finally saw them.

No blood.

Thank God again.

Chad went to work as if this was what he was born to do. By now, two others had joined them, helping pull out the casualties. Amazingly, they were all alive, coming out of varying stages of unconsciousness. Sergeant Russell took the worst of it, based on his location in the vehicle and probably due to his past history. He'd taken several IED blasts in Iraq. While the medics worked, Paul called in the 9-line MEDEVAC request, like he'd done so many years before, alongside Chad and JD. That was training, when life was simpler. Now it was real.

Staff Sergeant Underwood, Specialist Lopez, and Specialist Coleman were naturally shaken up, but otherwise passed Chad's questions and concussion assessment with no issues. They'd still be on the bird though, just in case. Better safe than sorry, especially with the first blast. It was hard to believe there would be more. They were just beginning their tour. The helicopter was now on the way. The enemy wasn't shooting any longer, which worried Paul. Just then, he saw another convoy of Strykers approaching from the opposite direction. Suddenly, a cloud of dust appeared, followed by another explosion.

How could we let this happen? thought Paul angrily, again wishing they had killed those men earlier.

This time, the enemy was nowhere in sight as the dust settled over the Stryker blast. Sunset was fast approaching and it was clear they'd be spending the night here. After an IED blast, it wasn't as simple as turning around and going home. Unless there was an extremely urgent threat, they would recover all their equipment before leaving. If it was too hostile, then they'd destroy the equipment. Luckily, that wasn't the case here.

Word came over the radio that there was an urgent casualty in the blast on the Stryker. Strykers simply weren't made to handle the IED blast like route clearance vehicles. Most combat vehicles were not, which was why route clearance was generally the first on the route each day. An urgent casualty meant that the casualty had to be seen within two hours in order to save life, limb, or eyesight. That instantly diverted the MEDEVAC from the 824th soldiers. Their casualty classification was luckily routine, meaning that their casualties required evacuation within twenty-four hours, but their condition was not expected to significantly deteriorate. It was hard to believe this was routine, but they were in combat now.

Praying, they waited, hoping the Stryker soldier would pull through. Again, they had that strange feeling. Something just wasn't right. The MEDEVAC response time was actually phenomenal throughout Afghanistan and Iraq and credited with saving many lives. What seemed like an eternity was really only a matter of minutes.

Finally, the MEDEVAC arrived. Sadly, it was too late for the soldier. Another dead hero. This time it was Lieutenant Edwards who they had partnered with only days earlier. A Wisconsin boy, just like most of them. The next time Paul saw his face would be in a photo hanging on the wall of the Brigade headquarters, along with dozens of his other fallen comrades. He dreaded that moment, but now he must focus.

Another helicopter arrived soon after, and the pair whisked the casualties away.

After locating as many of the parts as possible, they began the long wait. The next day, two wreckers would arrive and haul back the destroyed property. Until then, they'd set up a security perimeter with their infantry brethren and wait for whatever happened next.

Luckily, the night was uneventful, although this made Paul feel anything but relaxed. There was something about the silence that was eerie and had a hint of foreboding. The next day was different. The vehicles were recovered, the convoy was consolidated, and they were loaded up and ready to depart. Out of nowhere, with sudden, jarring explosions, mortars began raining down all around them. From where, they couldn't tell. Not able to fight back without first locating the mortar launch locations, they continued their departure instead. They had to be quick, but smart, because another common Taliban tactic was to distract the Americans and have them run right into another IED.

To avoid that, they'd let the eye in the sky do their bidding. Like clockwork, they heard the whistle from above and then the explosion. More dead terrorists and no more mortars.

They were extra cautious on the return trip, so much so that they used MICLICs. The MICLIC, or mine-clearing line charge, is a rocket-projected explosive line charge designed to clear conventional mine fields. First it is launched from a platform, or in this case an Assault Breacher Vehicle (ABV), courtesy of the Marines who had joined their return convoy. MICLICs are three hundred and fifty feet long and contain C-4 explosives all the way down the line. They can clear a lane of all mines and IEDs approximately twenty-five feet by three hundred feet when detonated. Cautiously, they used them at every danger area as they made their return. No other vehicles were hit, and no one else was hurt.

Slowly they rolled to what had quickly become their home.

Considering the chaos of Afghanistan, things basically stabilized once they returned. Entering the winter, many of the Taliban fighters would head back to Pakistan. Even though the majority of fighters were gone, the violence in no way stopped completely. It was just more sporadic and unpredictable. This gave Paul and his guys an opportunity to settle into a good rhythm and they became really good at finding IEDs. Excellent, in fact.

This quiet time also gave Paul many opportunities to catch up with Marie, who was lonely, but holding up well. Marie sometimes put the phone near Paul Jr. so Paul could hear his coos and squawks. Video chats were great but made Paul ache with sadness that he was missing so many exciting parts of his boy's life. These calls and chats gave Paul the motivation he needed to keep going.

During the winter months, there weren't as many Taliban fighters, but they were sneakier, often employing suicide bombers. Twice, Paul felt the ground shake as these madmen killed others by killing themselves. This really rattled the troops. Paul couldn't imagine strapping himself with explosives and pressing the button, with the express intent of killing others.

How do you defeat that kind of ideology?

Paul just couldn't understand it. One particularly gruesome scene would always haunt Paul.

A few weeks after that initial IED blast, Paul was out on mission on his birthday. They were conducting a humanitarian mission and trying to build goodwill. Sharing pictures of his boy to the owner of the market, Paul had won his trust. In doing this, he confessed that by meeting with them, the Taliban would now kill him if the Americans ever left.

As if to prove the point, just at that moment, the ground shook.

On the next road over, a vehicle-borne IED drove into a remote outpost, killing six Americans and wounding several more. By no coincidence, it was the same remote outpost that Secretary of Defense Robert M. Gates had visited only days earlier. It was also just down the road from what had come to be known as the birthplace of the Taliban. No doubt retaliation.

Just as they were becoming expert IED hunters, the Army had bigger plans for the men of the 824th Engineers. Soon, they would be training Afghan National Army (ANA) engineers. Nearly every infantry and cavalry unit they worked with also worked hand-in-hand, and shoulder-to-shoulder with their Afghan partners. The idea was to build the Afghan forces so they could secure their own country. Fighting was difficult in so many ways but easy to train. Everyone understood the basics. Engineering, logistics, and all the support to enable the fighters was the tricky part for foreign militaries. Soon, the 824th would be doing their part to rectify that.

CHAPTER 36

At the end of winter and the rainy season that followed, fighting season was quickly upon the soldiers of the 824th and enemy activity increased everywhere they operated. The trees were starting to bloom and so were the poppies. The financial incentive of the poppies used for the drug trade and the increased concealment of the vegetation contributed to the increased fighting. Plus, the temperature was rising, meaning the harsh inclement weather would soon come to an end. All these factors and more combined to bring Taliban fighters back to the region. With heavy NATO presence, Taliban factions were now afraid of losing control of their heartland in Kandahar Province.

Increased IED finds, blasts, and firefights, plus random grenades, mortars, recoilless rifle shots, and the occasional suicide bomber throughout their area of operations made the days long and unpredictable. Combined with the fact that Paul's unit would soon be training and then partnered with the Afghans on nearly every mission, they lived in a state of constant anxiety.

That unpredictability was what kept them all up at night. Each IED hit and firefight added to that anxiety. They had been lucky so far—no major casualties. Relatively small blasts destroyed vehicles, but the soldiers could generally escape with only minor injuries. There were concussions but everyone was returned to duty. For a route clearance company, that was pretty good.

And then it happened.

1st Platoon was travelling on a relatively new route—one they had helped build. They passed the sites of the two suicide bombers two months earlier and the mosque where Mullah Omar had allegedly started the Taliban movement. There had been several IEDs in this area and infantryman were constantly engaged in firefights. A few short weeks earlier, the 824th came across a bloody scene not too far from this same location where an attack using recoilless rifles had caused multiple casualties. Recoilless rifles were a common weapon used by the Taliban; they were effective because they could penetrate armored vehicles. By the time the 824th showed up on scene, it was too late. The 824th soldiers did all they could to help and save the casualties but there was nothing that could be done. Several brave infantrymen had made the ultimate sacrifice.

This time, 1st Platoon passed the outpost and was approaching a row of trees. They didn't see the triggerman who was waiting for this very moment. When they passed the row of trees, hell was unleashed on the lead vehicle as it rolled over an old buried culvert filled with explosives. This IED wasn't like the others. Rather than forty to eighty pounds of explosives, eight hundred pounds of premium grade explosives ripped the vehicle to scrap metal. Instantly ripped into two main pieces, other fragments were scattered throughout the surrounding area.

The other soldiers quickly cleared for secondary IEDs, while the medic, Specialist Bryant, rushed in, followed closely by Staff Sergeant Roberts, one of the 1st Platoon squad leaders, and their interpreter Abdul. What they found when they reached the vehicle was dismal. The soldiers inside were all unresponsive and they couldn't easily get into the vehicle. As with a typical IED blast, the vehicle was in thousands of pieces. However, unlike most blasts, the distance that those pieces were thrown was immense. That included what was left of the cab that housed the three unresponsive soldiers. The doors were jarred shut due to the angle it was lying on the ground. Other means of access were closed off by the jagged metal of the damage. They had to go in through the gunner's hatch, which was covered by Specialist Carter's lifeless body.

"We've got a pulse," Specialist Bryant shouted above the chaos.

Although unresponsive, all of the soldiers were still alive, for one reason only. Their seatbelts and restraints had all been properly fastened, thanks to the diligence of their leaders.

Without them, there would have been no chance for survival. Unfortunately, many of the units they worked with didn't bother with this safety precaution. Whether it was arrogance, laziness, or just thinking it would never happen to them, they were playing a game of Russian roulette. The brave soldiers of the 824th never took that kind of chance, and it saved their lives that day.

Specialist Bryant didn't have the time to contemplate the miracle of their survival. "Get me a knife or something to cut his restraint; all these guys will be going on backboards. I'm not taking any chances."

With patients, the combat medics were the ones in charge. Orders were passed swiftly down the line and seconds later, Specialist Carter was cut loose, being carefully placed on the backboard.

"They're alive, they're alive," Specialist Bryant echoed again to the growing group of 1st Platoon soldiers ready to help after he finally made it to Sergeant Stewart and Specialist Hill, "but this is going to be tough getting them out through these hatches," he admitted to Staff Sergeant Roberts as he cut through their seatbelts. "I'm almost positive at least one, if not both, have a broken back, but we can only fit one guy down in here."

"I'll do it," said Sergeant Evans, one of the other 1st Platoon team leaders. He was one of the strongest guys in the group and was getting in as quickly as Specialist Bryant was getting out. Two more soldiers were already up on the vehicle ready to pull them up as Sergeant Evans lifted.

"It's going to be hard, but you have to be as careful as possible not to jerk them around. Straight up. Same with you guys up here. Support his body the whole time and carefully get them on the backboards. I'll strap them in," Specialist Bryant advised.

Even though most had never seen a wounded soldier before, and certainly not one of their own, they operated with the experience of true warriors. Their training took over and they worked carefully and quickly. Meanwhile, the rest of the platoon was providing security under the direction of Lieutenant Dodge, waiting to repel a counterattack.

Luckily, it never came.

Staff Sergeant Collins, the new Platoon Sergeant for 1st Platoon, who had replaced Sergeant First Class Sullivan who was now working with the Afghan National Army, was diligently relaying the information from Specialist Bryant to form the MEDEVAC request. Everyone had a role. Even their interpreter Abdul helped position the backboards for the MEDEVAC arrival.

With that level of coordination, the MEDEVAC was arriving just as Specialist Bryant and the others got them to their designated landing zone. This was an area that was cleared of IEDs and open enough for a helicopter to land. Marked by a special panel just for this occasion, the link-up occurred quickly and they were in the air less than thirty minutes after the IED exploded.

But then something went wrong.

Instead of going to the Kandahar Airfield medical facility, they were brought back to FOB Alexander.

As soon as Paul found out, he rushed to their hospital.

"Where are they?" he asked, with First Sergeant Primer and Sergeant Price, their company medic, at his side.

"Right inside there, but you can't go in until they're—" the attendant never got the chance to finish as they raced inside. Quickly, they could see why they were not allowed inside; it was a small room and, with three casualties, the combat medics, and military doctors, there was barely any room for them. Paul didn't care, he had to see how his men were and why they were still here and not heading toward proper medical facilities.

Paul went to Sergeant Stewart first. He was covered with debris, his clothes were ripped in multiple locations, and he was strapped tight to the backboard that he was delivered in on. For some reason, he was being covered with some sort of plastic. Perhaps, to keep his body warm or cold, to prevent shock, contain the body, Paul didn't know. He almost thought he was dead at first, but his eyes were open and seeing.

Not knowing what to say in a situation like this, Paul defaulted to his usual positive approach, "You're looking good, Sergeant Stewart. You're going to be alright. Can I get you anything?" Sergeant Stewart's eyes moved, but he made no sound, and he didn't move. He hesitated, feeling unsure about what to say next. "We'll let the guys know that you're doing alright and be in touch soon. And we'll get those bastards for you." That last sentence came out without thinking. Seeing his soldiers like this, unsure of the damage, made him vengeful.

"Okay, you guys have to get out of here," said the female Staff Sergeant who was diligently attending to Specialist Carter. "The other helicopter is almost here, and we have to load them up and get them down to KAF."

Quickly, Paul visited Specialist Carter, who was coherent and responsive, and Specialist Hill, whose eyes darted everywhere in confusion, to echo his message of reassurance. Then, they were loaded up and gone. The trio lingered for a moment and then began the slow walk back.

"Hard to believe this is just the beginning of the fighting season," Primer spoke solemnly. "I always knew this could and probably would happen, but it's still a shock."

"Yeah, hard to believe," Sergeant Price agreed. "But at least they are alive."

Both looked at Paul, expecting him to say something. What they saw instead was a spark of fury, confusion, and guilt that they had never seen before. Paul remained silent, consumed in his own thoughts, blaming himself for allowing this to happen. Both recognized their own feelings in Paul's and carried the same burden yet said nothing as they continued their walk in silence.

After that flight, none of the injured soldiers would return to base to join their deployment brothers. They'd all be sent to Landstuhl, Germany and then sent home for recovery. Home to the largest US military hospital outside the United States, the Landstuhl Regional Medical Center was often one of the first stops for those severely wounded in Iraq and Afghanistan. It was a place no soldier wanted to visit. From the combat medics in the field, to the MEDEVAC crews and flight surgeons, up to the medical specialist at Landstuhl, soldiers were given the best care the world could offer. The military medical personnel saved many lives and performed medical miracles on a routine basis, but oftentimes there was only so much they could do, considering the extent of the injuries.

Sergeant Stewart would never walk again. Several vertebrae in his back were fractured. He'd be in a wheelchair the rest of his life. Specialist Hill also suffered severe back damage. It would be months before he could walk normally again, and he'd experience excruciating pain throughout his life. Surprisingly, the gunner, the only one outside the vehicle at the time of the explosion and fully exposed to the blast, suffered the least physical damage. After a massive concussion and flying through the air, Specialist Carter would carry the internal scars with him forever. Wounds like that never heal and never completely go away; the only hope is to learn to deal with the pain.

Brutally reminded of the ever-present dangers, the soldiers of the 824th needed to refocus quickly. This had made everything more real and showed them all what could happen. They knew it was only a matter of time until it happened again.

Another new road was being built, Route Jefferson, and of course the Taliban wanted to deny them access. This route was built to connect a remote outpost that was previously only accessible by foot. Cavalry scouts that patrolled the area were involved in daily firefights. The 824th experienced their share along this route as well. Multiple IED finds, RPG attacks, and some random firefights, but no casualties.

A week or two after the attack on 1st Platoon, Paul and Chad were on mission together again with 3rd Platoon, slowly clearing the route. This time, the Husky was out front using the ground penetrating radar for searching. As usual, it was getting a lot of false positives; they'd dig, but it would be nothing or just garbage. It was always better to be safe than sorry, however, and the dangerous thing was not the false positives, but rather failure to signal when an actual IED was buried.

Rolling along slowly, the Husky failed to detect an IED in their path. The explosion wasn't huge, but it was enough to rip up the vehicle and send the detached Husky cab flying. Since Huskies were designed to take a blast, the cab could come apart and usually the driver was fine.

Today was different.

Immediately following the explosion, Paul and Chad quickly exited their vehicle after the rollers had cleared their approach and the perimeter had been secured. The disorientation that Paul had encountered with his first IED was long gone. By now they had become more confident, and less cautious. This tendency is not the ideal situation, but an unfortunate reality that emerges the longer a unit is exposed to combat. They weren't complacent, but comfortable. Comfortable with the environment, the culture, the mission, the different situations, and the danger.

When they got to the cab, Specialist Murphy couldn't feel his legs. Just like 1st Platoon, their training took over. They got the spine board and called the MEDEVAC, all working together like a well-oiled machine, despite the adrenaline and fear pumping through their veins. Another broken back and another soldier who would carry his wounds with him forever. Once the helicopter left, the wrecker arrived to recover the broken Husky.

They quickly returned to the vehicles and continued the mission. It wasn't easy, but they must accomplish the mission no matter how many vehicles were blown up. A lot of people depended on them for their safety. Just as they began to move again, there was another explosion. This time there had been a secondary IED, designed to kill as they dismounted, which the rollers had not found the first time through. Paul and Chad, now safely strapped back in their vehicles, had been only inches away from that fate, having just walked through that very location. Thankfully, hardly any damage was sustained by the blast, only serving to annoy and anger the men in the platoon even more.

One week later, they were on the same route, with the same platoon and even the same Husky. Their mechanics, along with their contractor support, put together damaged vehicles with amazing speed. They were even better at recovering blown up vehicles. The 824th mechanics took special pride in getting them loaded as fast as possible. This kept the mission going and got their brothers out of harm's way quickly. While there were sometimes internal conflicts between line platoons doing the patrols and those supporting them, the 824th had none.

They were truly one team.

Today, there was a new driver, Corporal Cook, since Specialist Murphy was already back in the states recovering. As they rolled along, almost in the same place as the last IED, Cook stopped. This was now a hotspot and a place they checked closely. Thoroughly searching, he found nothing. Just as they began to roll again, the cab of the Husky turned into a blistering nightmare. Not from an IED below, but from a recoilless rifle shot that rang out from the wood-line over four hundred feet away. The rest of the platoon watched in shock before returning fire on that location. Just as quickly as it had engulfed the cab, the fire subsided.

Chad quickly exited his vehicle, fearing that Cook had to be dead. The cab of a Husky is relatively small, just enough room for one person to slide in. Any shot, especially one from a recoilless rifle, would surely cause massive, deadly damage. Only a miracle would save Cook. Off and running, Chad climbed up onto the vehicle, praying for that miracle.

Swinging open the hatch, Chad found Cook was still alive and responsive. It took a moment for Chad to realize what had happened, and it was the miracle he had asked for. Recoilless rifle bullets are designed to explode upon contact. This shot penetrated the window, right next to Cook's head. Due to the thickness of the bulletproof glass, the round's trajectory changed. Instead of a direct shot to the head where the round came in the window, it was diverted toward the windshield and dropped at his feet while exploding. Minor burns covered his arms and shrapnel punctured his hands, but other than that, Cook was relatively unscathed. Amazingly, he was even able to drive back to base.

Taliban activity was increasing. Nearly every day, they would find an IED. Or one would find them. Firefights occurred daily in every battlespace. To counter, US/NATO operations picked up as well. Kinetic operations, once rare, now involved 824th soldiers on a regular basis, both mounted and dismounted.

One day, prior to clearing their routes, they coordinated for aerial reconnaissance. At one of their usual hotspots on Route Red Bull, two men stopped on a motorcycle. They looked around, looked up suspiciously, and then walked a short way away to retrieve a shovel and three yellow jugs, which they used to house their deadly concoction. As they were beginning to dig and emplace their deadly explosives, Specialist Cooper, who was monitoring the situation, coordinated for a Predator strike. Seconds later, there was an explosion on the same screen they had been watching. One less terrorist in the world. His partner quickly grabbed what was left of the body and drove off on their motorcycle.

It was a nice, quiet day on the route after that.

Unfortunately, the Taliban struck back a few months later.

The CONOP request was a fairly simple one. At least, it seemed it would be. They were asked to clear a road that they cleared every day. Although this time they were asked to do it twice, this was still something they had done many times, so they carried on, unfazed. The plan was to travel from east to west during the first pass and from west to east on the second pass. The first pass would be their first route in the morning. Then, they'd finish their other framework operations before returning for the second.

The local infantry battalion had been conducting patrols through a known Taliban stronghold. This stronghold was directly linked to an IED emplacer, so if the infantry could eliminate this cell, they would ideally eliminate some IEDs. The 824th's sweeps would keep the road open for the infantrymen to freely maneuver. One of the core missions of the combat engineers was mobility and it was one they took great pride in. This road, Route Red Bull, was a busy one for the 824th. A grenade attack, several firefights, and a recoilless rifle round once passed through both sides of their Buffalo. There were also several IED attacks that destroyed vehicles and rattled the soldiers, but no serious injuries. Like most routes, they found many more IEDs than those that found them first.

Paul sat quietly, eyes always searching, body always on alert, but his mind was thinking about how he should have called Marie that morning. He tended to think that during every mission he was on. Today, he couldn't quite shake the feeling but tried to focus on the task at hand. Everything was going smoothly on the first pass. The hope was that the Taliban, especially the IED emplacers, would be pre-occupied by the offensive and unable to place IEDs. As the patrol came to their danger zone, or area of interest, the first vehicle passed by with no contact. As did the second vehicle, the third, the fourth, and the fifth. With only the sixth and final vehicle left to pass through, they thought they were in the clear. Most of the IED blasts occurred on the first vehicle, with only a handful on the second. In their experience, none had occurred on any of the other vehicles.

Suddenly, as Paul was about to call in that they had passed the danger area, he felt himself thrown forward, stopped only by his seat restraints. This violent upheaval occurred simultaneously with a concussive boom and violent flash. When the dust from the explosion settled, communication over the radio relayed that the RG-31 sat on the road, missing the front end. The attack was well-coordinated but not well-timed. Specialist Bryant arrived on the scene and found everyone, including Paul, in the vehicle was perfectly fine. The front of the vehicle took the brunt of the blast and was completely disabled.

However, they still needed to finish their mission. Within minutes, recovery was on their way with a new vehicle.

A short time after the QRF arrived with recovery assets, the route clearance package was on mission again and the QRF was returning to base with the disabled vehicle. The QRF, or quick reaction force, was a unit on standby, who could rapidly respond to developing situations. Chad had arrived in the new vehicle, replacing Specialist Bryant, who escorted Paul and the other soldiers from the blast back. Everyone seemed fine, but it was just a precaution. Oftentimes, traumatic brain injury (TBI) symptoms such as confusion, having difficulty concentrating, or behavioral changes aren't detected immediately. Also, the idea of a back-to-back blast for anyone was something they didn't want to experience. Better safe than sorry was how they treated anyone in an IED blast, no matter what the size.

As planned, the patrol completed their framework operations before returning to the same route again only two hours later. With the kinetic operations in the area and an IED attack already that day, they were again hoping for a quiet route. It had already been a long day, and this was their last road. They were ready to return to base.

Paul, after clearing his post-IED medical check, was meeting with the Afghan National Army (ANA) leadership when the platoon started the route the second time.

"Sir, another IED blast and casualties," reported Sergeant Reed, who was monitoring the communications with all their battle space owners, the infantry units that lived on and operated in the areas the 824th also operated, and the 824th platoons out on routes. "MEDEVAC was already requested so they don't need our medical support, but our QRF and recovery is getting spun up now."

Paul's heart sank during the initial uncertainty, never knowing what to expect next. Their staff knew the procedure by heart now, having learned through experience. Paul had a CCIR, or commander's critical information requirement, where he was to be notified immediately if certain events happened. IED blasts and wounded soldiers were both on the list.

He ushered a few of the ANA leaders, including a bright-eyed lieutenant named Nasir who Paul had taken a liking to, into headquarters, to await news and observe the decision-making process.

"What do we know so far?" Paul questioned, hoping for a minor blast but very concerned that MEDEVAC had already been requested.

"Reports for our patrol have been limited," Reed explained. This was standard protocol for 824th patrols since it was more important for them to communicate with their battle space owners and MEDEVAC during hostilities. "But, based on what we've received, the vehicle is badly damaged and the IED appears to have penetrated the cab."

"Shit, that hasn't happened yet, has it?" Paul asked but not expecting a response. Their faces said it all. Not even the eight-hundred-pound IED had penetrated the cab. When that happens, the soldier's body takes the brunt of the explosives rather than the vehicle. "How the hell does this happen? Didn't we just clear that road?"

Again, the questions went unanswered as all of them were thinking the same thought. They waited for the next report, helpless. Paul hardly noticed the ANA as they sat silently, watching.

Meanwhile, it was chaos out on the patrol. Those few quiet moments after the IED blast were quickly filled with shouting. Unable to maneuver, Staff Sergeant Roberts yelled for help. Looking over at Specialist King, he saw blood going everywhere. Spurting against the interior of the cab, the sight of blood momentarily paralyzed him. He felt himself going into shock. Their communication systems were down, and he felt helpless. His own leg was clearly broken, but he felt no pain.

Amidst the pandemonium, he found clarity. In order to save King, he had to act now. Pulling his tourniquet from his left pant leg pocket, the same place they'd been trained to carry them for months, he quickly assessed the wound, and realized there was more than one. His tourniquet would not be enough. Bright, red blood oozed out of wounds on both legs. Quickly picking the one with the most blood, he wrapped the tourniquet around the right leg and pulled the strap as hard as he could. Circulation was now cut off to that leg. Within seconds, the bleeding slowed. The left leg continued to seep blood. He grabbed for King's left pant leg pocket but couldn't reached it as it was pinned against the door, so he rummaged through the rest of his pockets, hoping against hope. Having no other tourniquet at the moment and unable to open his door, he cut his seat belt and crawled out the gunner hatch.

Specialist Howard, their gunner, was draped over the hatch, still attached to his restraint. Breathing, good. No blood, good. A quick diagnosis told Staff Sergeant Roberts it was a concussion. Priority was to get another tourniquet; he'd look at the concussion later. Plus, with their communications down there was likely no MEDEVAC request yet. Subconsciously apologizing for momentarily overlooking him despite his injuries, Roberts rummaged in his pockets for a tourniquet and this time found his target. He carefully moved Howard to the side as he prepared to dive back inside, then hesitated when he heard gunfire lighting up the distance as the infantrymen pursued the culprits. Turning away from the gunfire, knowing it wasn't meant for them, he saw Chad heading their way, followed closely by Sergeant Gray.

"King needs a tourniquet for his right leg," Roberts yelled toward the duo. "I've already done one for his left and have the other one here. Grab it," he yelled throwing it to Chad. "I'm going to find Lieutenant Dodge and relay the information for the MEDEVAC."

Chad took control. "Gray, grab me the morphine from the kit," he said with his usual calmness as they carefully climbed in the hatch. Noticing Howard, drifting in and out of consciousness upon entry into the vehicle, he quickly directed Gray to loosen his restraints. "I'm going to give King some good stuff to take away the pain and get this tourniquet on him, then we're going to get him out of here, so while I'm working, get Howard down and take his vitals."

Checking Specialist King as he talked, Chad knew the situation was grave. Despite all the blasts, this was the worst he'd seen.

It would take a miracle.

Chad closed his eyes for a second and prayed, *I know I don't do this often, but we need a little help, God.*

Calling for someone to bring the backboard from the vehicle next to them, they careful placed it on the opposite side of the firefight. Two gun trucks were securing that side while the other gun truck and Buffalo were watching in the direction of the engagement. Three-hundred-sixty-degree security. Now, came the difficult part. Hoisting King through the gunner hatch, they eased his inert body up and out. Gently, they placed him on the backboard.

"Let's get Howard on the other board now," Chad directed as Staff Sergeant Roberts re-joined the group. "What's the ETA on that chopper?"

"Enroute and coming from Alexander, so it should be quick," Roberts replied, already moving to help with Howard.

"Wait a minute, Roberts," Chad called as he limped away. "Let me take a look at that leg."

"I'm fine, let's get Howard and then you can check it."

"I think your leg might be broken and I need to take a look

at it," Chad insisted more strongly this time. "Sit down here."

"Look Snow, I know this is your job, but I'm not leaving my men. Not today and not for a minor leg injury," Roberts adamantly replied.

"I get that; I understand," Chad said. "I'm not asking for you, I know you would tough it out. I'm asking for him." Chad pointed to King. "He's going to wake up in another country and feel lost. He needs someone there to comfort him, a familiar face, his leader." Chad paused, watching Roberts' face. He was as tough as nails but had a heart bigger than most. Chad knew that.

Roberts glanced at King before turning back to Chad. "OK," he said simply.

Only minutes had passed since the explosion. All the casualties were ready, and the MEDEVAC was coming.

Over the radio, they heard, "Can't land, LZ not large enough, need alternate location, over."

"No!" shouted Chad. *This can't be happening.* "His pulse is dropping. If we don't get them out of here soon, he doesn't stand a chance!" Chad had barely left King's side since they pulled him from the vehicle, doing anything he could to help. At this point, that wasn't much. They needed to get him out of there or they'd lose him.

Roberts tried to stand up, but Chad held him down firmly with one hand and motioned for Gray to find their lieutenant and get an alternate location. There was no time to delay. Deciding on an abandoned school playground three hundred meters away, they quickly began moving in that direction.

The MEDEVAC helicopter touched down just as they arrived. Two attack helicopters circled above, daring the Taliban to begin shooting. No shots came. They loaded the three soldiers into the helicopter and just like that they were off. Chad watched as it took off, not knowing if he'd ever see Specialist King again.

The long, lonely wait began.

Reports trickled into Paul and the rest of the company slowly. 2nd Platoon had already been dispatched with a wrecker to help with the recovery.

"Multiple injuries, one urgent, MEDEVAC enroute, over."

Moments later, they discovered which vehicle and knew it was King, Roberts, and Howard.

The whole process was taking longer than it should. They had no idea why and couldn't do anything. They felt helpless. They could only wait for updates, worrying with unabated anticipation.

Finally, they received word from the patrol that they were headed back.

Paul greeted them when they arrived. He sat with them and listened to the debrief. Not many words were exchanged, so Paul just let these brave men shed their tears. He embraced each, knowing they would be right out there again tomorrow, putting their lives on the line to keep others safe. He'd never felt more pain and uncertainty, yet pride in his soldiers kept him going.

Chad was the last person he spoke to that night. Coincidentally, or maybe not, they both came to visit the blown-up vehicle before turning in that night. Dried blood was splattered everywhere. Examining the wreckage, they could clearly see why this had been worse than most. There was a massive hole in the driver's side of the vehicle and mangled metal between the seat and the pedals.

"Any updates on King yet?" Chad asked, knowing there probably wasn't.

Paul shook his head and Chad could see the sorrow in his eyes. Neither felt they'd see King alive again. "Nothing yet, but we'll be monitoring it all through the night," Paul replied. "The guys are going to wake me up if they hear anything and I'll let you know."

"Wake me up, too, will you, Paul?"

"Sure, I can do that," Paul said, turning to face Chad. "Thanks for what you did out there today. Without you and the other guys knowing exactly what to do and getting there right away, he didn't stand a chance."

"It's what we do," Chad said. He shoved his hands into his pockets and clenched his jaw. They both stood for a while, staring into the wreckage.

"It's more than that and you know it. I never did tell you, but that day you showed up at the headquarters, I was just thinking how we needed a great combat medic to help our team. Never thought it would be you, but I'm sure glad it was."

"Me too, Paul, me too," Chad said. He thought for a moment and then said, "This is what gives my life meaning, to make a difference, to save lives. Like I said, it's what we do, and I wouldn't change that for anything. Just wish I could do more."

For a few moments longer, they stood there in the darkness. Then, they headed back to their beds for a sleepless night of waiting.

Most IEDs destroyed the vehicles, not limbs or lives, but these were different. These changed people's lives forever. It was uncertain whether Specialist King would survive. Only the miracles of modern medicine could save him. Even if these injured men ended up being alright, physically, many others would never be the same, physically, mentally, or emotionally. All the IED hits stayed with Paul, but these in particular would never leave him. Altogether, nearly half of the soldiers had already been involved in IED blasts, twelve had already received Purple Hearts for their wounds, and nearly everyone received a combat action badge for engaging with the enemy. Now, only one area remained as a Taliban stronghold. It was the area between Route Washington, site of the eight-hundred-pound IED, and Route Red Bull, site of their latest tragedy. This area, with Route Jefferson in the center, was where the 824th would be headed next with their cavalry brethren.

CHAPTER 37

The friendship between Sergeant First Class Sullivan and Nasir continued after they arrived at Camp Arghandab, which the Americans called FOB Alexander. Nasir had a feeling this man had influence. And he was right. The way he befriended everyone at basic training, probably meant he did the same thing at his base, with his people. It seemed that his personality and ability to earn respect were the reasons he was sent to train with the ANA. Ultimately, he knew that Sullivan could help him get what he needed to accomplish his mission.

On the first night, after arriving at Camp Arghandab, they got settled into their new home. On the second night, they were introduced to the American commander, Captain Foster. He seemed sincere about working with them and helping the ANA take back their country. During his speech, he reminded them of the United States' own struggle for freedom. Most of his company was convinced and came away with a favorable impression of the Americans.

The Americans aren't sincere in trying to "give" us freedom, they are here to control us. Nasir didn't let his skepticism show, but he sensed something else from this commander. Foster's kindness could certainly be his weakness. Nasir and Sullivan were becoming better friends and he fully expected to get information from Foster as well. *Information which will be crucial to fulfilling my mission here.*

They didn't waste any time getting started on training. Nasir and the others were all assembled the next morning, waiting for training to begin. Two Americans and an interpreter walked in.

"Good morning, my name is Sergeant Russell, and this is my assistant Specialist Lopez." The American paused to let the interpreter translate. It took more time but was the only way that this type of partnership would work.

"I'll be the trainer for your platoon and going through all the training with you over the next few months." Russell looked at the interpreter as he paused again before continuing. "Today we'll be covering different types of IEDs that we've found, as well as TTPs used by the Taliban."

The interpreter began but then paused, turning to Russell. "What is TTP?"

"Sorry, I'm so used to saying acronyms," Russell spread his hands as he explained. "TTP stands for Tactics, Techniques, and Procedures."

"We've translated copies of our tactical standard operating procedures and there is a copy for each of you," Russell stated, pausing once again for translation. He was beginning to establish a rhythm. "And we will teach you each and every one of them."

"After we've completed that training, your platoon will go through scenarios and be evaluated." Sergeant Russell paused, looking each recruit in the face. Nasir made sure to meet the Sergeant's gaze. "Once you pass these tests, we'll be ready to do fully partnered missions together."

And I'll be ready to carry out my mission, Nasir thought.

Nasir knew that trust was the real underlying reason behind this training. Building that trust between two different worlds would not be easy, but it was vital, for both the American operation and for Nasir's mission.

"Alright, let's break up into two squads. Half with me and half with Specialist Lopez," commanded Russell as the training day began.

First, they would be trained on all aspects of the American operation. One of the first things would be learning how to drive Humvees. They would be using these vehicles to find IEDs. Of course, they weren't given the complex, fully up-armored vehicles like the Americans. Nor all their gadgets. Their primary detection device would be the good old-fashioned mine detector. On foot, they would patrol alongside the vehicles.

Naturally, learning to use these mine detectors was another one of their training objectives. Utilizing mine detectors was actually a very effective tactic, since most IEDs were command wire-operated, meaning someone was watching for them and pushing the detonator when they were in the right location. Find the wire, find the IED. And maybe the triggerman. However, Nasir knew how combat worked. That tactic would work for a while, but then the Taliban would counter. Pretty soon they would place pressure plate IEDs, activated when a person stepped on them or a vehicle rolled over them, along the routes they walked, or set up ambushes for the dismounted soldiers. When the Americans adjusted to that, they'd find something new. Nasir knew because he had done it time and time again, which is why they focused on detailed reconnaissance. That was exactly why he was here. Not only would they be taught how to find IEDs, but also exactly what to do when they did find one. And how not to get blown up in the process. That was the most important part.

As Paul watched the training, his gaze fell on Russell. Russell had not been chosen for this assignment at random. Neither had Sergeant Hughes from 3rd Platoon, nor Sergeant Rogers from 1st Platoon. First off, all three were carefully selected because they had certain characteristics to be successful in such a difficult situation. These included the ability to teach, the patience and understanding to lead soldiers from a different country, and experience. The other criteria were more circumstantial and less subjective. They had all been in three IED blasts or more between their previous deployments to Iraq and this current deployment and were beginning to see the cumulative effects. To protect the health they had left, they were assigned as instructors. Paul thought back to the stories he'd been told about their previous blasts in Iraq, and shook his head. How many more Americans would be hurt by these wars? And who knew what injuries lay beneath the physical ones, the mental injuries, the PTSD? Would it ever go away for them?

Russell was among the first soldiers blown up when they arrived in Afghanistan. Both he and his training partner, Specialist Lopez, had suffered the blast. The difference was that Lopez had been out on missions since the blast, but Russell had not. Headaches had persisted now for several months, despite several visits to the doctor. More than once he'd woken up dizzy and barely able to walk. His balance returned only after sitting for several minutes. Then, there was something wrong with his eyes. Sometimes light irritated them or made his headaches worse. He often threw up for no reason. Back and forth it went, with no way of knowing what to expect from one day to the next. Definitely too dangerous to go back on mission, but he still filled valuable roles liked these.

More than once, Paul approached him about getting the treatment he needed and sending him home. "No chance," was all he'd say. Paul didn't push the issue because he knew that he'd be the same way in their shoes. For their own good, he wanted to force them to seek treatment, and he often did, but he knew that these men wanted nothing but to fight and serve. Then, Russell would proceed to tell Paul about all the things he could do, like training the ANA. Every time, he'd assure Paul he'd get the help he needed when they got home. Every time, Paul knew that he probably wouldn't, just like the other soldiers who would live the rest of their lives forever changed. Paul resisted, but he knew Russell was right, even if it felt wrong. They had a mission and not all of it was outside the wire.

Sergeant Hughes was a special case. He had been on bed rest for weeks after a large explosion in Iraq several years earlier. Multiple soldiers had approached Paul, telling him how Hughes would get easily confused. Sometimes he would be talking about something and then completely lose his train of thought. Paul could have chalked it up to normal aging human behavior, but this was different. Hughes' train of thought rarely returned and it was what followed that made it scary. Instead of accepting the situation, Hughes would become angry and frustrated. It was like he became a different person. Each person told Paul, "It was never like that before Iraq," as if they were telling the same story. Paul knew that Hughes kept to himself now and preferred to be alone. Paul suspected that he suffered from severe anxiety and depression, but Hughes had never sought treatment, so his medical records said very little about his situation.

These were two of the most severe cases, but it was no-where near all the suffering Paul encountered. Nearly every week another soldier would come forward, talking about feeling differently, acting differently for no reason, or how things just didn't seem right, yet they couldn't explain why. They just knew that something was wrong. Each reacted different-ly, but all were noticeably frustrated.

Nasir spoke with the American soldiers at every opportu-nity. That was how he learned about Hughes, Russell, and Lo-pez. It still amazed him at how welcoming they all were. He expected a front, but not genuine concern. Nearly every week, he'd sit down with Sullivan and Captain Foster, along with his commander, to discuss how the training was progress-ing. The Americans were always curious when they thought that they would be ready to fully partner on missions. "After the training," was all his commander would say. No specific dates, no timeline. The Americans always accepted and were never too pushy. They had overall say over what happened and when training was complete, but they wanted the ANA soldiers to feel confident as well.

Another sign of weakness.

Inadvertently, their conversations led to discussions about life. Captain Foster, or Paul as Nasir came to call him, would talk about his wife and happily show off the picture of his baby boy. Each time he would pull out one of those pictures or discuss his family, Paul would always get sentimental. He wanted all Afghans to get the opportunity to raise their chil-dren in peace. Despite himself, Nasir always smiled and ex-pressed the same hope, although he knew that it was just a dream, not reality. Sometimes he'd let his mind wander to the times when life was simpler, when he just wanted to live life with his family, providing for them, learning from his father. But then he'd wake up from his reverie and realize the situa-tion he and his country were in.

Peace is not possible in Afghanistan, Nasir thought, with only the slightest hint of disappointment. He knew that most Afghans accepted this and harbored no distant American dreams of peace and prosperity. *However, once we are firmly in control again, there will at least be order.* Even with this knowledge, Nasir had to pull himself back repeatedly, trying not to think about the boy he used to be and what he used to stand for. He was different now, he had to be.

Religion was another popular topic, but the Americans treaded lightly. They were mostly curious about Islam, passages from the Quran, and how they had learned it. Paul was well-versed in Christianity and was quick to point out the connections between their religions. He was currently reading the Quran. This piqued Nasir's interest since he had never gotten that opportunity, although his father had recited many passages. The passages he recited were all from memory. They had no Quran, nor had anyone in his village when he was younger. He'd seen them since, but not many. That alone caught his attention, knowing that Paul had one in his possession.

"Islam is a gentle religion that has been corrupted by the Taliban, Nasir," he remembered his father saying many years earlier. "You must always remember what is right by Allah, not the Taliban, for Allah is your true savior. Do not be led astray, as a lost sheep. The wolves will be waiting."

Nasir had forgotten that until this moment. *You were right, Father. The wolves were waiting. But it was not the Taliban, it was the Americans that you should have warned me about. The Taliban remembers Allah; the Americans murdered you.*

According to Paul, Abraham was a central figure in both, and Jesus was highly regarded in Islam as well, though not their savior, as in Christianity. In fact, Islam and Christianity, along with Judaism, really worshipped the same God. That was something Nasir certainly had never heard before. Many of the stories were similar, and themes of peace, love, and forgiveness could be found throughout both the Bible and Quran.

When they would talk about their personal lives, Nasir would make up lies to share and build the connection. He would tell them what he thought they wanted to hear and knew that would gain their trust. He spoke of his family, desire for peace, and settling down to raise his own family. Nasir had become a master of deception, living two separate lives. However, these conversations about religion really sparked his curiosity and his responses were sincere, just as he had been with his father.

If only he had more time to learn from his father.

One thing that amazed him about the Americans was how much they cared for each other. Time and time again, they would come in, blown up from another IED. No one cared that they hadn't found the IED, that they had failed. No one cared that the vehicle cost nearly a million dollars. Their only concern was for each other.

Nasir remembered clearly the day that Specialist King and a few others had been blown up. They had been in a meeting when Paul first got the message of an IED blast. Not knowing the extent, Paul invited him to their headquarters as they waited for information. Partnered missions were hopefully starting soon, so Captain Foster, Sergeant First Class Sullivan, and their other leaders wanted to ensure they were included in decisions and information. Then he received some type of message that must have shown the severity of the injury. The training was over. Paul's only concern was finding out what happened and doing anything he could to help. Nasir lingered for a while, hoping to discover more. No more information was forthcoming, and knowing he was overstaying his welcome, Nasir decided to speak up.

"Captain Paul, will you find me tomorrow and tell me about King?" Nasir asked, and was surprised to feel a genuine concern. "I hope he is alright."

"Of course, Nasir. Thank you." Nasir could see he was deeply troubled, because his usual positive demeanor was gone. He just looked tired, and worried.

Nasir had difficulty sleeping that night. Dreams that had once haunted him now returned.

"Nasir, I think he's going to make it," Paul said, sounding optimistic when he found him the next day. "But it's going to be a long recovery."

They talked for a while longer and Nasir learned that both his legs had to be amputated, two fingers were gone, and his jaw was broken with several missing teeth. The internal damage was immense. Nearly every internal organ had some level of damage, but at least they were intact. Nothing penetrated his chest cavity, thanks to the body armor. Despite his extensive injuries, it was the blood loss that had almost killed him. Only the quick reaction of his soldiers saved King's life that day. Tears came to Captain Foster's eyes, but never quite fell as he described how his life had been saved.

After Paul left, Nasir was filled with mixed emotions. Nasir's concern had been genuine, and he was truly happy that King would live. He shared in Paul's amazement that they saved his life despite all the injuries. But why was he happy about that? Wasn't he here to kill them? It didn't make any sense. Maybe he needed to leave and return to the field. He was getting too close to the Americans. He was beginning to care and that was dangerous.

Again, the dreams returned that night, waking him in a cold sweat. Nasir knew the nightmares were bad but could never remember them once he was awake. That was probably for the best. Maybe they were of his father's death. Or about his family. Or of all the people he had killed. And their families. Or maybe it was about the people he was plotting to kill next. It was certainly nothing he wanted to remember or relive.

The concern the Americans had for each other also spilled over to the ANA, now that they were partners. Nasir could tell the Americans went above and beyond with the training. They showed so much patience and respect for their Afghan counterparts, taking the time to make sure that they understood everything completely before moving on to the next training topic. Plus, they didn't have to get to know them. There was no obligation. This was only business. They'd be going home soon enough. Yet they did and seemed to truly enjoy the connection. The Americans went so far as to build them a prototype of one of their Humvees with a mechanical arm, to make it just like their equipment. The Americans sensed the reservations they had with their light equipment, the Humvees, and tried to find a solution.

Finally, all the training was complete, scenarios were passed, and the all-important trust was established. They were ready to begin partnered missions. To mark the occasion, they all had a hand in helping to tear down the wall to the Americans' tactical operation center (TOC), making it into a joint TOC. Perfect. Now he'd have access to everything.

His mission was right on schedule.

CHAPTER 38

"Renegade, this is Pegasus, over."

"Pegasus, this is Renegades. Go ahead."

"We've got a patrol that would like to travel down an old route and we were wondering if you could clear it before they came down it? We saw you in the area."

No doubt they had seen their icon on the Blue Force Tracker. This GPS-enabled device allowed all coalition forces to see where other friendly forces were in the area. With the ability to designate enemy situations as well, it worked well to identify where units were engaged with the Taliban, possible IEDs, or other danger areas.

Lieutenant Dodge responded, "Absolutely. What's the route name?"

They weren't technically on mission today, but rather making a local supply run and picking up a couple of soldiers that needed to move between bases for training and coordination. However, the way Dodge saw it, you were always on mission, whether you were inside or outside the wire, but especially outside the wire. The Taliban had no rules.

"No name on this route, but it starts at EG3456239485 and ends where it links up with Route Washington. I'll send the coordinates, over," the unknown person behind the Pegasus call sign replied.

"Roger. We'll be there in ten minutes and confirm with you when it's clear."

Along with their typical vehicles, they had two additional vehicles today. A wrecker and a Heavy Expanded Mobility Tactical Truck (HEMTT) Load Handling System (LHS), which they picked up as part of this mission. This vehicle worked exceptionally well for hauling equipment but paled in comparison to the RG-31 and other route clearance vehicles in their ability to take an IED blast. In fact, LHS vehicles generally were not allowed on route clearance missions due to the high probability of striking an IED, but they would be passing by the requested route and aiding mobility was their mission, so Dodge decided to accommodate the request.

Approaching the road and leaving Highway 1, they didn't give it much thought. It was a short route, only a few miles long, and then they would be on their way back to base, back home. Perhaps the unnamed road should have been a warning, but their desire to help took control. Turning onto the road, they had no idea what was coming next.

It looked like every other route, only with no travelers. Another bad sign. Farmers worked their fields, several houses dotted the landscape, and a flock of sheep moved in the distance under the watchful eye of the child that trailed behind. Activity on and near the road, however, was almost nonexistent. Dodge leaned forward, his eyes narrowing slightly.

Something wasn't right.

Suddenly, they came to a disturbance in the road, a large, oddly placed rock, so they sent the Buffalo to dig. A foot or so down they found wires. A little more digging revealed four plastic jugs. Eighty pounds of explosives. Finally, they found a pressure plate device. There was no command wire here, which made sense, given the minimal activity. The explosives were perfectly placed so that when a wheel hit the offset pressure plate, the explosion would happen directly under the cab. Looking at the exact placement, Dodge frowned. *Someone had done some careful measurements.*

No one was qualified to blow them in place, so they waited for EOD. Fortunately, the wait was short. Some well-placed C-4 by the EOD robot destroyed the IED. They could still see Highway 1 to their rear as EOD departed.

On they went, moving more deliberately.

Where there was one, there might be more.

Halfway through the route now, they slowly continued.

Seeing Route Washington, they knew they were nearing the end. Specialist McNally, one of the drivers, was just happy to be out on mission. He rarely got to leave the wire. Mostly, he just wanted to be one of the guys. When they needed an extra driver today, he jumped at the opportunity. As they neared Route Washington, he and Sergeant Rudolph were taking turns telling jokes and laughing. They didn't know each other well but could already tell that they would be good friends.

This was the part of Route Washington where they rarely ventured. This battle space belonged to a different route clearance company. Since there were no tracks to follow, each vehicle took a slightly different path. The lead RG reached Washington first, turned left and moved ahead to stage for the rest of the convoy. The second RG joined them. Just as the Buffalo turned onto the route, a cloud of dust suddenly appeared behind them.

In front of their very eyes and before they knew what had happened, the LHS was a twisted mass of plastic and metal covered in desert sand.

All vehicles came to a halt. This wasn't supposed to happen. Not today. They weren't even officially on mission. As usual, Chad was the first one out of the vehicle. He had a sick feeling this time. Approaching, he saw the vehicle was destroyed. This was not like the others. Instead of the cab coming off in the blast, it was torn open. Chad looked inside, the sick feeling worsening. McNally was unresponsive as he checked for signs of life.

Looking over at the TC seat, Rudolph seemed fine and was relatively untouched. However, Chad could see that he was quickly headed toward shock. Chad nodded to himself. Shock was to be expected. He turned his attention back to McNally. The blast had occurred almost directly under him.

He hadn't stood a chance.

All vital checks confirmed Chad's initial prognosis. Just to be sure, Chad went through his entire repertoire, everything he could think of. He noted the multiple wounds, the amount of blood that McNally was losing. With tears pricking at his usually dry eyes, he frantically pulled several packets of combat gauze and tourniquets from his medical kit, but then slowly placed them in a pile near the immobile body.

No amount of QuikClot would save this man. He was desperate, but there would be no miracles this time. Nothing they could do would bring him back. McNally was gone. Chad got down on both knees, put his face in his bloodied hands, and wept.

Back at camp, Paul was wandering through the tents, making sure everything was in order.

"I'm sorry, Sir, but . . ." a voice called from behind him. Paul turned in that direction, "I'm the one who said I would tell you . . . We've had a KIA."

Paul looked up, and time seemed to stop, his thoughts stuttering to a halt. He stared at Sergeant First Class Rodriguez, trying to understand what he had just heard.

Rodriguez hesitated, averted his gaze, then quietly said it again. "KIA, McNally."

Paul shook his head, unable to speak as Rodriguez gave him the details. It couldn't be. The report must be wrong. A mistake. All patrols were done for the day. 3rd Platoon was out for a quick supply run. That was it.

KIA.

Why were they on that route? Did I know that? Should I have known that? Why didn't I stop them? Why was the LHS with them? This is my fault.

The sun was too bright, and his thoughts were too loud. He couldn't look at Rodriguez, couldn't control his emotions.

Paul turned, looking for a place to be alone. Their meeting tent loomed in front of him. Inside it was dark and empty. Paul collapsed to his knees, tears blurring his eyes as he sobbed, gasping for air.

KIA.

Every interaction that he ever had with McNally replayed through his head. The kid loved telling jokes, playing cards, and playing pranks on his buddies. He always had a smile on his face and wanted so badly to be a badass, to the point that he would beg to go out on missions. He gave his all when it came to training and duties, and Paul valued that greatly.

KIA.

Finally, he knew he must come out and face reality. One of

his soldiers had just been killed in action. There was so much to do to honor their brother, support the family, and continue to lead the men that he had grown to love. It wasn't until that moment that he really knew how much they all meant to him.

"Sir, what do you want us to do now?" Rodriguez asked as soon as he stepped out of the tent into the sunlight. His faithful Operations Sergeant, who had the difficult job of delivering the tragic message was still waiting for him outside the tent. Paul had no idea how much time had passed since he received the initial notification. They were all unsure. They hadn't faced this situation before.

"Get me a flight to Kandahar," Paul started, trying to gather his thoughts. He knew the body would leave for Dover that night. Dover Air Force Base was the stateside arrival for service members killed in Iraq and Afghanistan and a place no one wanted to think about. "Please let me know when the patrol gets back so I can talk to them. Might not hurt to get the chaplain either." He turned to another faithful presence. "First Sergeant Ponder, can you please work with battalion and start arrangements for the notification."

"Absolutely," he responded without hesitation. Like Paul, his eyes were still red.

Paul couldn't think about the family quite yet. There was too much to do and too much at stake. He needed to keep himself together. Thinking about the family would cause him to break down again.

Paul continued, "Pull the internet; no calls home until the family is notified." They had been through this drill before, too many times, for others, but never for their brother.

Even as Paul rattled off orders, it was all he could think about.

KIA.

Those three letters would forever be etched in his mind, as would the moment, the surroundings, and that sick feeling.

"Sir, I'll get a team going on the funeral arrangements as well," Ponder confirmed, keeping their communication simple. Hard conversations and tears would come later. Days, months, and years later they'd still be consumed by it. Everything was still too raw. Too unexpected. They had just lost one of the men they were asked to protect. How could they look McNally's mother and father in the face and tell them?

We have failed.

"Sir, they're back," Rodriguez said reluctantly.

Paul met them in the motorpool. No words would make it right, so he didn't say anything. Instead, he hugged each of his men as they exited their vehicles. Paul saw tears in each person's eyes. Even those who were rarely shaken, were now clearly troubled. Chad had a blank, paralyzed stare; when Paul hugged him, he barely responded.

When he embraced the last soldier, he looked deep into his eyes. Specialist White had been McNally's best friend. They had grown up together, enlisted together, and joined the 824th together. Their friendship had only grown from there. They shared a corner of the tent and helped each other through the hard times. Through times like these.

Now, he was gone.

"I'm sorry," Paul whispered.

Turning, he noticed many were still present. Paul wasn't sure why. Maybe they didn't want to face reality yet, leave their vehicle, leave each other, and acknowledge the loss. Or maybe they were reaching out.

Paul took a deep breath. Not really knowing what to say, he began slowly, "Specialist McNally was a great friend to many of you, a hell of a soldier, and always ready to help. He always gave 110%. I don't have the words to make this better, and nothing anyone could ever say will make this better. Time will be the only thing that can possibly ease this pain, and taking the fight to the enemy. The chaplain is here if anyone wants to talk, and of course, you can always talk to me. Cherish your brothers, men, and those you love, because they could be gone tomorrow."

As he finished, Paul's voice began to crack, and his legs began to shake. Recognizing this, one of the soldiers put his arm around him. Paul managed a nod, grateful for the support. Comradery this deep, between this many, was often only developed during sustained hardships.

One by one, others opened up, discussing the pain and shock of it all. The others sat back and listened. Processing this information was different for everyone. Paul just listened. His natural inclination was to bury himself away, see no one, and begin processing everything. But, he wanted to be there for his guys. Needed to be there for them. And he needed them, too.

Rudolph, still covered in blood, had helped bring him to the MEDEVAC after getting over his initial shock. "We knew this could happen, in the back of our minds. Heck, we've seen it happen to other units all around us and have had too many close calls ourselves." He covered his eyes with his balled-up fists. "I just, I don't know, never really thought it would happen."

After a moment, Sergeant Evans added, staring blankly in front of him, "Guess it's something we didn't want to think about."

"Why, why does this have to happen? I don't understand. He didn't do anything wrong, other than being in this god-forsaken place. I can't wait to get back out there and kill those mother fuckers who did this!" a soldier in the back angrily cried.

No one responded.

No one disagreed.

Everyone there was questioning everything at that moment. Their purpose here in Afghanistan. Why McNally and not them? Would they make it the rest of the way? Why would God do this to one of the best among them? Maybe it was completely random. Maybe they had no control over their destiny.

For nearly an hour, they helped each other through those first difficult moments. There would be many more hard days to come, but each knew that tomorrow was a new day. The missions didn't stop. They couldn't call in sick. The rest of the company needed them more than ever. The safety of so many depended on their success.

Paul looked around one last time as the circle became quiet with a silent finality. "If you guys ever need anything, or just want to talk, day or night, let me know. I'm always here for you, both here in Afghanistan and when we go back home, because we are all going back home together," Paul shared.

He had hoped that Chad would speak up, but when he looked around, he was nowhere to be found. He hoped he was doing alright, but knew he was probably hurting.

The night was crisp and quiet after they all left. Instead of walking back to pack, knowing he was leaving for Kandahar soon, Paul went in the opposite direction. Tucked in the corner of their small base was a training area that was rarely used. Paul went here to think. Usually, he thought about upcoming missions, brainstormed how to deal with a delicate situation, or thought about home.

Today, he could only think of McNally. Evan McNally. Why him? Why today? This random act of murder—did it help their cause? Did it mean anything to what they were trying to accomplish? His first instinct was revenge, just as many of the soldiers had expressed, but he knew that wouldn't help. In fact, it would only make things worse and hurt their cause. That was exactly what the Taliban was hoping for. Paul knew he must move forward carefully to prevent things from spiraling out of control. If not, the violence would escalate and they would no doubt lose more young soldiers. The Taliban would win. His approach could make all the difference. Quietly he whispered a prayer, asking for the strength to lead his soldiers honorably and to bring them all home just as he had promised moments earlier.

"Sir, I've been thinking," Ponder said as Paul came to the TOC to say goodbye. "We should probably keep White off missions for a while. Last thing we need is to repeat this horrible day because someone's mind isn't in the game. There are a few others that I'm watching closely, too."

"I think you're absolutely right," Paul agreed. "Thanks for speaking up and thanks for staying back here to get the funeral arrangements ready. The guys need you right now, more than ever."

"I know. I wish I could come with you to say goodbye, but one of us needs to be here. Especially now."

"Absolutely. I'm glad we're in this together. Take care of the guys, First Sergeant, and thanks. I'll see you tomorrow."

Then, he was off to Kandahar.

Left only with his thoughts, it was a never-ending cycle.

Away from the soldiers and alone, his thoughts turned to the family. He couldn't imagine if the tables were turned and it was *his* door they were knocking on, to tell Paul that *his* son was dead. How could he live after that?

The plane was staged at the tarmac, ready for Dover when they arrived. The casket was draped with an American flag when Paul slowly climbed the ramp. McNally's lifeless body was lying below. As Paul placed his hand upon the corner, it was too much. His knees buckled and he cried. Paul really didn't know how long. Time didn't matter.

Finally, Lieutenant Colonel Wabash placed his hands on Paul's shoulders. "I'm so sorry Paul, but we've got to go."

There were no more thoughts as they walked away. His questioning mind was replaced with emptiness.

CHAPTER 39

Nasir watched as they approached. Analyzing their every move, he needed to know exactly how they would react when he fired. They were all trained on the same battle drills, but each unit reacted a little differently. Hitting the ground was generally their first step, followed by returning fire. Some were slower. Some were more aggressive. Most were afraid to maneuver too much, for fear of IEDs. They preferred to wait for artillery or the helicopters. Nasir would be timing it all, planning as they progressed.

His Taliban forces had slowly trickled in from Pakistan and other parts of Afghanistan. They had grown to the point where they were ready for a decisive fight.

Not today though. Today, he was alone. He'd simply fire from afar and watch. Then, he'd disappear. Three days later, he would return. He knew what the Americans' next mission was and his forces would be ready. That was the beauty of his new-found access and the trust he had built.

Settling in a large grape hut three hundred meters away from the road, he had perfect visibility of their approach. These grape huts were prominent structures dotting the landscape and their slits allowed him to see everything. As he watched for their appearance, he could smell the grapes and dust mixing together in his nostrils, and it brought him back to that day. The day his father was shot, murdered by the Americans, amongst grape huts so like this very one he crouched in. Lost in his memories, he almost missed his chance.

Nine of them came up the trail with the robots that Nasir was tasked to stop. Another nine were making their way parallel to the first squad. Their objective was to cover the other squad's movement and they were slowly clearing each building they encountered. Rows of grapes would slow them down, but Nasir would have to think through that dilemma. He hadn't expected the overwatch. If he selected the perfect location, then the rows of grapes would provide an over-whelming obstacle. Mentally, he made his notes.

Wisely, they were all spread out and very alert. Everything that didn't look right, they'd check for IEDs. When it was a particularly concerning area with disturbed earth or at a crossroads, they'd fire up their robot and expand their search. This was why his leaders wanted to get rid of these robots so badly. Controlling the network of roads and limiting the American's ability to maneuver was vital to their cause. The robots were finding too many IEDs and the Americans were moving with confidence. That must stop. Slowly, methodically, they approached. He scanned each one with his scope. By now, he recognized many of their faces, although their infantry partners were new to him.

Scanning, he wasn't surprised to see Chad. He was always there, a true warrior. Of all the men, he respected Chad the most. He was always helping others; Nasir had seen him rush to the aid of the Afghans with no thoughts of his own safety. Continuing to scan, he was surprised to find Paul with them that day. Despite his operational intelligence, this surprised him. Although Captain Foster went out on missions on a regular basis, Nasir also knew that he was responsible for everything that happened to the company. With that, he knew that he couldn't be out there every day. Just as he had for Chad, Nasir had gained a significant amount of respect for Paul in the short time they worked together. It wasn't from his ability to talk about the Quran, or his knowledge of military operations, but rather his genuine dedication to helping others. Nasir had rarely seen that trait growing up, except in his father.

Seeing the two men gave him that unsettled feeling once again. The feeling had been stronger and more frequent lately, just like his dreams. Being embedded was harder than he had originally thought it would be. No longer could he separate these friendships from his mission to kill them. Now he knew them personally. And he respected them. They weren't monsters intent on destroying his people and culture as he had been told, nor were they imperialist pigs trying to take over his people's land. They had families. They had lives outside the military. And they truly cared for each other. They even cared for the Afghans. They had a mission to help Afghans take back their land for themselves and they were devoted to it. They believed in freedom for all. Most importantly, they trusted him. Trusted him liked a brother.

Pushing those thoughts from his mind, he refocused.

Remember Allah, Nasir. We act for him.

The group had made significant progress. They were nearly to the strike zone and this would be his only chance. Soon, the bounding squad would be too close. Still, that nagging doubt loomed.

Remember why you're here. Stick to the mission. We must reclaim this land. Reclaim it for Allah.

Nasir fired.

CHAPTER 40

Marie looked at the clock—two a.m. It looked like it would be another sleepless night. She hadn't heard from Paul again. At least Facebook was quiet. That was usually a good sign. There was usually chatter shortly after an event happened, as everyone scrambled to put together the pieces. Facebook wasn't even a thing when Paul had been in Iraq just a few short years earlier. Now, it was their lifeline to information. It also drove her nuts.

She loved the families. It amazed her how strong the bond had formed and how the deployment brought them together. She found herself looking forward to the Yellow Ribbon events, when she'd get to see everyone again. It was a time to let loose and share burdens with those that understood. It was the best kind of therapy. It kept her spirits up and was a reason to get out of bed in the morning, other than Paul Jr.

Then, everything changed when Evan McNally died. They didn't get any messages that day. That wasn't abnormal. There were lots of days where the soldiers didn't have access to internet or phones, days that they were out on operations and couldn't contact them. Family members also all understood that communication must cease when someone in their area died. They just hoped that the lack of messages wasn't because of that. Up until that day, it had always been another unit. Now she knew they weren't immune to that pain. That increased their worry and anxiety. Every time they didn't hear from Afghanistan, they began to worry. Now it was even worse than before, and Marie had trouble sleeping. It didn't help anything, yet here Marie lay at two in the morning, nowhere near sleep.

She thought of where Paul might be, of the men he led. She wondered if he would ever be the same. McNally's death had changed him. He was more distant now, more reserved. They still kept up their regular conversations, but there was no spark. Paul stopped talking about the missions, their Afghan partners, and the Afghan culture. He used to have so much passion for what he was doing. He loved the adventure. Now, nothing. Sometimes it felt like she was talking to herself on the phone, talking too much about stuff that didn't matter, that sounded silly in comparison to what he was going through. She kept talking, only because she felt that normalcy would help him stay connected to reality. That drastic change, this listless Paul, scared her.

Would he ever be the same?

Everything about Evan's death continued to haunt her. The phone was permanently planted on her nightstand. But since Paul left, it never rang at night. Not until that night. Paul had called her several hours after finding out, after the next-of-kin had been notified and the communications blackout was lifted.

"Hello? Paul?" she said into the mouthpiece, rubbing the sleep from her eyes.

She heard muffled sounds on the other end, what sounded like sobs.

"Paul? Is that you? Is everything okay, baby?" she asked, heart beginning to race. She sat up and pressed the phone to her ear to try to make out the words Paul was trying to say.

"Marie, he's dead. He . . . he died. He's gone. He's gone. He's gone," Paul said, repeating himself in between sobs.

"Who? Who's gone, Paul? What happened?" Marie asked, beginning to cry. She wondered if it was Chad, and hoped that for Paul's sake, it wasn't. She heard him take a long, shuddering breath.

"McNally. You remember him, a great kid. Such spirit, always ready for anything. It's all my fault," Paul managed to say, before breaking down again.

The words came out jumbled between his sobs, but the message was clear. Specialist McNally was dead. The news took Marie's breath away. For a moment, she didn't hear anything. Couldn't believe it. How many others would there be?

In the following days, she purposefully stayed away from

the news. She didn't want to know. Didn't want to see the death tolls or pictures of soldiers that had died. Didn't want to see crying parents and wives of those that had paid the ultimate sacrifice. Or the children that would never see their parents again. That was the hardest. That's what haunted her the most. She didn't want to be one of those.

Nights like this brought her back to Evan's funeral. Remembering the grave faces of his parents made her cry every time. Her heart broke for them. Losing a child is always a horrible thing. Having a child murdered in a distant country only added to that pain and confusion. Naturally, they questioned everything, and she agreed. What was this war really for? Was his sacrifice worth the cause? Why him? Why would God do this? Why did He take their son, and what was to stop Him from taking her husband?

The funeral was worse than she imagined. At this point in her life, she'd been to a few funerals. But the people had all been older; they had lived full lives. Their families knew the inevitable was expected. That's how it was with her grandparents. Of course, it still hurt. Death always leaves that painful void. But it was nothing like this. The shock. He was so young; too young to pay the ultimate price for his country.

So much left unfinished, she thought, remembering his fiancé off to the side, weeping uncontrollably. His life had really just begun. Then, it was all taken away in an instant.

These thoughts ultimately led back to Paul Jr. She couldn't imagine losing him. Just one year old, he was perfectly carefree of the agony that haunted her. How she longed for the carefree, death-free days. She cried every time Paul Jr. was glued to the TV, watching Dada read him a book on video, courtesy of the USO. She couldn't stop thinking about if Paul didn't come back. How would she do this by herself? What if their child grew up without a father? Not to mention, after several phone calls of one-sided conversation, if he did come back, what if Paul remained this different person, too changed to focus on his son? That wouldn't happen, would it? No matter how she tried to justify them, the questions persisted. The McNally's probably thought their son would come home, too, like all of the crying spouses did. No one ever truly thinks it will happen to them, despite thinking of little else when they are gone.

Marie's thoughts sometimes turned to JD and Lynn. Although Marie didn't personally know them very well, she felt as if she had known them for much longer. Paul's high school and college stories always came back to JD. Naturally, Lynn was in a lot of them, too. The way Paul talked about them they were the iconic match made in heaven. Soulmates. And now they barely talked. What changed? In a word, Afghanistan.

I won't let that happen. I will be ready for the change and do whatever it takes.

No matter what, she'd support him.

Just bring him home to me, she prayed.

CHAPTER 41

Reporting the progress of the day, Nasir went looking for his local Taliban commander, Hamza. He wasn't too far away, preparing for another mission in Nalgham. Americans were slowly encroaching there as well, and he wanted to make them think twice.

It didn't take Nasir long to find him. He was the kind of man that drove fear into people wherever he went. They all knew he was there, where he had been, and where he was going. But, they'd never tell the Americans. They knew who truly controlled the land. Those who would stay long after the Americans left.

"Nasir, grab that shovel and pretend to rake that field," he said with a sneer. "I have the feeling we're being watched."

And he was right. Not too far away, an American patrol was progressing along the river valley. "I'll get your update in a minute, but first you must watch this."

A boy who couldn't have been more than eight years old emerged from the house. His eyes were wide with fear and uncertainty.

"Strapped to his chest is enough explosives to take out at least two of those Americans. Then we'll talk as we head the other way," he said matter-of-factly. Nasir watched in horror. Of all the killing he had seen in his life, this was too much. This was going too far. Several other children were approaching the soldiers as well.

From what he'd seen, some generous soldiers threw water bottles to the children who approached them, others gave out snacks or the highly sought after calom. Off those children ran, proud to show off their treasures and trying not to get beaten and have it taken away.

More than once Nasir had witnessed the Americans give

something with the best intentions, like a soccer ball, only to have the kids all but destroy each other to claim the prize. Usually, the biggest and toughest emerged victorious, or a village elder intervened. That's the way it went in Afghanistan. Children learned at a young age that they got what they wanted through violence.

The boy had already begun walking toward the soldiers asking for a calom. Nasir knew his goal was to get close enough so his master could detonate the bomb. The Americans had devices to stop the signal, but Nasir had recently discovered that they were rarely using them because they were unreliable. He felt a pang of regret now that he had revealed that intelligence, now that his boss was about to exploit the newfound weakness at the expense of a child.

The soldiers were mostly ignoring the children, trying not to get distracted. They were focused on their mission. This was a hot area and they must be on full alert.

Slowly, the walking child-bomb made his way toward the patrol. Fear was all over his face. Every step closer, it got worse. He didn't want to die. Despite his obvious apprehension, it was doubtful the soldiers would notice. Their eyes were focused on the horizon. Looking for the enemy, they overlooked the children. Children were everywhere and running amongst them. As the human sacrifice moved toward them, Nasir saw many of the children begin moving away from the soldiers. They sensed something was wrong, even if they didn't understand the cause.

"Follow me, Nasir," Hamza commanded. He moved toward a building tucked on the edge of the wood line, no doubt heading for concealment.

Nasir hesitated.

"Nasir, you don't want to be around when this bomb goes off."

Still shocked, Nasir knew he was right, no matter how badly he felt. They were unsure how the soldiers would react. They would likely begin questioning, probably even detaining, bystanders. Maybe putting them into their machines. Less disciplined units would begin shooting wildly, with no intended target. Stray bullets didn't discriminate. They could kill him just as easily without intention. Pausing one last time, he hesitated, then turned his back and followed the commander.

As they walked, Nasir distantly wondered how this situation happened. He knew it could be any number of reasons. An orphan being exploited. A family offering a sacrifice for protection. Perhaps, it was to save others. Maybe it was a punishment. Retribution for the family or tribe turning their back on the Taliban. Nasir couldn't pretend he hadn't seen this before. Never this young though. Never with so much fear in a child's eyes. Why? He could understand how, but he couldn't understand why? Surely, there were other ways to defeat and kill the Americans.

What would Allah think?

Nasir didn't have time to ponder. Just as they stepped into the abandoned buildings, the child reached the soldiers. One soldier stopped, lifting his hand in a fist. The whole patrol halted. The alarm on the child's face grew. They knew something was wrong. Slowly, they backed away, but Hamza was watching their every move. Pressing the button, he watched with what could only be called a smile. Nasir's breath caught as a wave of nausea swept over him. Three soldiers lay on the ground. Two weren't moving and the other was grabbing his groin, screaming. The child was unrecognizable.

"Nasir, what are you doing? Follow me, you fool."

He couldn't move. Lost in a trance, he once again tried to rationalize. *Why?* But he would find no answer. The soldiers were spreading out, and, as predicted, beginning their questioning. No doubt reinforcements were on the way from sky and land. The sound of gunfire finally broke his trance. Not sure where it was coming from, he didn't wait to find out. He turned and left in the opposite direction, following the man who had created this destruction.

"What was that?" Hamza screamed. "Are you trying to get us captured or killed? Haven't you ever seen someone die before?"

Of course, he had, and Hamza knew that.

Nasir remained speechless.

"Well, speak up, you fool." "Fool" was his favorite insult

and Nasir had heard it many times, but never as much as today. When Hamza demanded answers, he usually got them.

Finally, Nasir spoke, "He was only a child."

"Is that your problem? That child wanted to die to glorify Allah and look at the glory he brought. Is it the child or killing the Americans that is bothering you? Perhaps you are getting too close to the enemy? Perhaps we picked the wrong man for the job . . ." Hamza's questioning trailing off.

There, he said it. The thing that consumed Nasir's thoughts, haunted his sleep, and made him doubt everything. He must not let Hamza know of his doubts.

"Of course not. It brings me great pleasure to see the Americans die and I look forward to seeing their grieving faces when I return. But the child. Surely, there is a better way. Isn't my mission enough and yours?"

"No. Nasir, your heart is too big, just like your father's. Always has been. You're a dreamer. You don't live in our reality. Now tell me your plan."

Hamza didn't realize what he had done. That was the worst thing he could have said. The reference to Nasir's father changed something deep down for Nasir. Or perhaps didn't change it, so much as returned something to his spirits.

Nasir replayed the highlights of the day and carefully laid out his plans. Little did Nasir know, those plans were about to change.

CHAPTER 42

That night the nagging feeling wouldn't leave Nasir. Watching Chad, Paul, and the rest of the 824th approaching in his scope had been unsettling. He pulled the trigger, but fired well over their heads, studying their reactions. They counterattacked effectively, but by the time they reached the grape hut he was nowhere to be found. Even though he hadn't planned to kill them this time, he was beginning to wonder whether he'd be able to go through with his original plan. Knowing his next mission was only three days away left little time for doubt.

Then, he'd be there to kill.

Watching the child kill soldiers as a homemade bomb was too much. And the sneer of his master as he pressed the button. Like most, Nasir didn't respect the man, but he feared him. The man wouldn't hesitate to use Nasir as one of his pawns. Just like the child.

How many sacrifices had there been? thought Nasir. It didn't matter. It was all for Allah. That was why he continued on. To glorify Allah.

He had long ago forgotten the dreamy boy of his youth. He had long ago forsaken what was left of his family. What would his father think? Maybe his father would at least have been proud of his soldiering skills and his dedication to Allah. Allah was always first for his father as well. What would he say about the Americans?

They killed him, he thought angrily.

Of course, he wanted his revenge. But he couldn't imagine any of the Americans he worked with killing in cold blood. They showed restraint. Even after an IED blast, they didn't fire randomly. They only fired when they were under fire. He knew he couldn't do the same. He wouldn't. In fact, in three

413

days he'd be the one to pull the trigger first and watch the Americans drop.

Again, he saw Chad's face, and Paul's. Then, Malang and the face of the slain American soldier, Evan McNally. Then, his father's again, always his father's. So much death. So much pain and confusion. This mission was different. He had never known those he'd killed before. Never thought about what they were like, why they were here, and their families. Never thought about the fact that they were someone's father or son.

The hour was late, and sleep eluded him. Every night he'd see death. Recently, he began to imagine the lives of each one of the tick marks on his rifle.

Were their loved ones mourning their deaths, just as he mourned his father?

Over and over again, he envisioned each of their deaths along with all the loved ones he'd lost. He'd relive them as if he was there. These painful thoughts were hard, but the nightmares were even worse. Now he could remember the dreams.

Sometimes, he would see his own death. Different every time, it was always brutal and usually at the hand of Hamza. He'd make it slow, painful, and tortuous for disobeying. What was worse was when, before he killed him, he'd go after his family. Slowly, methodically, he'd torture them until the life left their bodies and Nasir couldn't help them. Somehow, his father would still be alive in his dreams, but unable to stop them either. With that sneer, Hamza turned back to Nasir, advancing toward him. That's when he would awake, drenched in sweat, breathing rapidly. There would be no more sleep. Night after night, he endured this struggle. The dreams were never exactly the same, but always painful. Nasir knew that these nightmares would become a reality if he failed his mission. As he had, time and again, Nasir wished his father was here to offer his wisdom.

He closed his eyes and fell asleep. Somehow the deep sleep that had eluded him for many months finally came.

Nasir found himself in the grape fields. It was night. He looked around, sure he had lost something. His rifle? A water jug? Nasir looked up and he was there. His father. Whole and alive. Nasir caught his breath, reached out his hand, and then he stopped.

His father wasn't alive. It was just an image.

The face was still the same though, warm and loving. So was the voice. "Nasir, my son. I've been watching you. Look at the man you've become. I'm very proud. You are truly my child."

Nasir closed his eyes, hoping his father wouldn't see his guilt, wouldn't see who he had actually become. His father paused, and Nasir glanced up. His father knew. His father seemed to be looking directly into his soul and seeing all the horrible things Nasir had done and endured. But his eyes were still gentle and loving.

"Nasir, you harbor too much anger, too much pain. And it's because of me. *Listen*, Nasir. Listen to Allah. This is something he taught me so long ago."

Nasir reached for his father again, but the image was gone.

Before he could speak, there was another voice. Not deep and powerful as he had imagined, but comforting and thoughtful. It reminded him of his father.

"You follow me faithfully, but you follow me blindly," Nasir's true master began. "'O, you who believe! Enter absolutely into peace. Do not follow in the footsteps of Satan. He is an outright enemy to you.'"

"Those are my words written in the Quran. Where is this peace, Nasir? Muslims are killing Muslims, both in your land and beyond. You all worship the same Allah. You all worship the same God—Muslims, Christians, Jews—yet use religion as an excuse for war."

Enter absolutely into peace. The words were familiar. Nasir suddenly remembered his father telling him that. *Enter absolutely into peace.* He had forgotten. With all the chaos and hatred since his father's death, he had lost sight of that. Now he remembered and he'd never forget again.

"Nasir, I want you to spread my message. My real message. It's the only way to make change, the change you've dreamed of since you were young. It won't be easy, but you know what to do."

Nasir found himself shaking his head, trying to understand.

"I don't know what to do," Nasir pleaded. "I'm not strong enough to do what you ask. I've never even read the Quran. All I know is what my father taught me and the words of my mentors. How can I spread your real message?"

"I know you've never read the book, like so many of your countrymen, but understand this, Nasir. The book is powerful. People can find words within it to justify nearly anything. Because of that, some people use it for evil. For manipulation. They twist the message. That is exactly what has happened in your country. But that is not why the book is there. It is to promote peace and love throughout the world. This is the message I want you to find and the one I want you to spread. I'm calling on you to end this cycle of violence. You don't need to read the words to feel that message. Remember that feeling you had as a child. Find that and listen to your heart. Lead your nation to peace."

Bolting upright, Nasir looked around the small room with relief. The field was gone, and so was the voice. It was just a dream. This one wasn't like the others, though. Despite his deep sleep, he was now wide awake. Walking outside, the night air was cool on his skin. Extremely hot days made even warm nights feel that way. He looked around. *What am I doing here? Not just here at this moment in time, with my mission at hand. What am I doing here on earth? What is my purpose? How did I get to this point? My choice or circumstances?*

"It was just a dream," he whispered, as if trying to convince himself.

Just a dream. But it had seemed so real. His father had been there, almost close enough to touch. And then Allah. Had he really asked him to spread his word? And lead his country to peace? Even though it would likely mean death.

Death here on earth, perhaps, but eternal life with me, a thought came as if it was a whisper in his ear. *Faith is not always easy, Nasir. Remember, if Allah is on your side, none can overcome you.*

Although he didn't know how he would do it, Nasir knew he had to follow Allah. Despite the dangers, Nasir was filled with peace. He had a new mission.

CHAPTER 43

Three days later, Nasir was ready. The sun hadn't risen yet and the sky was just becoming light when he was again set up in a grape hut overlooking the Americans' expected approach. It was a different grape hut, but the concept was the same.

Only, this time, one thing was different.

Around Nasir, a large force of Taliban fighters was waiting in an ambush. Based on his reconnaissance, he knew exactly where to place them. They now listened to his every word. He had earned their respect. Nasir also knew the most opportune moment to fire to catch the Americans off guard and pin them down at a vulnerable location. His fighters were in place and ready.

Now, they would wait.

Just as before, the Americans were staggered along the road, using their IED finding robots as they approached. Scanning in his scope, he could see their faces clearly. Nasir stopped scanning for a second. Chad was there, of course. Nasir knew he would be, out with his guys. He always was, no matter what.

The day was warmer than it had been only three days before. And yes, here was the other squad bounding along with the main patrol. This time they were on the opposite side. That's exactly why he did his reconnaissance. It was difficult for the supporting squad to provide effective fire on the opposite side. On a typical day, this would give them maximum time to inflict casualties with their ambush. But this was not a typical day. This was a new day. A new beginning. This was the moment he had trained for during the last year. It was the mission he had trained for all his life.

Twenty more steps and they'd be in the ambush.

Pausing now, they looked around as if they were being watched. Nasir knew better and so did the soldiers. Armed and on patrol in a foreign land, they were always being watched. Especially in Afghanistan. Oftentimes, the person doing the watching was waiting to pull the trigger or push the button. Many times, they couldn't be seen. The ones that could be seen were rarely a concern.

Whatever apprehension they had passed, and they continued.

Ten steps.

Now, Nasir had the two operators in his scope. The robotic IED finders each had a remote control. One of the operators would steer the machine along the trail with their rollers. That machine was out front in the hopes that it would set off a pressure plate IED before they were on top of it. The other machine had a flail which was used to tear up the ground when they came to a hotspot. This was how they dug up IEDs of all kinds, but especially those controlled by a command wire, since the roller didn't work on them. This was also the exact reason Nasir's commander wanted them eliminated from the battlefield. They were simply finding and destroying too many IEDs.

Five more steps.

Nasir focused in on the lead operator. He recognized this soldier but couldn't place him. He didn't recognize the other operator.

Three more steps.

Yes, of course. Now, he remembered. This was the soldier that was so excited when they first met during training. He was teaching him what to do when they needed to dismount their vehicles, how to look for secondary IEDs.

Two more steps.

He's about my age, Nasir thought distantly. The American couldn't have been more than twenty years old. Young for America. Old for Afghanistan. It's amazing how war and violence aged their people.

One more step.

This was the moment Nasir had been selected and trained for. But, he was on a mission from Allah now. He fired. Just as quickly, he fired again. Within seconds, the wood line to his right lit up in gunfire. Without hesitation, the Americans opened fire in return.

Nasir's plan worked perfectly. He placed his Taliban fighters on a slight rise overlooking the trail. Hidden in the vegetation, Nasir would wait until the Americans were in front of their location. His accuracy would make the initial kill, bogging them down in the kill zone while his Taliban brethren coordinated their ambush. It had worked perfectly so many times before, but Nasir had another plan today. A higher plan from above. He fired the same as always but well over the heads of the operators again. They were certainly scared, but they were alive.

Instinctively, his Taliban forces fired but couldn't see the Americans. Nasir had fired early, when they were around the bend. The Americans couldn't see them either. The firefight raged on, but it was relatively ineffective for both sides. The Americans let loose with their grenade launcher, finding the Taliban location. One was hit and instantly killed. Another took shrapnel through the stomach. Two more moved positions to find the Americans. They were hit with gunfire when they stood.

Just as quickly as the fight started, the Taliban began their retreat.

Everyone was retreating except the wounded fighter. He didn't follow the others. Intrigued, Nasir watched from his grape hut. Usually, Nasir would fire his two shots and disappear. He wanted to see what happened. The wounded fighter was now the only one left. All others had retreated, taking the three dead fighters with them. The fighter placed his weapon in some thick brush. Instead of following his comrades, he staggered toward the Americans. The whoop-whoop-whoop of helicopters could be heard in the distance. With almost a dozen weapons pointed at him, he raised his arms.

"Look at his chest," cried Chad. "He's wounded."

With the interpreter and two others, a few of the soldiers approached the man.

"Check him for weapons," Chad directed, as he began questioning him through the interpreter.

"He's clean," the search team declared. As soon as Chad heard those words, he jumped up and began helping the injured man. Cutting off his shirt, he quickly bandaged the wound to stop the bleeding.

"Says he lives over there and was hit by a stray bullet when the fighting began," the interpreter said, giving Chad a skeptical look.

"Of course, he was," Chad agreed in a similar tone, both assuming he was Taliban. "Doesn't matter though. We take care of them just like we would our own."

To prove the point, the supporting squad had just arrived on scene and were already calling in a MEDEVAC. Just as they would for their own.

Nasir sat back and smiled. There was nothing fake about his smile this time. This smile felt good. He finally understood his true purpose. While he was sad at the loss of the three men, Chad proved that he had done the right thing. Now he must continue his mission at all costs and lead his nation to peace. He knew that he'd have to explain what had gone wrong, and would probably be blamed for it, but hopefully Hamza was feeling merciful. Nasir knew he was valuable as a sniper, and the men looked up to him.

When he got back to his camp, just as he predicted, his leadership were furious with him.

"How did the fight go so wrong? Why did you fire so soon?" one commander shouted at him.

"How could you have missed? You had a clear shot, nothing in your way, how is it that our best sniper would miss such an easy target?" another raged.

"We lost some good men because of you, I thought you were supposed to be the best!" the first commander continued. He stepped toward Nasir with a menacing look. Nasir knew he was not safe from their anger. Luckily, just then, Hamza stepped in, holding up his hand to stop the angry shouting.

Pulling him aside, Hamza said, "Nasir, you've done a lot

to help our cause, but if I ever see that again, I'll throw you to the wolves." Nasir nodded, smiling on the inside. He remembered who his father thought were the real wolves. Hamza left, muttering something Nasir couldn't quite catch about the Americans. The other commanders stood glowering at Nasir but said nothing further to him, instead choosing to make plans for another ambush. He was safe, for now.

How quickly one goes from idol to target, Nasir thought.

While they conferred with each other, Nasir noticed something he hadn't before. Skepticism and doubt. One of the Taliban soldiers, sitting beyond the debating leaders, had the look that Nasir knew so well. He knew it because he had felt it most of his life. He would approach this soldier, befriend him, and give him an avenue to express his doubts. That was an avenue Nasir never had. Converting this soldier and having him join Nasir's cause would be his next objective in his journey for Allah. That would be his first checkmark to promote peace. He hoped that he would have more checkmarks than he accumulated from his old lifestyle when his journey was through. Nasir vowed to atone for the lives he had taken.

CHAPTER 44

Looking back, Paul thought Nasir had seemed a little strange that morning. Nasir had come into their TOC, which wasn't unusual. However, his demeanor was different. It was almost as if he was saying goodbye. He had a certain way about him. A purpose. Paul hadn't really thought about it then, but he was certainly thinking about it now. That was the last time they had seen Nasir. It wasn't uncommon for ANA soldiers to go AWOL, but no one expected it to be Nasir. Now there were rumblings from the ANA community that he had been an insider. A member of Taliban all along.

The day Nasir disappeared, they had encountered a relatively short but intense firefight. No one got hurt. *Thank God.* The ambush appeared well-coordinated, but poorly executed.

Maybe there was a reason for that, Paul mused now. Interestingly, with Nasir gone, the ANA had also begun striking IEDs. Maybe the rumblings were true. But why had the well-coordinated attack failed that day? There had to be more to the story. Deep down, Paul couldn't help thinking that if Nasir was indeed Taliban and had been involved in the attack, he might have had a part in the attack's failure to cause any American casualties. They'd never know for sure.

Sitting at the flight line, waiting to go home, Paul was trying to put everything into perspective. He leaned back in the uncomfortable waiting room chair and propped his feet up on his duffel. After the botched ambush, they had a few more IED blasts, but nothing major. Nothing that would change people's lives physically. The 824th had already made more than their share of sacrifice, but Paul still felt lucky. It could have been worse and was for so many other units. Paul thought about each of their losses as he looked down the line.

The soldiers who remained had their wounds as well.

These wounds weren't visible. They remained hidden, and would emerge as something else, at another time. Some symptoms were already surfacing. He could hardly get two words out of Chad, and many of his usually optimistic soldiers mostly kept to themselves now instead of the rowdy games of horseshoes or cards they used to indulge in. Even those emotions and symptoms that were buried deep would re-emerge at some point. Everyone would deal with their demons in their own time. Paul hoped they would reach out for help when that time came, even though he knew he would struggle to do the same.

Paul was proud of what they had accomplished. All of them had done their job and done it well. They cleared over one hundred IEDs from the battlefield, possibly saving that many lives or more. They had built strong relationships with their neighbors that helped them all succeed. He thought fondly of all the military coins and gifts that these neighbors had given them as a token of gratitude. They also reached out to the Afghan people at every opportunity. He remembered bringing supplies to a local school, with lots of treats and sports equipment for the kids. The smiles on the kids' faces had made him feel so good and had reminded him of the little baby boy he was missing at home. This initiative won recognition all the way up to General Petraeus, commander of Afghan forces. The 824th had perfected using DOK-INGs, the robotic mine clearance systems, to clear IEDs for dismounted soldiers. That tactic was now being used throughout the Afghan theater. Partnering with the Afghans was a challenge, but one they embraced with pride. Each and every mission, they tackled with that same dedication. They could all take pride in the positive impact that they made on the region. Now, it was up to the ANA to sustain.

Paul smiled to himself, thinking of the vision Sergeant First Class Sullivan had spoken of often. Sullivan imagined they would be flying out, leaving Afghanistan for good, and they would look down and see the ANA on patrol. Waiting for his plane out today, Paul thought that might just come true.

Looking around at the other men waiting, Paul found

himself smiling. They had worked together as a team and shared the true bond of brotherhood. Each hardship brought them closer. Every catastrophe made them stronger. Paul was proud to serve with each of them and proud of what they accomplished, no matter what happened in the future.

Thinking of the future, Paul couldn't help worrying. What would happen to each of them now? They all deserved to live long, prosperous lives, but he knew it would be hard. A sad thought crossed his mind. He knew that he might never see some of these great men again. You become so close to people, form a deep bond during the time you spend together, and then people go back to their normal, busy lives spread across the country. He smiled, imagining the younger soldiers getting married, having children, and settling down. Thinking of seeing Marie and Paul Jr. again, he imagined how happy the others would be to return home to their families. He wished that euphoria would never fade. He knew the sad reality was very different. Making a marriage last was already tough. Combined with the hardships they faced and dealing with their new realities would lead many down a path he didn't want to think about.

Paul wondered how many would stay in the military. He imagined them as the future Army leaders. Imagined what they would become outside the military. Some would go on to finish college. Some would return to their jobs. For others, their old jobs just wouldn't be enough anymore. They'd want something more. Something to challenge them just like their responsibilities here in Afghanistan. Paul hoped they would find that success, but again the sad reality set in. Paul knew that many veterans went on to successful careers, but too many struggled. It was hard to imagine, but some of them might even become one of the too-many homeless veterans across the country. They were such a great bunch—hard working, willing to do anything, even die for their country.

Many would struggle while others would have everything they wanted and still not be happy. That was also difficult, because people just couldn't understand. These men had gone through a truly life-changing experience. This was not a week-long spring break trip where someone comes back and says,

"This trip changed my life." The events they experienced had become part of them. Those experiences had changed them. How they dealt with that, determined who they would become. Some would never move past this phase of their life. It would haunt them forever. For this moment, waiting to leave the place that had changed each of them, Paul wanted to just remember them for who they were. They had all made him proud. With these men by his side, Paul was proud to be an American, and proud of what they had accomplished. They were the best that their country had to offer, and he would miss them dearly. More than they would ever know.

Paul would forever remember the fun times, too. Like when one of his soldiers shaved off a bit of his eyebrow to mimic Paul's own eyebrow scar. Tagging himself on Facebook as Paul Foster got a lot of laughs. Or the picture of some of the guys wearing nothing but Speedos. Rounding the corner, he once saw one of their robots with a dollar bill in its grip. It was heading toward one of the guys who was pretending to be a stripper.

You couldn't make this stuff up, thought Paul with a smile.

Another time, one of the guys belly-flopped into a mud puddle, only to find out it was only a couple inches deep. Of course, there was the infamous dance video uploaded on Facebook that was quickly removed when some of the leadership caught wind of it. The vehicle sing-alongs, where they belted out Miley Cyrus and other songs you wouldn't expect from a bunch of hardened combat veterans. Each month they gave out a Reenigne, the word "engineer" backwards, award for the most bizarre antics for that month. Amazingly, none of the situations Paul just recalled had ever won.

The winners were too crazy to even think about, Paul thought grinning again.

That wasn't what he'd miss most though. He would miss the bond they shared. Conversations about life that lasted all through the night. Helping each other through life's problems. Discussing the future—hopes, dreams, and ambitions. Sharing everything because they were all miserable together. That common bond from the misery they shared led them to an unbreakable bond. It didn't matter if they never saw each other again, that bond would remain unbroken.

Paul hoped that the bond with Marie grew stronger as well. Together, they had now weathered two long deployments. Helping each other through each tragic event made them realize just how much they loved each other. They would never take their love or time together for granted. They would appreciate every moment. Being open and honest, they communicated as much as they could, given the circumstances, even though Paul knew many times it was mostly Marie who spoke. Sometimes he was tired, and just wanted to hear about real life, normal life, home life. Everything led them to a love that continued to grow, despite the absence. Or maybe because of the absence.

Paul missed being a father, too. He had left just as Paul Jr. arrived. Being away meant they couldn't be the family Paul had dreamed of yet, but he was almost home.

Paul again thought of Afghanistan and the person he was a year earlier. He still couldn't help envisioning Paul Jr. being able to study here someday. He still had visions of peace and prosperity for the entire country. However, he had a lot more respect for the reality of the situation. He knew the dreamer in him had become a realist. This conflict wasn't like others. Each was unique. It wasn't fair to compare it to previous wars and expect similar results. The people were different. The situation was different. Mission success was defined differently as well. Everything was different. This fight would take time and a lot of brave people here in Afghanistan. Americans could help but they couldn't do it alone.

At that, his thoughts returned to Nasir. Something was still unsettling about that situation. Paul had always felt that the bright-eyed Nasir would go far and be a force for change. Their intelligent conversations told him that, as well as his intuition. This disappearance had thrown him for a loop, and he just felt like something else was at play here. Maybe he was an infiltrator like the rumor suggested and maybe he was the one who orchestrated that attack, the same day he disappeared, but Paul couldn't help but feel like Nasir had some good in him, too. How could someone switch sides like that, without blinking an eye? There was something there, something good.

The ANA soldiers could help bring about that change as well. More effective units like them could help tip the scale against the Taliban. This made Paul proud as well, working with the ANA and watching them grow. It started in small groups and would spread. They would have to prove to the people of Afghanistan that they were secure. Only then would change occur. It was a start, but there was a long way to go.

In the distance, Paul heard one of the sounds that would forever haunt him. The blades of a helicopter would no longer excite him as they did in his youth. Instead, he would think about this place. He would see his soldiers getting carried away, unsure if they would survive. He would see them raining their firepower down on the enemy. And he would always see Evan McNally.

Quickly, they loaded the helicopter.

Paul was the last one in, with First Sergeant Ponder by his side. They both took one last look. This place was such a big part of their life. Although they would likely never return, it would always be with them. Flying, they could see their battlespace. It looked so small from the sky. They could see the routes where they had spent so many hours and sacrificed so much. There at the end of Red Bull was hope. Sullivan must be smiling, because as they looked down, they could see the ANA out on patrol.

CHAPTER 45

Coming home was hard. Certainly, more difficult than Paul had expected. That was true for most of the guys that he spoke to. At first, he spoke with some of the soldiers each week. Life seemed to be going well. After several weeks, conversations became a monthly thing. Problems were beginning to creep into different areas of life. Almost a year later, most of the soldiers barely spoke at all. As expected, life had taken over. They all tried to keep up with the others, but each had their own challenges and opportunities. Paul got lost in his own world as well.

Reuniting with Marie wasn't difficult, but it wasn't easy. The first month was great, like another honeymoon. After that, they went on like always, and rarely talked about the deployment. Paul wanted it that way. Paul saw other relationships follow a similar path, but for some it didn't take long for everything to fall apart. Divorces were no longer surprising. Both people had changed. Sometimes, one person didn't like who the other had become. More often, it was just a lack of communication, understanding, and patience. Although they understood that everything was different, many couples didn't take the time to discuss it and truly re-connect. They didn't take the time to have their second honeymoon and fall in love again. Those that did often emerged even stronger. Those that didn't tended to grow apart.

Paul and Marie were somewhere in between. They talked openly during the first part of the deployment, but the conversations had been more superficial since Evan died. Paul had turned inward and that worried Marie. He withdrew more than normal and spent long periods alone, tucked in the dark basement. When he re-emerged, he had nothing to say.

Luckily, their time and attention were centered around

Paul Jr. Although his son treated him like a stranger at first, they quickly overcame that with some quality time playing on the floor, reading books, and snuggling during Mickey Mouse Clubhouse. They were lucky that Paul Jr. was only a year old. Many of his soldiers told Paul of difficulties with older children and teenagers. Sometimes the bond was permanently lost and never restored, which was often made worse by marriages breaking down. Other times, it took years to rebuild. Paul knew he was lucky on that front and he was grateful.

The hardest thing was that most people they encountered in society simply didn't understand. The overwhelming support was amazing but didn't change that fact. The harder they tried to relate, the worse it often made it. He couldn't imagine what it must have been like for Vietnam veterans going through the mental anguish of returning from combat as well as being outcast from society, spit on, and cursed.

What a dark time for America and the military, Paul often thought sadly. Returning from combat was already hard enough without being treated with utter disrespect. Now, because of the Vietnam veterans' hard work in welcoming home troops from Iraq and Afghanistan, they were treated with respect and gratitude. Paul had dozens of people thank him for his service every time he was in uniform and more than one offered to buy him a meal. It helped, but it didn't change the fact that people didn't understand. How could they, really? Even though Paul was in the military, he certainly didn't understand what it was like before he was sent to Iraq and Afghanistan.

One of the things no one seemed to understand is that, after spending a year with a great group of guys, they were like a family, bonded by hardship. It hurt each day they were apart.

I wonder what he's doing today, or *I wonder how they're dealing with the reintegration,* crossed his mind daily. Mostly, he missed their company. Every day, they would risk their lives for others, for him, for each other, and do it without complaint. They found a way to enjoy life despite the horrendous conditions. It amazed him. Now they all returned to their regular lives.

Paul encountered an unexpected side effect of deployment when he would find himself getting uncharacteristically angry at times when he would be out running errands or just out in public in general, because everything and everyone just moved so slowly. Nothing was done with a sense of purpose, not like in Afghanistan. People didn't care, they were just minding their own business, but it enraged him. There were men outside the wire, sacrificing their lives for these people, and they just didn't care. Sometimes he had to go out to his car to sit in the silence for a bit, because just being around people took such a toll. These spells didn't happen too often but when they did, they always took him by surprise.

There was also the disturbed feeling he got like he was never alone, always being watched, wondering what would happen next. It was eerily similar to that feeling he got when he watched a scary movie or saw something disturbing in the news. Afterwards, he found himself looking over his shoulder, checking in dark places, and keeping an extra watchful eye over his son. He always had to have his back to the wall so he could watch everything. The problem was that sometimes that feeling persisted. He couldn't rationalize it away because it had become a way of life. A way of survival.

Just when Paul thought he was finally getting back on his feet, the unthinkable happened. Specialist White committed suicide. It knocked him and the rest of the company off whatever progress they had made. After all the suicide prevention awareness and training they went through, and after the entire company was so close for so long, no one saw it coming. Nothing could have prepared Paul for the awful reality. Losing someone in battle was extremely tough. Losing McNally had been hellish. Even so, there is always that chance in combat. It's still hard, but it's on your mind every day. Losing White after they returned home and were supposed to be safe, caught Paul completely off-guard.

Paul learned that White had said some pretty cryptic and morbid things to another one of the soldiers the previous evening. Knowing the signs from all the training, he felt that something was off and called the police, but because White acted normal when they arrived, the police left.

The next day he was dead.

No one in the 824th had known what had happened the night before, nor had there been any other indication. Now, it was too late. The unexpected reunion for the wake and funeral was somber and not at all the circumstances they wanted to see each other. They vowed to make their upcoming Welcome Home Ceremony a more memorable affair.

Finding another job was also a miserable process. Paul simply wasn't ready to go back to work right away. He had to clear his mind. Leaving a great job was a difficult decision, but it would have been a mistake to return. Eventually, he had no choice; he was too stubborn to take unemployment and the money they saved from the deployment was finally running out. After months living off their savings, he still wasn't ready to go back to work, but he had to start looking.

Considering his qualifications, Paul figured it would be easy. He was a combat veteran who had deployed to both Iraq and Afghanistan as a Company Commander. The level of responsibility easily exceeded that of CEOs and presidents of small companies in many aspects. Company Commanders directly managed and were responsible for the lives of hundreds of people, planned and executed complex operations, owned millions of dollars of equipment, and were exercising the extension of the American government's foreign policy in a hostile nation. Yet, after dozens of applications, the first job offer came in months later for ten dollars an hour as a customer service representative. The next was a little better, but still dismal. Finally, he landed a job, but nothing that would satisfy him for the long term. It would do for now, until he could figure things out. From most people's perspective, it was a good job as an office manager, with some responsibilities. But it was nothing like what he had been doing. Maybe his expectations were too high, but he didn't want to settle.

His soldiers fared even worse. After leading combat patrols, many were now back on the production line with little to no responsibilities. Employers didn't understand and some just didn't care. Many lost jobs before they left, after their employers learned they'd be gone for over a year. Others simply left a job they didn't like, hoping to find something better when they returned. With all that, they still had military duty, and that made employers leery.

Despite the continuing struggles, Paul and the others were looking forward to their first reunion. There was an official Welcome Home one year after their return. Despite the distance that naturally came from their separation, they were quickly that same strong team that they were in Afghanistan. Now they had the new common bond of trying to re-integrate into society. Most conversations led down that path, along with stories from the past. Those brought smiles to everyone. Everyone except Chad. He seemed disconnected, like he was in another place. Away from the crowd, Paul approached him.

"Hey Chad, how's it going?" Paul began enthusiastically. "I miss seeing you every day."

He couldn't help but recall their unexpected reunion a little over two years earlier. There had been so much enthusiasm. So much excitement at the opportunity to deploy together. Now, there was just distance.

"Hey, Sir," Chad said, briefly meeting Paul's eyes. "Good to see you." No warmth or humor like before. Not even a name. Still "Sir," just like deployment.

Paul nodded, trying to adjust to Chad's behavior. He frowned, concern leaching into his voice. "How have you been, Chad? I've been worried. Everyone has. No one can reach you and no one has heard much since we got back."

For a moment, Chad didn't say anything, just looked back toward the crowd.

"I know, Paul," Chad finally responded, "I've just been working on some things, just like everyone else."

Paul waited, but Chad wasn't going to continue. Finally, Paul said carefully, "I know. It hasn't been easy, but I want you to know that I'm here for you if you ever need anything at all."

Chad turned away from the crowd briefly. "Thanks. I know, but it's not that easy. I think you know that, too. I've been looking forward to this yet dreading it." Chad sighed. "Seeing McNally's parents is great. I'm glad they're here, but there is only one thing I think about when I see them. Same with White. It brings me to tears seeing all the guys walk across the stage, but also brings me back to those moments. And others. But, that's nothing new, right?"

"I get it. I do the same thing," Paul started to say, but Chad went on as if he hadn't heard.

"Everything is just different now."

Paul had been concerned after their conversation two years earlier, based on his experiences of September 11th. He'd been keeping a careful watch in Afghanistan, but Chad showed no sign of issues. No anxiety, depression, or anything like that, at least in the beginning. Nothing more than anyone else. He seemed to be in his element, doing what he was meant to do. Now, Paul was worried. He knew Chad was a master at deceiving people of his true state of mind, but Chad wasn't hiding anything now.

"Yeah, things are different, always will be now," Paul said, not really knowing what to say. "Why don't you come over tonight and have dinner at the house?"

"I figured you might ask," he said, finally cracking a slight smile. "That sounds great."

Seeing them all laugh and smile again, made Paul think back to that day as they were preparing to leave. He smiled, thinking that life was kind of like that. Moments that stand out so vividly, never to be repeated. Moments like this. Paul wanted to step back and frame this in his memory. Another great moment to remember. Another great moment that will never happen again.

The Welcome Home Ceremony was perfect. It was a great opportunity to re-connect and celebrate their successes. Their unit received countless awards—Presidential Unit Citation, Reserve Officer Association's Outstanding Company of the Year, the Army Engineer Regiment's Itschner Award. An amazing feat for any unit. Later, Paul looked in the local papers but didn't find any acknowledgment of the event or their many accomplishments. Instead, road construction, a recent robbery, and a local business that was considering expanding covered the front page. Once again though, unfortunately, most people didn't understand or care. But Paul knew what they had done and that was all that mattered at this moment.

Each in turn received an encased, folded American flag to

display proudly as they walked across the stage greeted by local dignitaries.

They also had a huge feast for lunch, laughing and joking the entire time. Paul could see they were happy to be back together. His own joy and sense of connection was reflected in everyone around him. Their stories made sense to this crowd. They understood the jokes. They were even laughing at some of the nuances of coming home—how weird it was to drive again and how they hit the deck when they first heard loud noises. Instinct just took over. Even looking over their shoulders and not trusting anyone made sense to this group. They felt at home with each other. They enjoyed the moment and were all sad to see it end.

As planned, Chad arrived for dinner after the ceremony. He seemed better, more at ease. Paul hoped Chad had been withdrawn just because of all the emotions that he was feeling earlier. Normally, he would offer him a beer, but he was extra cautious after seeing JD's relationship with alcohol. Their conversation started on a light note, describing more of their college antics to Marie.

"I never knew that, Paul," she teased, but couldn't help being concerned. Here was yet another friend of Paul's who was struggling. She knew Paul's next crash would follow.

Later on, Chad changed the subject. "It's great catching up with you and reliving the old college days. I sure wish we could go back to that sometimes. No real worries. Didn't really think about the rest of the world or care really. It was just enjoying the moment, even though we were doing nothing but anticipating the future. Kind of ironic, isn't it? Now that we know the reality of how people live and die, and the way people are treated around the world, it's hard to think about anything else."

Chad was looking right at Paul as they sat in the living room. Marie had disappeared to check on Paul Jr., who had woken up crying.

"I know you're worried, and everyone else is, too, but I'm doing okay," Chad continued. "Last time we were here, I told you all about September 11th and what happened, but I didn't tell you everything."

At this, he told Paul all about Steve's death, meeting Mel, and all the other dead bodies he had encountered during the clean-up. And in his dreams. He opened up about Allison and Vanessa Bradshaw, his trip to Nebraska, and how he made the decision to join after that moment. Before that, he confessed that he had been going nowhere and miserable with life. Being a combat medic gave his life meaning.

"It's what I was born to do," Chad stated proudly, showing his trademark smile. "Seeing King walk across the stage at the Welcome Ceremony after all that happened brought me back to that moment that I got to him, when we were in the shit, but the feeling was not all bad, because he's here now. He's enjoying life. That's more than a lot of people can say that have all their limbs. I want to give more people that opportunity. I'm planning to go back as soon as I can. Even join active duty if that's what it takes. After that, I'll get my nursing degree, EMT certificate, too, and keep helping people. Like I said, it's what I was born to do."

Paul was stunned. Chad wasn't the one who was lost. He knew his purpose and was waiting to get back to it.

"That's amazing, Chad. I'm really happy for you. I never really got the chance to talk to you, to tell you, but thanks for taking care of the guys," Paul said, opening up now himself. "You are going to do a great job, wherever you go. Just do me a favor, okay?"

"Absolutely."

"Stay in touch," Paul said with a smile. "We missed you. I miss you."

"Sure, Paul. Ali and I fell into that trap after I left New York, and so did JD and I after I left college. We just didn't keep in touch like we should have and lost the closeness. Luckily, I'm still friends with both, but not like it was. Don't worry, I won't make that mistake again," he replied, then hesitated. "To be honest, I've been worried about you. Sorry I haven't been around to check in on you."

"Me?" Paul raised his eyebrows in surprise.

"Yeah. I know how you are, bottling everything up. Don't be afraid to let people in. The reason I haven't been around much the last year is that I've been traveling, visiting Stewart and Murphy, and some of the other guys. Volunteering at veterans' homes, hospitals, wherever people need help. We've all changed, Paul. There is no way around that and no way of going back. It's not just the deployment that makes things harder. Having kids, getting married, leaving your hometown, holding down a job, losing loved ones, things like that will always change people. That's a good thing. We will never be able to go back to the carefree days, but it gives us a deeper appreciation of life. And that's much better."

Paul couldn't believe what he just heard. Chad had it all figured out. Paul had completely miscalculated his state of mind. *What an amazing perspective and so true.* Marie came back and smiled when she saw Paul's expression.

Chad stood. "There she is. I was just waiting for you to get back to say goodbye. Take care of him, will you?"

"Of course. It was great seeing you, Chad," Marie said, giving him a big hug.

Paul walked with him to the door. Still amazed, he smiled. "Great seeing you again, Chad. It really was. I'm glad you have everything figured out and I wish you the best of luck on your upcoming adventures."

"I don't have everything figured out. No one does. That's not really the point. The point is just to enjoy and appreciate what you have."

"When did you get so profound?" Paul joked.

"I learned from this great leader I had in Afghanistan," Chad replied, just as quick with that smile again. "And don't worry. I'll stay in touch this time."

Paul went to the basement again, but this time with a little different perspective. Just as his outlook darkened a little bit more with each event in Afghanistan, it was beginning to brighten with each moment and each day like this. Paul couldn't stop thinking that, with all the hardships they encountered, maybe today was what he needed to finally move forward.

That hope would be short-lived.

Two days after their welcome home ceremony, Sullivan, the eternal optimist and dreamer, killed himself. Shocked again, this time the company assembled and all the smiling faces from days earlier had vanished. Nobody understood how this could happen again, and so soon. They had just been laughing and joking, now this. It didn't make any sense.

Repressing all his thoughts about the deployment kept Paul in a vicious cycle. It was one he didn't understand. This latest suicide pushed him deeper. To avoid thinking, Paul would fill up every spare minute of his time. He couldn't shake the pure dread of facing life's inevitable challenges. Even simple things created an oppressive anxiety. It was as if he was getting ready to jump out of a plane, give a presentation to a stadium full of people, or take a game winning shot with the world watching. In that kind of situation, adrenaline is needed to rise to the occasion. Paul didn't need it in everyday life, but he got the feeling for everything now and it simply wouldn't go away. Things like house projects, simple conversations, even family get-togethers would cause this anxiety. Deadlines or any real stress would only heighten it. His body stayed in a perpetual state of stress and fear. Paul only become more frustrated and exhausted. For years, he endured the stress of combat, made decisions that changed people's lives, and solved complex problems without prolonged anxiety. Now, he could barely leave the house. It wasn't just the anxiety, either. It always spiraled into severe depression.

Paul's Mom and Marie collaborated to throw a huge party for Paul to try to help pull him out of his inner turmoil. It would be a late welcome home party for those he hadn't seen since before he left.

JD was there.

Lynn was not.

Paul didn't ask.

Every communication they had over the last year essentially told him it was over.

"We're trying," JD would say. From what he could tell, Paul guessed the "we" was really Lynn. Before the major festivities began, they slipped outside to discuss one of their favorite topics. Ever since they were young, they had a dream to go out west, camp in the mountains, and chase big game.

"I know I said it before when you actually got home, but it's great to have you back home. Heck it's been over a year, but seems like yesterday," JD said. "Great party, too. Your mom always knows how to throw a great party." He took another drink, finishing his beer. Paul wanted to say something about the alcohol but didn't want to ruin the mood. He was feeling okay for the first time in a long time, and JD seemed to be having a good time as well.

"Thanks, JD," Paul replied. "It's great to be home. Sure makes you appreciate everything after you're gone that long and see the way they live." He hesitated and then continued, "How are you doing, JD?"

"Let's get another beer and I'll tell you," JD said, already walking toward the drinks.

"Sounds like a plan."

Now huddled around the coolers, JD changed the subject back to their original conversation. "Can't wait for that trip, man," he said. "Hard to believe it's actually happening. Finally. How long have we been talking about this?"

"About the time we started talking," Paul replied with a smile.

"That's about right. Now it's just a few short months away. Is Marie okay with you leaving again?"

"Oh yeah, she's an angel," Paul said, seeing an opening to ask about Lynn. "She actually thinks it will be a good opportunity to clear my head. What about Lynn?"

"That, my friend, is a conversation for another day," JD replied. "Perhaps in the Colorado mountains. For now, let's get another drink."

Paul's was still nearly full.

It didn't take long before JD was drunk. Again, nothing unusual for a party, thought Paul. Before long, he was challenging everyone to shots. Not long after, he was lying on a table covered in vomit. Everyone just thought he had partied too hard. Paul was a little more concerned than that. He couldn't possibly know that this had become an almost daily routine for JD, but he did know something was very wrong. He had begun to suspect that alcohol was JD's way of dealing with his demons but couldn't find the right time to talk about it. After the party, they went back to their separate lives and Paul fell back into crippling depression.

He would sit in the basement for hours, pondering life. To solve his problems, he turned inward, instead of relying on family and friends. Paul couldn't say why, nor did he give it much thought. Like most, he never really felt comfortable having serious conversations about things that bothered him. He didn't want to burden others. They had their own issues. Why put this on them when they might not even be able to do anything? After going to five different mental health professionals, he wasn't sure anyone could do anything to help.

So, he closed himself off from the world. He had given up trying to suppress his memories and struggles of deployment. Just like JD, Paul kept replaying every event in his head. Desperately, he searched for anything he could have done differently. Over and over again. What if? Maybe Evan would still be here. Maybe King would still have legs. Maybe Stewart wouldn't be wheelchair bound for the rest of his life. Maybe Murphy and Hill wouldn't have had broken backs. And now – maybe Sullivan and White wouldn't have killed themselves.

If only I had done that. If only I could have stopped it.

On a certain level he knew he had done his best, but he still blamed himself.

Paul also questioned his military service. All he had wanted to do was help, to serve his country, to protect his family and friends. He wanted to make sure there was never another September 11th. Yet, he felt that world was more chaotic and dangerous. Look at Iraq. Over four thousand lives lost. Now, the U.S. was leaving, and the country was falling apart. In many ways, Iraq was worse off than when they had arrived. The constant instability created a power vacuum, enabling chaos and evil to thrive. Who knew what would happen with Afghanistan? It was already America's longest war, but Paul had to wonder what was really being accomplished. The Taliban was still operating relatively freely. They still controlled the country and the population through fear.

At the moment, the likelihood of Afghanistan being a base to launch another September 11th was slim. But if that was the objective, Paul wondered why not just monitor and destroy it when the intelligence indicated? The U.S. knew Osama bin Laden was there, knew he was planning something, and had eyes on him. If they had killed him in early 2001 or before, that horrible day may never have happened. Maybe they would have never gone to Afghanistan. Who knows? He thought about all the other places where an attack like that could be planned.

We can't be at war with all of them. Paul shook his head. *What are we trying to accomplish? What is it all for?*

In quiet moments, these questions and more continually circled through Paul's head. There were no real answers. Only questions. Only what-ifs. He sometimes wondered if he was wrong about everything.

These questions weren't the worst thing though. They opened up larger questions. Why was he here on earth? What was his purpose? It scared him that he didn't have a clear answer. One thing that he did know was that he could no longer serve in the military. He needed a break. He just couldn't do it anymore. Leaving the military, having a job he disliked, distance between family and friends, even some distance with Marie, left him questioning everything.

Maybe ending it all is the best choice?

It scared him every time those thoughts popped in his head.

Trying to snap out of his depression, Paul made it a point to visit all the wounded soldiers. It warmed his heart to see their progress. They were so optimistic. Despite their injuries, they were ready to take advantage of life's opportunities. Some of them told horror stories about the self-loathing that plagued many of their fellow soldiers with similar injuries. No surprise, but recovery suffered for the pessimistic. His soldier's positive attitude made all the difference.

Paul tried to use this as motivation to try to enjoy life. For a day or two, it would work. His faith would be restored, and he would be ready to tackle anything. Then, the anxiety would creep in again. Then, he would begin to blame himself again. Then, he would begin asking the questions that had no answers. Thoughts of suicide would creep in. Again, he withdrew. The dark basement became his sanctuary. That's how the cycle went. For a while, everything would be okay. Then, he'd flip through the channels on the television and see the headline, "Entire squad dies in IED attack near Kandahar."

Paul would be right back in that moment.

Or, he'd be grilling on the back deck, enjoying a beautiful day with his family. In the distance, he'd hear the dreadful sound of a helicopter. "KIA" was all he could think. Unable to stop himself, he would replay every horrible moment in his head. More than once he'd forget what he was doing when these spells struck, resulting in lost conversations and burnt hamburgers. Again, he would withdraw, and the cycle would repeat.

Or, he'd be enjoying a baseball game. Until the fireworks came, then it lost all enjoyment. All he would see was a vehicle disappear in a cloud of dust, feeling sick with the uncertainty of whether his soldiers were alive. There wasn't much that didn't remind him of Afghanistan. Each time he would withdraw, and the cycle would begin anew.

Marie watched this cycle with concern. Paul made it clear that he really didn't want to talk about deployment. She imagined he didn't want to relive it. Understandable, but she still worried. He tried talking to several counselors, but never really saw it through. Each time, Paul would attend only a session or two and then say they just weren't working for him.

"They don't understand," he told Marie, as they were leaving the office of the fourth therapist. Marie didn't know what to say. She knew they probably didn't understand, but she wanted to him to talk to someone, to get the help he needed.

What scared her most was what seemed like his new split-personality behavior. Around friends and family, or just interacting with people in general, he seemed fine. He would chatter away, charismatic, and sociable like old times. Nobody would ever suspect anything was wrong. Then, they would get home and he seemed to withdraw from the world. He couldn't focus and his whole demeanor would change. Conversations were nonexistent and he'd just stare listlessly at his plate while they ate meals together. Then, he would disappear into the basement for hours. She wondered what he was thinking about, wishing she could help.

Eventually, he would re-emerge, give her a big hug, and pretend everything was fine. She was glad when the episodes ended after a short time, because they would often last for days. Other times, instead of going to the basement, he would lounge around the house. They would still interact, he would still play with Paul Jr., but he never smiled. There was no emotion. Those times truly scared her. Over and over the cycle repeated. She always offered to help; told him she was there if he ever needed anything. Time and time again, Paul insisted he was fine. She knew he wasn't.

CHAPTER 46

Unable to sleep, Paul opened his eyes and sat up. Brightness from flames could still be seen through the tent.

That's weird, he thought, as he looked around. The fire should be out by now.

Looking over, he saw that JD's sleeping bag was empty. Then he noticed JD's silhouette in front of the fire, sitting there in the darkness. Paul hesitated, then unzipped his sleeping bag. He shivered as he was enveloped by the cold. He dressed quickly and added an extra layer before hurrying out to the warmth of the fire.

He opened the tent door and stopped. JD was sitting completely still. He seemed to be mesmerized as he looked down at his new pistol. All week long he had flaunted his new gun, showing it off, saying it would keep the bears and cougars away. It wasn't that farfetched since many backcountry campers did the same. But sitting here in the dark, Paul was unsettled watching him with his new weapon. The bottle of Jim Beam that was unopened when they went to bed was now only half full. Or, rather, judging by JD's drastic change in personality over the past few years, he would guess half empty.

As Paul approached the fire, JD didn't look up.

"Remember how we imagined this as kids?" he asked. Paul nodded. "How could I forget? It's all we ever talked about."

Neither remembered where the idea originated but this trip had been a dream of theirs since they were children. They used to talk about how, armed only with the essentials, they'd hike deep into the Colorado Rockies, searching for the majestic elk. The original plan was to sleep under the stars. They had tempered that idealism a little in favor of a tent. They had also planned to only eat what they killed. Good thing they changed that idea as well since the only thing they had caught was one small brook trout, which didn't go very far. They had thought there would be animals everywhere but were sorely disappointed.

JD smiled bitterly. "Now here we are and what a disappointment."

Paul shifted uneasily. "I wouldn't say that, JD. It's still been a heck of an adventure, camping here in the middle of the mountains, just the two of us. It's still a dream come true."

JD was shaking his head. "No, it's just like life, too. We have all these big plans. Meeting the women of our dreams, living happily ever after. The big house on the corner with the perfect yard. Travelling. Seeing the world. Great job, all that. Look at us and the military. Neither of us could wait to go and now both of us wish we never had to. Wish that no one ever had to."

"JD, man, what's really going on? What can I do to help?"

JD finally looked up. "There's nothing you or anyone else can do. It's just time to make some changes."

What does that mean? JD's cryptic words only increased Paul's uneasiness.

"I'm not going to lie, seeing you like this scares the hell out of me." Paul hesitated. "Especially sitting there holding that gun with half a bottle of whiskey in you."

JD didn't answer. Paul didn't know how to ask what he felt he needed to, so he took a little different approach. "Suicide has already destroyed too many military families," Paul began. "I'd be crushed if I ever lost you."

JD let out a sudden, wild laugh. "I'm not gonna kill myself, Paul. Is that what you really think?" He quickly became serious again. He didn't have to see Paul's face to feel guilty. Both he and Paul had lost too many friends to suicide.

Paul looked away. "Come on JD, that's nothing to laugh at. Look at how many veterans kill themselves every day. How many people we've served with that have done it. It's an epidemic and you can't blame me for asking."

JD nodded. "You're right and I'm sorry. I know how it must look and sound."

Paul thought that JD was letting his guard down for the first time during their conversation, yet the silence lingered.

Finally, Paul said, "JD, I have to admit that I really didn't understand what you were going through when you came back from Afghanistan. But I understand a little better now. There is not a day that goes by that I don't think about what happened. I feel guilty. I blame myself. I wish I could change places with them. Sometimes, I think it would be easier to just disappear. Or worse." Paul shook his head, trying to find the right words, "We've never had a conversation about it, but I wish we would."

In the flicker of the fire, Paul saw JD brush a tear away. He let the silence remain, waiting for JD's response.

JD didn't look up, but he finally said, "I never knew you felt that way, too. I thought it was just me. The truth is that I think about it all the time. Can't stop really. Just wish I had died over there. At least then my mind would be at peace."

"I know. I think about it, too, JD," Paul confessed. "I think about killing myself just to put a stop to this endless cycle of thoughts running through my head. But I don't want to lose you, JD. You're my best friend. Always have been, and always will be."

"You're my best friend, too. Brothers for life," JD said. "I think about killing myself every day and this sure doesn't help." He raised the bottle with a grimace. "The gun isn't for that though and it's not for bears or cougars. Truth is that I'm just scared shitless everywhere I go. I don't trust anyone, and I always feel like something bad is going to happen at any moment. Do you feel any of that?"

"Yeah, I do. Not necessarily scared all the time but I try to cram as much as I can into every moment, so I don't have time to think about all that. It never works though. Just makes things worse actually." Paul paused, struck with a sudden realization. "You're right, though. I don't feel like I'm going to live to be an old man and I never realized why until this moment."

JD nodded, and Paul wondered if he was feeling the same thing; like a little bit of the weight was lifted.

"Lynn has really tried, but she doesn't get it," JD said suddenly. "Although . . . that's mostly my fault," he admitted. "She tries to help but I know she can't, and I get so frustrated I just end up exploding. The drinking only makes that worse, too."

Paul nodded, though JD wasn't looking at him. "Marie tries to help, too. I know, it's hard."

"And then my dad being military, I really just didn't want to listen, wanted to show him I was tough, so I've never even given him a chance either." JD put the bottle down and poked at the fire.

Paul wasn't sure how to respond. JD and his father had always had a pretty contentious relationship. "Well, I think the important thing is to try, right?"

JD looked up, smiling slyly. "You can't just give that advice like you don't need it. You should try to give therapy another chance."

Paul drew back, surprised. "How—"

JD laughed. "I may have heard something through Lynn. She and Marie talk occasionally."

Paul couldn't help laughing. "Okay, yeah. I should give therapy another chance. I mean, they may not understand what we've been through, but they can still help us get through it."

JD nodded, suddenly solemn. "Yeah. Maybe I can cope with this and take back my life, but I need help to do it."

They talked all through the night, adding more wood to the fire when it burned down to coals. Paul realized that JD had been trying to be strong, as well, not wanting to burden others. Paul was so grateful for the time they had together; just talking to each other and being understood was a relief from the constant anxiety.

Conversation shifted between the "good ol' days" and the struggles they were facing. JD confessed his relationship with Lynn was over. He already had plans to leave. Paul was sad to hear that, but not really surprised.

"It's just been too negative over the last few years," JD said. "I'm not sure we can ever get past it and Lynn deserves better."

Nothing Paul said could convince him otherwise. He was

determined. Paul decided not to push further, thinking about his own relationship.

"I can see Marie and I heading down that path, too," Paul finally said, catching JD off guard. "Unless I make some changes."

JD leaned forward. "Don't let her get away. Don't make the same mistakes I did, Paul. You'll regret it forever."

"You know, it's not too late," Paul said, trying one last time.

JD shook his head, "It is though. We're not in love anymore. That's the difference. I let her slip away, not just since I came back either. I was obsessed with war, obsessed with deploying, obsessed with killing bad guys, you know that. Through all that I forgot what was truly important. It's just time for a change."

"What kind of change are you thinking of?" Paul said quickly, suddenly worried again.

"Nothing like that, man," JD responded quickly. "Just a change of scenery. You're right. It's pretty nice out here."

Paul just had to smile. JD smiled right back.

They never did get an elk. They didn't even see many animals, but it didn't matter. They finally felt reconnected. Paul felt closer to JD than he had since they day they had both graduated college. Just like after his conversation with Chad, Paul's outlook on life was a little brighter. However, he knew that there was something he had to do to keep moving forward.

For the second time that week, Paul stayed up all night talking. This time with Marie. He finally opened up, told her everything, confessing his darkest thoughts. Instead of pushing him away, she pulled him closer. His biggest fear was all in his head.

"I had no idea, love. I knew you were struggling, I just didn't realize how much. I'm so glad you told me and just want you to know that I'm always here for you."

"I love you, Marie. Thanks for listening. Sorry that it took me so long to talk to you. I was just lost in my own little world and thought I could do it myself. I didn't want to burden you."

"You could never be a burden," Marie cut him off and

gave him another hug. "Actually, I never thought I could love you more, but I was wrong. I feel like I know you better now."

The light was getting brighter still.

The following weekend, he stopped to see JD, wanting to continue to build on their connection. He knocked on the door and waited. Paul was just about to knock again when Lynn threw open the door, sobbing.

"Where the hell is he, Paul?" she screamed, hitting him on the chest, barely coherent. "What did he say to you? What did you tell him? Where is he, Paul? I'm so scared." Quickly, she lost steam and fell into long sobs. She couldn't stop trembling as Paul wrapped his arms around her.

"Listen, Lynn," he began. "I'm sorry, I don't know. I don't know. What happened? Is JD okay?"

She backed away, looking intently at his face. Seeing sincerity, she handed him a note. "This is all I know. He's gone."

The note was short, but there was no missing the meaning.

Dear Lynn,

I'm sorry that I let my darkness tear us apart. And I'm sorry that I have to leave. I just don't want to hurt you anymore. I'm not sure where I'm headed, but I'm going to search for peace. It's my only hope. Remember that day down by the lake when we skipped school and we were the only ones there? I told you I loved you that day and that will always be true. Please remember that.

Love, JD

CHAPTER 47

"Paul!" Marie shouted. He was in the hall, playing with their son. Paul couldn't help laughing as Paul Jr. made a surprised face and yelled back, "Mommy!"

"Yes, it is," Paul agreed with a smile.

"Someone just pulled up to the driveway," Marie called. "I'm going to let you handle this one."

"Okay love, thanks," he said, giving her a kiss as they passed each other in the hallway. "I love you."

She beamed. "Love you, too."

Paul opened the door and stared in amazement. Nasir was standing in the driveway. Paul thought he'd never see Nasir again and always wondered about him. Yet, here he was.

Finally, Paul found his voice. "Nasir! I . . . Good to see you, old friend. How did you get here?" he blurted out, before remembering that Nasir didn't understand English very well. To Paul's great surprise, he responded in nearly fluent English.

"Well, Captain Foster, that is a long story," Nasir said as he held out his hand. "Do you have some tea?"

"Of course, come in." Paul was skeptical but curious. He brought Nasir to the kitchen table and offered him a seat. Before he could sit, Marie came in and smiled, holding out her hand. "This is my wife Marie and that"—he pointed at Paul Jr. as he ran by—"is the little boy you've seen in the pictures."

"Not so little anymore, is he?" Nasir asked with a smile as he shook Marie's hand with both of his. Paul was surprised again at the ease with which he accepted Marie's hand. He assumed that Nasir would have reservations about touching a woman who wasn't his family or wife.

"Honey, this is Nasir. He was one of the Afghan soldiers I worked with in Afghanistan. Really bright, intelligent, and friendly."

"Hello," she said. "It's very nice to meet you."

"Nice to meet you as well," Nasir said.

"Have a seat," Paul said. "I'll get some of that tea ready, although I must warn you that it is a little different than the tea that you're used to."

"Captain Foster—"

"Please call me Paul," he said, interrupting.

Nasir nodded. "Okay, Paul. I think it would be best if we talked somewhere else, perhaps outside?"

"Sounds good," Paul replied, looking toward Marie and smiling to reassure her. "Downstairs should work."

"I'll make some tea and knock on the basement door when it's ready," Marie said, waving them away.

As they walked downstairs, Paul said, "Nasir, now I'm in suspense. You have to tell me your story."

Nasir nodded as Paul gestured to a sitting area, "It is very good to see you Capt—I mean, Paul." Nasir looked at him solemnly, "It's been a long journey and I wanted to stop here as soon as I came to America. I'm glad there aren't many Paul Fosters out there, because otherwise I wouldn't have been able to find you."

"I'm glad you did," Paul smiled. "I must say, I'm impressed with your English."

"Thank you. I've been working hard. Paul, do you remember when I met Sullivan at training?"

Paul nodded, wondering where this was going.

"That was no accident." Nasir proceeded to tell him about everything. His father. Running away from home. Malang. Becoming a sniper. His undercover mission. And finally, his dream.

Paul listened intently, horrified to learn that he had been there to kill them. Paul's naiveté at the danger caused him to start to noticeably shake. Here he was. In Paul's house. With his family. A Taliban killer. Paul started thinking about what he could use as a weapon if things went south. He gripped the armrest of his chair and watched Nasir carefully. Just then, Marie knocked on the basement door and Paul jumped up to go grab the tea. He gripped the mug in his hand tightly as he handed one to Nasir.

Nasir had been expecting Paul's fear, and noticed Paul's hands shaking as he set the tea tray down. He held his hands up in peace. "Please do not misunderstand me. I'm sorry if I alarmed you. That was not what I wanted. I wanted to tell you this story. I'm not here to hurt you, by Allah. I'm here to ask for your forgiveness."

"It's just a lot to take in, so please forgive my alarm. I'm happy you're here and I'd like to hear the rest of your story," Paul said still fidgeting in his chair nervously, but trying more to hide it now.

"After my dream, I couldn't do it. I fired at your men that day, but I missed. I missed on purpose. From that day forward, I've been trying to foster peace."

Paul sat speechless, so Nasir continued.

"It wasn't easy, but I made allies and had some close calls. Eventually, I made it to Kunar Province and told them I could help them find Osama bin Laden. I had to go undercover again. Each week, I would return with new intelligence. Each week, I would try to get further. They said they would help me get to the US if I helped. I'm not sure how much I did, but we got him the other day. I was hoping it would help end this war."

"Me, too," Paul said, as his disbelief deepened. When Nasir had disappeared in Afghanistan, Paul thought there was something deeper.

Paul shook his head, trying to clear it. "Nasir, I had no idea. I don't know what to say. I guess a start would be to thank you for your work to eliminate the world's most wanted criminal. I'm still in shock."

"I understand. I would be, too. Just thinking about how Allah has directed my journey is overwhelming," Nasir smiled. "I really want to thank you and your soldiers. You showed me you cared, you treated me like a brother. Without that and wisdom from my father and Allah, I would not be sitting here today. So, do you forgive me?"

Unbelievable, thought Paul. *Here is proof that we made a difference to someone.*

"Of course and thank you for saving the soldiers that day.

You had their lives in your hand and chose the path to save them at the risk of your own life. It takes a brave person to do that. And now you have done so many other great things and I have no doubt you will continue to do more great things."

They discussed Nasir's journey a little while longer, before heading back upstairs to refill their tea. Just as they had promised, the Americans had helped Nasir get asylum by getting him on a plane and getting in contact with the State Department after his intelligence proved to be correct.

"This is a treat to be having tea here with you in America, but I must say I like the tea in Afghanistan better," Nasir said with a smile.

Paul nodded, laughing. "That's fair."

Nasir grew serious. "I can see what you were fighting for Paul. You have a wonderful life here and a beautiful country. I hope the same is true in Afghanistan one day when I return. My mission isn't complete yet." He stood and set his mug down with a sigh. "It's been great to see you Paul, but I must leave. Please take care."

"You, too, Nasir, and thanks for sharing your story. It is one that I will never forget."

Paul followed him to the door and stood in the open door, watching Nasir drive away.

Then he turned and went to find Marie and Paul Jr, embracing them both.

He really did have a great life, with so much to be thankful for, but he's been carrying around baggage for far too long that prevented him from enjoying it. He knew what he must do. Nasir had come here for forgiveness, facing one of the people that he had been sent to kill. It was time for Paul to face his demons.

Talking with JD in the Colorado mountains had released some of that baggage, that anger and depression that residing in him. Opening up to Marie upon his return proved to be great therapy and brought them closer together. If he was ever going to defeat the evil inside of him, he must face it head on and not let it control him.

Paul made a vow to do just that. Each day, he would block out time to dig deep and think through the things that haunted him, put them into perspective, and accept that they were part of his past. But they didn't have to be part of his future. Reflecting on all the great things in his life – Marie, Paul Jr., family, friends, the amazing people he served with, their home, their freedoms here in America, and so many more – he would focus on these and let them overpower the wicked thoughts that tried to control him. Paul also knew he must continue to open up and talk, not suppress everything inside. With that, he walked over to the phone. There were some conversations that he had waited too long to have.

She answered after two rings and he recognized the voice in an instant. It had been a couple years shy of a decade since they last spoke, but it brought him rushing back to their last miserable month together.

"Hello?" Dawn asked for the third time, her voice growing frustrated and Paul knew she was about to hang up.

"Hey Dawn, it's Paul."

"Paul? Why are you calling me? Sorry, I'm just surprised to hear from you. How are you?"

From her response, Paul could tell that she was still bothered by their unresolved past as well.

"I'm doing good and I know this must be a surprise, but I had to talk to you. How are you doing?"

"I'm okay, I guess, just trying to keep up with everything, you know."

"Yeah, I know all too well."

Paul remembered the day that she told him they were no longer having the child, and the depression that followed. He had never talked about it since. It was the worst day of his life at the time and the first time he completely suppressed his true feelings, just bottled them up and pretended it never happened. But it was always there, deep down. Now suppressing his feelings was the norm and he could tell it got worse each time.

"I wanted to tell you, well, that, I'm sorry," Paul said, holding back emotions.

"Sorry for what?" Dawn asked.

"Sorry for everything, I guess, but mostly that I was so harsh on you for the decision you made. As much as I hated it, it was probably so much harder for you and you didn't deserve that, so I'm sorry."

Dawn was silent on the other end, except for a few muffled sniffles that came through. Finally, she spoke, her voice shaky. "Thanks, Paul, that means a lot. You're right, it was the hardest thing I ever did, and not a day goes by that I don't think about it, regret it, wish things had turned out differently. But they didn't, and now I have to live with that. You have no idea how much this call means to me though. Thank you."

"I'm sure glad I called, too, and wish I would have done it sooner."

"It's never too late to make a call like this, is it? Better than living with the pain. But, I'm sure you know all about that. How are you really doing, being back from overseas and all? I still chat with Dr. Hamm from time to time and it sounds like you spent a lot of time over there."

"I'm not going to lie, it's been rough. Rougher than I thought, but I'm starting to see the light. Moments like this help. I've got a little boy now and another on the way, and they help show me how great life is. Even saying this to you is not something I would have done a year ago, or even a few months ago, so I guess that says something."

"That's great, Paul. I'm so happy for you. I've actually got two little ones now, too, and they are my pride and joy. Can't imagine life without them. Sounds like things worked out for both of us."

"Yeah, I guess you're right. You mentioned Dr. Hamm, how's he doing these days?"

More silence.

"I'm sorry, you must not have heard. He passed away a few weeks ago. They're going to have a memorial service for him when the students come back this fall. I'm thinking about going."

"No, I didn't hear that. What a shock. He was such an inspiration to me. In fact, he was actually the first to tell me that I should be a professor and that's ultimately what I ended up doing. Probably because of him. He'll definitely be missed."

That same feeling was pulling at him again, the one that told him to repress his sadness, be tough, disappear into the abyss, and not talk about it. But, Dr. Hamm would have never wanted that, would have had some lesson to him about doing the opposite and enjoying every moment, not knowing when it would be his last. "Yeah, I think I'll go to memorial service, too. It would be great to remember all the wisdom he passed on to me and say thanks. Plus, I haven't been to campus for years. It would be great to relive some of those memories, maybe go to a football game or something."

"Good idea and maybe we'll run into each other, meet each other's families, who knows."

"Yeah, maybe," Paul said wondering how awkward it would have been had they not had this conversation. Now, things wouldn't be so bad if they ran into each other. Some of the darkness had faded with this call and the light was shining brighter. "That sounds like a plan."

"It was great talking to you, Paul, and thanks again for the call."

"No, thank you, Dawn. Take care of yourself."

"You too. Bye."

"Bye."

CHAPTER 48

The next day, as he was rushing to a meeting, Paul couldn't stop thinking about Nasir's story and his conversation with Dawn. His phone, vibrating in his pocket, interrupted his thoughts. Since he didn't recognize the number, he was about to return it to his pocket. He didn't usually answer unfamiliar numbers, particularly when he was in a hurry, but something stopped him. He clicked the button to answer.

"Hello?" he asked.

"We finally got that son of a bitch, didn't we?" The voice made Paul stop and stand still. There are some voices in life that you never forget, and this was one of them for Paul. It was JD. Paul wasn't surprised that JD had emerged from hiding to call him about it.

"We sure did. It feels pretty good, doesn't it? Even if it doesn't change much." Paul started walking again. "Wait, before we talk about that, how the hell are you?"

JD laughed. "You know Paul, I'm doing great, I really am. It's great to hear your voice again. How are you and Marie? How many kids you got now?"

"Only one, smartass, but another on the way. Marie's great, really loves being a mom, still working hard, doing it all. Me, I'm alright. No complaints. Glad to hear that you're doing great. I've been wondering about you."

There was a brief moment of silence as Paul hesitated to ask another question. *Where are you, what are you doing, why'd you leave?* Shaking his head, he decided not to ask and the moment slipped past.

"That's really great, man, and no surprise. You two always had what it took to make it through."

Paul heard JD pause briefly, as if considering what to say. Finally, JD said, "Paul, I owe you an apology and an explanation. Last time we saw each other, in the mountains, I was messed up. I'm sorry that I just left like that, but I had to get away. I felt like I was going to explode, go crazy, you know. But, talking to you really helped and for a moment I was at peace up there in the mountains. So, that's what I did. Just disappeared in the woods for a while, like we did when we were growing up. And it worked. I guess I had my Lieutenant Dan moment." He cleared his throat. "I had already lost Lynn, and I'll always regret that, but at least I didn't lose myself. I was afraid of that."

Paul listened intently, his meeting already forgotten. This was far more important.

Before Paul could reply, JD continued, quick to tell him about his new life. "Now I'm helping other veterans recover through nature. Pretty neat, huh? And it's really rewarding. I love it. How about you? What are you up to these days?"

Of all the times he had imagined what JD was doing, he never envisioned it would be something as amazing as this. Paul sat down, disbelief, pride, and happiness converging within. He'd been recognizing moments, things to be thankful for, like these more now as part of his therapy. At that instant, he realized that this was one of those moments. Here he was having a conversation with his best friend after not hearing a word for months. He knew that he would always look back at this moment and smile, knowing things would never be the same again. Life was always changing. It always would. For now, he would just enjoy the moment.

"Wow, bud. That's incredible. Congratulations! You know, it's funny you mentioned that because I've made some changes, too. I had a great job, but it just wasn't right. It wasn't what I really wanted to do. So, I'm going back to school and planning to be a professor. I even went back in the Reserves. Hard to believe, huh?"

Paul could almost hear JD's smile. "No, not too hard really. After two deployments, the hard years should be over, with everything winding down now. Hard to beat the benefits and who knows, maybe they'll send you some place nice one of these days? Back to school, huh? Wow. Well, all that must be keeping you pretty busy. What about Chad? Talk to him lately?"

Paul didn't say anything for a second, just smiled. JD hadn't asked about Chad in years. Paul thought it was another great sign.

"He's good, yeah. Back overseas. Says that's where he needs to be." If anyone would understand that sentiment, Paul thought JD would.

"Good for him." JD's voice was earnest. "Tell him I said hi when you get a chance." JD hesitated and then said, "Hey Paul, do me a favor, will you?"

"Of course, anything," Paul said quickly.

"Just tell Lynn I'm sorry. She was right all along, but I didn't want to listen. I didn't want to get help. Didn't want to talk about the fact that I was hurting. Feeling guilty, blaming myself. Her love never faltered, but I stopped loving myself, which made it impossible to see that. Please tell her I'll never forget her, and I'll always love her."

Paul tried to reply but had to clear his throat a couple times. "Sure JD, I'll do that." Paul swallowed hard. "You know, it's never too late to win her back."

"We'll see. Just not quite ready yet," JD said, leaving room for hope. "I've got a little more work to do, but I just wanted to call and let you know I was good and to say thanks."

"No need for thanks. That's what friends are for, man. And you know you'll always be my best friend."

"I know, and right back at you," JD responded. "I'm planning a trip back home soon and I'll give you a call. Right now, I've gotta run. Great talking to you and glad to hear everything is good."

"Great talking to you, too. You had us all wondering, but I'll let everyone know that you are doing good."

"See you, man. Don't forget to tell Lynn, Okay?"

"You got it. Talk to you soon."

Paul stared at the phone for a moment. Instinctively, he wanted to search the area code, know where he was, go find him. But knowing he was doing fine put him at ease. He was happy that JD had found his path. Just like Chad. *And I guess me as well*, he thought, as he smiled at the beautiful day.

Already missing his meeting, Paul didn't go back to work

for only the second time in his life. The first came under completely different circumstances. That was the day he found out he was going back to Afghanistan. So much had happened since then. Looking back on it, Paul would never have guessed where his life would lead, nor those of the ones he loved. He knew now that everyone must find their own path and take their own journey. No one can live for somebody else. That was difficult for him to accept, because he wanted to help so badly when people were in need. Not just the countries that he invested so much of his time and energy in, but the individuals that he loved that were hurting. Even though it may seem that you are not getting through to people, Paul realized that the important thing is to keep offering that assistance. Some may go it alone for a while, but everyone needs someone eventually. Paul knew that many simply reach out without saying anything. Their actions indicate their need, even if they can't find the words. Paul wanted to be there when that time came. The important thing is to never stop trying to help those that you love.

Paul thought about the pain he experienced and how he learned to cope with it. It never really goes away, but rather becomes part of you. However, his response to it had changed. The pain no longer debilitated him, but rather motivated him. Motivated him to take advantage of life and enjoy every moment. So many people go through something similar, experiencing that crippling pain, in their lives. Losing a loved one, whether a spouse, brother, sister, friend, or child fundamentally changes a person. Brushes with life-threatening illness or traumatic events do the same. Chronic pain. Physical, mental, and emotional abuse. Fires. Accidents. Natural disasters. The list could go on. Most people face terrible situations and difficult decisions at some point in their lives. Paul had seen that with so many that were exposed to violence and traumatic events while deployed. People handle the inevitable pain and change differently, but the important thing is to never stop trying. That's what he vowed to do.

Everyone struggles with something, but there is so much good in the world, too. Paul decided that he had to remember and focus on that. *It's best to just enjoy every moment you can. Just like Professor Hamm told me all those years ago.*

Paul thought of his service differently now that he had emerged from the depths of his basement and the depths of his mind. Veterans should be proud that they were ready when their nation needed them. They would be there again in a heartbeat if their nation called. The United States had its fair share of conflicts when becoming a nation—the American Revolution, War of 1812, and the bloody Civil War—but had since enjoyed an unprecedented period of peace. Discounting Pearl Harbor and September 11th, there has not been an armed conflict in America for one hundred and fifty years. Paul didn't know for sure if many other countries could say the same, but he doubted it was many. Certainly not in the places he had been.

The freedoms that defined America were simply amazing. *We're truly fortunate*, Paul thought. Although people would debate the merits of the United States' actions in Iraq and Afghanistan, Paul had confidence in the fact that it was done with the best of intentions. Paul had been trying to protect what he loved and give more freedoms to others by eliminating evil. His own life hadn't gone as planned, and neither does war. Ultimately, people as well as countries must decide their own fate.

"Come sit on my lap buddy," Paul said to his son as Paul Jr. was getting ready for bed that evening, patting his lap as he grabbed a book from the nearby coffee table. It was one of his favorites, actually both of their favorites—*"Daddy and Me."* Paul Jr. smiled and lunged into his father's arms. "Actually, how about a story tonight?"

"How about a book and story?" he said, bargaining like children often do.

"It's a deal."

First, they read the book. Then, they began the story.

"Once upon a time, there were three brave men. They set out to help people in need and make the world a safer, better place for everyone. They wanted to change the world."

"Just like superheroes!" Paul Jr. shouted.

"Yes, just like that," the proud father beamed back at his son, before continuing the story. "They trained hard and were ready when the time came. Bad guys were hurting people and they had to stop them."

"Why did the bad guys hurt people, daddy?" his son asked, hanging on every word.

"I don't know, buddy. I've figured out a lot of things but that's something I'll never understand. Now let's keep going with our story. They travelled to a faraway land, way over the ocean, and tried to help as many people as they could." He glanced at his son and smiled at his attentiveness. "They were on a team with the bravest people they ever met, but some of their friends got hurt really bad, and some even got killed. It made them so sad and the bad things kept happening. They didn't understand. The heroes did everything they could but felt helpless. They hurt inside.

"Then one day they looked around and realized they had changed the world. They were safe in great land called America with their family and friends. They had so many freedoms that others do not. Places like Europe, Kuwait, South Korea, and many others are safe because of these brave heroes. The three friends were a small part of the history that made that happen and a part of the many more heroes that will be waiting to keep all of us safe in the future no matter what happens."

Marie entered the room just as he finished the story. Paul Jr. didn't notice. His eyes were still locked on his father's.

"Did you like the story, buddy?" Paul asked his son.

"Yeah, but you forgot something?" Paul Jr. asked innocently.

"What's that, bud?"

"You forgot to say they lived happily ever after."

"Of course, you're right," Paul said. He thought about JD and Lynn, Chad and the other guys of the 824th, Nasir, Professor Hamm, his parents, siblings, family, friends, and all the others that had touched him in his life. They had all felt pain and persevered. Paul thought of their journeys and his. He smiled up at Marie, now clearly showing with their second child, and thought of the life they built together. Then, he looked at his son. He was more right than he knew. "And from that moment on they vowed to enjoy every moment and cherish their freedoms and by doing that they all lived happily ever after."

ACKNOWLEDGEMENTS

There are so many people to thank for this book. As with everything in my life, I want to thank my family and friends for their enduring support. A special thanks especially to my wife, Angie, who not only endured so much through the long deployments but has been an encouraging, supportive, and loving influence in my life ever since. I thank my lucky stars every day that we are together.

Jansina, of Rivershore Books, worked with me every step of the way on the publication and I owe her an enormous debt of gratitude. The same goes to Jessica Ryker, Elizabeth Miniatt, and family members who provided valuable insights as they proofread different sections.

Most importantly, I want to thank all of those that I've had the privilege to serve with, not just for what you've done and meant to me personally, but for volunteering to keep our nation safe no matter what is thrown your way. You are what makes this nation great. Even though some of us may never cross paths again, there is always a special place in my heart for you and I love you all dearly.

RIVERSHORE BOOKS

www.rivershorebooks.com
info@rivershorebooks.com
www.facebook.com/rivershore.books
www.twitter.com/rivershorebooks
blog.rivershorebooks.com
forum.rivershorebooks.com

Made in the USA
Monee, IL
11 September 2020

42041362R00277